7-7-22

P9-CQA-913

DISCARDED BY THE
LA PORTE INDIANA
PUBLIC & COUNTY LIBRARY

SIGNATURE

L P'89 07153

THE
COCKROACHES
OF
STAY MORE

Books by Donald Harington:

NONFICTION

Let us Build Us a City: Eleven Lost Towns

FICTION

The Cockroaches of Stay More

The Architecture of the Arkansas Ozarks

Some Other Place. The Right Place.

Lightning Bug

The Cherry Pit

THE COCKROACHES OF STAY MORE

a novel by

Donald Harington

A HELEN AND KURT WOLFF BOOK
HARCOURT BRACE JOVANOVICH, PUBLISHERS
San Diego   New York   London

HBJ

Copyright © 1989 by Donald Harington

All rights reserved. No part of this publication may be reproduced or transmitted in any form or by any means, electronic or mechanical, including photocopy, recording, or any information storage and retrieval system, without permission in writing from the publisher.

Requests for permission to make copies of any part of the work should be mailed to: Permissions, Harcourt Brace Jovanovich, Publishers, Orlando, Florida 32887.

Library of Congress Cataloging-in-Publication Data
Harington, Donald.
The cockroaches of Stay More: a novel/by Donald Harington.—
1st ed.
p.   cm.
"A Helen and Kurt Wolff book."
ISBN 0-15-118270-1
I. Title.
PS3558.A6242C6 1989
813'.54—dc19   88-18054

Designed by Dalia Hartman
Printed in the United States of America

First edition

A B C D E

MAY 1 8 1989

*For my daughters: Jennifer, Calico, and Katy,
and my stepson Mickel, who never heard
a bedtime story like this one.*

The author is very grateful to Jack Butler
for a careful reading of the manuscript.
He found what was good and said so;
he saw what was missing and wrote it himself.

CONTENTS

THE
COCKROACHES
OF
STAY MORE

INSTAR THE FIRST:
The Maiden

1.

One time not too long ago on a beginning of night in the latter part of May, a middle-aged gent was walking homeward along the forest path from Roamin Road to the village of Carlott, behind Holy House in the valley of Stainmoor or Stay More. The six gitalongs that carried him were rickety, and there was a meandering to his gait that gave a whole new meaning to the word *Periplaneta*. This wanderer gave a smart nod, as if in agreement to a command, though no one had spoken to him yet. His wings were not folded neatly across his back and were neither tidy nor black but flowzy and brownish. Presently he was met by a plump parson whose wings were very black and long and trim like the tails of a coat, and who was humming a hymn, "The Old Shiny Pin."

"Morsel, Reverend," said the flowzy gent, and spat, marking his space.

"Good morsel to ye, Squire John," said the pudgy parson, and spat too.

"Now sir, beggin yore pardon," the wanderer said, spitting again, "but we bumped inter one another last Sattidy on this path about this same time, and I said, 'Morsel,' same as now, and you answered me, 'Good morsel to ye, Squire John,' same as now, didn't ye?"

"More'n likely I did," said the parson, and spat.

"And seems like once before that, maybe Friday."

"I might've, now ye mention it."

"Wal, Reverend, then how come ye called me 'Squar John,' please tell me, when I'm plain ole Jack Dingletoon, as everbody knows?"

The fat parson strode six steps or twelve nearer. Their spaces intermingled and overlapped.

"I jist had a urr to do it," he said. The minister's huge eyes twinkled and his voice had an impish seriousness. "Don't ye know, I've been researchin and studyin folkses pedigrees all over Stay More, if the day comes when Man shall ask of me to call the roll and account fer ever blessit one of you'uns. I've crope inter ever crook and nanny of town and talked to everbody about their foreparents as fur back as they can recollect. And it'll surprise ye to learn, Squire, that you aint a Dingletoon atter all. Nossir, 'Dingletoon' is jist the way that one of yore ancestors long ago got in the way of mispronouncin 'Ingledew.' "

Jack Dingletoon pondered this. "Naw!" he remarked. "You don't mean to tell me!"

"Shore as I'm astandin here," said the parson,

and requested, "Tilt up yore jaws thataway, Squire, and let me look at yore face. Yes, that's the Ingledew touchers and sniffwhips, I'd bet on 'em, a little adulterated, ye might say, no harm meant, please sir. Why, you're descended from ole Squire Jacob Ingledew hisself, the first roosterroach to set gitalong in this valley."

"So's everbody else, aint they?" Jack observed.

"Wal, not edzackly," declared Brother Tichborne, for that was his name, and he was no descendant of Jacob Ingledew himself, but of relative newcomers generations later, who were Manfearing Crustians without any record of incest. "As fur as I kin figger, the Dingletoons was a branch what broke off from the Ingledews way back afore the time of Joshua Crust Hisself. You know, the Lord Joshua weren't no kin of the Ingledews, and matter of fack He prophesied the Ingledews would wester off from the face of the earth, jist lak they been a–westerin. Not on account of the sin of incest, though, but on account of the sin of pride."

Jack Dingletoon chuckled. "Wal, we couldn't be no kin of the Ingledews nohow. We aint never had nothin to be proud of."

Brother Tichborne smiled in agreement. "You shore aint. But maybe the Dingletoons has got jist as much right as the Ingledews to dwell in Partheeny."

Jack snorted, but all six of his gitalongs tingled. "Haw! That'd be the day, us a–movin inter Partheeny, or even Holy House. That would be the day!" He moved closer and lowered his voice, although no one was eavesdropping except a quartet of crooning

3

katydids and some grazing roly-polies. "Preacher, how long has this news about me been knowed? Have the Ingledew squars been told I'm their kin?"

"Nossir," said the parson, "nary a soul but me and you knows it." He explained that he had come across the information while interviewing old Granny Stapleton, virtually deaf, deprived of both her sniff-whips and near west from arthritis but still possessed of exceptional memory. Brother Tichborne had a great talent for separating history from legend and tall tale, and had been able to determine from Granny's information that the Dingletoons were indeed long-ago scions of the Ingledews. "At first when I heared it, I tole myself, wouldn't be no sense in passin it along to ye, nohow," said the parson. "The knowin of it aint got the power of itself to rain down morsels upon ye. But I figgered it won't do ye no harm neither to know it. Maybe it could uplift yore spirit and take the hump outen yore back."

Jack Dingletoon involuntarily straightened his pronotum, elevating his shoulders and even his head. His large kidney-shaped eyes seemed to moisten, and the tips of his wings trembled. "Preacher," he declared solemnly, "that is the best news ever I learned in all my born days. Jist wait till I tell Josie! Won't her eyes pop outen her skull! But first, let's us me and you go celebrate with a little drap of brew. Reckon they'd let me inter the cookroom if they knowed I was a Ingledew?"

"Thanks jist the same, Squire John, but I reckon I'd better not," declined the minister, not from any scruples against intoxicants but from a reluctance to mingle with the frequenters of the cookroom's beer cans, scarcely a Crustian among them. "I'd best be gittin on back to the Frock."

"Don't ye reckon they'd let me jine 'em in the beer can if I was to tell 'em I'm a Ingledew?" Jack Dingletoon repeated with less confidence.

"You could try," Brother Tichborne allowed. "But more'n likely they wouldn't believe you. Best not let yore knowin of yore own name git ye inter lordliness. Have you ever tried to enter Holy House afore?"

"Course not," Jack declared. "But if *you* was to go with me . . ."

"Not tonight, thank ye, Squire John," said Brother Tichborne, and turned to resume his journey. "Say hidy to Josie for me. And a long good night to ye." The obese parson hitched up his gitalongs and skittered off into the darkness.

Jack walked on, six, nine or eighteen steps in a profound reverie before lowering himself down upon the substratum, beneath some towering grasses silhouetted against the moon, and gave himself over to consideration of the significance of being an Ingledew, not a mere Dingletoon. The whole world was changed. The night was twelve shades of blue now, and thirteen shades of ultraviolet, and the air was beginning to fill with lightning bugs. Within range of Jack's sniffwhips and eyes a lady lightning bug was perched upon the end of a blade of grass, testing and fine-tuning her lantern. Jack paid her no mind although his ocelli twitched at each neon flash of her summons. Choral groups of katydids were serenading in four-part harmony; here and there a cricket could be heard warming up his instrument of challenge, and in the distance sounded a background of countless *Hylae* peeping and piping.

The peepers were a variety of frog, mortal predators upon any roosterroach who came near them. The music of the night had its ominous overtones and also its discordant noises: somewhere nearby a huge nightcrawler worm was laboring noisily uphill with many shiftings of gears, backfirings, and faulty rumblings in its transmission. It was sending out signals: "BREAKER ONE OH. DO YOU READ? HOWBOUTCHA, BIG MAMA? UP THIS HUMP HUNTIN FOR BEAVER LOOKIN FOR A NAP TRAP AND GOTTA LOG SOME Z'S. PEELIN OFF? TEN TWENTY? GIVE A SHOUT." Lost in thought, Jack ignored the worm, whose language was not in his ken, anyway. From some distant rise another worm answered: "TEN FOUR AND BODACIOUS, GOOD BUDDY. WHAT'S YOUR HANDLE, BUFFALO? ROGER ROLLER SKATE. ONE FOOT ON THE FLOOR, ONE HANGIN OUT THE DOOR, AND SHE JUST WON'T DO MORE. SIXTY-NINE? STACK THEM EIGHTS. WE GONE."

Jack lowered his sniffwhips and his tailprongs, tucking them all beneath him so that he was no longer confused by the flowering cacophony of sounds and scents, the strident bloom of seeking odors, the yearning blare of efflorescing aromas, the redolent reek of craving commotions, the purple smell of boisterous desires, the lascivious essences of unfolding tones, the rank voices and perfumes of swollen lust.

6

Although he tuned out the sounds and scents, he could not avoid the spectacle of two katydids mating right in the road beside him, fork-tailed *Scudderiae* scudling in the dust to the tune of the male's continuing lavender croon: "Tzeet, baby! Tzek, baby! Oh, tzuk, baby, yeah, yeah!"

Jack had already had, beginning at the crack of dusk, an immoderate dose of Chism's Dew, the fermented essence of honeydew, scorned by serious drinkers as nothing but rotgut. All his life he had craved a sample of the genuine beer that was a feature of life in Holy House, beyond his reach and station, but he had never even tried to enter Holy House, let alone the cookroom beer cans there, although the cookroom was full of holes and he could have crept through any of them. Now, with the aid of the nerve given him by Chism's Dew, he might pass through one of those holes and, if accosted and challenged, declare, "Boys, have I got news fer you'uns! I aint a Dingletoon but a Ingledew!" Wouldn't they jump, if they believed him? If they believed him. . . .

The copulating katydids had flounced jointly on down the trail out of sight, and were replaced by a young roosterroach swain skittering along and whistling "Down in the Arkansas."

Jack Dingletoon raised his sniffwhips, lashed them back and forth, and called out, "Hey, sonny, come here."

The lad stopped, turned his head, twitched his tailprongs, flicked his own sniffwhips with considerably more alacrity than Jack could muster, and replied, "Wal, look who's tryin to boss me around! Why onch *you* come *here*, ole Jack?"

Jack did not budge. "I ast ye fust, boy. And don't ye call me 'ole Jack'. I'm Squire John Ingledew, boy, and I aint askin you to come here, I'm *a-tellin* ye to."

"You and who else, Jack Orv Dingletoon?" the youth taunted, spat, and tossed his head. "Drunk as per usual, I see. Who'd ye say you was?"

Jack drew himself erect, and for a brief moment rose up on his hind gitalongs in the mantis-threat stilt walk, causing the pre-imago adolescent to cower and turn as if to flee. "Now you lissen a me, Freddy Coe! If you know what's good fer ye, you'll pay me some mind and not give me no more of yer sass. I'm a Ingledew, boy, and Master of the Cosmos! I'm a cousin of Squire Sam Ingledew or maybe even his half-uncle! Don't ye know I got the *power*?" Jack swished his sniffwhips across each other and hoped for some phenomenon to occur to give proof to his power. He hoped the dark blue sky would suddenly fill with lightning. Or that the Great White Mouse would come into view. Or that at least all the sounds of the spring night would join to play the Purple Symphony. But instead, as very ill luck would have it, a centipede suddenly appeared, *Scutigeria forceps*, scooting forcibly up the trail in search of prey. This centipede, or Santa Fe, as they call it in the Ozarks, had only twenty-eight gitalongs, not a hundred, but its fangs were already dripping with the deadly poison that kills roosterroaches in an instant.

Poor Freddy Coe was so paralyzed with fear that his six gitalongs lost their automatic escape response and he stood there trembling and screaming. *I'm a gone rooster*, Jack Dingletoon told himself, thinking how briefly he had been allowed to enjoy the pleasure of being an Ingledew before his wretched life was snuffed out by this dragon of a Santa Fe. He felt the multigitalonged monster's sniffwhips already singling him out for special attention. What would Squire Hank Ingledew do in such a situation? Pray? No, everybody knew Squire Hank and all the Ingledews neither feared nor worshipped Man. *My number is up*, Jack realized, as he braced himself for the Santa Fe's fatal lunge. Instinctively he rose again into the mantis posture, a poor sham which wouldn't fool a Santa Fe even if centipedes were afraid of mantises. This Santa simply smirked with evil mirth and opened its forceps wide. *So long, cruel world*, Jack said to the cruel world, and prepared for his west.

But in the split instant that the centipede lunged, Squire John Orval Ingledew, without stopping to re-member how to unfold and flap his forewings let alone his hindwings (the prescutal process laterally projects close to the tegula which lies medial to the base of the remigium of the wings), took to the air! As if in awe (or was it only the beating of his wings?) the air was filled with the strains of the Purple Symphony in triumphant prelude almost out of keeping with the clumsiness of his blast-off.

He knew he could not maintain the flight for very long, two seconds at best, but he was out of reach of the fatal fangs of the centipede, who did not even pause to register disappointment before diverting its attention to Freddy Coe, still quivering and howling in abject cowardice and terror. Jack's joy at his own escape was tinged with pity for poor Freddy, who

9

had no wings yet and could neither fly nor flee. But Miz Coe had eleven more just like him in her brood and she might not even notice him missing. He was a snotty kid, no loss to anyone.

Then—he must have been hearing the voices of his brave Ingledew ancestors castigating him—Jack suddenly felt dastardly and selfish, shamed and debased, and he used the last ounce of his flight's energy to divebomb the Santa Fe's neck, where he got a good hold and took a good bite and then kicked free from the wildly thrashing gitalongs. He had not really hurt the Santa Fe, but he had scared the shit out of it, and it was beating a quick retreat, leaving a shower of feces in its wake. It disappeared into the forest of the tall grass.

"Now *that*," he said to Freddy, "is the way a true Ingledew orter handle the situation."

Freddy was speechless for a long moment before he could say, "Holy Locust! Squire John, you're a wizard! I reckon you really are a Ingledew, aint you?"

2.

No, thought Brother Tichborne, as he approached a choice orifice punctured into the wooden wall of Holy House, beyond which he could no longer hear nor smell the scene of Jack, Freddy, and the Santa Fe, that feller aint any more a Ingledew than I am, so why did I have to go and tell him he was?

10

He had wanted to get Jack Dingletoon to enter Parthenon, that was why, to get him to penetrate that stronghold of irreligious Ingledews who did not even bow down and worship the Woman who lived there. The Reverend Tichborne had seen Her more than once, from afar, or from not any closer than the front yard of Her house, upon the porch of which She sometimes sat at dusk, after Her supper, the leavings of which, if any, were bestowed only upon those two lucky Ingledews who were the squires of Stay More, just as Ingledews had always been squires since the beginning of time, although, true to the Lord Joshua Crust's prophecy, they were now fast disappearing, and only two remained: Squire Hank and his son, Squire Sam.

It simply wasn't fair that those two should have Parthenon all to themselves, as if it were a royal castle. All of the other houses of Stay More had been abandoned by Man, except of course for Holy House, where Brother Tichborne made his residence along with most of the other quality roosterroaches of Stay More, who were reduced to fighting each other for the residues of Man's table (as well as of His bed, His cheer-of-ease, or wherever else He chose to sit and eat). Brother Tichborne thought it a terrible irony that the Ingledews had the exclusive right to whatever morsels were left by the Woman in Parthenon, although they never prayed to Her. The Ingledews were not only atheists, but it was also commonly known that our Lord Joshua Crust had been pinnified by a person of the Ingledew name, a human person. We all take our names from Man.

11

We take our names from Man, who is our rock and our salvation, although His wrath is great and unceasing. Man had a habit of routinely taking up and firing a revolver at the roosterroaches who dwelt in His house, with westerly accuracy depending on how much He had had to drink. Other ministers before Brother Tichborne had determined that this shooting and westering of chosen roosterroaches was both a form of punishment and an expression of Man's love, and therefore the shooting, or the act of being shot, was called not a westering but a Rapture.

There are two forms of Rapture, good Crustians believe: there is the instant Rapture of the bullet from Man, which is a guarantee that one will live upon the right hand of Man in the sweet heaven of the hereafter; but there is also the promise of the Rapture after The Bomb, when Man will lift the righteous off the floor and give them eternal life. The good Crustians will be raptured, but the faithless will perish in that holocaust and go to Hell. Hell, as everyone knows and fears, is a place of work. Unless we are righteous and obey the Lord's commandments, we will find ourselves in Hell, the dominion of the Mockroach, hard at work.

The bullets which Man fired to rapture the chosen Crustians always pierced the floor as well, the wall, the ceiling, a door, or a windowpane of the house, which was called Holy House because of all these holes. Each new hole created a new entrance for more roosterroaches, but it was not permissible for any "furrin" roosterroach to enter Holy House. Each hole also created drafts, and this past winter had been terrible, causing even Man Himself to take to stronger drink than beer.

If there was any consolation for Brother Tichborne in the gross injustice of the overpopulation of Holy House and underpopulation of Parthenon, it was that the Woman was such a fastidious keeper of Her cookroom and table that rarely did a crust or crumb fall from her table, lap, plate, pan, countertop, or mouth corner. Our Man of Holy House, by contrast, bestowed upon the multitudes a great continuous feast of crusts and crumbs, to say nothing of the countless dregs of beer that kept most Holy Housers nearly as intoxicated as Man Himself. Brother Tichborne was old enough to observe that Man's use of beer, and of the more poisonous bourbon, was increasing.

The ways of Man are inscrutable. Man giveth, and Man taketh away. Blessed be the Name of Man (though Brother Chidiock Tichborne, who had a fine old name himself, had to admit that he did not know the name of his Man, nor of the Woman either).

Such were his thoughts as he climbed the pier of native fieldstone stacked into a cube which supported one corner, the southeastern, of the abandoned room of Holy House, a room containing a hodgepodge of relics, junk, castoff effects of generations of Man who had inhabited the house. Among this detritus was a heavy and crumpled frock coat, single-breasted, of black alpaca, narrow lapels, three pockets, which still bore traces of the sacred aroma of the sweat of some Man who had worn it an eon ago, possibly before the time of Joshua Crust. Chidiock Tichborne and his fifteen brothers and sisters had been born inside the folds of this frock. He had spent his first instar exploring the smooth lining of Italian cloth, playing hide-and-seek with his siblings through the tunnels of the sleeves, and visiting with other children who lived in the pockets and beneath the tails, for this frock coat had been home and birthplace not just to several generations of Tichbornes but to the Murrisons, the Chisms, the Duckworths, the Plowrights and other fine families of Stay More who, because they lived closest to the cookroom—much closer than the closet-dwelling roosterroaches who lived in an old smock, not a frock—were the higher strata of society in the village, the most prosperous, and, Brother Tichborne would have you know, the most devout, Crustlike, Manfearing, and faithful.

All of Stay More had only one minister, and this was Brother Tichborne.

Brother Tichborne returned home to the frock from his "gloaming constitutional," as he called it, to find that his wife, Ila Frances, had risen and started breakfast for herself and their children.

"Morsel, Sister Tichborne," the minister greeted his wife, whom he was wont to address formally. He wished she would do the same, but:

"Mors, Chid," she said. "What-all's the news out yander in the world?"

"Hit's purty nice and fair, the night a-comin on," he observed. "Six zillion stars out and up."

"Only six?" she said. "Last night they was seven."

"Paw, kin we go to the play-party tonight, us younguns?" requested Archy, one of their sons, past

14

his imago, and indicating himself and his siblings, mostly identical brothers.

"Naw, Archibald," the minister said. "They's liable to be dancin at thet there play-party."

"Aw, we kin jist watch," Archy declared.

Mrs. Tichborne suggested, "They kin keep their sisters out of trouble."

"Shore, I reckon," said Archy. "We kin watch out for our sisters."

"No dancin," said Brother Tichborne wearily. "None of y'uns do no dancin."

The dozen-odd Tichborne offspring sprang away from breakfast—the boys skittled away, while the girls flittered away.

Alone together, Brother and Sister Tichborne discussed their plans for the night. Sister Tichborne wanted to go visit her sister, who was married to a Smockroach. Brother Tichborne considered going with her; it would be an opportunity to convert a few of the Smockroaches. His ambition, if he lived long enough, if Man's bullets did not rapture him and send him west, was to convert everyone into Crustians . . . even the Ingledews, whose domicile, Parthenon, he wanted to consecrate to Crustianity.

But tonight there was a more pressing chore: Chid Tichborne needed to plan and rehearse his next Sunday prayer meeting and worship service, which, for the first time, he intended to conduct right in the presence of Man, right at Man's feet, as it were. This bold move would be sure to convert some of the faithless.

And when he had made those preparations,

he had better drop in on that play-party, just to make sure that the young folks were behaving themselves. . . .

3.

Sam Ingledew preferred crusts to crumbs, especially when it was crust of Brie, Camembert or Boursin; when it was crust of pretzel or waffle or éclair; when it was crust of brownie or macaroon or ladyfinger; his favorite of all edibles was apple fritter. The crust of *beignet aux pommes* was the measure of its quality: he could not conceive of a good beignet without a thoroughly crispy crust.

But he was not a Crustian, not in the devotional sense. Certainly he *believed* that there had existed in ancient Stay More a certain roosterroach with the name of Joshua, who was called the Crust, and Sam was even ready to accept the possibility that this Joshua Crust had been impaled upon a pin by a Man, or Manchild, who had had the venerable Stay More family name of Ingledew. But Sam could not accept the commonly held belief that the roosterroach Joshua was the *son* of Man, any more than he could accept the idea that roosterroach Ingledews were descended from human ones. Enough, that we adopt the names and ways of Man; too much, that we should claim biological lineage.

By temperament as well as by residence, Sam felt

removed from the battles between Crustians and non-Crustians, Frockroaches and Smockroaches. Holy House was a world away, although the two buildings were only a couple of furlongs from each other, at opposite ends of the Roamin Road, which had been the Main Street of the village of Stay More when Stay More was still being proliferated by Ingledews, human and roosterroach alike. Sam's father, Squire Hank Ingledew, loved to talk of the old days, although Squire Hank himself had never known them, nor had Hank's immediate grandsires or great-grandsires, all the way back to Isaac Ingledew, who had led the roosterroaches into exile during the generations when Stay More had been totally abandoned by Man.

Ingledews had always been leaders, long before the time of Joshua, and if Sam did not feel inclined to lead anyone, it was because he had even less taste for politics than for religion. A philosopher, an epicure, a naturalist, and a bon vivant, he felt that he was a stranger to the folkways of his kindred. He was a cosmopolite in a world of rustics.

And unless he got busy and overcame his shyness and found a girlfriend, he was the last of the Ingledews. His father, Squire Hank, though still physically powerful, was psychologically impotent and would never again sire offspring. Sam had no brothers and sisters. When his mother had laid the ootheca which had been his prelife capsule, her easteregg, she had slipped away from his father and climbed the mantel above the unused fireplace in the Woman's bedroom. She had entered this very Clock and deposited her easteregg carefully in one corner, far from the slow gnashing of the Clock's gears and the swinging of its pendulum, safe from any spiders or scorpions. It was her third easteregg of the season; the other two had entirely failed to hatch.

An ootheca hatches through the combined simultaneous and spontaneous inhalation and exhalation of its fourteen to sixteen inhabitants. Sam remembered—it was his first memory—the awful effort of sucking in and puffing out his abdomen, which failed to crack the crust of the ootheca, failed to hatch the easteregg, and the panic when he realized that the other fifteen "passengers" in the ootheca were not helping because they were west, or rather had not succeeded in eastering. They were stillborn, all of them, and Sam would have been also, despite his frantic and most desperate efforts, had not the Clock exclaimed "SUGARPLUM!" and begun striking seven times with such noise and vibration that the sound alone seemed to rupture the ootheca's case and release him, squalling in fright and singing in triumph in the same breath, into this life.

His mother had not crusted him "Sam"; that was not his "real" name. There were no Ingledews of any generation, human or roosterroach, with that given name, nor with the name his mother actually gave him, which has been forgotten, even by him (she had been west, lo, since Sam was in his fourth instar and an infestation of the cockroach mite, *Pimeliaphilus podapolipophagus*, carried her off). She had crusted him with a special name symbolic of the season in which he was born.

"When ye git growed up," she had explained,

"when ye reach yore imago, you can call yoreself anything you like. Names is sorta sniffwhips on the front of yore face. You can wave 'em about, and use 'em to find yore way around in this world, and keep 'em clean all the time, and ye can touch things with 'em, and talk to other folkses with 'em, and all such as thet, but a given name is jist a sniffwhip."

So in his maturity—he was no longer young, but had lived a full circuit of the earth around the sun— he had dropped his Crustian name and chosen to call himself Gregor Samsa Ingledew, the full meaning of which was known, or appreciated, only by himself. How he learned the significance of it is one of those mysteries as puzzling as the fact that every rooster-roach is born with all the knowledge that he needs to get him through to his west.

When the Clock conspired with his mighty efforts to crack the case of his easteregg and he found himself alone with fifteen stillborn siblings on the floor of the Clock, he had no mother to care for him. She was somewhere down below, or in another part of Parthenon, where his infant cries could not reach her. No roosterroach mother can know the instant her easteregg hatches unless she keeps constant watch on it. Few do.

He found himself alone and hungry and ignorant of his strange surroundings, the wheeling gears and meshing cogs and the swinging pendulum, the clacking rack and bobbing cock and ticking deadbeat escapement. He thought the Clock was his mother, but her mechanisms did not quite fit his imprinted genetic memory, and when he tried to talk with her in her own language—rapid clacking verbs, clittering adjectives, thrumming nouns, with tinkling commas, dingling periods, and bonging exclamation points, she would not respond to him. When she said "FONDUE!" he repeated her exactly, but she ignored him. For three days, he went hungry. His first night's absolute whiteness, which frightened him, as if he were a ghost of himself, mellowed into amber, and then into tan. He prowled the length of the mantelshelf, greatly intimidated by the heights. He considered eating one of his stillborn siblings, for nothing is tastier to a roosterroach than a westered embryo, but somehow he understood that the toothsome delight under consideration was his sister.

One night (he kept to the darkest corner of the Clock whenever there was a bit of light), he saw the Woman. She stood near the mantelpiece, near enough for his sniffwhips to detect with ravenous recognition what She held in Her hands—in one hand a glass of milk, in the other hand an Oreo, that fabled delectation of chocolate crumbs. He knew She must be his mother, although She looked even less like a mother roosterroach than the Clock did. He felt an overpowering filial love for Her, which was a love not merely for the food She was bringing to him but for Her great beauty; for the golden waves of hair spread upon Her shoulders as white as his own body had lately been, for the surpassing sweetness of Her face, for the grace with which She moved, for the dulcet tones with which She created words—"Now is this Friday? Or is it Saturday? Why, yes, I do believe it's Saturday."

Baby Sam returned the words: "Why, yes, I do believe it's Saturday." But She, like the Clock, ignored him. She did not even see him. Nor did She give him any of the food which She was bearing. She set the glass of milk down on the mantelshelf and abruptly opened the glass door on the face of the Clock, startling him into withdrawal further back in the shadows. With the hand that had held the milk She steadied the Clock, and with the other hand, the hand that held the Oreo, She stuck a key into the Clock face and began to wind it. The Clock made new sounds that Sam had not heard before, the scritching of the key, the spranging of the spring being tightened.

She turned and turned the key, and in the long course of this labor a tiny corner of the Oreo She held crumbled off and fell to the floor of the Clock.

This minute fragment of Oreo sustained young Sam for over a week, until his true mother arrived and led him down from the Clock and into the world and began explaining to him all the things he did not understand.

She explained to him that certain things are "not nice." For example, it is not nice to vomit your food while others are watching. "Gobble yore food, but puke in solitude," was one of her many maxims. Although it is acceptable to speak of discharges from the front end as "puke," it is not acceptable to speak of discharges from the rear end by any of the numerous scatological words that many roosterroaches, particularly males, employ daily. It is better to speak of "making water," or "going out" or "going out to see how high the moon is," or even "heading for the john to do number two."

Above all, his mother explained, it is not nice, ever, to use the word "cockroach." The simple reason is that "cock" is one of the unmentionable words for either the male generative organ or the female receptacle of same, depending on who uses either, the word or the organ. His mother called his organ a tallywhacker, and he knew what she meant and wished she would drop the subject, it embarrassed him so. In his sixth instar, just before his imago, Sam learned of the Spanish word *cucaracha*, which is the origin of the English "cockroach," and has nothing to do with the male member or even male chickens, but in Stay More nobody with any decency would ever say "cockroach," nor would they speak of cock in any form, such as cockeyed, cocksure, coxcomb, let alone peacock, and it was best to avoid any utterance of pecker, dick, peter, jemmison, prick, root, ducey, dinger, dood, yingyang, tool, goober, horn, rhubarb, okra or even penis.

Why this prudery? Being already possessed of the uncommon wisdom of the Ingledews, which he refined through countless hours of meditation, Sam Ingledew understood in time that the essential reason for all sexual modesty is to give sex mystery, without which it would be dull, commonplace, obligatory, and uninviting. Modesty makes sex hard-to-get and therefore challenging, and therefore worthy of all one's waking obsessions and half of one's dreams. If it were otherwise, the generations would not generate.

"Roosterroach" seemed ludicrous to Sam when it was applied to a female of his species, but, he supposed, no more ludicrous than "cockroach" itself. The female "cock," he learned from his childhood companions, was called the twat, snatch, pussy, twitchet, moosey, monkey, or simply cunt, a word which his mother, first making him take a bite of a rancid bar of soap after he uttered it, told him should always be replaced by "gillyclicker," the feminine equivalent of tallywhacker. "Gillyclicker" sounded forbidding and mechanical to Sam, but was still better than *gonapophyses*, which is unpronounceable.

Sam had to chew soap whenever he spoke the wrong word. When he simply misused a word, he was sniffwhipped. On penalty of a severe sniffwhipping, he was told never to use the shortened "roach" as a substitute for "roosterroach," as Man does, because properly speaking a roach is a small, silvery freshwater fish, *Rutilus rutilus*, and in its several slang associations it means such things as a roll of hair, or the cut on the edge of a boat's sail, or the butt of a marijuana cigarette—a form of "roach" which Sam's mother once took him on a long jaunt to the edge of Stay More to examine, from a safe distance: it was still smoldering upon the ground, and its faint smoke, if allowed to enter one's spiracles, would make one drunker than Chism's Dew. "Now, son, *that* is a 'roach,' " his mother had said, "unless you ever see the fish kind of roach, which will eat ye quicker'n ye can git word to Man. So don't never let me hear you say 'roach' when you mean *us*. Us is always 'roosterroach.' "

When Sam's mother westered, he properly grieved for two days, staying awake all during the daylight to mourn, and then he had no further maternal instruction to digest or injunction to obey. His loneliness sometimes compelled him to leave his Clock, whence he had returned to live alone during his fifth instar, and venture out into Stay More to attempt the cultivation of other boys his age, but because he was an Ingledew and destined to be a squire, and because he lived in Parthenon two furlongs away from all the other youth of Stay More, and because he was by nature "different" from other pre-imago roosterroaches his age, he did not succeed in finding a best friend, and the extent of his acceptance by his peers into the youth culture was his learning a few bawdy jokes and bits of gossip about various girls, and learning the practice the boys called "jacking off," which involved a complicated manipulation of one's tallywhacker with one's hind gitalong.

"Jacking off," a substitute for the act of mating with a female, caused a spermatophore to burst forth from the endophallus with a high degree of physical and emotional pleasure. A favorite game of the hot-blooded imago males of Stay More involved using the ejaculated spermatophores as small, maneuverable spheres in a contest of sniffwhip dexterity within a circle drawn in the dirt; one's own spermatophore was one's "shooter," and the object of the game was to shoot and capture the other spermatophores. The game was known as "marbles."

When he reached the age of imago, Sam indulged in the game of marbles whenever he could find a group playing it, and sometimes he played it alone, by himself, producing marble after marble, and he scorned those Crustians who claimed that the game was sinful, wicked, and could cause one to lose all one's marbles, or to go deaf, or blind, or to have hair grow on the sides of one's sniffwhips.

When he began to lose his hearing, he thought that he had been wrong, the Crustians right, but he learned that none of the other players of marbles were losing theirs. Maybe the other players never played alone, by themselves, as he did. Maybe it really was sinful to play with yourself, and it worried him to the extent that he quit playing the game alone, then quit playing it with others. But still his hearing grew worse.

Although he told no one, it was very difficult to conceal the fact that he was nearly deaf. More and more he kept to himself and to his Clock. In time he had no friends among the Smockroaches or the Frockroaches. He was the Clockroach, and he could still hear the striking of the Clock. But he missed, he sorely missed, being able to hear the Woman. All of the months of his growing up, he had listened to Her. She talked to Herself. Much of what She said to Herself he could not understand, but most of it he was able to figure out, and Sam felt that he probably knew Her better than any other creature knew Her, certainly better than Man knew Her.

Once in a while She talked not to Herself but to a black hard plastic device shaped like an oversized ant, which usually rested upon the back of another black hard plastic device shaped like an oversized beetle. Somehow a person's voice, another Woman, or, very rarely, a Man, spoke through this device to Her. Usually She spoke back to it, and Sam, before he lost his hearing, could listen to the conversation.

But often She simply twiddled a dial on the beetle and then listened without speaking. Before his hearing began to fail him, Sam had heard a number of these lectures, or whatever they were. A voice would say, "You have dialed Tel-Med program number 147, 'The Lady Living Alone.' Through choice or necessity, many women choose to live by themselves. This can result in medical problems as well as social problems. We want to talk to you about them."

Part of Sam's education, before his hearing began to go, was to eavesdrop on these Tel-Med programs. More than once he had heard Number 42, "I'm Just Tired, Doctor"; Number 693, "Weight Control While Quitting Smoking"; Number 694, "Why a Woman Should Quit Smoking"; Number 6, "Breast Cancer"; Number 323, "Are You Afraid of the Dentist?"; Number 35, "Understanding Headaches"; and Number 728, "When Should I See a Psychiatrist?"

The last program that Sam heard clearly, a month or so before his hearing went, was Number 945, "So You Love an Alcoholic?"

4.

As for Carlott, it was . . . well, the most charitable thing to be said for Carlott is that it was the most *natural* of environments, but even that is arguable if we agree that the true native habitat of the roosterroach is the household of Man, within Man's providence, bounty, and grace. It was a rare day indeed when a Carlotter tasted any food provided by Man.

All roosterroaches are scavengers in the best sense, not of feeding on westered or decaying organic matter, but of cleaning up the leftovers carelessly neglected by other creatures, Man chief among them. But three hundred and fifty million years before Man climbed down out of trees and learned to cook, roosterroaches were finding *something* to eat.

The residents of Carlott, though most of them were Crustians and believers in Man, lived on what they could find in the forests, fields, and yard behind and beside Holy House. They never entered Holy House except by invitation from their kinfolk among the Frockroaches and Smockroaches. The Carlott community took its name from the circumstance that its dwellings—rotten logs, hollows in trees and in limbs, concavities beneath old boards and metallic junk—were centered around the rusting hulk of an inoperable automobile, a Ford Fairlane of ancient vintage which was said to have delivered Man to Holy House but was no longer used, and a still operable Ford Torino of more recent manufacture, which Man occasionally drove away and returned in, parking it

27

beside the older car in a small yard in the rear of Holy House. The chassis of the older car was also inhabited by a large nest of *Polistes annularis*, the paper wasp, who was strictly a daytime creature and never bothered the roosterroaches.

The family Dingletoon, of whom Jack was paterfamilias, occupied a hollow fallen limb or branch of maple on the weed-forested side of Carlott, within sight of the great ruin of the edifice known as the Three-Hole Privy, long ago abandoned entirely by Man, and the exact purpose of which remains a mystery to modern roosterroaches, although legends abound, particularly concerning the ancient victuals provided there. Jack Dingletoon remembered as a child hearing Gramp Dingletoon tell wondrous tales of how generation upon generation of Dingletoons were sustained and even nourished by the edibles provided in the cellars of the Privy.

But Tish Dingletoon, Jack's eldest daughter still at home, had not cared for these stories of the Privy food; the stories she picked up from her girlfriends concerned the viands available at Holy House and the rumors of incredibly delectable treats consumed at Parthenon, or Partheeny, as it was pronounced. Tish had never tasted a Twinkie, and could scarce imagine it. She was tortured by descriptions of bismarcks, fritters, crullers, saratogas, danish, and doughnuts glazed, raised, and jellied. The closest she had ever come to sampling any of these was a bit of white fluff given her by a Smockroach swain, Jim Tom Dinsmore, who said it was "Wonder Bread." Tish had suspected that Jim Tom was simply preparing her

28

with an appetizer, as it were, to entice her to taste the affy-dizzy of his tergal gland, a forbidden and dangerous potion.

Her mother had taught her always to resist the temptation to lick affy-dizzy, as the exudate of the male tergal gland was called. Some of her girlfriends had tasted it, but Tish had not. To reach it, you practically had to climb up on the boy's back, beneath his wings, and if you did that, he had you where he wanted you, and might make you take one of his marbles. Taking a marble was supposed to be a right smart of fun, but it also meant you'd soon have to carry a big easteregg sticking out of your rear end for several days before you could drop it somewhere.

Tonight would be a dance. Now as the near woods and the far fields and even the impossibly distant mountainsides began to echo with both the sound and smell of the Purple Symphony, from every covert cranny and hidden nook of Carlott, and down from the holes of Holy House too, crept forth dozens of maiden roosterroaches, who gathered into two long parallel snaking lines, sniffwhips to one another's tailprongs, end to end, two by two, side by side, and began to promenade all over the glens and glades of Stay More, stepping, nearly prancing, in tune to both the smells and the sounds of the symphony.

Some of the girls in this double processional tapped their abdomens to the ground to keep a beat for the others to march to; all of them held their heads high and swung their sniffwhips rhythmically to and fro in the air, and their tailprongs from side to side. Their numbers made them into one giant centipede, nay, a millipede, and the authority that towers in numbers frightened off any predator as well as any harmless creature that might stand in the path of this great undulating chain of femininity. Crickets and katydids alike leapt frantically out of their way, and nightcrawlers plowed off the road and into the median strip with cries of "MAYDAY!" and "THIRTY-THREE!" and "BLOOD BOX!" A great warty toad, *Bufo americanus*, who ordinarily would have made a meal out of several of these girls at one lick, westered of heart failure. Some of the girls giggled at the sight of his hammy legs in the air, still kicking in west.

The night, and the air, and the music, not to mention the calendar, conspired to make each of these virginal roosterroaches broadcast her own personal perfume, until the downdrifting dew was thoroughly saturated with pheromones, irresistibly sensual, and the mingling of these vampish vapors seeped into every lair of Carlott and hole of Holy House, and even as far away as Parthenon, and all the male roosterroaches banged their heads against the walls of their hiding places in an effort to give themselves the willpower to keep their tergal glands from leaking all their affy-dizzy. For these maidens were only teasing with their powerful pheromones; they did not mean business; they were not ready for mating . . . yet. The long double chain wound and wound around the hollers and hummocks of the little village.

In certain isolated coves of the Ozark Mountains, up until the most recent times, the folk (both humanfolk and roosterroachfolk) still celebrated, particularly in May as the earth began to grow, what can only be called Cerealia, rites in honor of Ceres, the godhead above the god of Roman Man, or rather goddesshead: Mother Earth herself, protectress of all the fruits of the earth and from whom the sacred word "cereal" comes. The young of Man had often conducted their "play-party" as a form of Cerealia, and the roosterroaches, following Man in all things, did likewise.

This double file of promenading females sashayed up and down the Roamin Road almost as far as Parthenon, almost within sight of the Woman, a substitute for Ceres, who sat on the porch of Parthenon, in Her rocking cheer, not Mother Earth but a sort of Earth Mother although She had never had any children herself. From within Parthenon, through the open screen door behind Her, came the sounds of Her stereo, but it was not the source of the Purple Symphony, and indeed She probably could not hear the latter, even with Her stereo off. Nor could She see the hundreds of roosterroaches turning their train around in Her dooryard.

As the double file of maidens came prancing back down the Roamin Road, one of the females exclaimed, "The Lord-a-Joshuway! Why, Tish Dingletoon, if there aint yore pappy tryin to ketch holt of the end of our train!"

Tish Dingletoon turned her head at this exclamation and swung her sniffwhips to try to detect the distant tail of the roosterroachipede, where Jack Dingletoon was staggering along in pursuit, seeking to imitate the sway of the girls' sniffwhips with his own, and doing an awful job of copying their prance and posture.

Jack's head was tilted back and he was singing in

31

cadence to the march: "Hi yoop! I aint no Dingletoon no more! By cracky, I'm a pure dee pure blood In- gledew now, and a *squire* to boot!"

All the girls tittered, giggled, and pointed, except Tish, in whom a slow heat rose.

"He's had too much Chism's Dew, is all he has," she said hastily, "and he don't know what he's sayin."

One of her companions giggled and said, "Bet he don't have a Ingledew's pecker on him! Haw-haw!"

"Now looky here: I won't march another inch with you'uns if ye say any jokes about him!" Tish cried, and cast down her eyes and her sniffwhips, afraid to hold them up and see if indeed by some hideous chance her father's tallywhacker might be ex- tending itself or his tergal gland might be leaking affy- dizzy. She would be mortified beyond hope if he were even involuntarily exposing himself or releasing affy- dizzy in the presence of all these females. Tish could not look, nor smell, and she concentrated upon the steps of her own six gitalongs, lest one of them hit a twig or miss a step, and thus, by ignoring whatever spectacle her sire was making of himself (in time she could no longer hear his voice), she managed to con- tinue with the double parade to its conclusion at the Platform, as they called the one door of the Ford Fairlane which Man had removed from its hinges and laid into the weeds, where it served as a pavilion for dances as well as political rallies and an occasional pulpit for Brother Tichborne.

Tish Dingletoon at this time of her life was not yet a beauty, still retaining some of the awkwardness of her pre-imago girlishness: you could sometimes

32

see her fifth instar in her cheeks, or her third instar sparkling from her eyes, and even her second instar would flit over the curves of her mandibles now and then. She assumed that she was just one more Dingletoon female, no more, no less: an attractive, even "cute" country girl, but not a "looker."

Nothing more was seen, heard or sniffed of Jack Dingletoon in his sportive conduct at the end of the train, and when the parade entered the glade of the Cars, its allotted and magic space (all creatures having a space their very own, wherein they are safe from harm or molestation), the dancing began. The maidens climbed the Platform and formed themselves into "squares" of four and eight for a play-party dance, without partners, or with girl partners, at least in the beginning. Later, when the fumes of the pheromones had settled down, and a virile male could appear without leaking affy-dizzy, the braver, bolder, more self-possessed youths among the idlers and pedestrians might venture to join the girls.

There was an old story, nearly a year old, that Man had appeared in Carlott one night while a play-party was in progress, had violated the magic space of the roosterroaches, had tripped over the Platform, westering several roosterroaches in the crush of His falling, and then, standing up again, had urinated all over the Platform and environs, westering a few more. But that was long ago, almost a whole year, and none of this generation of girls had been born then. They had been told of it by their mothers as a warning always to fear Man, to obey His commandments, to live righteously in reverence of His wrath.

Since lowly Carlotters could not enter Holy House and subject themselves to the possibility of Rapture by bullets, this memory of Man's violation of the Platform gave some Carlotters the hope and expectation of Rapture by piss.

Several squares of the play-party were danced by the girls alone, including "Pig in the Parlor," "Frog up a Stump," and "Possum Trot," before the first males appeared as lookers-on. Among these first brave watchers were several sons of the Frockroach preacher, Brother Tichborne, and one of these, a bold swain named Archy, was the first male to climb the Platform.

"What you fixin to do, Archy?" asked one of his brothers.

"I got a hankerin to jine the dance," Archy declared.

"You're out of yore fool haid," said the brother. "What if Paw was to find out?"

"You aim to tell 'im?" Archy challenged. "Come on, Felix, and the rest of you boys too. Let's us have us some fun."

But none of Archy's brothers would join him. He turned to choose a partner. The girls waited breathlessly to see which of them he would pick. Tish Dingletoon took notice of him, a fine strong handsome boy, and she told herself that her chances of being chosen as his partner were slight, and thus she did not, as some of the other girls were doing, primp and pose and prettify herself.

Sure enough, he did not even seem to notice Tish but selected Spicy Bourne, another Carlotter, like her sisters a feisty beauty and, also like her sisters, rather conceited and smug, but a vivacious dancer.

Archy's appearance emboldened several other males, who climbed the Platform and joined sniff-whips in a ring for the singing and dancing of "Skip to My Lou":

> Flies in the buttermilk, two by two,
> Flies in the buttermilk, shoo fly shoo,
> Flies in the buttermilk, two by two,
> Skip to my Lou, my darlin.

This was not a "square" so much as a circle, everyone ringing around the dancing couple, who one by one drew others into the center of the circle. Tish hoped she would be drawn by Archy, but she could only stand at her place in the ring, all six of her git-alongs tapping expectantly to the beat of the dance, and fix her eyes and her sniffwhips steadily upon him while he danced with Spicy Bourne. Like most males, he did not devote his attention to his partner; in fact, he seemed to ignore Spicy with his eyes and sniff-whips, which kept roaming around the circle in search of another girl, but the girl he picked was not Tish but Rosa Faye Duckworth. Tish could only wait until he was once again through with his partner and chose a new one.

The play-party is meant to be an innocent frolic. Compared with the more adult and more exciting square dance, the play-party is supposedly a chaste gathering, approved by the most hidebound Crust-ians, but still the occasional incident of unrestrained lust will occur, off in the "brushes," the forest of weeds on the edge of Carlott. The couple abandoning the Platform and giving in to their desires do not reappear during the whole night, for the act of sexual congress is a complicated congeries of anatomical hookups, end-to-end splicings and interconnections, from which the couple cannot extricate themselves until the male's marble has been thoroughly enthroned within the female's chamber, a process, literally, that takes hour upon hour.

Thus, tonight, while Tish was still waiting for Archy to take notice of her, and the repertoire of games had gone from "Skip to My Lou" to "Shoot the Buffalo" to "Humpin the Santa Fe" and "Spinnin the Spider," the party was suddenly silenced by the abrupt appearance of Brother Chidiock Tichborne, who was dragging into view the still-conjoined bodies of a youth and maiden whom he had discovered "making the beast with two heads" off in the brushes.

The unfortunate couple were embarrassed beyond all mortification, not simply for having been surprised in the act by the minister but also for their inability to separate, to unclasp, to unlink, to undo all the various latches, clamps and sphincters that linked them together, tail to tail in opposite directions. The girl was weeping piteously, and the boy was growling in helpless rage, with their faces so downcast as to make them unrecognizable.

"Looky here!" shouted Brother Tichborne in a voice that surely carried all the way to Holy House. "Sinners! Afore the sight of the Lord! All of y'uns bow down on yore knees!"

The assembled crowd of young folks, or at least all the Crustians among them, knelt, or crouched, in attitudes of fear and submission. A few remained flagrantly unbowed at first, but Brother Tichborne's voice and his lashing sniffwhips soon stunned them into prostration.

"These here play-parties and dances has got to stop!" the minister boomed. He expatiated on the temptations of the flesh, the pitfalls of dancing, and the teachings of our Lord Joshua Crust, who had expressly forbidden any activity that might exalt physical pleasure. But he held his ultimate censure for the end of his sermon:

"And who do we have here?" he thundered, and kicked the offending boy under the chin, and then moved along the length of their conjunction to kick the girl also. "Hold up yore heads!" he yelled at them. "Raise yore faces and let all the world and Man see who ye air!" He kicked them again, and the boy and girl slowly raised their eyes to look woefully at the congregation, who, however, did not need this proof of their identity, having already identified them by smell through trembling sniffwhips. The boy was clearly Isham Whitter, a Carlotter, and the girl was just as obviously Lucy Whitter, his sister.

"IN-CEST!" shouted Brother Tichborne. "He that lieth with his own sister is damned to eternal shame! She that lieth with her own brother shall bear monsters as children! Cursed be them both! No sin is more worser in the eyes of Man!" Brother Tichborne began tripping over his own tongue: "The insectuous incest—the incestuous insect is the low-downest, unmanliest, kickworthiest sinner in the world!" And he kicked the couple again.

The minister could have used the awful example of Ish and Lucy Whitter to harangue and exhort the multitude for the rest of the night, but behold! a sudden blinding light flashed upon the scene from the open rear doorway of Holy House, and there stood the towering silhouette of Man Himself!

If the assembly had not already been overwhelmed by Brother Tichborne, they were petrified by the appearance of Man, and all of them crouched as low as they could get. Then when He moved, they all found their gitalongs and scurried in every direction until they were hidden from the sight of Man, either beneath the Platform or into the deepest forest of the grass and weeds.

Brother Tichborne alone, or rather alone with the offending incestuous couple, who still could not unjoin themselves and flee, or were attempting to flee in opposite directions and thus canceling each other's attempts, remained on the Platform. The minister genuflected into most devout prayer and worship.

A thousand—nay, two thousand, for everyone has two—sniffwhips and four thousand eyes watched warily as Man came stumbling down the back steps of Holy House and staggered out into the direction of Carlott. Man was not carrying His terrible swift revolver. His hands were empty, and free to swing through the air, grab at the air, to balance Himself, to grope His way out into the darkness.

As He approached the Platform, Brother Tichborne raised his head and clasped his touchers and his fore-gitalongs together in abject entreaty. "Lord, if it be Thy will," he prayed, "piss upon me!"

But Man did not reach the Platform. He stopped, and held His great hands to the sky. "SHARON!" He called in the most deafening voice, and two thousand tailprongs were lowered away from the sound. Even louder He called again, "SHAY-RONNNN!"

Then He pitched forward and fell headlong into the grass of Carlott, where He lay inert and seemingly lifeless for the rest of the night.

Brother Tichborne announced, "The Lord but sleepeth. Let us pray." He led them in an unenthusiastic prayer, and then he made a few routine announcements: the Crustian Young People's Fellowship would hold a sunset-to-sunrise hymn-sing Saturday night. And at the Sunday night worship service and prayer meeting, open for the first time to Carlotters, who were free, for the duration of the service, to enter Holy House, there would be a special call to Rapture, right before the very eyes of the Lord Himself. Everybody welcome!

"I'll believe it when I see it," a voice said beside Tish, and she turned to see that the roosterroach standing next to her, brushing her body with his own, was Archy Tichborne. He smiled handsomely at her, noticing her for the first time in his life, but she was too bashful even to smile back.

5.

If Greg Sam Ingledew's tailprongs had not been long since stunned into deafness by the continual announcements of his Clock, he might have heard, all the way to Parthenon, the calling voice of Man, who had cried the name of the Woman twice. She had heard it, across those two furlongs of empty town.

Although Sam could hear only the imagined steady tocking of his little chateau, his sense of sight and smell were greatly refined in compensation, and he could detect the slightest changes in Woman as She Herself picked up the distant calling of Her name. She was sitting in Her cheer-of-ease, a marvelous piece of furniture with a high back of padded cushions to support Her spine, other cushions to support Her bottom, other cushions to support and rest Her arms, which ended in lovely hands that held a book, in the wan light of a kerosene lamp on a round table beside Her cheer-of-ease. Sam appreciated that She preferred, although electricity was available to Her, to light Parthenon only with the comfortable glow of kerosene lanterns and lamps. It was easy on all four of his eyes; his ocelli, or stargazers, did not alarm the bejoshua out of him every time She lighted a lamp.

When the distant wail, "Sharon," wafted through the open screen door of Her room, the Woman dropped Her book into Her lap, involuntarily emitted three different scents of fear, annoyance, and excitement, which Sam's sniffwhips thoroughly perceived and classified, then spoke aloud, after the second sound of Her name, "Oh, for crying out loud! Larry, why don't you just drop dead?"

Sam did not hear this, but he could clearly determine that She had heard something from afar, that She was disturbed by it, and that She had spoken out against it. She did not immediately resume reading Her book.

Sam's mother had in his second or third instar explained to him the circumstances, handed down from Grandpa Ingledew, whereby Woman inhabited Parthenon, which, in ancient Stay More, had been one of the general merchandise stores for a whole population of Man, or Men, as well as Women and Children. The ancestor of this Woman, Sam's Woman, had been a proprietress of this merchandise store, which occupied the central room of her dwelling, her bedroom and sitting room occupying one side of Parthenon. The ancestor-Woman, a fabled demigoddess named Latha, had later abandoned Parthenon, and it had remained unoccupied through countless generations of roosterroaches, just as all the other buildings of Stay More were uninhabited and most of them disappearing through rot, neglect, windstorm and rainstorm, fire and vandalism. A generation ago (a roosterroach generation from east to west is about two whole years), this Woman, Sharon, suddenly returned to Stay More and reoccupied the dwelling-part but not the store-part of Parthenon. Sharon, Sam had discovered before he lost his hearing, was the actual granddaughter of Latha, and the two Women still communicated by the instrument which

41

sat permanently on the same round table which held the kerosene lamp.

Sam had even seen the ancient demigoddess Latha on more than one occasion, when that Woman had come to visit Her granddaughter, and the two had sat together in rocking cheers on the porch in the dusk, although usually when Latha came it was daylight and Sam was fast asleep. But the one time Latha had come at night and Sam had crawled boldly beneath Her rocking cheer to listen to the two Women talk, his hearing had been excellent and he had been able to catch enough of the conversation to deduce that his Woman, Sharon, although She had grown from earliest childhood to adulthood in Stay More, had gone away and lived for years in a city, then in a town, then in a city again, before coming back to Stay More to clean up and fix up the old Parthenon and live in it alone. The grandmother, Latha, had been concerned that Sharon might become very lonely in the dead village, but Sharon had protested that She would not be. This had been before the Man had come.

Because of his lifelong residence in the Woman's bedroom, Gregor Samsa Ingledew knew a few things that no other roosterroach of Stay More actually understood, and one of these was the name of the Man, which was Larry. Since the only roosterroaches who now inhabited Parthenon were Sam and his father, Squire Hank Ingledew, and since Squire Hank spent most of his waking hours hanging out at Doc Swain's place, only Sam had been present on the one occasion when Larry had actually come to Parthenon, one night, and had talked with the Woman at length, had argued with Her, and, about the time the Clock struck "TUTTI-FRUTTI," had removed the garments which covered Her body, had removed the garments which covered His body, and had climbed together with Her into Her bed, where, beneath the quilt required by the chill of autumn, He and She had made movements which Sam could only conjecture about. Then They had slept. Sam had remained awake beyond dawn, waiting for Them to awaken, but he had finally drifted into sleep and had awakened to find the Man gone and the Woman complaining loudly to Herself about Her stupidity and Her hangover and Her need for a cigarette.

Now Sam watched Sharon, who had heard the calling of her name twice, followed by a long silence. Sam's sniffwhips detected an unmistakable scent of yearning. The bristles on the lower tier of sniffwhip segments are especially sensitive to scents of yearning, wanting, inexpressible wistfulness, in either one's fellow roosterroaches or in Man, and it is considered good luck to pick up, on one's sniffwhips, such a pining smell. There is a popular saying, "More rare than pine is the smell of pining"—which is rare indeed, for there are few pine trees in this part of the Ozarks.

Sharon pined. And because he clearly detected it, Sam grew excited, knowing that some good luck would occur to him. He was not ordinarily superstitious, certainly not like the vast majority of roosterroaches, who could not even turn around without observing some of the most ridiculous beliefs and practices, but Sam believed that superstitions are more credible rules of conduct than religion, for which he had no use whatever: he knew enough to conclude that Woman had not created him; certainly Sharon had not. He did not believe that Joshua Crust had been the son of Sharon or of Larry or of any of Their ancestors. He did not believe that Sharon would continue feeding him only if he sang praises to Her . . . although he felt like singing praises to Her anyway. He did not believe that when he westered he would go to live forevermore on Her right hand. She wouldn't want him on Her right hand or Her left. And as for this Rapture business which that mountebank Chidiock Tichborne preached and extolled, Sam would love to be raptured by the Woman but not in the westerly sense, and certainly not by a firearm, which the Woman did not own.

But he did believe that the scent of pining brought good luck, and the very best luck he could wish for, which sometimes he dreamed about in his daily sleep, would be some magic that would either transform the Woman into a roosterroach, or, better, metamorphose Sam into a Man. And yet, desiring this with all his heart, he realized that such metamorphosis was sheer fable.

Sam stepped out from his Clock and crept to the edge of the mantelshelf. The Woman was picking up the black talking-instrument and cradling it against Her ear, while one of Her fingers twiddled the belly of the other half of the instrument around and around. Sam wondered if she was only calling Tel-Med, perhaps for a program with a name like "What to Do When Your Ex-Lover Drunkenly Yells Your Name

44

in the Middle of the Night." But she began talking into the thing, and one never talks *to* Tel-Med. Of course Sam could not hear what she was saying, nor could he, this time, even imagine it. Could he hear her if he moved closer? Very close? Say, right up the cheer-of-ease? Dare he?

First he wanted to be sure that he was scrupulously clean, although he had already had his evening bath and it was too early for his morning bath. He scrubbed his head vigorously, then washed both of his sniffwhips, counting each segment as it passed between his lips, 356 segments in all, each responsible for absorbing some information about the world around him. Next he washed and scrubbed his tailprongs with his rear gitalongs, and tested each prong, wiggling it and standing it erect, for although his tailprongs were no longer sensitive to sound they were still capable of full erection. He could also use them, if the occasion required, for feeling his way backwards; reverse sniffwhips, as it were.

How does a fastidious genteel roosterroach know when his nightly (or thrice-nightly) ablutions are finished? Of the 178 segments on each sniffwhip, the last two, at the very tip, have as their sole function an appraisal of one's own cleanliness, tidiness, and aroma. Sam no less than any other roosterroach would rather have lost both his tailprongs and been totally deaf than to lose the tips of his sniffwhips. Whenever an individual loses these, through accident, battle, or failure to keep them clean, that individual is almost certain to be dirty, stinking, and flowzy . . . until he regenerates the tips.

For all Man's repugnance toward him, the roosterroach is the most immaculate of insects, permitting no speck of dirt or disease to remain upon his body. And Gregor Samsa Ingledew was the most immaculate of roosterroaches. Not just in his person but in his surroundings: he kept the interior of the Clock, and most of its exterior too, spotless. The Woman, who was a fastidious housekeeper Herself, would have been proud of Sam, if She knew he existed. She did not. Didn't She ever wonder, when She was dusting Her room, why the Clock and the mantelshelf never needed to be dusted?

Sam climbed down the mantel and gained the floor. He was about to approach closer to a female, other than his mother, of any species, than he had ever been since his life began. For all his excellent grooming, which along with his intelligence, squirehood, and residential situation made him the most attractive and eligible bachelor of Stay More, Sam had a congenital flaw more damaging than deafness: he was enormously and painfully shy of females. All Ingledews had been, as long as anyone could remember. It was a family legend, nay, a longstanding family joke: if every Ingledew male had been the subject of some great story of heroic deeds, he was also the butt of some hilarious anecdote involving his shyness toward females and the extraordinary circumstances of fate or feminine intrigue that had permitted at least one male Ingledew in each generation to marry and perpetuate the family name . . . as well as the congenital dread of females.

But his terrible shyness toward any member of

the opposite sex would not now prevent Sam from approaching Sharon, for he did not intend to let Her see him. She was absorbed in Her conversation over the black talking-instrument. He selected the best route to get as close as possible to Her voice without being seen, and climbed up the very back of the tall cheer-of-ease, an easy task of crawling gitalong over gitalong through the nap of the fabric. Reaching the summit, he climbed down the other side, right behind Her head. He was very careful not to touch Her hair, and very careful to keep an escape route in sight in order to vanish in an instant in the unlikely event that She began to turn Her head in his direction.

From this proximity, Her voice was almost booming, although She spoke quietly. He could hear, if not every word, at least some of it.

". . . and feel so sorry for him but don't see that there's a blessed thing I or anyone could do . . ." She was saying. She was, Sam assumed, talking to Her grandmother. He had anticipated that She might be putting a call through to the Man Himself, but Holy House did not contain a talking-instrument. Sam was surprised to discover that he was glad She wasn't talking to Larry, which would have made Sam jealous. *Jealous?* he said to himself, in wonder. *I am jealous of Man?* Well, why not?

". . . if he could just give up and go away," She was saying. "Vernon has offered to evict him if I only tell him to. Vernon really hates what he's doing to that house, letting it go to ruin and shooting it full of holes. No, no, Gran, I'm not worried he'll shoot me. I never go near the house. He only shoots late at night, when he's blotto, I guess, and maybe his demons are pursuing him. Yes, maybe he's shooting at his demons. . . ."

Sam smiled. He would like to tell his kindred the Holy Housers that She had called them "demons." The Woman suddenly reached back with Her hand, and Sam thought She was going to swat him, but She only wanted to scratch the back of Her neck. Her fingers were lovely. If there was one way in which the Human creature was really superior to the roosterroach in design, Sam reflected, it was in the fingers. Roosterroaches had nothing like them; a roosterroach's touchers were clumsy stubs by comparison. One of Sharon's fingers was enwrapped with a dazzling metallic band more yellow than Her hair; the light glittering off it, reflected from the kerosene lamp, nearly blinded Sam.

". . . don't you think? It must have been at least the hundredth one, I don't even count them. What? Oh, of course I keep them, I've got a shoebox full of them. I wouldn't *think* of throwing them away, they're so beautifully written, such elegant language. I can hardly resist the urge to answer one of them, to write him back, at least to tell him that he'll never get his work done as long as he spends all his time writing letters to me. . . ."

The Woman turned Her head to one side, not enough for Her to see Sam even with peripheral vision, but enough for him to see the iris of Her eye. Her eyes were blue, a lighter blue than any of the shades of the evening air, a blue like the eggs of robins whose nest had fallen in a March storm into the yard of Parthenon, where Sam had come upon it. Rooster-roaches do not have the color vision to detect most hues of blue. Their color vision is most perceptive in ultraviolet, which Man cannot even see (one reason Sam was convinced that Man was not the omniscient ruler of the visible world). But Sam could clearly perceive that Sharon's iris was the azure tint of the robin's egg. The eyes of all roosterroaches are irides-cent shades of green. Sam adored Sharon's eyes.

". . . at least he's *supposed* to be doing a long critical essay on Daniel Lyam Montross, which is why he says he has to stay here. No, he hasn't written any more poetry himself for years. At least he doesn't write any of it to *me*, or if he does he doesn't show it to me. He said he's having trouble getting started on the Montross thing, but at least he's started it. . . ."

In those metamorphic dreams he sometimes had, when he became Her lover, Sam preferred not to bring Her down to his level and give Her pheromones, but instead raised himself to Manhood, keeping his affy-dizzy however and tempting Her with it, crawling into Her bed and—no, "crawling" was the wrong word. He was not all that clear what he would do with Man's body if he had one.

He was so transfixed by Her beauty and his day-dream of making love to her that he had not noticed the voice had stopped entirely, the voice had said "Good night, Gran, sleep tight," and the Woman had returned the talking-instrument to the table beside Her cheer-of-ease. Now She was standing up. Now She was turning. . . .

49

Sam's gitalongs went into action and he sprang for the crevice between the cushions of the cheer-of-ease. But he was just a fraction of a second too late. She saw him. He heard Her gasp.

In all the time the Ingledews had enjoyed the privilege of dwelling in Parthenon, they had never allowed themselves to be glimpsed by Her. Sam had violated this tradition, and he felt just rotten and awful. His father would wester him.

6.

Doc Colvin Swain was the seventh son of a seventh son, which Ozark tradition indicates as infallibly as the daily setting of the sun that he was destined to become a physician, even in spite of himself. He was born of a Swain (it is an old, old family name not to be confused with "swain," the name for an immature pre-imago male roosterroach, the male equivalent of "nymph") who was the last, or seventh, swain to emerge from his mother's easteregg, and Colvin himself emerged from *his* mother's easteregg last in line following Irvin, Gavin, Alvin, Marvin, Steven, and Vincent.

If being seventh was not enough to doom him to medical practice, Colvin Swain's name and its sake, which he never had the inclination to change, would have kept him from being a "normal" roosterroach, because the human Colvin Swain had been the greatly beloved physician to the village of Stay More in its last years of existence as a community, eons ago. Not only that, and not even to mention that Doc Swain the roosterroach had taken on Doc Swain the long-westered human's personality, his speech, his character, and even his habit of making "house calls," Doc Swain occupied the ruin of the old Swain clinic, on Roamin Road halfway between Holy House and Parthenon, that is, one furlong from each. The collapsing Swain clinic had no inhabitants except Doc (a widower) and a family of Daddies-long-legs who considered Doc too large to eat, and several families of *Theridon tepidariorum*, your ordinary house spider, whose webs had covered every corner of the interior of the clinic but who, like bats, ate only insects who flew, something Doc hadn't done since his last escape from the Great White Mouse. Indeed, Doc was rumored to have practiced medicine on various of these arachnid housemates of his; in any case, he was on good terms with the spiders and had the run of the clinic . . . or rather the hobble of it, since he was missing three unregenerated gitalongs, two on one side, one on the other, lost to the bite of his nemesis, the Great White Mouse, who had ambushed him on one of his errands of mercy into the backbrush . . . or so he claimed, although an eyewitness had hinted that the mysterious monster-mouse might have had provocation, that Doc was seen attempting to bite off its tail to use in one of the philters or nostrums that he occasionally concocted. It was said that the tip of an albino mouse's tail is an essential ingredient in the remedy for gout, which afflicted several of Doc's male

51

patients. But Doc swore the attack of the Great White Mouse upon his person was totally unprovoked, and he constantly plotted revenge.

"Heal thyself," nobody ever said to him, but ought to have, because he was a wreck of a specimen himself. In addition to the three missing unregenerated gitalongs, his heart was irregular, his digestion faulty, his ocelli, or stargazers, were nearly blind . . . and he appeared to have the gout. But his mind was sound, and next to Squire Hank Ingledew he was considered the wisest sage in the world.

In fact, next to Squire Ingledew was where he wanted to be, the two old codgers preferring each other's company to that of lesser mortals, and they could often be found together, of an evening, lounging on the porch of Doc's clinic, watching the world go by, commenting upon it, and holding court for the various other loafers, mostly older male roosterroaches, who liked to gather there, being forbidden by Squire Hank from congregating on the porch of Parthenon, and leaving the porch of Holy House to other folk.

On any given night, after breakfast, a couple dozen or more members of this Loafer's Court could be found lolling around Doc Swain and Squire Hank, listening to them holding forth on the ancient stories of Stay More, swapping tall tales, and waxing prophetic about their favorite subject, which was The Bomb, particularly the irreligious, anti-Rapture view of it held by many, who did not believe that Man would save the righteous from that great explosion but rather that Man himself would perish in the ho-

locaust, and the roosterroaches would have the oner-
ous responsibility of inheriting the earth, something
they did not particularly desire. No one could conceive of any explosion louder or worse than Man's
bullets, and there were many who thought that Man's
shooting was itself The Bomb, but the True Bombers
told the Anabombers that The Bomb would make the
explosions of bullets from His revolver seem like mere
clearings of the throat.

Tonight, Doc Swain, Squire Hank, and the Loafer's Court had watched the parade of damsels go sashaying down Roamin Road to Parthenon and back,
had seen drunk Jack Dingletoon straggling along in
pursuit, and had made comments, jokes, and insin-
uations about various of the girls, about Jack, about
one another, and about anything within the visible or
sniffable world.

When the end of the train hove into view and
there was comical Jack Dingletoon yelling, "Hi yoop!
I aint no Dingeltoon no more! By cracky, I'm a pure
dee pure blood Ingledew now, and a *squire* to boot!"
the members of the Loafer's Court cast glances and
sniffs at Squire Hank to see his reaction, and one of
them, O.D. Ledbetter, remarked, "Now what d'ye
reckon has guv that fool sech a notion?"

"Chism's Dew allus makes a feller feel bigger
than he is," observed Elbert Kimber. "That's what
it's suppose to do, aint it?"

Squire Hank did not comment, but spat, and
made ruminative gestures of his cheeks. No one could
remember when he had ever been silent before.

"Naw," remarked Doc Swain, "that aint it. He's

jist out of his head, maybe, because I tole him a little while ago that he aint got long for this world afore he goes west. He ast me to look 'im over, and blamed if his old Malpighian tubes aint all kivvered with fatty bodies."

The loafers stared at Doc and at one another. "Is that a fack?" several said, and "You don't mean to say so," said others, and one even said, "What's a malpigeon tube?" Each of them spat, each in his turn. Most of them had good reason for spitting, not to mark any territory (for all of *this* territory belonged to Doc), but because among the many other blessings bestowed upon them by Man, He left cigarette butts scattered throughout Holy House, from which an abundance of chewable leaf was salvaged and masticated by most of the male roosterroaches of Stay More. Tobacco did give one's head a pleasant giddiness and ease, but the chewing and spitting of it was essentially a ritual way of asserting one's identity and masculinity and the merging of one's identity with that of the male group.

"The Malpighian tubes," Doc explained, "are part of the digestive system, sorta wrapped around your gut like little wires. Man calls them 'kidneys'."

"Aw, shore," said Tolbert Duckworth, "I allus have a little drink fer my wife's kidneys."

The other loafers laughed, but Doc said, "Not *that* kind of kidney. This kind is sort of midway between yore gizzard and yore butthole. It sorta strains all the juice that runs through yore system."

Several of the company nodded their heads in understanding, spat, and Lum Plowright observed, "So ole Jack's strainer is on the blink?"

"Wal, the fatty bodies has shore squoze up his Malpighian tubes," Doc declared, feeling just a little guilty for breaking the Hypocritic Oath by openly discussing a patient's problems.

"His wife is a real fatty body," Fent Chism remarked, and the assembly guffawed, picturing Josie Dingletoon, a still-shapely dish despite her many and frequent litterings of eastereggs.

"She'll be a mandamn widow-gal, shore, afore long," Doc remarked.

This comment caused each loafer to reflect, as loafers will, upon his own mortality, the widow he would leave behind if he were not already widowered, the children who would survive and mourn or not for him, and the nature of west and of life, if any, after west. Such meditations naturally introduced one or the other of their two most popular topics, Janus-faced: the glorious history of now-almost-westered Stay More, and the any-day-now (or any-night-now) advent of The Bomb.

Tonight the court lingered upon each subject until it was exhausted. Perhaps it is unfair to call this assembly "loafers," because all roosterroaches are by nature gentlefolk of leisure, nonworkers, even vagrants, as the name *Periplaneta* suggests. Especially in contrast to the busy bee, the hyperactive ant, the industrious termite, the various nest-builders, daubers, potters, borers, and biters whose diurnal or nocturnal existence is of ceaseless activity, the roosterroach, once he has found his nightly share of morsels, crust or crumb, does nothing, knocks off, loiters about, putters, piddles, takes his ease without any responsibility other than the heavy chore of finding ways to

55

fill up the time between dusk breakfast and dawn supper.

No wonder roosterroaches are fond of gossip, philosophy, kidding and kibitzing, jokes, stories, tall tales, legends, superstitions, and half-baked religion. In this natural inclination, roosterroaches are ideally suited to imitate the Man of the Ozarks, or at least Ozark Man as He used to be, in the legendary days of Stay More's past, when Man, although a farmer, and a capable one, devoted only enough labor to His farm to provide food for His family and His devoted roosterroaches, and spent the major portion of His life in unhurried idleness.

Although there was only one Man left in Stay More for these roosterroaches to depend upon and venerate, and although He was not nearly as interesting as the fabled Stay Morons of yore, He was at least, like them, devoted to leisure. He did not work. He did not farm, though there were rumors that He spent a tiny portion of His daylight hours, late afternoon, before any roosterroach awoke to watch, puttering in a tiny vegetable garden across Roamin Road from Holy House. One night a delegation of roosterroaches had gone there and inspected His puny lettuce. The last of the human Ingledews had been gardeners, if nothing else, famed for their ability to grow onions as big as apples, but also pronouncing them "ingurns" as in the first syllable of their name. This Man did not pronounce them that way . . . or perhaps He did. It was hard to tell, because He never spoke. He had no one to speak to.

The loafers, if we must call them that, admired

their Man because He was a total loafer too, but pitied Him because he had no one to loaf *with*. None of the roosterroaches now living could ever recall when there was more than one Man, and indeed most of the fundamentalist Crustians believed that there was only one Man in all the world, but the old stories which the loafers told and retold on the porch of Doc Swain's place always involved a Stay More peopled with many Men, and Men (as well as Women and Children) living together and loafing together in an idyllic Golden Age.

The Golden Age of Stay More would remain only the subject of endless legends and embellished conjectures among the tale-telling roosterroaches until after The Bomb, when according to Crustian belief, Joshua Crust Himself would be resurrected from the west and take everyone in a Rapture to live on the right hand of Man in the perfect Ozark Golden Age of yore. Even those roosterroaches who were such infidels that they could not accept the idea of Joshua Crust and His resurrection still believed that life after The Bomb would become a new Golden Age.

Doc Swain alone did not believe this. Cheerful philosopher as he was, he was an utter pessimist on the subject of The Bomb. The Bomb, in his opinion, was inevitable. Whatever catastrophic form it took— asphyxiation, earthquake, famine, or, most dreadful for heat-loving roosterroaches, a big freeze—it would be horrible.

Roosterroaches are omnivorous, but that would do them no good if there was nothing to eat. "Fellers, if it comes to it," a loafer posed the question, "can we eat caterpillar shit?"

"After The Bomb," Doc pointed out, "caterpillars would be the first to wester."

The one drawback of the roosterroach's durability, longevity, adaptiveness, and imperishability was that being the last creature alive after the holocaust would pose a great problem: Who, or what, would the roosterroach eat?

"I'd shore hate to be the last roosterroach still east," Doc remarked to the assembled loafers.

"Nor me neither," said several of the other loafers, and spat, thoughtfully but decisively, each in his turn.

"Wal, Doc," Squire Hank Ingledew spoke up, "if you was the last, you'd have to whup me first afore you could commence eatin me, and once you'd et me, then yore biggest problem would be to figger out which part of yoreself to eat first, next."

The loafers guffawed, and O.D. Ledbetter suggested, "Me, I'd eat my hind end first."

"Haw," said Elbert Kimber, "then you wouldn't have no butthole to ee-liminate what you'd done et!" All the loafers snorted or snickered.

"I reckon I'd eat my sniffwhips first," said Tolbert Duckworth, "since I wouldn't be needin 'em no more nohow, what with nobody else around to sniff at."

"Then you'd never know how much you stunk," Squire Hank observed.

"Wouldn't make no difference nohow," Lum Plowright put in. "But me, what I'd do, since it'd be my last meal on earth, I'd enjoy myself and eat my stomach first!" Several others nodded in agreement, and spat.

"That'd wester ye right off," Doc Swain said. "Now I tell ye fellers, assumin I could whup Squire Hank and be the last 'stead of him, and assumin I'd done already had the satisfaction of watchin that White Mouse wester a slow, painful west, I reckon I'd jist not eat none of me, but slowly starve to west, and take a last stroll down to Banty Creek and back."

"Might as well hop in it and drown," Squire Hank said, and spat.

"Naw," said Doc Swain. "I'd jist look all around me, at ever livin thing that had westered, includin that putrefied White Mouse, and I would know that I was the very last mandamn livin thing on earth. Wouldn't that be a satisfaction? Wouldn't that be a reward for what-all I'd had to live through? Jist to know that? Jist to say to myself, 'I am the last mandamned livin thing on earth?' "

Since these were mostly heuristic questions, or rhetorical, or both, no one responded. The company of loafers lost themselves in meditation, imagining the scenario that Doc had pictured. At length, Tolbert Duckworth, who was a good Crustian and an elder in the church, remarked, "Hit shore is enough to make a body glad that our Lord Joshua Crust is gonna rapture us and save us from all sech as that, if Man Himself don't rapture us first."

Several others nodded, and spat. Neither Squire Hank nor Doc Swain nodded, but they spat.

7.

Tish Dingletoon tarried beneath the Platform long after the play-party had been broken up by Brother Tichborne and everyone had gone home or elsewhere. She wondered if she would ever again have a chance to attract Archy Tichborne to her, ever to get him within range of her pheromones when she was ready to use them. No, probably the Fate-Thing intended for her to marry a Carlotter. How vain of her to aspire to the attentions of a Holy House roosterroach. Sure, Jim Tom Dinsmore would be glad to have her and would take her to live in the Smock if she would marry him, but he was a puny and unsightly specimen, compared with Archy Tichborne.

Might just as well be getting on back, Tish told herself, and crawled out from under the Platform and turned her steps sadly homeward. But as she sought the path to the hollow log that was the Dingletoon home, she bumped into one of the fingertips of Man, who lay prone with his arms outstretched in the grass of Carlott. The closeness of Him overwhelmed her, even more than His great size. Tish passed her sniff-whips slowly over the tip of His fingernail and attempted to identify the plethora of traces of all that Man had touched, scratched, tickled or tapped within the past several hours. This was the closest she had ever been to Man, and she had never approached any of the things He had touched, scratched, tickled or tapped, so she could not readily identify these strange new sensations on her sniffwhips. She was in total awe, but not in fear. *Fear the Lord thy Man*, she had

60

heard, again and again, and yet she was not afraid of Him. As she moved closer to the tall grass into which His face was pressed, and then drew so close that the tips of her sniffwhips could touch the tips of His beard-whiskers, whatever fear or worship she was supposed to feel for Him was replaced by a sudden compassion, something she had no business feeling, as if she were better than Him, or more fortunate than Him, or at least much more sober than Him, or not smaller than Him at all but His own size. This would have amounted almost to blasphemous condescension had it not been a pure impulse of sympathy, without any vanity behind it.

"Pore feller," she said aloud, knowing He couldn't hear her. "You're just a critter, like me. Whatever's troublin Ye aint all that different from the kinds of troubles I got. You git hungry too, don't Ye? And You git sad too, I bet. And most of all, Man, You git lonely all the time."

Never mind that if He awakened, and had His gun, He would rapture her quicker than the wink of a stargazer. For this moment, Tish loved Him, and it was not the sort of love that all Crustians spoke of when they said, *Love the Lord thy Man*.

Tish knew that the Fate-Thing was more powerful than Him, that He was under the dominion of the Fate-Thing just as much as she was. Did the Fate-Thing have a better name? Was its name "Sharon"? Had He been calling out to the Fate-Thing, Sharon? If Sharon was the name of the Fate-Thing, then Tish ought to address her prayers not to Man but to Sharon.

Experimentally, Tish called out, as He had done,

"SHARON!" Again she called, louder but questioningly, "SHAY-RONN?" But if that was the Fate-Thing's name, it—or She—did not respond, any more than it—or She—had responded to the Lord Himself.

Meditating on her walk homeward, Tish realized that perhaps "Sharon" was not the name of any Fate-Thing, but, rather, of the Woman who dwelt in Parthenon. Or perhaps the Woman *was* the Fate-Thing. Tish had had her very first glimpse of the Woman earlier tonight when the parade of maidens turned their train in the yard of Parthenon, that fabled house which was a private castle for the squires Ingledew. Although Tish had seen Squire Hank around the village often, she had never seen handsome Squire Sam, who, her friends told her, did not mix. Tish's girl-friends were always having nightdreams in which they were endlessly noticed and courted by Squire Sam, like a commoner by a prince, and perhaps wedded by him and made into a princess and taken to live in his fabulous Clock. Tish could not even conceive of what a Clock looked like, although she heard it distantly every hour, and somehow she associated the sound it made, its chiming of "BUN," "TART," etc., with Squire Sam, as if in a sweet pealing voice he were calling out the times of night for her.

These were the thoughts that filled her young head as she walked slowly homeward. As she neared the Dingletoon log, she heard certain rhythmic sounds which she recognized as her mother's crooning to Tish's infant siblings:

"Joshua bless yore pitchy eyeses! And yore waxy cheekses! And yore cherry mouthses! And yore scraggly legses! And ever bitty bits of you'unses' bles-sit bodies!''

There were so many of them, in the several broods of Jack and Josie Dingletoon, including a freshly hatched litter of fifteen scarcely out of their milk-white babyhood and with their easteregg open like a huge zippered purse in the center of the loafing room. In addition to these babies, who were scampering madly all over the place in search of any scrap that was chewable, there was another brood of a baker's dozen in their third instar, and still a third brood in their fifth instar, making for quite a large family. Of course the older children of this family could just as well set up their own homes and lives, but the Dingletoons had always been family-oriented and possessed of a strong flocking instinct, like many poor Carlott families—the Flockroaches of Stay More. Tish was the only one of her generation of siblings to remain in the household, and thus a share of the supervision of the younger ones fell upon her.

Mother of them all and veteran of many nights of hauling easatereggs around at the end of her abdomen, Josie Dingletoon still retained much of the freshness and even the plump prettiness of her youth, and it was clear that whatever attractiveness Tish possessed had been inherited from her mother.

"I'll dance with 'em a while for ye, Momma," Tish offered, and sought to relieve her mother of the responsibility for keeping the children entertained.

But Josie, always blithe, seemed even more cheerful tonight. "We'll everbody dance!" she exclaimed. "I'm glad ye've come, Letitia hon, but not to spell me with these younguns. We've all got reason to party and dance! Jist wait'll I tell ye!"

"Maw . . ." said young Jubal, touching his sniff-whip timidly to her, but he was ignored.

"Does it have anything to do with Daddy makin such a joke of hisself tonight?" Tish asked. "Did you hear about it? I was so mortified I wanted to sink into the ground and disappear or be gobbled right up by a frog!"

"Now daughter, that was jist him a–celebratin the news. It has been diskivvered that we air quality folks, and yore father has good reason to be proud! We've all got reason to be proud as Punch! We belong to a great fambly that goes back past the time of Joshua Crust Hisself, the time of the fabled pagan Ingledews of yore!"

"Maw . . ." the boy Jubal attempted to gain her attention again but was again rebuffed.

"What on earth are ye talkin about, Mother?" Tish asked.

"Lissen a me, Tishy hon!" exclaimed Josie, nearly beside herself with excitement. "These news will make yore bosom swell! I swear if we aint all Ingle-dews! Yore dad wasn't jist cuttin a dido when he said that! That were no flimflam windy lie-tale he picked up! He's the rightful descendant of all the big Squire Ingledews!"

"*Maw!*" persisted the kid Jubal and claimed her notice. "Air we all of us squires now?"

Josie looked down and sniffed down at her son. "No, you fool," she said to him. "Jist me and yore Paw."

"I'm right glad to hear it, Mother, if it's true," Tish said, "but will it do us any good?"

"Why, naturally, chile," Josie declared. "We kin all go live in Partheeny!" She paused to let these words caress the lengths of every listening pair of tailprongs. The older siblings whispered dramatically among themselves, *Partheeny!* and the middle siblings began explaining to the infant siblings what and where Partheeny was.

Tish could not believe this fabulous likelihood, and she began casting about with her sniffwhips in search of her father, to have him confirm the possibility. "Whereabouts is Daddy at?" she asked her mother.

Josie took on a flustered look. "Now don't you go a-bustin out mad at yore pore ole pappy, Tishia gal, but he got so excited with the news that he went to see if they wouldn't let him into the cookroom at Holy House."

"*What?*" Tish exclaimed. "Why, he's off his rocker! How could you let him do such a thing?"

Josie hung her head. "Wal, he's allus had a hankerin fer some real beer, and who'm I to deny him? But I reckon I'd best go fetch him, afore he gits his fool self shot by the Lord."

"The Lord aint a-rapturin nobody tonight," Tish said. "He has passed plumb out in the middle of Carlott. I touched Him myself."

"You did *which*?" Josie asked, aghast.

"Not with my touchers, just my sniffwhips, I touched Him while He lay, jist to see if He felt real," Tish declared, with no little pride.

The entire room fell silent. None of the middle siblings, let alone the younger ones, had ever had a glimpse of Him, although every morning they said their prayers to Him at bedtime. To think that their very own big sister, Sis Tish, had actually not only seen Him but also actually and truly really *touched* Him! They all gathered around her and tried to touch her, as if some of the magic would rub off on them. They all began babbling in excitement at once.

"Hush, you'uns!" Josie demanded, then turned on Tish. "Daughter, I don't know what to think of ye! Aint I never taught ye no sense? Don't ye know that you must never, *never* touch the Lord?"

"But He's out cold, west-drunk jist like Daddy gits sometimes," Tish tried to explain.

Josie slapped her. With both sniffwhips the mother lashed the sides of Tish's face, bringing tears to her eyes. "Hesh yore wicked mouth!" she exclaimed. "That's blasphemy! The Lord is probably jist a-sleepin, this time of night, and you might've disturbed His rest."

"But He's drunk as a biled owl!" Tish wailed, telling the truth, although truthfully none of the owls she had seen, of which there were several in the woods of Stay More, were either boiled or drunk.

Josie gasped, hmmphed, and made the sign of the pin with her sniffwhips. "I had best go take a look fer myself," she said to herself, then told her oldest daughter, "I'd best go look fer yore father." She began a thorough cleaning of herself in preparation for departure.

"Momma, you aint lightin out for the cookroom too, are ye?" Tish asked.

"If I have to," Josie said, nearly beside herself with nervous excitement: even if she didn't get to touch the Lord herself, she might find her husband in the cookroom, where she had never been before, and might get to sample the fabulous edibles there. And maybe she might even be allowed to enter one of those cans of beer. "Now lissen a me, Tish," she gave instructions, "if I aint back afore daypeep, make shore none of the least-uns watches the mornin star, and git 'em to say their prayers, and keep Jubal outa the sisters' hidey-hole, and don't let none of 'em git in the storehole where Paw keeps the morel mushrooms, and be sure nary one of 'em watches the sun rise. Kin you remember all that?" Tish nodded her head, although the list of the injunctions was long, and still another one remained, a formality: "And watch out for the badgers, bats, and beastly bugs!"

"Be keerful, Momma," Tish said, as Josie left the log, and Tish found herself in charge of the whole family. A dozen or so tickled up to her and begged her for a story, but she put them off, saying she'd give them a story at bedtime. She supervised them as best she could, as they left the log to forage for bits of algae and fungi, edible but not palatable fodder. Her tailprongs picked up the sounds of their stomachs grumbling like a pack of hungry ants. Almost absently, Tish reached up and took one of her sniffwhips into her mouth and began simultaneously to wash, taste, smell, and "count the beads" on it. This process provided her with information about her environment: the temperature (73° and falling), tomorrow's forecast (partly cloudy, scattered thundershowers), the present locations of each of her brothers and sis-

67

ters, what they were eating, which ones had intestinal problems or mental problems, which ones had constipation or diarrhea, and how many worms, crickets, and katydids were in the vicinity. Thus she kept track of the passing of the night.

She could no longer find her mother within range of her sniffwhips, so assumed she had reached Holy House and perhaps actually entered the cookroom. Would she ever see her parents again? She tuned in the area of Carlott where He had been lying, and discovered that still He lay. The night passed on.

Continually vigilant toward her siblings, she kept count and discovered one missing. She called Jubal to her, and said, "Jubal, I caint find Joe Don."

Jubal replied, "Something et him."

These were sad words. It was sorrowful news when, if a child westered, the reason was announced as "Something he et." It was more sorrowful if the last two words were transposed. Tish tuned her sniffwhips and picked up the scent of a green frog, *Hyla cinerea*, but it was climbing back up whatever tree it had come down out of to make a meal of Joe Don. Tish called the rest of the siblings in out of the yard, and told the ones who did not already know that their brother Joe Don had gone west, into the crop of a green frog. Everyone grieved together for a few minutes, and several of the older children declared, "Hit's the Lord's will," but Tish knew that the Lord's will, at this moment under the influence of alcohol, wasn't.

"Now tell us a bedtime story, Sis," Jubal requested, knowing they needed something to take their minds off the westering of Joe Don, and the siblings chorused, "Yep, a story, yep a story Sis."

She gathered them to her and began, "One time
. . ." She had learned to begin all her stories this way.
Such a beginning carried the suggestion not only that
the story being told had occurred once upon a time
long, long ago, but also that it had occurred only once,
a one-time-only unique event. She searched her store
of favorite stories, and decided to tell them one about
the Mockroach. "One time there was a little roosterroach. He disobeyed his pappy and momma, who
told him to be sure and go to sleep at the first
peep of light, and to sleep all day. He wanted to
stay awake during the day, so's he could see what
was happenin in the world while roosterroaches
sleep."

And she told how the foolhardy roosterroach sallied forth into the daylight and found himself among
the diurnal creatures who prey and eat by light, birds
of all kinds who fly by day, and snakes and lizards
who roam by day, and four-footed animals like squir-
rels who prowl by day. All of these monsters would
have eaten the roosterroach, but he was protected by
the Mockroach, who had a test for him.

The Mockroach protected the roosterroach so
that he could stay east in the daylight long enough to
decide whether he truly wanted to be a day-bug or
go on being a night-bug as Man had intended him to
be.

The world of daylight was wonderful. Not only
was it full of Man, and His Woman and Children, all
running around and working and playing in the sunshine, but it was full of open flowers that close at
night, and the music of birds that sing only by day,
not as sweet as the nightingale but more of them, and

there were colors everywhere, not just the hundred grays and blues of night, but yellows and greens and reds!

The roosterroach thought everything was lovely, but the Mockroach told him that if he wanted to remain a day-bug he would have to decide to be changed either into a day-bug who eats grass or a day-bug who eats other bugs: a herbivore or a carnivore.

Of course no roosterroach had ever eaten grass or eaten another bug, at least not a live one. The Mockroach made him try a sample of each. The roosterroach chewed and chewed on the blade of grass, but he couldn't swallow it and spat it out. The Mockroach gave him the head of a fly to eat, and he chewed it and chewed it, and swallowed it, but it made him sick, and he puked it up.

The Mockroach told the roosterroach that if he could learn to eat grass, he could become a grasshopper, and dance and sing in the meadows and pastures all day long, all summer long, a happy pastoral life. He could jump great distances and fly with bright yellow wings, and it would be an easy, idyllic existence.

And if the roosterroach could learn to eat other insects, he could become a praying mantis with long powerful forelegs to seize any small thing that flew his way. He could stay put and not have to run around, and could eat anything that he caught, any insect that flew or crawled, and even lizards, frogs, and small birds! The mantis could eat the grasshopper, but the grasshopper couldn't eat the mantis.

Tish paused, and looked around her at her forty-two brothers and sisters, who were hanging on her every word with their mouths agape in wonder and their small brains almost visibly churning. "Children," she asked them, "which would you choose to be?"

"The grasshopper!" said Jubal, but he was drowned out by nearly all the others, who were clamoring, "The mantis! The mantis! The praying mantis!"

Tish would have given her story a different ending, if they had voted for the grasshopper. She would have told how the roosterroach was changed into a grasshopper and enjoyed a truly Arcadian life, which, however, ended when he was eaten by a meadow lark. But because they wanted the mantis, she said, "Okay. The Mockroach changed the roosterroach into a praying mantis and told him to pray to him, then hopped on his back and said, 'Giddyup! You've got to be my horsey!' and the poor mantis had to carry the Mockroach everywhere he went, forevermore. That's why Man calls the mantis, 'devil's horse.' "

The children were downcast with disappointment at the fate of the mantis but, Tish was certain as she ran them off to their beds, they would think twice before ever wanting to be changed into anything.

She herself, if she could be changed, would have chosen to become a cecropia moth, and remain nocturnal. The cecropia had a wingspan of nearly seven inches and was the most beautiful insect Tish had ever seen. But she would wait until the children were older

71

to tell them the story of the cecropia. The best thing about it was that once it was grown up, the cecropia didn't have to choose between eating vegetables or being a predator. The adult cecropia ate nothing. Its only purpose was love.

INSTAR THE SECOND:
Maiden No More

8.

Sam waited in the weeds beside the porch of Doc Swain's clinic for the Loafer's Court to break up. He would have been welcome to join them—no Ingledew was shy toward his fellow males the way he was toward females—but Sam didn't want to have it known that he was becoming progressively deaf. He hated even to let Doc himself know, but that was now inevitable. Sam would wait until the others, including his father, had gone.

His father was the last to leave, in the wee hours, well past midnight. It seemed he would never leave. Squire Hank and Doc Swain could talk all night, and often did, and often simultaneously, neither listening to the other, but neither needing to, since they agreed on almost everything and never argued. Once Squire Hank had remarked to his son, explaining his nightly attendance at Doc Swain's, "Hit shore beats listenin to myself talk."

In his fifth and sixth instars Sam had sometimes followed his father to the porch of Doc Swain's clinic, and had listened to them talking with what struck Sam as an uncanny ability to appear to listen to the other's words while speaking one's own. At these get-togethers, Sam had learned all there was to know about the glorious past of Stay More, and almost all there was to know about the eventual coming of The Bomb. Sam suspected that Doc Swain knew a few things about The Bomb which he would not even share with Squire Hank.

Sam could not hear these final words that his father spoke to Doc Swain:

"Best be gittin on down back. Come go home with me."

Nor could he hear Doc Swain's reply:

"Reckon not tonight. Stay more and spend the day with me."

But Sam had heard this exchange countless times when he still had his hearing and he knew that they were exchanging polite leave-takings, neither meaning sincerely the formalities he said. Squire Hank would not even consider actually inviting his best friend to Parthenon, and Doc Swain wasn't really interested in having Squire Hank sleep over through the day. But still the old roosterroaches continued for at least fifteen minutes:

"Caint do that, I reckon. Whyn't ye jist come along down to my place?"

"Better not. You make yoreself pleasant and stay the whole day."

"Time to light out fer home. Come and keep me company."

"Not tonight, Squar. You jist move in here and have you some vittles."

"Thank ye, Doc, but I'm a mind to git on home. You come with me."

Neither roosterroach was willing to yield the last word to the other, and thus these invitations and declinings and counter-invitations continued through infinite variations, until finally Doc Swain made a slight change:

"Wal, come again, then, and fix to stay a week."

"If you'll come stay a week with me, first. Let's go."

"Won't do it tonight, I reckon, Hank. You keep a eye out for the White Mouse for me."

"I'll watch fer 'im. See ye tomorrow night."

Squire Hank got the last word, and Doc, as a courtesy, let him have it, and Squire Hank hitched up his gitalongs and shuffled along homeward. Sam waited a little while, until his father was completely out of sight and sniff. Doc Swain was alone now, crouched upon his porch, his sniffwhips lying at rest alongside his body, his wise old eyes staring outward into the blackness with a sad expression, as if he were still thinking about The Bomb.

Doc's sniffwhips snapped to attention as Sam approached. He required a full second to recognize Sam, and then he spat and said, "Wal, if it aint Samuel! Aint seen you in a locust's age, my boy."

Sam could not hear this, but he said, "Hidy, Doc. How's ever little thing with you?"

"Jist fine," Doc said. "I'm same as usual but what about you? I figgered that Clock had done went and et ye."

75

Sam decided not to pretend further that he could hear, and told the kindly physician, "Doc, I'm near about deaf."

"Huh? Wal, it aint no wonder, that old Clock has done et yore tailprongs, maybe. Want I should look 'em over fer ye?"

Nor did Sam hear this. Doc repeated himself, louder, and Sam saw his mouth working and even felt a waft of his voice along his sniffwhips, but his tailprongs registered no sound. "Am I getting old, Doc?" he asked.

"That aint it. Here, let me have a look at yore prongs," Doc insisted and moved around and lifted and lowered each of Sam's cerci, counting the articles on each. "Nineteen is the most anybody could hope to have, per prong," Doc assured him, then minutely examined the filaments on each article. "They're all clean as new pins," he remarked. "No blasphemy meant." He abruptly bit one prong.

"Ouch!" Sam said.

"Reckon whatever it is," declared Doc, "it aint likely organic but functional. Know what I think? Samuel, my young friend, I'm afraid that Clock has done went and stunned yore prongs beyond repair. Most all yore life you've heared that Clock strike ever hour much too close. It would drive anybody deef."

Sam heard none of this, but he asked, desperately, "What can I *do*?"

"Wouldn't do ye no good to move out of the Clock now, I'm afeared," Doc said. "The damage is done done."

"I caint hear you, Doc," Sam said.

"I SAID, THE DAMAGE IS DONE DONE!" Doc shouted. "WHAT I RECKON YOU NEED IS, IS A WIFE TO TAKE KEER OF YE!"

Sam heard this, and blushed. "Aw, Doc . . ."

"I fergot," Doc apologized. "None of you Ingledews has ever had the least bit of nerve when it comes to courtin females. How're we gonna git ye a wife?" Since Sam could not hear this, Doc was talking more to himself than to Sam, but he was good at that, and continued, "Of course, any gal in Stay More would give her left sniffwhip to be yore wife, but you'd have to perpose, and you'd sooner wester than look a gal in the eye, wouldn't ye? JIST A MINUTE," he raised his voice, held up a foreclaw, then disappeared into his clinic. More than a minute passed before he reappeared, dragging behind him something that was almost too heavy for him to pull. It was a pill, of sorts. He presented it to Sam. "HERE," he said, loudly. "Now don't ye tell a soul I gave ye this, but haul it along home with ye and keep it, and whenever ye find a gal who strikes yore fancy, why, jist take a nibble or two outen this here pill, and it'll give ye the nerve to say 'hidy' to her."

Sam heard none of this, except the "here." "What's this?" he asked.

"HIT'S *SANG*," Doc Swain explained. "Root of the ginseng, and powerful scarce to come by." Sam's befuddlement was obvious and Doc had to yell and repeat himself and then yell and repeat a complicated explanation of how ginseng root works, and what it tastes like, and what the indications and contraindications were for its use. When, after much yelling and gesturing, Doc was convinced that Sam understood him, Doc said, "Well?"

"Doc," Sam declared, "I came to see you about my deafness and you give me a remedy for impotence."

Doc guffawed, and then he explained, loudly and with many repetitions, that the ginseng root would indirectly help Sam's deafness by giving him the nerve to woo and wed a wife who would become his surrogate tailprongs and do his listening for him.

"But can't anything be done directly for my tailprongs?" Sam asked.

"Wal . . ." Doc said, and hesitated, and tried to review in his mind all the cases of deafness that he had heard about or treated. Then Doc held up a foreclaw. "There's only one substance, and it aint scientific like ginseng. It aint even medical, but it never fails. It aint even somethin I've seen work before myself, but my education has been sort of classical, ye know. Most likely you'd call this jist one of them oletimey superstitions, and maybe that's all it is, but it works."

"Speak up, Doc," Sam said. "What is it? Do you have to coat my prongs with mandrake sap or something?"

"Worse than that," Doc said. "I could go out tonight and find all the mandrake sap you'd ever hope to want, but that aint it. What you need is grease from the mountings of a church bell, and it has to be a church bell recently rung."

Sam stared at Doc and shook his head, and Doc repeated himself so loudly that the bats in the air folded their ears and covered them with their wings. When the prescription had finally registered, Sam exclaimed, "Joshua H. Crust!" without blasphemy to Doc, since Doc wasn't a Crustian either. Sam tried to picture in his mind's eye a church bell. The only bell he had ever seen was the bell in the Stay More schoolhouse, which long ago Men had used on infrequent occasion as a church.

"Grease," Sam said, and let several moments pass before adding, "from the mountings," and a long silence ensued before his next words, "of a church bell," followed by an interminable hiatus preceding his repetition of the words, "recently rung." Then he sighed loudly and said to Doc, "History has it that that bell in the Stay More schoolhouse was never rung except for school . . . or for a funeral. There are no more schoolchildren of Man . . . or of Woman. And for there to be a funeral, one of Them would have to wester. Who will it be? Well, thanks a whole lot, Doc," Sam said with no little sarcasm. "It does me a lot of good. Let me know if you hear of any reason They should ring the bell. Or let me know if you hear the bell." Sam prepared to leave.

Doc did not bother with the "stay more" ritual. All he said was, loudly, "DON'T FORGET THIS HERE SANG ROOT."

Sam stared at the "pill" of ginseng idly, remembered what it was for, and idly dragged it along home, where he ensconced it in a corner of his Clock among his other preserves and collectibles.

9.

Foredawn, that lambent time when the world becomes westerly quiet and still for nocturnal as well as diurnal creatures, Squire John Ingledew, a.k.a. Jack Dingletoon, found himself belly-up atop a liquid medium. The state, condition, or position of "belly-up" is so characteristic of west that some folks seeking to avoid the unpleasant associations of the word "west" employ the euphemism "belly-up." No insect would consciously lie on its back unless it were west . . . and if it were west, it would not be conscious. Any insect who accidentally gets into the belly-up position will, like a turtle on its back, kick and struggle like mad to right itself. But Jack did not kick or struggle. He was happy. He was feeling better than he could ever remember having felt, although he was vaguely troubled by an inability to remember clearly how he had reached this state, condition, or position.

He had been amazed at the welcome he had received in the cookroom of Holy House. He had expected to be denied admission, or at least challenged, and he had been prepared to assert the authority of his lineage. He could not have known that Squire Hank himself had quietly spread word throughout Stay More that Jack Dingletoon should be treated with respect and cordiality, that if Jack actually were an Ingledew then he was due such courtesy, and if he were only deluded into thinking he was an Ingledew he ought to be "humored."

Jack had been prepared to barge into the cookroom lashing his sniffwhips right and left and declaring, "Outa my way, boys! I'm a Ingledew, by cracky, and I aim to get my share!" But he'd scarcely had the chance to speak before he was greeted with loud exclamations of "Hidy, Squar John!" and "Proud to see ye, Squar John!" and "Light down and set, Squar John!" and before he knew it they were leading him to a right fair-sized puddle of beer on the linoleum. Between lapping up the brew and pausing to munch a morsel of potato chip or something they thrust upon him, he never got a chance to say a word.

Late in the night, or rather early in the morning, he had been surprised to see a female come sashaying into the cookroom, and despite his intoxication, or because of what his fellows were saying about her, Jack learned that the female was his own wife, Josie. The cookroom was an all-male preserve, with strict rules governing attendance and excluding all females, but, strangely, the male roosterroaches had shown Josie the same courtesy and welcome they tendered to Jack, and it had gone to Josie's head, making her giddier than the beer on which she was allowed to fill up.

Floating belly-up, Jack wondered, idly, what had become of his wife now. The last he'd paid any notice, she was flirting with Troy Dinsmore, a Smockroach, but it was all just innocent trifling, and old Troy was too drunk to get serious anyhow. Jack turned his head to one side, extended his touchers into the liquid and brought them to his lips. It was a fresher brew than what had been on the linoleum. It still had some fizz to it. Jack wiggled his tailprongs and made it foam a bit.

Then he noticed the other roosterroach, also

floating belly-up. It wasn't Josie. It appeared to be Jaybird Coe, a Frockroach, who, Jack realized, had within the past few hours become his best buddy.

"Aint this the life?" Jack said to Jaybird, and demonstrated how he could paddle with his tailprongs and actually scoot around on the surface of the beer, around and around within the confines of the metal tank. Tailprongs normally are sticking up overhead, or rather overtail, but if one is lying on one's back, belly-up in beer, then they are extending downward into the liquid. Jack hoped his example would inspire Jaybird to paddle around too, but Jaybird wouldn't do it. He just lay there, floating on his back. Jack dipped a sniffwhip into the brew and splashed Jaybird with it, right in the face, but Jaybird didn't seem to mind. "Drunk as a wheelbarrow," Jack observed, although the only wheelbarrow he had seen, across the road in the Lord's Garden Patch, was a teetotaller.

Jack studied the ceiling. There was a slot-shaped opening in it, through which poured the first light of dawn. It didn't bother Jack, but he was vaguely bothered by the memory of having dropped through that slot to reach where he was. That implied, somehow, a problem, though at the moment he couldn't put his sniffwhips on just what the problem was. He nudged Jaybird. "Hey, Jaybird," he said. But Jaybird didn't respond. Jack tickled his face with his sniffwhip. "Come on, Jay, pop out of it," he urged, and bumped up against Jaybird forcefully, but his friend lay as still as west. *West?* Jack thought, and began to feel a rising panic.

He heard a distant voice calling his name. Or

calling him by the name he used to have, Jack. Now he was Squire John, but this voice didn't seem to know that. It was a high-pitched female voice, and Jack tried to identify its owner with his sniffwhips, but all he could pick up on his sniffwhips was the smell of the beer all around him, along with a steadily growing scent of westwardness, the west of the belly-up feller beside him, Jaybird.

"Jack, whar air ye?" came the voice, again and again, and Jack realized it was Josie.

He called back, "Josie? I'm down here inside of this beer can!" Soon he saw her face peering down at him from the slot overhead. How had she got up there, to the top of the can? She had no wings. Had someone boosted her up? "Keep back from the aidge!" he cautioned her. "You'll fall in, too."

"What're ye doin down thar, Jack?" she asked.

"Jist a-layin here, floatin around and feelin fine," he declared.

"You aint drownded, air ye?"

"Noo, but it 'pears thet ole Jaybird might be."

"How did ye git down thar, Jack?"

"Same way you're liable to git down here if ye don't step back," Jack warned her, but the words were not out of his mouth before he saw her tumbling headlong down into the can. With a gentle splash she landed beside him, and got a snootful of beer.

"Mmm-mmm," she purred, licking her mandibles. "This is the real stuff!"

"Now look what ye've done went and done," he pointed out. "Now we're both trapped in here." He had figured the problem out.

83

She noticed belly-up Jaybird. "Is he really westered off?" she asked.

"That, or he's drunker'n a fried coot," Jack said.

Josie had never seen a fried coot. But she sniffed
the distinct odor of westwardness that emanated from
Jaybird's corpse, and she felt both a mingling of sorrow for the westered and a sense of responsibility: she
wondered which, if any, of the few edibles stored in
her larder she could take to Samantha Coe for the
funeral feed. Josie didn't have a scrap of sweetstuff
anywhere in the log, what with her big family, but
the other ladies would be sure to bring Samantha a
bit of pie or cake or at least cookie for the funeral
feed, and Josie would look cheap, as usual. She complained to her husband, "I don't have a blessit thing
to take to the funeral feed."

"Lorgamercy, Maw, is thet all ye kin think of,
at a time like this?" Jack demanded. "It aint Jaybird's
funeral we're concerned with. It's our own, if we caint
git out of here."

Josie took another sip of the beer that surrounded
her, and wondered how long it would take her, with
Jack's help, to drink all of it. "How deep is this, hon?"
she asked.

"I aint tried to touch bottom," he declared. "And
I aint so certain I'd keer to try."

Josie attempted to explain her plan. If they drank
all the beer, they couldn't drown in it.

"Now thet is real, real clever," Jack commented
with sarcasm, tapping his forehead with a toucher.
"But jist think about it a minute. Whar is all the beer
we drink gonna *go*?"

Josie thought for a minute. "Oh," she then said. She lapsed into worried silence, and paddled around idly with her tailprongs, but the fun of it rapidly palled. "Jack," she asked, "kin ye turn right side up?"

"Maw, I wush ye'd stop callin me 'Jack.' You don't have to call me 'Squar John' but at least 'John' would be a heap of improvement."

"Wal John, if you're shore enough a Ingledew, you orter be able to turn right side up and spread yore wings and fly out of here."

Jack had a vague but pleasant memory of having recently escaped from a Santa Fe by using his wings. It was worth a try. He rolled to one side, and kicked all six of his gitalongs, but could not flip over onto his stomach. "Give me a shove," he told his wife.

Josie tried shoving him, to turn him over, but she only succeeded in pushing him across the pool. She pushed him up against the metal wall of the tank, and there, by continued shoving and his own splashing efforts, she was able to turn him right side up. He tried to spread his wings, but they were soaked with beer, and he quickly discovered that he had no buoyancy in this position. He could only float if he was belly-up.

"Halp!" he cried, and sank.

"Oh, Lord, save us!" Josie cried out to Man, who was still sound (or unsound) asleep in the back yard. "Climb the wall, Jack!" she begged her husband, and shoved him hard against the aluminum wall, and he scrabbled with his foreclaws and scratched with his hind claws, and clutched with his touchers and thrashed with his tailprongs and lashed with his sniffwhips, but could get no purchase whatever on the smooth metal. All his frantic efforts only had the effect of flipping Josie over onto her stomach, so that she no longer had any buoyancy either.

They were sinking together. As he had done in the instant before the Santa Fe tried to seize him, Jack reflected upon his life's brief moment of glory: how fleetingly he had been allowed to enjoy the privileges of Ingledewidity, how transitory the pleasure of fame. But this time he had neither wings nor courage to save him.

Josie thought of her daughter Tish. Would Tish know how to receive properly all the guests who came bearing funeral feeds? Would Tish be certain that each child had a proper share of the bits of pie, cake, or cookie? Would she make certain that the log was scrubbed clean and that each child was thoroughly bathed and spruced up? Then, when the funeral feed was over, would she, as Josie had told Jubal to tell her to do, present herself at Parthenon and claim kin to the Ingledews?

"Tish has got to claim kin to the Ingledews," Josie said to Jack as they both floundered and sank.

"What?" Jack wondered what nonsense his wife was babbling in her moment of west. "What's that got to do with us a-westerin? All I kin think of, is when I git to Hell I'll have to go to *work*."

10.

"If a bird gits me, I deserve it, O Lord," Brother Tichborne said aloud, as the dawn came up. There was not quite yet enough light for a bird to see him, and the earliest bird would get the worm, not him, but he knew that if he kept going in the direction he was heading, he would never get back to the safety of Holy House before he was visible to all daytime creatures, and west in the clutches of a bird or reptile would be no Rapture at all.

Yes, the Lord still lay. In His profound stupor, He had slightly shifted, no longer flatly supine upon the grass of Carlott but twisted to one side with one of His knees flexed upward toward His chest, and His butt elevated like one of the mountain peaks that rimmed Stay More valley.

It was this peak that Brother Tichborne boldly climbed, having no trouble gaining its summit but feeling shocked at his own audacity in scaling the Lord's Butt. At the crest of the bluejeans-covered prat he sat, or crouched, and surveyed the world below and around, slowly lightening in the foredawn. He studied the Lord's profile: a face never seen so near nor so lit up before. How many of his fellow rooster-roaches had ever had such a view? There were certain unholy heathens particularly among the closet Smockroaches, who claimed to have crawled upon the Lord's person while the Lord was in His bed; but Chid Tichborne doubted that any of them had seen His face with so much light upon it.

It was a magnificent face, although the strong, firm jowls were hidden beneath a scraggly, gray-streaked beard. Brother Tichborne would have preferred, somehow, that the beard be all white, more in keeping with his concept of a deity, but the several white hairs or whiskers among the darker ones were enough to give the Lord a scholarly look. Some folks claimed there were other Men in the world; although Chid Tichborne preached against this polytheism, he admitted to himself that it was a possibility, even if he had never seen one of the other Men. But surely no other Man was as smart, as strong, and as all-powerful as our Man.

. . . Unless, Chid Tichborne thought with a violent shudder, the Lord had westered. Was He stirring at all? Did His chest rise and fall perceptibly with His shallow breathing? In Brother Tichborne's knees, as in the knees of all roosterroaches, there were special sensors which could detect the slightest vibration in the substratum, but the patch of jeans upon which Chid was perched was totally inert.

If the Lord were west, what would become of His roosterroaches? Of course they would not starve, but they would get powerfully hungry, and they would have to leave Holy House. Few of them could forage in the woods, like common Carlotters, eating raw algae and fungi. Most of them would want to invade Parthenon, which is exactly what Chid was planning, although everybody feared the Ingledews almost as much as they feared the Lord. Silly of them, because the two Ingledews were vastly outnumbered, no matter what legendary powers of combat they were purported to possess.

If the Holy House roosterroaches conquered the Ingledews and took over Parthenon, Chid realized, he would have to make revisions and alterations in his religion. He could no longer preach the Kingdom of Man, but would have to speak of the Queendom of Woman, and he was not certain he could do that. He had nothing against matriarchy itself; he simply didn't have much use for females. A female, whether Woman or roosterroach, was all right as far as her functions went: bearing and raising children, keeping the house and all, but you couldn't very easily base a whole system of theology around one of them. Chid tried to imagine himself beginning a prayer "Our Mother who art in Parthenon . . ." and felt ridiculous.

Chid's sniffwhips caused him to shift his gaze from the Lord's handsome but possibly westered countenance to the grass of Carlott surrounding the Lord, where daytime life was beginning to stir. A nightcrawler had come to a stop near the Lord's nose and was broadcasting, "BREAKER ONE OH. HOWBOUTCHA, GOOD BUDDY? GOT A DEAD WHALE TO STARBOARD. TUNNEL SIXTEEN BLOCKED." This was followed by a buzz of static and then a distant nightcrawler on the other side of the Lord answered, "FOUR ROGER. TAKE A SHAKE TO TUNNEL TWENTY-SEVEN, AND SKIRT THE MOTHER. NO BLOCK ON TWENTY-SEVEN. DO YOU READ?"

The nightcrawler shifted gears and changed direction, down the length of the earth beside the Lord's body in search of another hole in the ground, but he had not gone far before a robin swooped out of the sky, took one hop, and seized the entire nightcrawler and lifted it, wriggling rig and all, off into the sky, its pitiful last message rapidly fading: "WE UP AND AWAY TO GLORYLAND, THREES AND EIGHTS. . . ."

Brother Tichborne scanned the sky nervously for other birds. In the grass near the Lord's hindquarters Chid saw a lizard, fearsome as a dragon and swifter than a snake, its darting tongue serving as a pronged sniffwhip and already catching the scent of Chid, and approaching.

"Lord, hear this sinner," Chid prayed aloud, also silently praying that the Lord was not too westered to hear his prayer, "I have done wrong, I know, Lord, and I confess. I have jined ends with my own sister, Lord, and got her with marbles and eastereggs, and married her. I have jined in adultery with other ladies, Lord, amongst them Josie Dingletoon, who hardly ary feller could resist, but she never tempted me, it was my own sinfulness. Now wilt Thou permit the beasts of the field and the critters of the air to consume me, instead of Thy divine Rapture? Lord, I pray that I be saved, to stay east and preach Thy glories to all roosterroachkind, or, if it be Thy will, to be raptured by Thy hand and Thy sacred shootin-arn. But if I am to be westered off by a beast of the field or a critter of the air, let it be swift, O Lord, swift as Thy rapturing, and take me to live on Thy right hand in the Heaven of Stay More Forever. In Joshua's Blessed Name I pray, Amen."

And behold, the Lord opened one eye.

Even though the Lord held His one eye opened

for only a few jerks of a second and then closed it tightly again, Chid Tichborne took this as a sign that the Lord had heard him and intended to spare him, that the Lord forgave him for his transgressions. A chill shiver ran through Chid; no, he realized it was not his own chill shiver, but one running through the Lord Himself, the Lord's whole body quivering. Chid saw a bird swooping downward, aimed right at him, but he feared no evil, for the Lord was with him, and the Lord twitched an elbow, which caused the bird to swerve and miss and rise back out of sight. Likewise the lizard in the grass retreated.

The Lord began to rise. He got His knees up under Himself and spread His palms upon the ground, and arched His back. Chid did not want to fall off into the grass, where lizards, snakes, birds, or Lord knows what-all might get him. He clung to the Lord's jeans and sought to crawl into the Lord's hip pocket, but the space was too tight. As the Lord rose to His knees, Chid climbed above His belt to the back of His shirt, and as the Lord continued rising to a standing position, Chid crawled up beneath the back of the Lord's shirt collar. There, out of sight of any creature, even the Lord, he hid, and hung on, as the Lord staggered around the yard of Carlott for a while, kicking into pieces of car junk, then tottering toward the back porch of Holy House.

Although this height and his own boldness made his nerves tingle, Chid felt elevated above his former station in life and almost sanctified, almost possessed of godhead himself. Wouldn't those infidel Smockroaches be astonished into piety if they could see him?

91

But all roosterroaches had retired for the day into deep slumber, and none were abroad to witness the minister's daring ride on the back of the Lord's neck.

The Lord shuffled along through Holy House to His cookroom. He swung open the great door of the Fabulous Fridge, and a blast of cold air pierced Chid and made his mandibles chatter. The Lord just stared for a long time at the interior of the Fridge, as if trying to decide what to take, or perhaps only checking to see that nothing was missing (no roosterroach had ever succeeded in sneaking into the sealed interior). Then the Lord closed the Fridge's door without removing anything. He bent low over the double-tub Porcelain Sink, a place of frequent wading parties for roosterroaches, and placed His head directly beneath the Fantastic Faucet and turned on the water, causing a great gush of it to splash all over His hair and even the back of His collar, where Chid crouched, only partially sheltered from the spray. For what seemed like a full minute, the Lord held His head beneath the rushing water, then raised His head and shook it vigorously, as if to dry it.

The Lord stumbled against the cookroom table, and in doing so jostled a pile of books stacked on the table alongside an opened beer can. Some of the books fell to the floor but the beer can only tottered; the Lord grabbed it and raised it to His lips. The Lord took a lusty swallow. The Lord gagged, coughed, opened the door leading from the cookroom to the front yard, drew back His arm, and threw the beer can and whatever contents remained across the yard, westward across the weed-grown Roamin Road and into the edge of the Lord's Garden and Refuse Pile.

Then the Lord made Himself a pot of coffee. The aroma offended Chid, who had once attempted to eat a ground of coffee and been sickened by it. The Lord poured himself a large cup of the stuff, then took down from the cupboard a box and out of the box He drew an oatmeal cookie. Crumbs fell to the floor, and Chid fought the great temptation to drop down from the Lord's collar and help himself to the food on the floor, but it was full daylight now, and no roosterroach ever dines after dawn.

With His cookie and coffee, the Lord left the cookroom, crossed the eating room and loafing room, and entered the ponder room. Usually all the Lord ever did in this room was sit in a swiveling chair at His desk and stare out the window and ponder. Occasionally the Lord was known, at night when roosterroaches could observe Him, to take one or more or several of the many books which lined the walls of the ponder room, and sit in the loafing room and read. One of the first lessons that roosterroaches were taught in the second or third instar was to leave alone the tempting glue in the bindings of these books. Edible though it was, nutritious though it was, tasty though it was, the consumption of bookbinding glue would be a serious offense unto the Lord, an unforgivable sin, and no roosterroach bothered the books.

But this morning the Lord neither pondered nor read a book. He sat at His desk, at the machine which was called, from the label Chid deciphered on it, Selec Trick, referring perhaps to the tricks which the Lord made it do, usually by tapping the beast's fifty eyes,

93

which caused a dancing globe to spread words upon sheets of yellow paper. But this morning He chose white paper and put it into the Selec Trick.

Resisting the powerful urge to scamper down and fetch one of the several crumbs of oatmeal cookie which continued to fall from the Lord's hand, and trying to avoid the fumes of coffee that insulted his sniffwhips, the Reverend Chidiock Tichborne sat on the Lord's shoulder and watched Him perform tricks on His Selec Trick.

The first letters were the day of the week, Saturday, no problem for the minister to decipher. These were followed by the month, May, and the date, and the year. The Lord pushed and poked eyes on the Selec Trick which made its dancing globe run and bounce. And the Lord typed: "Dear Sharon," and paused but the briefest moment, then did tricks all the morning long, and much of the afternoon.

11.

Surely, thought Tish, as she woke at the first dim of dusk to find that her parents had not returned, they will come home any minute now that the sun is set. She made all the children wait, before foraging for the night's first meal, in order to welcome the return of Daddy and Momma. But the full dark came, everyone was ravenous enough to eat dirt, and still there was no sign of the parents. The older children kept their sniffwhips finely tuned in search of the first hint

94

of Jack and/or Josie Dingletoon, and eager Jubal received permission from Tish to leave the log and walk out across Carlott in the direction of Holy House to reconnoiter the expected return. When Jubal did not come home after an hour, Tish went out in search of him, and found him sitting atop the deserted Platform, staring toward Holy House and swinging his sniffwhips slowly but steadily in every direction.

"Reckon ye might as well come on back home, Jubal, boy," his elder sister said to him. "They're not a-comin tonight, it don't look like."

The boy rose up and glanced around. "Where did the Lord lay?" he asked.

"Right yonder," Tish pointed a sniffwhip. The impress of the Lord's body was still detectable in the grass. "His head was there, and His feet were way over *there*, and out yonder is where I touched His finger."

The boy climbed down from the Platform and walked slowly homeward beside his sister, retracing their steps. After a while he raised his bent head and with upturned face, with stargazers and big eyes alike, he gazed at the stars, whose cold pulses were beating amid the black hollows above, serenely removed from these two wisps of roosterroach life. Jubal asked Tish how far away those twinklers were, and whether Man was Lord of all those worlds as well as of this one.

"Did ye tell me wunst the stars are worlds, Tish?" he asked her.

"Yes."

"All like ours, with roosterroaches all over all of 'em?"

"I reckon so, Jubal."

95

"Do they all have to go west, everywhere, jist like us?"

"Everything goes west, sooner or later. Even those whole stars, each and ever, sputter and go dark and go cold and go west."

Jubal grew very reflective. "And is our world ever going to go cold?"

Tish realized that Jubal was too young to remember the last winter. She herself had been still too young during the worst part of it to realize its severity. "Yes," she said. "It will become very cold."

"When we go live in Partheeny, can we stay warm all the time?"

"Why, Jubal, what gives ye the notion that we could ever go live in *Partheeny*?"

"If you was to marry a Squar Ingledew, we could!"

Tish could not suppress a great laugh. "I'm not about to marry no Squar Ingledew!" she said. "Whatever give ye such a notion?"

"Momma said."

"Huh? What-all did Momma say?"

"She said if ever anything happened to her and Daddy, you was to remember that the Dingletoons was actually Ingledews, and that you orter go and visit the squires and claim kin."

"Claimin kin is one thing," Tish told Jubal. "Gittin married to one of 'em is a gray moth of a different color. Besides, if we was kin, it'd be incest to marry one. And Brother Tichborne says there's nothing worser than incest."

"When will ye claim kin?" he wanted to know.

96

She was confounded, nay, dumbfounded, by the prospect. From the woods all around came the opening bars of the Purple Symphony, but she mistook these sounds for strains in her own heart: someone had told her that when you hear the Purple Symphony it makes you yearn for something. The lower bristles of her sniffwhips tingled with the scent of pining, and even though she realized the scent was coming from herself, it still meant good luck. Would she have good luck if she tried to claim kin to the Ingledews?

"When will ye claim kin?" Jubal intruded on her reverie once more, and Tish discovered herself back home in the rotlog hovel, surrounded by her siblings, all of whom were picking up Jubal's question and drumming it at her: When will ye claim kin? When will ye claim kin? *When will ye claim kin?*

Tish suddenly felt overwhelmed by her responsibility, her duty, and the burden of the knowledge that they were Ingledews. Why had this knowledge come so abruptly, almost as a foretokening of tragedy? If her father had not discovered, on the same night of his westering, that he was an Ingledew, his children would have faced the vicissitudes of their lot in life with the same resignation and the same acceptance of reality that all roosterroaches possess. They would have been content to go on living as Dingletoons. Somewhere, somehow, Tish might have crossed paths with Archy Tichborne again, whom she had encountered so fleetingly at the play-party. "Just to think," she said to herself morosely, "only last night I danced and laughed!" Now, as the oldest survivor among the Dingletoon children, she had to take over the household . . . or find a way to move to Parthenon.

"Better claim kin tonight," Jubal prodded. "Grab time by the sniffwhips, as Momma allus said. The early worm fools the bird."

"Just leave me be!" Tish wailed, and fled from the house. She climbed the Great Rock to the north of Carlott, a boulder almost as high as Holy House itself, which was in its shadow. On the top of this Great Rock was a small level place, which Man Himself had never visited and could scarcely reach, where a group of small rocks, column-like, had been arranged, some flat ones, post-and-lintel, capping and spanning others, into a circle. According to legend, powerful roosterroaches years before the time of Joshua Crust had placed the rocks into this circle, although it was not conceivable that *any* roosterroach, not even a crew of mighty Ingledews, could have budged or nudged any of these stones. Still this circle of stones was a special place, pagan, non-Crustian, and perhaps witchlike, where few roosterroaches ever went any more. One had to traverse deep mosses to reach it. It had been called Hinglerocks, long ago, and Tish knew the name but had never heard anyone else speak of it, or go there. To her Hinglerocks was a private ruined temple, where she could go to escape the puzzles and vexations of life, or, now, to mourn the westering of her parents and try to give herself nerve to claim kin to the Ingledews. Because nothing except moss grew there to tempt any food-searching creature, she was never molested, except en route, when she might encounter a hostile cricket, a Santa

Fe or scorpion, or meet up with some fat nightcrawler whose lingo she could not fathom.

From Hinglerocks Tish could see all the way to Parthenon, two furlongs distant; the house-long-ago-converted-into-a-general-store-and-now-back-into-a-house was silhouetted in the moonlight against the holler in which it nestled, a single light burning within one room to the left, a kerosene light, pale as a distant star. The weed-forested Roamin Road led to it; the closest Tish had ever been to Parthenon was the edge of this forest on the Roamin Road just the night before, when the parade of damsels marched there. The Lord never drove His vehicle over this road any more, nor did He even walk it any more, except to put envelopes into the Woman's mailbox.

For what must have been an hour or more, Tish sat at Hinglerocks gazing out toward Parthenon and summoning her courage to venture there. At last she decided at least to approach the place, and sniff around it.

Another hour was consumed in her journey: as she approached the forest of weeds that loomed between her and her destination, she almost hoped to be spared arrival by some forest-creature: the oblivion of a shrew's gullet would be preferable to the rigors of interviews with Ingledews. She would rather encounter a badger, a possum, even the weird rare armadillo, than face an Ingledew. Then she remembered that her own dear late father had been an Ingledew, and there had been nothing fearsome about him. For that matter, *she* was an Ingledew! Suddenly she became very self-conscious, and as she entered the forest of weeds she examined herself. Weren't her hips and thighs too long and fat? All six of them, or at least four of them? Were her gitalongs too tiny? Was her thorax full enough?

Before she crossed the front yard of Parthenon, she paused to give herself a thorough bath, washing her sniffwhips twice each, and cleaning every spike on her gitalongs; she felt that this was the most important bath she had ever given herself, and she was thorough and meticulous. She passed her sniffwhips slowly over her entire body and examined the result. Did she detect the faintest trace of fragrant pheromone? If so, it was from excitement, not from lust.

She crossed the yard. Among the random patches of grass, the unceremonious expanse of smooth dirt was strewn with commemorative statuary: here a copper penny, there a wad of tinfoil; here a threaded screw and a washer, there a poptop from a beverage can; here a glass bead, there a nacreous button. Tish paused to examine a round glass marble, a Man-child's plaything, streaked with colors, transparent, wonderful. She considered the contrast of this yard of Parthenon with that of Carlott, which was littered with roller bearings, rusting cotter pins, oily couplings, bent valves, sparkplugs, the miscellaneous detritus of automobile parts. Tish could have spent the whole night examining Parthenon's marvelous yard, but there ahead of her was the porch of Parthenon itself.

Stone piers supported the porch, and she climbed the one nearest to the window whose light she had seen from afar. She scaled the wooden wall to the ledge of this window, and looked through the screen.

There, in a cheer-of-ease, sat the Woman. Tish had heard many legends, reports, histories, descriptions, and rumors about the Woman, but had never seen Her so close before, big as life, bigger than life, almost as big as Man. But Man, when Tish had seen Him the night before and even touched Him, had been deeply asleep, if not drunker than a pied piper. This Woman was wide awake, Her eyes open. She was reading. In Her hands She held some sheets of paper, white, and She was reading one of these. Her hair was as yellow as a comet moth's wings, and Her smooth mouth was turned up at one corner in a smile. She had a very kind and gentle expression. Tish would have liked to climb up into Her lap and talk with Her, but Tish was old enough to know that the Woman would not tolerate the touch of a roosterroach any more than the Man would.

High on one wall of the room was a mantelshelf, above a boarded-up fireplace, and on the mantelshelf rose a clock, *the* Clock, of which Tish had heard so much, and whose chimes she had heard all her life. But those chimes, from the distance of Carlott, had sounded like only so many little pings and pongs. Now, as Tish waited and watched, the Clock began to strike the hour, and it said "BUN!" nearly startling Tish off her perch. Then it said, "TART!" A third time it struck: "TRIFLE!" Tish counted a fourth: "FUDGE!" And a fifth: "FONDANT!" The Clock pealed six: "SCONE!" And the Clock struck seven: "SUGARPLUM!" Tish was debating with herself whether it had really said all these things, when it said "EGG!" For nine o'clock, the Clock said "NOU-

GAT!" Then it struck ten: "DIVINITY!" with a reverberation that seemed to shake the very ledge that Tish sat upon. The last thing the Clock said was "ECLAIR!" Tish waited for a twelfth chime, and was prepared to count it, but it never came.

The Woman yawned and raised Her long arms overhead. She smiled again. Then yawned again. Then She folded up the sheets of paper and placed them inside an envelope, which She placed inside a book, and closed the book. She stood up from Her cheer-of-ease, blew out Her kerosene lantern, returning the world to its normal intensities and colorations, and then She climbed into Her bed.

12.

Gregor Samsa Ingledew was so startled to detect, with the whole length of his sniffwhips, the approach of the scent of none other than his own father, that he instinctively prepared himself for combat, something he had been required to do only once before in his life in the Clock, when a scorpion had attempted entry. The scorpion, a mortal foe of all roosterroaches, is an arachnid, like a spider, but an overgrown one, with crab's pincers, and a tail like a crane tipped by a deadly stinger. Like the roosterroach, he is a night-prowler, but the roosterroach prowls for garbage and the scorpion prowls for roosterroaches. A favorite taunt or curse of roosterroach children is to say to one another, "Scorpy on you!" Sam had supposed his Clock a safe refuge from scorpions as well as all other creatures, but one night while winding the Clock the Woman had left the glass front door ajar, and the scorpion had crept in. Sam had often had dreams, or rather daymares, of being attacked by a scorpion, and he had thought he was asleep when he first saw it coming at him, thrice as large as he. He had hoped he would wake up, but discovered that he was already very much awake. If he *had* been asleep, it would have been his last sleep. Awake, he was able to summon up unrealized reserves of the Ingledew strength, cunning, and martial art.

The scorpion had been no match for him, really. Before he could stop to consider what he was doing, he had confronted it, attacked it, wrestled it, mutilated it. Deftly sidestepping the plunging poisonous stinger, he had bitten off one of the scorpion's pincers while grabbing the other and twisting, throwing the scorpion over onto its back, rendering the tail ineffective, and had chewed into the underside of the scorpion's thorax. The scorpion had screamed in pain and fright and had begged mercy in a language totally foreign to Sam, but with a universal sound of piteous beseechment so heartrending that Sam had been tempted to let it go. But he had quickly killed it instead, ripped out its heart and its brain, and dragged its carcass to the edge of the mantelshelf and kicked it off, for the Woman to find and dispose of. Only much later had he begun shivering with wracking fear.

Now he was confronted again, not by a scorpion

but a possibly worse intruder, Squire Hank Ingledew, who had never visited the Clock before in the time Sam had lived there, namely, all his life. *"Dad?"* Sam said in great astonishment, even before catching sight of his father.

Squire Hank hove into view. "Morsel, son," he said, and immediately began looking around him, and above him, at the great intricate innards of the clock-works, the appurtenances and impedimenta of Sam's apartment. "Right spiffy-lookin place ye got here," Squire Hank observed.

Sam could not hear a word. "Morsel, Dad," he said, and politely asked, "To what do I owe the pleasure of this visit?"

Squire Hank laughed. "Queer, aint it? I never wunst clum up here afore." The elder Ingledew got misty-eyed and waxed reminiscent, "The whole time ye was growin up, yore Momma had all the say in yore raisin, and I hardly never saw ye. Ever since she went and westered off, I've been meanin to come drap in on ye, and say hidy and all, but I reckon I've jist not had a good reason. Not until now."

Sam, hearing none of this, assumed his father was awkwardly trying to make conversation about the weather. "Yes," he said, "I expect we might get a thundershower any time now."

"Worser than that, I reckon," his father said. "It's a gal. A female."

"But I suppose the flowers need it," Sam said. "It's been awful dry."

"I aint so certain we need *her*," Hank said. "She's come to claim kin to us, and maybe move in on us.

One of ole Jack Dingletoon's daughters, him that thinks he's discovered he's a Ingledew. Now she says he's probably west, and Josie too, and it's her duty, bein head of household and all, to claim kin to us. So what should I tell her?"

Hearing-impaired persons are good at detecting the asking of a question, even if they do not understand the words. Sam could hear the rising inflection of the question mark, and he assumed his father had shifted the topic of discussion from the weather to Sam's personal well-being, so he answered, "I have no complaints."

"You mean you don't care if she moves in or not?" Squire Hank was incredulous. "You want her to bring her whole caboodle of brothers and sisters too?"

Two question marks. "I'm doing okay, thank you, and finding plenty to eat." Sam gestured at his neat array of food fragments, of which he was proud. The dozens of them were arranged and catalogued, at least in his own mind, and he had specimens of everything the Woman had ever eaten.

Squire Hank surveyed the larder. "Heck, they'd eat all that plumb up quicker'n ye could count."

"Thank you," Sam said. "Yes, that one there is a rare dab of lemon meringue. And this piece is almost a year old, a croissant demi-sel. Here, try a taste of this one, a butterscotch marzipan."

Squire Hank idly chewed upon the offering. He asked, "Do you want a slew of them rotlog Dingletoon clodhoppers a-stompin all over these goodies?"

The question mark led Sam to assume that his

father was asking for samples of other specimens. He offered a taste of peanut brittle. Then he offered a taste of . . . "No, I don't think you want this one. This is a pellet of ginseng root, recently acquired from Doc Swain, which he claims is good for—"

Squire Hank snickered. "Yeah, he guv me a dose of that stuff, wunst. It works, I tell ye. But what use is it fer a feller my age? Come to think of it, *you* might jist be a-needin it, if you have to talk to this gal I'm tellin ye about, this Letitia Dingletoon, says her name is. You *want* to talk to her?"

His father was being awfully inquisitive. What was he asking now? Had Sam tried the gingseng himself? "Sure," he said.

His father stared at him in wonder. "Then you'd better bite off a big hunk right now," said the elder Ingledew and held out the pellet of gingseng. "Here," he said. "Eat. EAT!"

Sam heard a word, the first word he had heard his father speak. A command: eat. Although Sam did not understand why his father was insisting on it, he knew that the previous night, when he had sampled a taste of the ginseng, it had given him a kind of convivial glow, which perhaps was all it was intended to do. "I will if you will," he said to his father, taking a bite and passing it back.

"Maybe I'll need it too," said his father, and took a little bite, "if I got to go back down thar and talk to that gal and 'splain to her that she's got to come up here and claim kin to you yourself."

Sam wished he could hear his father. Possibly his father intended that the two of them share the ginseng and work up a pair of convivial glows that would allow them to be good friends, not just father and son. Sam was on the verge of confessing to his father that his hearing had failed him, but if he did that, there would be no further point in having a conversation with his father anyway. Hoping for quick intoxication, he took another, larger bite of the ginseng. "It has a rather strange taste," he observed. "Don't you think? Not like a food but like a drug."

This comment did not lead to further camaraderie. His father seemed preparing to leave. "Well, it's your Clock," Squire Hank said to his son, "and I aint about to tell ye how to live yore life. But iffen it was me, I shore would discourage that gal from any notions she might have about movin in on ye." Squire Hank gave Sam a mock-cuff on the side of the head, and said, "Allrighty, I'll send her on up. Don't do nothin I wouldn't do, ye hear? Hawr-hawr."

No, he didn't hear. Squire Hank made his exit. "So long, Dad," Sam called after him, a bit disappointed the visit had been so brief, and so unproductive of any further bond between the two Ingledews. One of these days, Sam told himself, I'll just have to tell him that I'm deaf.

13.

Sure enough, her nervousness was about to make her involuntarily release a molecule of pheromone. Like an effort to suppress a belch or a sneeze, the anxiety weakened the effort, and the fragrant pheromone escaped, preceding her like a herald of trumpets into the Clock.

Of the three possible intruders into the Clock—scorpion, father, strange girl—the latter struck Sam as the most to be feared, even with the aid of ginseng, a third and largest bite of which he chomped on the instant the molecule began dancing along the length of his sniffwhip.

The interior overwhelmed her. The parts of the Clock were moving, some swiftly, some imperceptibly, but they all moved, whereas the various cogs and gears littering Carlott were all inert, lifeless. She could not separate the minute quiverings of the mainspring from the tremblings of her mainheart.

Sam, after the initial shock of the cavorting molecule of pheromone had paralyzed his sniffwhip, used his eyes to behold, up close, much too close, a female of his own species: a girl fully developed, with long and strong legs, all six nicely spiked on the tibia, the merons muscular and the trochanters shapely, the arolia small and dainty, the unguiae neatly manicured. Her face, although at the moment it was transfixed in fright, was a comely country girl's with pastoral beauty and the most delicate suggestion of a feistiness: the scape of the sniffwhip was slightly recessed in its socket, and joined the pedicel firmly and assertively but with a touch of mischievousness. Her mouth had full paraglossae suggestively covered by smooth galeae, while the broad labrum rose up to the clypeus with audacity and authority. Sam thought he was about to faint, either from the sight of her or an overdose of ginseng, or both.

Tish felt sick to her stomach. She had had nothing

to eat tonight, but she felt as if she were about to puke, not from nausea but from nerves. It did not help, one bit, that Squire Sam Ingledew—for it was clearly he, handsome as all her girlfriends had gossiped he was—was looking at her as if she were something that had crawled out of a hole in the ground. It had been an effort to crawl up the mantel and reach the Clock, but she had made as dignified an entrance as she could.

Moments passed. Knowing nothing better to say, she asked, "Are you Squire Sam Ingledew?" which struck her as silly, almost like asking of Man, "Are you Man?"

It was the first time a female other than his mother had ever spoken to him, and even if he had heard her, which he had not, he would not have known what to say.

"I met yore daddy, down below," she went on, wondering if she was babbling, "who said he was Squire Hank Ingledew and is maybe yore daddy, if you're Squire Sam Ingledew, which I reckon ye must be, if this here is yore Clock. I mean, you *look* like Squire Sam Ingledew, although I've never laid eyes on ye before but you just look just like I just figgered you'd just look!" She ran out of breath and had to stop.

Sam managed two words: "Beg pardon?"

Tish took a deep breath, a very deep one, as much as her sixteen spiracles could draw in, and repeated herself, word for word. But Squire Sam only continued looking at her as if she were something on the end of a stick.

Was the ginseng taking effect? Sam managed to

mouth five whole words: "I don't hear very well."
He gave each of his tailprongs a wiggle as if to demonstrate that they were physically functional although
sensorially impaired.

"Oh," she said, and watched him wiggling his
tailprongs. They were cute. She moved closer to one
of them, cupped her touchers around her mouth and
shouted, "HELLO! I'M TISH!"

Sam jumped. "I'm not *that* deaf," he said. Then
he thought to ask, "Don't you know that roosterroaches aren't allowed in Parthenon . . . except for
us Ingledews, of course?"

Tish hung her head, and mumbled, "Yeah, I
know." Then she raised her voice and tried to explain.

Sam tried to listen. Something about her father.
Something about her mother. Something about her
forty-three brothers and sisters. Something about
claiming kin. He realized he must seem inquisitorial,
not hospitable. He reached out and selected a dab of
one of his collectibles, and offered it to her. "Vanilla
egg custard?" he said.

Her touchers told her it was edible, and she
wolfed it down, finding it more than edible: the most
delicious thing she'd ever eaten. But almost at once
she feared it could have been a dollop of affy-dizzy
from his own tergal gland, designed to seduce her.
Still she commented, appreciatively, "Yum-yum."

"Peanut brittle?" he offered. She tasted. He offered her tastes of several of his select little snacks.
The crumb of dark Oreo, in particular, seemed to
transport her.

"I never had any of that before," she said, sighing
with pleasure.

110

He led her down the aisles of the neatly arranged foodstuffs, pointing out and describing each, and offering her tastes. She was *so* appreciative. He was surprised at himself, the volubility of his own voice, talking to a female. Alas, if only he could have heard her random comments of appreciation, her sighs of pleasure, her purrs of delight, but just to see the expressions on her face was reward enough.

The Clock announced the twelfth and final hour: "TUTTI-FRUTTI!" Then it was silent. "Midnight," Sam announced, feeling inane, at a loss.

She wished she could talk to him. Squire Sam, she realized, although he was a mortal creature no greater than she, had something in common with the Fate-Thing: both were deaf. The Fate-Thing could not hear her requests or supplications; it was totally indifferent to her needs. Maybe, she realized, Squire Sam wasn't actually deaf but only indifferent, like the Fate-Thing. She wished she could ask him, at least, if he believed in anything like the Fate-Thing.

For want of other words, he offered, "Would you like to see the clockworks?" and without waiting for the nod of her head, he commanded, "Here, climb up," and started her on a hike upward through the intricate innards of the Clock, cautioning her not to catch her gitalongs in any of the gears. "This," he pointed out, "is the Great Wheel, whose ratchets are regulated by the mainspring, over yonder, which is wound up every eighth day by the Woman of Parthenon. Do you know Her? Now here we have the pinion which turns with the Great Wheel and thrusts through the clock face yonder to join the long, or minute, hand of the dial, which completes a circuit

111

of the dial each hour and thus measures the sixty minutes in the hour. This pinion has only one-twelfth as many teeth as the Great Wheel, see? Do you know fractions?" He attempted to explain to her the mathematical ratios of the sundry pinions and wheels, although math was clearly over her head, as were the pinions and wheels. As they ascended upward through the Clock, he said, "Now *this* is called the 'dead escapement,' or 'deadbeat escapement.' Do you know 'dead'? Humans use it as a euphemism for 'west.' Of course this thingumajig is neither east nor west, but its true function is to convert the energy from the spring to the swinging of the pendulum down below, and to 'fall dead' after each jerk—that is, go west after each jerk—watch closely there, see?— click, click, *dead*, click, click, *west*—you get the idea?" *How can I actually be talking so much to a female?* he asked himself, astounded at himself, and realized it must be the effect of the ginseng.

Why is he telling me all of this? she wondered, flattered that a handsome feller so painfully shy was actually opening up to her. Maybe, she realized, he is making me familiar with the place so that I can live here! Would he really ask her to live here? But would she really want to live in such a noisy place?

"The idea of the deadbeat escapement," he said, "is an almost poetic metaphor suggestive of escape through death, or escape by westering, which is getting us into eschatology and leading us dangerously close to the concept of Rapture espoused by your Crustian minister, the Reverend Tichborne. But you don't know eschatology, do you, Tish? I'll have to tell you all about it, but not tonight. Step up there, a bit more, we're almost to the top of the Clock. Yes, this bracket we're standing upon here—see how it overhangs yonder—is attached to the plate, *there*, to support the very tiptop of the end of the pendulum. This bracket is called the . . . the cock." He studied her closely for any blush or twinge, but there was none, so he bravely asked, "Have you ever heard the word 'cock' before?" But her face was blank, as if "eschatology" and "cock" were all the same to her. He wanted to explain how the cock hovers above the deadbeat escapement, and how the cock symbolizes or is a metaphor suggestive of The Bomb. Didn't she know about The Bomb? "Haven't you ever heard of The Bomb?" he asked. But again the blank, expressionless, innocent look. "You know, you could sort of nod your head yes or shake your head no when I ask you something."

She nodded her head. But then she shook her head, no, she had never heard of The Bomb, nor Cock, nor any of it.

He led her down from the clockworks, back to his loafing space, where he offered her a taste of crust of apple fritter, his favorite of foods. Her eyes gleamed in rapture as she devoured it. *Rapture?* he said to himself, and thought to try to explain to her the complicated distinction between the artificial concept of Rapture as the Crustians saw it and the actuality of the holocaust of The Bomb. She had difficulty grasping the explanation, especially the part about why Man would do it, in the first place, why Man would set off The Bomb, which, she at least understood, was zillions of times more powerful than Man's bullets, which were awful enough.

She hazarded a word: "Why?"

"Did you speak?" he asked, surprised.

She nodded her head again, and said, right at his tailprongs: "WHY?"

"I have an idea," he suggested, having a fine idea: he and she could devise a kind of sign language between themselves, a system of gestures, signals, using their sniffwhips, touchers, even tailprongs. "For example, if you wish to ask 'Why?' you put a sniffwhip to your forehead and then spread your sniffwhips to make the letter 'Y,' like so." He demonstrated, then waited to see if she could do it. It was much easier, she found, than merely nodding or shaking her head.

She signed, "Why?" A second time, she signed "Why?" It was almost like a game.

"That's good," he said. "Your first word. Now, let's devise the rest of the alphabet. How would you make a V?"

She held her sniffwhips close together, but spread to form a V.

"Very good!" he exclaimed. He touched the tips of his sniffwhips together and slowly spread them into a V, saying, "This slow spreading of my sniffwhips, the slow drawing apart of them, could represent 'very' as our first V-word. For 'good,' just touch your sniffwhip to your mouth and then place it across your other sniffwhip."

"Very good," she signed.

"Very good!" he signed and said. "This is fun." He flicked the base of one sniffwhip with the tip of the other. "Fun."

"Fun," she signed. "Very good fun," she signed.

He laughed. "This is easier than I thought it would be." He brushed a sniffwhip upward against another several times in quick succession. "Easy."

"Easy," she signed.

"Your turn to make up a sign for a word," he offered. "How would you do 'I,' meaning yourself but also the letter I?"

She needed only a moment to come up with the idea of the tip of a sniffwhip pulled down close to her face and held up in a vertical position like a little i. He signed it after her.

"And 'you'?" he asked.

"Even easier," she signed, and simply pointed the same sniffwhip at him for "you."

He crossed the lengths of his sniffwhips and drew them to his chest as in an embrace. She was transported by apple fritter, he by ginseng. "This is the sign for 'love,'" he said. Quickly, without thinking, she imitated the sign for "love." He made the sign for "I," he made the sign for "love," he made the sign for "you."

"I," she signed. "Love," she signed. She hesitated. "Not very easy," she signed.

He blushed, abashed at himself for his audacity. They made up new words, new letters, tried them out, created sample sentences of safer declarations and questions. A question mark is easy: a crooking of the tip of the sniffwhip to describe the figure of the question mark, or both sniffwhips to be emphatic: "??" An exclamation mark is even easier, a stiffening and straightening of the sniffwhip high overhead: "!" Double sniffwhips are twice as exclamatory: "Watch out, there's a scorpion behind you!!" He was only kidding, and frightened her, but she forgave him, and, entering into the spirit, became the inventor of the combined question *and* exclamation: "Now why would you have scared me so?!"

Their communication became articulate, their gestural statements prolonged and increasingly complicated. They even reached the point where she could tell him about her belief in Fate-Thing. The sign devised for "thing" was a mere shifting and dropping of one extended sniffwhip, but "fate" was so difficult that, like many of their words, it required not the sniffwhips and touchers alone but also a gitalong or two, a shifting of the body, a semaphoring of the tailprongs.

Tish "talked." Sam "listened." The night passed. Their conversation was slowed by the need for stopping to invent a new sign for a word here and there. They were so caught up in their dialogue that neither of them noticed the Clock strike "BUN" or even "TART." When they had nearly exhausted the subject of the Fate-Thing, she asked him again her original question, "Why The Bomb?" and he attempted as best he could to explain it to her in signs. He even seized upon her conception of the Fate-Thing to support his own theory: that someone or something, perhaps the Fate-Thing, would prevent Man from destroying the earth with The Bomb.

"TRIFLE," said the Clock.

Sam and Tish "talked" so much their sniffwhips began to ache, a rare occurrence for their species, who keep their sniffwhips in motion anyway all the live-

116

long night, and even, often, during the day, in their sleep.

Tish realized she had "talked" more with Sam than with anyone in her whole life, and when the Clock said "FUDGE," Tish used her new sign language to express astonishment and dismay and to sign, "Yellow fireball will rise up any minute now."

"Yellow fireball," Sam repeated the sign after her. He realized he had not spoken for hours; although she could easily hear him, he was talking only in the language they had invented for him to "hear" her.

"I must go," Tish signed, "or I shall get caught in daylight."

"You will get caught in daylight anyway if you try to go now," he pointed out to her. "Stay more and spend the whole day."

She thought he was making the polite but insincere formality, the traditional ritual of dialogue translated into signs, and she returned these signs: "Best be getting on down back. Come go home with me." She realized how ridiculous the invitation was, to ask a Squire Ingledew to come to her rotten log, but she knew he knew she didn't mean the invitation.

"Better not," he signed. "You just make yourself pleasant and stay the whole day."

"Time to light out for home," she signed. "Come and keep me company."

"Not this morning, thank you, Tish. Why don't you just move in here and have you some vittles?"

Oh, if only he meant it! "Can't do that, I reckon," she formally signed, reluctantly. "I am a mind to get on home."

"No, you are not," he signed. He was breaking the rhythm! He was interpolating! "You are a mind to stay more, and you are going to do it."

"Huh?" she signed, surprised at his extemporizing the formalities. "What?!"

"You heard me," he signed.

"But," she signed. She wondered what to sign next. She tried signing "but" once more, and yet again. She felt she was stuttering in sign language. "But my forty-three brothers and sisters will fear that I have been westered by a bird, chicken, or other fowl."

"If you leave now," he pointed out, "you *will* be westered by a bird, chicken, or other fowl."

The yellow fireball rose above Dinsmore Mountain, not yellow but orange and huge and hot. Through the screen door of the Woman's bedroom came the sound of the lifting of the morning breeze and then of birds, chickens, and other fowls reciting their matinals. Through the glass of the face of the Clock, Tish could see the Woman Herself turn over in Her bed and waken, then slowly swing Her feet off the bed to the floor.

"Behold," signed Tish. "The Woman, goddess of Parthenon, awakes and rises up."

"Yes," signed Sam. "Notice how she touches the flat surface beneath her bed with her left gitalong first."

"Why does she do that?"

"Maybe," Sam signed, smiling, "it is a superstitious propitiation—" the big words gave him trouble "—to the Fate-Thing." Then he finger-spelled, or, rather, sniffwhip-and-toucher-spelled, the Woman's name. "Her name is Sharon. S-H-A-R-O-N."

"Sharon," repeated Tish. "I have heard Man call out to Her." She watched as the Woman removed her nightgown and put on the red flower-print shirt and blue jeans that she would wear that day. "She is so beautiful, pretty, lovely," signed Tish.

"And lonely," signed Sam. The sign for "lonely" is to draw the very tip of the right sniffwhip down over the lips, almost as in making the "Shhh" sign for silence, implying "silent and alone." Sam offered, "Shall I tell you a story about Sharon?" Their sign for "story" had begun as a linking and pulling apart in quick succession several times the tips of the sniffwhips, but now that they had used the word several times between them they found that unconsciously they were joining the tips of one another's sniffwhips in order to sign it.

"Oh, please do tell me a story!" Tish requested, grabbing at the tips of his sniffwhips with her own.

Sharon, Sam explained, was the granddaughter of a demigoddess named Latha, who once had lived here but now lived east of Stay More. Latha was very old but even more beautiful than Sharon, and during the time of her life that she had dwelt in Parthenon, eons ago, she had lived alone too, and had been lonely, and yearning, and Parthenon had been filled with the luck-bringing scents of yearning. A Man from out of her past, whose name was Every, as in each and every, a different Man not related to the present Man of Stay More, whose name is Larry, had returned to town and become involved in the most fabulous of stories, which Tish must remind Sam to tell her, but not now.

This is the story of Sharon, who decided to move back to Stay More, where She had spent most of Her adolescent years, and not only to move back but to move into the very Parthenon. Was Sharon also expecting a Man from out of Her past to come to Her? If so, was that Man the same who now lived here, Larry? If this was true, why did Sharon refuse to have anything further to do with Larry?

"Yes? Yes?" signed Tish. "Go on. Go on!?"

"That's all we know, right now," Sam signed. "The story is continuing. Like the story of you and me."

If Tish caught the insinuation of this series of gestures, she did not let on. She seemed to sign to herself, "So 'Larry' is the name of our Man?" Having an actual name for Him seemed somehow to belittle Him, although thinking of the Woman as Sharon did not belittle Her. Tish watched Sharon, who had entered a small room leading off Her bedroom and sat upon a stool of gleaming white porcelain.

"What does She do?" Tish signed a question.

"She sits upon what is called a toilet," Sam explained in signs, with some hesitancy, as if the process bothered him. "Listen," he told her. Although he was deaf, he could remember when his hearing was good and he could hear the sound. Tish listened and heard it: a tinkling, as of rain. She looked at Sam in puzzlement, and Sam signed, "She is making water."

"Oh, water!?" Tish exclaimed in signs. Then Tish signed a question, "Has She ever had a rock-a-bye?"

Sam mulled the possibility. Although he had

once thought of Sharon as his own mother, he had long ago given up the possibility that he had hatched from an ootheca laid by Her. "I don't think so," he answered. "If she had rock-a-byes, none of them have ever come to Parthenon."

"How," Tish wondered aloud, signing absently, "do Man and Woman twist and pound rock-a-byes?"

Sam was charmed by her question and the artless gestures she used to ask it. How, indeed, did humans make babies? He remembered the one night, or rather early morning, when he had observed the Woman with Larry in Her bed. Had they been engaged in a baby-making thing? If so, the Woman had not had a baby as a result of it. "I suppose," he signed, "it is not too awfully different—" he crossed and uncrossed his sniffwhips, for *different* "—from the way that roosterroaches do it."

She laughed uproariously. Perhaps her embarrassment contributed to the excessiveness of her laughter, he thought.

"What's so funny?" he asked, speaking aloud for the first time in hours, but then he signed it: "What's so funny??"

She signed: "Just the way you sign 'roosterroach.' I recognized the sign, although we have not used it before. I never thought of roosterroaches that way before. I guess you have to see everything in a different language to understand it."

It was his turn to laugh. He repeated the signs after her: *You have to see everything in a different language to understand it.* Then he signed, "I love that." He loved this girl. He loved her so much that his tergal gland began to leak a drop of affy-dizzy. He backed away

121

from her, but not quickly enough, not far enough. She sniffed the heady male aroma. No vanilla custard, no apple fritter on earth, can equal it in attraction. She was tantalized, and involuntarily made a step in his direction, causing him to back into a corner of the Clock.

The Woman left Her toilet room, recrossed Her bedroom to another door. From another room came the sounds of pots and pans rattling.

Sam realized his back, all along the underside of his wings, was lathered with affy-dizzy.

Had hours passed since Tish had stuffed herself on fritter? She felt her appetite returning with a gush and whispered with timid signs (if signs can whisper), "Just a taste."

Now, there is no such thing as "just a taste" of the irresistible nectar of love which is called affy-dizzy. Like a bee drawn to a flower, a female is held by it, is lured to climb the male's back so that she can reach the fount of the affy-dizzy and greedily lap it up, the taste of which, unlike even the finest crumb fallen from Man's (or Woman's) table, is the most delectable substance ever to reach her touchers and her lips, and it stimulates her appetite to consume all of it, every droplet, and each taste of it excites her more.

Because no female had ever lapped his affy-dizzy before, but because he had in his dreams, and night fantasies too, imagined the procedure, Sam was surprised to take leave of his body, or, rather, to observe his body take leave of him: once the female has been maneuvered into position to reach and taste the affy-dizzy, one of three specialized clamps in the male's genitalia reaches up and seizes one of three specialized

122

latches in the female's genitalia. This clamp will remain firmly manacled to this latch for at least two hours.

When the clamp and the latch were firmly affixed, in an instant, Sam attempted to sign, "Oops!" but could only spell it, and Tish was too distracted to notice.

The intricate anatomy of the mechanisms of reproduction is astonishing: there are not one but two phallomeres, and it is the right one which first probes the female.

"Sam!" she cried out, and then attempted to spell it, "S-A-M-!-!" but he could not see her; their bodies were already turning into the opposed position, end to end at 180 degrees.

The second clamp, whose function is titillation as well as coupling, clinched a second latch and began tickling and was tickled in return. The third clamp grabbed the third latch.

The sunlight coming into the room, into the face of the Clock, brightly blinded both of them, clamper and latcher alike. Above them rolled the ancient ceaseless workings of the Clock; within them rolled the classic machinery of their sex, in which the complexities of movement were no less involute, convolute, and revolute. The Clock would scream "SCONE!" and then it would groan "SUGARPLUM!" before Tish and Sam were finished. Tish had wanted to know a simple answer to a simple question, how Man and Woman twist and pound their babies. Indeed, for humans it is comparatively simple; for the species of Sam and Tish, it took hours, and inward constructions beyond all imagining.

123

INSTAR THE THIRD:
The Rally

14.

When Tish awoke, not to any inner biological clock but to strange sounds, it was already beyond gloaming. She required more than a minute to determine not only the source of the sounds but her very location: above her head were not the familiar rotting grains of wood in her sleeping cranny at the log, a homey sight her eyes had seen every waking evening of her life, but instead the smooth wooden-toothed edges of gears and wheels, like a magnified daymare of the interior of some creature's gullet and gizzard, grinding away at her who had been swallowed whole. She tried to stifle a cry, the choked squeak escaping without disturbing the deep sleep of her companion, who, she suddenly remembered, was deaf. She stared at him, waved both sniffwhips over him to perceive the depth of his slumberscent, and determined that he was indeed far away in dreamland. There was a smile at the edges of his handsome mouth. But the sounds he was making! He was snoring. She had heard her late father snore, particularly during days after he had consumed too much Chism's Dew, but nothing like this, the snores of a feller who could not hear himself snore! It would have been bearable except that each of his twenty spiracles was snoring in a different pitch, so that the effect reminded her of an assembly of cicadas drumming and shrilling in discord.

She jumped, not simply in response to the grating sounds but in sudden recollection of the activity that had consumed most of her morning. She felt a fullness in her abdomen which was . . . it was quite pleasant, even wonderful, nothing at all like a stomach ache, but strange and somehow conclusive, *final*, as if to say to her, *That's all there is to it.* Her sense of immeasurable gratification and satiety was tinged with a certain sadness, a feeling of loss, not simply the loss of her innocence and virginity but the loss of all her life that had led up to this event, as if the adult cecropia, designed for love alone, discovers after the act that love was not worth all that bother and metamorphosis. Her expectations were not entirely disappointed, save for the gnawing realization that it could have consequences in the form of sixteen passengers in an easteregg. She licked her lips and could still faintly taste the affy-dizzy. Had it all been worth the taste?

And now she was hungry again! Not for more affy-dizzy, but for solid food, for breakfast. She explored Sam's larder, the row upon neat row of crusts and crumbs of every conceivable provision, more a hoard than a pantry. Her touchers told her that all of these items were arranged and catalogued not only according to variety and sugar content but also according to age, as well as to crustiness and crumbiness, and many of them were older than she, even older than he! She selected a bit of well-ripened Twinkie, consumed it with gusto, and followed it up with an assortment of dabs of pudding, bits of candy, flecks of frosting, and specks of meringue. She noticed that one wall of the Clock was hung with the six cast-off moults of the owner, Squire Sam: the moults ranged in size from a first-instar scarcely larger than her head to a sixth-instar as large as she, which would almost still fit him. Why had he kept them? Not to eat, surely. Souvenirs of his childhood?

Tish stepped out of the Clock to take her bath, and gave herself a thorough washing on the edge of the mantelshelf, while she surveyed the room, the Woman's bed-and-sitting room, which did not have Sharon in it at the moment. Everything looked cozy and comfortable, as Tish had noticed the night before—had it been only *one* night before? It seemed like ages.

A terrible noise almost knocked Tish off the mantelshelf. It was not the Clock. The Clock had said, almost politely, a few minutes ago, "NOUGAT," and Tish was becoming accustomed to the things the Clock said. This was a shrill noise coming from a gigantic black insect perched upon a small table beside the Woman's bed. The insistent tintinnabulation lasted for a full second before abruptly ceasing, but Tish scarcely had time to retreat within the safety of the Clock before it roared another long burst of the same skirling cry. She stood transfixed, staring at the creature, the like of which she had never seen, unless it was *two* creatures: a huge carpenter ant mounted across the back of a huge rhinoceros beetle. Yes, perhaps the ant was killing the beetle, and it was the wailing westering howls of the beetle that were making such an urgent, horrible jangle. The howls did not waken Sam, but of course he was deaf. Tish was tempted to shake him awake. A third time now the big beetle screamed for mercy, and the Woman Sharon Herself came into the room and seized the huge ant and plucked it off the beetle's back. But then, instead of comforting the stricken beetle, She held the ant against Her cheek tenderly and spoke to it, saying, "Hi, Gran." The ant was Sharon's grandmother?!? The ant spoke to Sharon, but Tish could not hear the ant's words. Sharon sat down on the edge of Her bed, still holding the ant against Her cheek, and listened to it for a long moment, then said, "Oh, the radio said that too, but we haven't had a sign of it yet, have we?" Then She listened to more of the ant's words, and said, "I tried oiling it, but still it sticks."

The ant, Tish perceived, had no sniffwhips nor gitalongs. It had a head and a thorax and an abdomen, and a long, long tail which, in fact, was attached to the beetle! It spoke some more to the Woman, who answered, "No, but I had another letter from him yesterday, and it took my breath away. He's never written so beautifully, and if he has to get drunk to write like that, he might as well stay drunk! It was all I could do to keep from rushing right over there and hugging him!"

127

The ant spoke for a long time to Sharon, who only contributed an occasional, "Yes, Gran," or "I *know* that, Gran," or "You're right, Gran." Then Sharon said, "At least I've done something I haven't done before. I've written an answer. No, I haven't mailed it. Where would I mail it? Oh? But this is Sunday, isn't it? Where? Oh. Is *that* his mailbox, that thing? Well, I guess I could just poke it in there, but would he find it? I feel I have to say something to him, and maybe it's the only way. I think he expects an answer. I told him in the letter that if he could just go for one solid week without a drink, I'd come and talk to him. I don't know. What? I'd just have to take his word for it, I guess. He thinks I might let him move in *here*. It's out of the question, the way things stand."

Sharon listened for a while longer, then said, "Well, thanks, Gran, I appreciate that. How's everything up your way?" Another minute of listening followed, and then Sharon said, "Take care of yourself too, Gran. Oh, wait, by the way, I meant to ask. The other night I saw a cockroach. Did you ever have those when you lived here?" Listening, Tish thought: *cock*roach? and wondered if she had heard correctly. The Woman would not have said Smockroach or Frockroach; all of those lived at Holy House and were never allowed to come here. Maybe She had said "Clockroach," and was referring to Sam? But would Squire Sam have allowed himself to be seen by the Woman?

". . . So I called this toll-free number up at Harrison, you know, the one called Tel-Med sponsored by the Arkansas Regional Medical Program, which plays these tapes with advice on everything. I dialed the tape called 'Cockroaches—Menace or Nuisance' and got five minutes of stuff about their history, they're the oldest insect on earth, haven't changed for three hundred and fifty *million* years, and there are fifty-five different kinds of them in the United States. It said they have filth all over their legs and bodies, because they like to live in filth, and they'll spread this filth all over your food, and they'll puke and crap in your food too. It said to look out for their eggs, which are sort of leathery pouches that look like tiny pinto beans, and if you see an egg, destroy it, because it's got a dozen or more baby cockroaches inside of it. The tape said that cockroaches are a sign of poor housekeeping, and that if you keep your house clean and sanitary, they won't bother you. I was so ashamed when I heard that! This house isn't dirty, Gran, you know that. . . ."

Listening. Listening. Was Gran giving Sharon advice on how to get rid of roosterroaches? Tish wished she could hear the voice coming through the ant, and she strained to hear, but could not.

At length Sharon said, "Well. The tape warned that the disgusting little buggers will give you salmonella poisoning, diarrhea, nausea, dysentery, and even polio and TB, so if I don't answer the next time you call, you know I'm bad sick!" Sharon laughed, and Tish heard some laughter from the ant, and then Sharon said, "Well, I guess I'd better go mail my letter before I die! Goodnight, Gran. Sleep tight."

The Woman returned the ant to the top of the

beetle, but the beetle did not scream again; truly it must have been westered by the ant. Then the Woman reached under the bed and brought out a shiny and silvery stick with one great eye at the end. The Woman squeezed it, and it lit up like a zillion lightning bugs flashing at once, only it remained lit and did not twinkle off. The Woman picked up an envelope and carried it out of the room and to Her porch.

Quickly Tish climbed down the mantel and followed, squeezing under the screen door as its spring closed it. The Woman was descending the porch steps as Tish gained the porch. Tish observed that the Woman was pointing ahead of Her with the great lighting stick, which was casting a circle of illumination out into the yard, and the Woman walked out into this circle. Overhead the dark sky was filled with heavy clouds full of water. Tish scrambled along behind the Woman as fast as her six gitalongs could carry her.

15.

The Loafer's Court, gathered around Doc Swain and Squire Hank on Doc's porch, had an unexpected visitor, who arrived right while O.D. Ledbetter was telling a really good 'un, raunchy as all git out, about this feller what claimed he had not just two pricks but *three*. "He was fixin to marry this gal up on Banty Creek," old O.D. was saying, "but she accidental seen him a-takin a piss one night behind the wall, and she commenced hollerin that the weddin was called off. 'That pecker a yourn is jist too big fer a little ole gal lak me!' she tole 'im. But he jist laughs and says to her, 'Sweetheart, I got three of 'em. One is the tickler size, another'n is the prober size, and the great big 'un is the depositer size. I always use the depositer size to piss with.'

"So they went ahead and got theirselfs married," O.D. told it, "and the first night he tried the tickler size, and everything was just fine. So the second night she ast fer the prober size, and he tried that 'un on her too, and it was just fine. Wal sirs, the third night she begged for the depositer size, and it was the best of all. Him and her had the finest couple a hours you could imagine, and it looked like they'd live happy ever after.

"But about three weeks after the weddin the girl woke up one evenin and she says to him, 'Hon, do you reckon you could find a rubber band anywheres?' And he says yeah, they's some rubber bands in Man's writin-desk over to Holy House, but what does she want with one? 'Wal, I jist thought of somethin,' she told him. 'If we can tie all three of yore pricks together, I might could git a *decent* fuckin for a change!' "

Every loafer laughed fit to bust a gut, and complimented O.D. that that was the best 'un they ever heard, and challenged Squire Hank to tell a better one, and Squire was jist hitching himself up to do it, when they noticed that one of the loafers, who hadn't laughed, was coughing pretty bad. They looked at

131

the loafer and discovered that he wasn't a loafer after all, at least not a regular one, but the preacher himself! Brother Chid Tichborne had climbed the porch unnoticed and moved in amongst them.

O.D. apologized, "Heck, Preacher, I wudn't never of tole such a brash tale iffen I'd knowed ye was *listenin*."

Tolbert Duckworth put in, "Yeah, Preacher, and I shore didn't mean to laugh, neither. Why, I thought that there was the *nastiest* story ever I heared. Phew!"

Fent Chism put in, "Yeah, and this is the Lord's Day, and all. We ort to be ashamed, tellin dirty tales on the Lord's Day."

"Wal, boys," said Brother Chid. "I hope I don't never hear of none you'uns stealin the Lord's rubber bands."

"Hit was jist a story-tale," O.D. protested. "Wudn't never nothin ever really happent lak thet, nohow."

"Naw," said Elbert Kimber. "Wunst she had been fucked with the tickler size, that was all she could take!"

Everybody laughed again, except the preacher, who frowned at Elbert's language. Everybody stopped laughing abruptly, and studied the preacher's frown, and waited for him to say something else. But Brother Tichborne only looked properly pious and disapproving.

Finally Doc Swain himself had the boldness to ask, "Wal, Reverend, what brings you to my place tonight?" This was a fine question to ask, because it reminded the preacher that he wasn't a regular member of the Loafer's Court.

At least half of the loafers, Chid had mentally counted, were Crustians, and members of his congregation. Tolbert Duckworth was even an elder in the church, and Fent Chism was a deacon. It was to these good Crustians rather than to Doc that Chid addressed his next words, "Brethren, the Lord moves in mysterious ways. Though He giveth thee the bread of life, He also planneth to taketh it away from thee."

"Amen," said Tolbert Duckworth.

"Praise His name," said Fent Chism.

"And as ye may know," Chid announced, "tonight we are havin the prayer meetin and worship service right at the Lord's gitalongs, with Him awake and all, and ready to cast judgment upon us."

"Amen," said Fent Chism, and "Praise His name," said Tolbert Duckworth.

"No doubt He will rapture right and left," Chid observed. "No doubt a many and a many of us will know Rapture. Amen. Praise His name. And et cetera. But fellers—" Chid paused for dramatic effect, changing his tone and his tune "—I am here to tell ye the news that the Lord is fixin to try to move into Partheeny!" Chid glanced at Squire Hank to see his reaction, but the Squire remained expressionless. The others, however, stared open-mouthed at the minister, and then at one another, and then at Squire Hank, to see what *he* would say.

Squire Hank squinted at Chid and asked, "How do ye know?"

How could Chid tell them? He had preached at them every Sunday, and sometimes on Wednesday night prayer meeting too, *never* to touch the Lord, never even to think about going near His Person, and here he had been up underside the Lord's shirt collar himself, and that was how he knew that the Lord had written a letter to the Woman of Parthenon, in which He had hinted, or actually requested—well, to be honest, begged—to be allowed to move His "things," including His self, into Parthenon.

"I have done seen a letter," Chid revealed. "I caint quote you His exact words, but He more or less informed Her that it was his intention to abandon Holy House and move into Partheeny."

Again all the loafers looked at Squire Hank for his comment, and finally the Squire declared, "I misdoubt that She would ever think of allowin Him to move in on Her."

"Maybe She invited Him, who knows?" suggested Tolbert Duckworth.

"Yeah," Chid allowed. "One way or th'other, He jist might do it, and then what would we do? Maybe we had better be ready to move out, ourselfs."

"Or maybe," Squire Hank said, "all of you'uns ought to be prayin to yore Lord to stay put."

"Good idee, Squar!" said Fent Chism. "Yeah, Brother Tichborne, maybe tonight at the prayer meetin when we're all assembled right there at the Lord's gitalongs, maybe we had ort to pray to Him and beg Him not to leave Holy House."

"That's what we ort!" agreed Elder Duckworth.

But Chid said, "Naw. It wouldn't do no good to beseech the Lord in that wise. Maybe the one we ort to beseech is Squire Hank, right here. Maybe we ort to be askin Squire Hank if he would ever let every last blessit one of us move into Partheeny when the Lord does."

All eyes and sniffwhips were upon Squire Hank. He ruminated. He spat. He frowned a bit. He ruminated some more. Then a trace of a smile crept upon the corner of his face, and he said, "Why don't you'uns ask *Her* that?"

"Speak of the Mockroach!" exclaimed Mont Dinsmore, who was sitting on the north edge of the crowd nearest that direction, and suddenly thrashed his sniffwhips. He exclaimed, "Hey, fellers, lookee who's a-comin yonder!"

Every one turned and tuned their sniffwhips, and beheld the approach of none other than the subject of discussion, the Woman Herself. The great circular beam of Her flashlight preceded Her, but only briefly did the flashlight illuminate the front of Doc Swain's clinic, and it did not shine upon the porch floor where the mob of loafers crouched. The Woman was strolling slowly down one rut of the Roamin Road. No one could ever remember having seen Her on this part of the Road before, approaching Holy House. Hardly was She out of sight when all the roosterroaches began a busy prattling amongst themselves.

"Wal strike me blind!" Tolbert Duckworth said. "If that aint the—!"

"Maybe She's a-gorn to visit Him!" Fent Chism voiced the thoughts of several.

"What're we a-waitin fer?" Chid Tichborne said. "Let's go see!"

At that moment a girl roosterroach came running down the Road, following in the steps of the Woman, but scrambling as fast as her gitalongs would carry her. When she came within sight and sniff of the Loafer's Court, she stopped, pausing for breath and to cast an anxious glance at all the loafers.

"Morsel, gal," called Doc Swain. "What's the rush?"

The girl looked from one to another of the loafers. She was panting. "Howdy, sirs, and morsels to y'uns," she said timidly, between wheezes.

"Somethin chasin ye?" Doc Swain asked. "Have you seen the White Mouse?"

The girl looked over her shoulder, and appeared uncertain. "Yessir, I think there's some kind of booger a-follerin me," she declared.

The loafers laughed, and one of them teased, "Was it white? What color was it?"

But the girl did not answer. Taking a deep breath, she resumed her journey, as fast as she could skitter.

"Now who-all was *thet*?" asked a loafer.

"I do believe that was little ole Tish Dingletoon, Jack Dingletoon's biggest gal," declared another.

Another loafer asked, "Did ye hear that ole Jack has done went and westered off?"

"Yeah, him and Josie both, together," said another.

"Maybe she's jist a-lookin for to find them," suggested still another.

"Wal, fellers, that's sorrowful news," commented Brother Chid Tichborne, "and I don't know about you'uns, but me, I'm gonna git right back to Holy House and see what's up." He straightened his gitalongs and rose up from the porch floor. He paused to see if any other loafer would budge, but the others

136

remained crouched. "Wal?" he said. "Aint none of you'uns interested in goin with me?"

Tolbert Duckworth asked Doc Swain, "Hey, Doc, what you aimin to do?"

"Me?" Doc said. "Why, I don't rightly know. How about you, Squire Hank?"

"Wal . . ." said Squire Hank, but showed no sign of budging from his crouch. Everyone watched him closely for a sign of a budge, and then they watched Doc Swain for a sign of a budge. Squire Hank spat, and said, "I thought maybe that booger she was afeared of might jist be my boy Sam, but it don't look like he's a-follerin her. Don't look like *any* boogers a-follerin her."

Chid Tichborne said, "Wal, I don't know about the rest of you boogers, but *I* aim to foller her." He took another couple of steps toward the edge of the porch, but there was no sign of a budge from any of the others.

Finally Doc Swain remarked, "Jist think, fellers. This might could be the only chance we ever have in our lifetimes to see Her speak to Him, or vice versa." Doc creakingly rose up from his crouch and stood upon his still-remaining three gitalongs, wobbling unsteadily, and moved over beside Chid.

Squire Hank said, "Could be She's jist going to tell Him to stay away from Her." He too rose up, stretched, and prepared to go. With the Squire leading, all of the assembled loafers decamped from Doc's porch and ambled off down Roamin Road in the direction of the Woman's flashlight, now just a pinpoint of light nearly a furlong away, rapidly merging with the light coming from a window of Holy House.

16.

But the Woman did not climb the porch of Holy
House. The Roamin Road skirts within sniffing distance of the porch, but the Woman stayed on the
Road, and Tish stayed on Her heels, or close behind,
almost to the edge of Banty Creek, where a small dirt
road led from Carlott to the old low-water cement
bridge over the stream and provided the Lord's vehicle
with access to the outside world. It also provided
access for the mail vehicle from the outside world to
stop at the Lord's mailbox, which was a piece of metal
junk, a World War II cartridge case mounted upon a
pole stuck in the ground amid brambles and brush.
Here the mail carrier, driving out of Jasper, the county
seat eighty furlongs to the north, stopped every morning to leave a copy of the *Arkansas Gazette* (daily),
the Newton County *Times* (Thursdays), the *New
York Review of Books* (biweekly), *Arkansas Times*
(monthly), *Audubon* (bimonthly), and *Poetry*, the
Southern Review, Poetry Northwest, and *PMLA* (all
quarterly), and various circulars, fliers, handouts, and
other promotional material and appeals from pur-
chasers of mailing lists for "literate middleclass
natureloving bookreading forties white males." The
only exercise the Lord was ever known to take, apart
from the late-afternoon inspection of the weeds in His
Garden, was to walk from Holy House to His Holy
Mailbox, a distance of maybe half a furlong. Very
rarely did He get a letter.

The Woman found the cartridge case with Her

flashlight, opened its lid, and dropped the letter into it. "There," Tish heard Her say to Herself, "I hope the mailman doesn't think it's an outgoing letter." Tish wondered what an outgoing letter was; one that was friendly and sociable?

The Woman did not pause before turning around, and Tish had to leap to get out of the way of Her footsteps as the Woman began retracing Her path. She walked faster on the return journey, and Tish did not even try to keep up with Her.

The loafers saw Her coming back. They were nearly abreast of Holy House, wherein their families were doing whatever they could to entertain themselves through the night, when one of the loafers shouted, "Yonder She comes back again!" and another bellowed, "Let's us git off the Road!" and all of them scrambled to get out of Her way. One of them, Luke Whitter, was a step too late, and was ground into the earth by the Woman's shoe. Doc Swain rushed to check him over, but Luke was pretty thoroughly squashed, and was groaning his last. There was nothing Doc could do.

"The Lord giveth, and the Lord taketh away," said Chid Tichborne. "Our Joshua Crust saith, 'Be thou faithful unto west, and I will give thee a crown of life.' " And he made a mental note to remember to include Luke Whitter's name among the several obituaries he would have to deliver tonight at the services.

"Amen," said the Crustian loafers, and turned Luke's carcass over into the belly-up position and covered it with blades of grass.

"Wal," observed Doc, "hit don't look like the Womarn was aimin to visit Holy House after all."

Mont Dinsmore announced, "Yonder comes that gal again."

Tish wanted to enter the forest of weeds to avoid walking through the mob of loafers, but the scent of west coming from Luke's carcass frightened her, and she passed onward among the roosterroaches.

"That booger still after ye?" Doc Swain asked her.

"Nossir," she said, smiling, "I reckon he drowned in Banty Creek."

"You aint a-follerin that Womarn, air ye?" he asked. Tish nodded her head. "Where'd She go? What's She up to?"

"She jist went to mail a letter," Tish said. "She mailed a letter to the Lord, and put it in His box."

Brother Chid Tichborne solemnly declared, "I shore wush they was some way we could find out what-all that letter says in it."

But not even the most irreverent among them was in the mood for going to the Lord's Holy Mailbox and attempting to tamper with His mail. Most of them still remembered the story of a family of Ledbetters who had gone to the cartridge case one night, dined on the gray flocking that stuffed the lining of a Jiffy bookmailing bag, and were sound asleep when the Lord surprised them there the next day, and swatted them all west with a rolled-up *Gazette*.

Instead of venturing onward to the mailbox, the mob of loafers entered Holy House, not through the same hole but through several. At a respectful distance, Tish followed. If nothing else, she could satisfy her curiosity about the interior of Holy House. She might even get some information about her missing parents. She kept as close as she could to Squire Hank, as if she might need his protection, and sure enough, just as she entered the loafing room she was accosted by a large lady roosterroach who challenged her territorial rights.

"Jist who d'ye think you *air*?" demanded Mrs. Kimber.

Squire Hank placed himself between the two females and said to Mrs. Kimber, "She's with me."

"Oh, beggin yore pardon, Squar, I didn't *know*," Mrs. Kimber apologized, and got out of the way.

The loafing room was dark except for one corner, and none of them went near it, for it contained the awake Man. A lone lamp cast its pointed beam upon the pages of a book held in the lap of the Lord. All the air around and over His head was swathed in the fumes of smoke from the cigarette burning between His fingers. On a table beside His Great Cheer-of-Ease was His Great Sacred Crystal Ashtray, a marvelous cube of glass with tapered corners rising to four concave troughs for holding His burning cigarette when He chose to put it down, and the interior of the cube was filled with extinguished butts. On one side of the Great Sacred Crystal Ashtray lay a pair of pencils, long yellow logs with rubber tips and pointed lead ends, and beyond those was a tall tumbler holding ice cubes and amber liquid. And beside the drinking glass was His Terrible Swift Rapturing Revolver Shootin-Gun.

141

One of the loafers announced, "He aint a–drinkin no beer tonight. They aint been a single blessit can opened out to the cookroom."

Another loafer observed with an expression of disgust, "Jist that pizen hard stuff. Old Granddad. Westerly as scorpion–piss."

Another loafer announced, "They's a couple of Fritos on the cookroom floor. Better hurry." Several dozen of the loafers decamped from the loafing room toward the cookroom.

Tish whispered to Squire Hank, "I wish there was some way to tell Him He's got a letter from Her."

Squire Hank did not respond, but continued observing the Lord. Was he as deaf as his son?

17.

The deaf son rose long after the deaf sun had set. The Clock had struck the news, "DIVINITY!" a reference not to any Godhead or Manhead but to the divinely delicious confection, white as a newborn nymph, stuffed with chopped nutmeats. Sam felt as if he were stuffed with chopped nutmeats. He required a long minute to realize the lateness of the hour, and the fact that he had done something unimaginable, something totally beyond his normal powers, something wonderful but terrible: he had planted a marble! But where was the girl? Frantically he searched the Clock. What had her name been? Yes: Tish. "TISH!" he called out, and realized that he was simultaneously sniffwhip-spelling it, and remembered the delightful means of communication they had devised. Further, he remembered with a shock that he was in love with her. There was no mistake. It was not simple lust, not merely a desire to give her a marble, nor even a wish to confer upon her the motherhood of the next and possibly last generation of Ingledews. He loved her!

But she was neither in nor around the Clock, and his sniffwhips could find no trace of her, save a faint lingering touch of the pheromone that she had sprayed the morning before. He climbed down from the Clock, and was vaguely disturbed by an out-of-the-ordinary situation: the Woman was not in Her cheer-of-ease, as usually She was during the hour of Divinity; Her stereo phonograph was not playing; Her kerosene lamps were all unlit; Her presence could not be detected within the Parthenon. She was not at home.

Sam rushed into the cookroom, hollering, "Dad! Have you seen a girl?" but his father was not there. It was likely that his father was hanging out, as usual, at Doc Swain's place. Sam scrambled out of Parthenon and gained the Roamin Road, and headed off toward Doc's place.

There was *no*body there! The nightly Loafer's Court was not convening. No patients waited to see the physician. Sam felt an unearthly sense of abandonment. *Where was everybody?* Sam was assailed by a metaphysical qualm: had the world of his ken and kin deserted him because of his sinning with Tish? But had it been a sin? Premarital fornication, yes, but had he seduced her? No, it had been entirely mutual; in fact, her pheromone had escaped *before* his affydizzy had escaped.

He decided to journey onward to Holy House in search of his fellow creatures. In his haste and near-panic, he bumped into a cricket. It is almost impossible for anyone with good hearing to bump into a cricket, because they are the most raucous of sound-producing insects, their so-called "chirp" audible from great distances, eight or nine furlongs. Actually the "chirp" is a monotonous reiterated challenge of the male to his fellow males, an expression, "Shy ye, feller, up," meaning "You, sir, back away from me." Unlike the calls of other male bugs, which are meant to attract females, it is meant to scare off the competition, much in the same way that the fighting of horn beetles and stag beetles is simply an elimination of the weaker. The loudest cricket wins. When two male crickets meet, they will holler "Shy ye feller up" at one another insistently until one of them gives way and retreats.

Even if he had not been in such a hurry, Sam Ingledew, not hearing the cricket, would have bumped into him. He gave the cricket a bad start, because no other bug had ever bumped into him before.

When he had recovered, the cricket said, "I say, shy ye feller up."

"Beg pardon," Sam returned, apologizing both for having bumped into him and for being unable to hear him. As a general rule, he detested crickets, but he was nothing if not polite.

"SHY YE FELLER UP!" the cricket repeated, so loudly that Sam couldn't help hearing him.

"Sorry," Sam said, and made to move around the cricket, but the hostile cricket shifted his position, blocking Sam's way. The cricket was not much larger than Sam, although he had the long thick thighs and gitalongs of an athlete; his sniffwhips were much longer than Sam's, and he had a belligerent expression on his face. "Look, buddy," Sam said, "if you'll just step aside, I'll give you no trouble." Again he tried to get around the cricket, but the cricket continued to block his way and continued to repeat his mindless warning.

One fact of life which had led Sam to question the infallibility and wisdom of Man—not particularly the Man of Holy House but all Men—was that Man venerated or at least cherished the cricket but despised the cockroach. Crickets to Man were cute, adorable, and charming, and it was thought to be very bad luck to kill one of them. Sam had never heard of a cricket being killed by Man . . . or by Woman. But cockroaches, of basically the same size, shape, color, and configuration, in fact more sleek and streamlined than crickets, simply because they lacked the stupidity to rub their wings together and make "music," were therefore not "cute," but objects of revulsion and enmity. It wasn't fair; it wasn't cricket.

"Listen, my friend," Sam said to the cricket, "I don't want your old lady. She isn't of the least attraction to me. Fat thighs look okay on a fellow, but on a girl they're lousy. Step aside."

If the cricket understood what Sam was saying

145

to him (and Sam doubted their intelligence too), he gave no sign of it, but only continued saying, "Shy ye feller up."

Sam decided that the only thing to do was to lower himself to the cricket's level and communicate in his own tongue. "Shy ye feller up, yourself," he said to the cricket.

This was a mistake. For a moment it stunned the cricket into silence, but then he resumed, louder than ever, "SHY YE FELLER UP!"

"Oh, for crying out loud," Sam said, and attempted to shove the cricket aside. But the cricket rose up on his long rear legs and cuffed Sam a blow on the side of his head that rang his bell. Sam slugged him back. The cricket punched Sam full in the face. Sam clobbered the cricket on his chops.

This scuffle drew the combatants off the Roamin Road and into the forest of weeds, and thus Sam was not aware that the Woman, Sharon, returning from her postal errand, had passed by, heading home.

Sam and the cricket circled one another warily with their dukes raised. The cricket jumped and bit Sam painfully on the abdomen. Sam remembered that crickets, though usually vegetarian, are capable of being carnivores. The cricket was now screaming at the top of his wings, "SHY YE SHY YE FELLER UP FELLER UP SHY YE FELLER UP SHY YE!!!" Sam lashed him with both sniffwhips, gave him a series of one-two punches with his touchers to the face, then kicked him over onto his back, jumped onto his chest and got in several good pokes into his soft underside.

Undaunted, the cricket arched his back, flipped over and threw Sam off of him, then sank his teeth into Sam's thorax and held on. Sam clawed furiously at the cricket, inflicting wounds all over the cricket's body until the cricket released his bite on Sam.

Sam was aware that a number of other male crickets had formed themselves into a ring of spectators around the fighters. Even if Sam was to defeat this cricket, might he not be attacked by the cricket's kinsmen? For a moment this prospect weakened him, and he caught two hard blows from his opponent.

He went down. *Remember you're an Ingledew*, he told himself, *and all Ingledews have the power*. He struggled to his gitalongs, righted himself, and realized the other crickets were cheering him! "Strike ye, feller, up!" one of the crickets urged. "Hit him, feller, up alongside his head!" another said.

Sam kicked out and tripped his foe off his gitalongs, and as the cricket went down, Sam bashed him a good lick on the side of his head, then a mighty blow on top of the head that plowed the cricket's nose into the earth. The cricket tried to rise, and made two good efforts at getting up, then collapsed all of a heap.

The other crickets beat their wings in applause. They clapped and smiled and cheered, and Sam took a little bow, then went on his way. The sky, he noticed, was fully darkened by clouds, and the weather segments of his sniffwhips had upped the chances of thundershowers from 30% to 85%.

His fears that he had been totally abandoned were soon relieved by the sight of the interior of Holy House, which was crawling with roosterroaches. The cookroom, which Sam visited first, was aswarm with Frockroaches and Smockroaches battling one another over bits of Frito on the floor, and upon the table there was a mob scene in the arena of a paper plate containing the remains of Man's supper: chicken à la king on toast. Although hungry, Sam did not join in. He moved unnoticed and unrecognized among the Holy House roosterroaches. He left the cookroom and entered the loafing room, where a crowd had gathered around Brother Chidiock Tichborne, who was preaching. Sam realized that it was Sunday night, time for the usual Sabbath service, but there was something different about this one: they were meeting right in the presence of the Lord, Who, however, did not seem to notice the hundreds of them gathered together in His Name on the floor around His cheer-of-ease, in which He sat drinking and reading.

"Sinners! Look in yore hearts!" the minister was exhorting the congregation, who were mostly Crustians and did not include those the minister considered true sinners. "Who amongst us can look in his heart and say, 'Lord, I am free from sin'? Up yonder sits our Lord Hisself, and verily I say unto ye, though He may have a book in His lap, His eye is upon ye, His all-seeing eye is lookin into *yore* heart, and He *knows* which of ye have kept His commandments and which of ye have sinned! Repent, for His terrible wrath is soon to be visited upon ye!"

Of course Sam could hear none of this, but he was impressed with the minister's ability to hold his audience, who included, Sam was startled to notice, his own father, Squire Hank, crouched at one edge

148

of the crowd, almost unnoticed except by a girl whispering at one of his tailprongs. The girl, Sam was further surprised to discover, was Tish, his own beloved. Why was his father here? Why was *she* here?

"Oh, what a blessed privilege it is," the minister went on, "for us pore sinners to come together tonight right smack dab in the Lord's Own Mighty Presence, where few of us has been before, to lay our hearts bare before Him and invite His judgment. Repent, I say, for the hour of reckoning is at hand! No one of ye is free from sin! Who amongst ye has tasted of the crumb when the crust would do? Who amongst ye has jined in lust and sin with thine own kindred in *incest*? Who amongst ye has adulterated? And who amongst ye has fornicated?"

Though Sam could not hear, he could see, and he saw Tish trembling. Was she a Crustian? He recalled her belief in the Fate-Thing, such a naive but passionate conviction, and he wondered if she had room in her heart for belief in the Crustian drivel espoused by Chid Tichborne.

"Oh yes, my friends, don't ye doubt for a minute that He won't rise up against the sinners in yore midst and smite them! He will smite thee with his bullets! His Holy Revolver is loaded and ready! Hit's up yonder right alongside His Great Sacred Crystal Ashtray, and it's ready to use! Look in yore heart, I tell ye, and ask: Is it *me*, O Lord? Am I the one who deserves Thy punishment? Have my sins offended Thee, O Lord?"

Sam was tempted to join his father and his beloved. He noticed that his father was the only member of the audience unaffected by the preacher's oratory.

149

The others, including Tish, seemed to verge on hysteric frenzy. Several had bowed their heads to the floor in abject propitiation. Others, mostly males, were rising up and wringing their sniffwhips together in anguish. Still others, mostly females, were raising both touchers and sniffwhips in the direction of Man, in imploration. All of these prostrated themselves when the minister shouted:

"Let us pray! Almighty Man, our Father who art Lord of all the world, we beseech Thee to heed our solemn prayer." So loud was Chid's voice, with his face turned upward toward Man, that one would have thought that Man, if not Sam, could have heard him. Indeed, Sam could catch a word or two here and there. "All of us are guilty of wickedness! And transgression! And iniquity! And unrighteousness! And *evil*! O Lord our Man, if it be Thy will, rise up against these sinners and smite them with Thy Holy Gun!"

And verily, the Lord rose up. He put His book down and stood. But He did not lift up His revolver. He lifted up His empty glass and took it to the cook-room, for a refill. He had not even appeared to notice the assembly of worship on the floor of His loafing room. Many of them had scrambled and scurried for the nearest hiding place at the instant the Lord's knee-hinges straightened Him upward. But most of them had remained crouched where they were, increasing the fervor of their prayer.

Tish, Sam noticed, was among those staying in place and praying almost aloud. Sam's father, he saw, was looking at her with pity.

18.

Chid was disappointed. It had been one of his finest sermons, and one of his most eloquent prayers, inspired not only by the occasion of their meeting for the first time at the Lord's gitalongs but also by Chid's having Squire Hank himself in the audience, though only on the fringe of it, not down front among the oldest elders and deacons, where he could rightfully crouch if he so desired. What was the Squire, that infidel, doing here, at all? Hoping to see Chid make a fool of himself? Well, the Squire would be surprised. Even if the Lord had not risen up with His revolver, as Chid had been almost certain He would do, the night was still young, the worship service was just getting started, the Lord hadn't consumed more than a halfpint of the quart He usually drank, and Chid, if he used his best devices, might yet get a rise out of Him.

"Brethering and sistering," he addressed the crowd, attempting to summon back those who had fled, "the Lord goeth away, yea, He goeth to His cookroom to open His Fabulous Fridge and get more ice cubes, but He shall come again! Be ye faithful and watchful with me, friends, ere the Lord returneth. Meanwhile, a few announcements."

The Ladies' Aid would next meet on Thursday night. The Gents' Saturday Prayer Breakfast would have a guest speaker. The Crustian Young People's Fellowship would go on an outing to Banty Creek Tuesday night.

"Brother Duckworth," Chid requested, "would ye kindly report on the membership rolls?"

Chid yielded the floor to Elder Duckworth, and Tolbert stood to announce, "Brethern and sistern, the elders and deacons of this here church is proud to announce that sixty-three young folks has done reached the age of imago and jined up; seven roosterroaches has repented of their past sins and atoned for their expulsions and has asked to be taken back into the fold. The deacons and elders is powerful sorrow to announce the following expulsions from the church: Brother Theron Coe, who has been found guilty of incest with seven of his daughters, is no longer with us. Brother Jesse Clendenen, Junior, has been found guilty of excessive profanity, and is expelled. Brother Hector Duckworth, who I am glad to say aint no brother a mine, has confessed to incest with five of his sisters and is removed from the rolls. Sister Nancy Whitter has committed incest with eight of her sons and is no longer amongst us. . . ."

Chid listened idly to this recitation of transgressions, backslidings, expulsions, and reprimands, and noted that it was no worse than usual. His eye and his sniffwhip roamed the congregation, to note their reactions to this tabulation of wrongdoing, and all of them were looking properly solemn and contrite . . . all except one, who was grinning. Who was that stranger? Why, yes, it appeared to be Squire Hank's boy, name of Samuel. What was Squire Sam doing here? Worse, why was he wearing such an idiotic grin during this public declaration of awful sin? Did he think it was funny that so many church members were being expelled and castigated?

152

Chid's eye and sniffwhip moved onward, pausing here and there, until he noticed his own family, his wife Ila Frances and some of their children—but where was Archibald? Oh, yes, *there* was Archibald, over to the other side of the congregation, near Squire Hank but talking to some girl, that same female who had been out there in the Roamin Road earlier this evening, who had seen the Woman mail Her letter to the Lord. Chid realized she was Josie Dingletoon's daughter, and, probably because she was the result of that there marble that Chid had given Josie in a moment (or two hours) of weakness and temptation, Chid's very own daughter too, therefore a half-sister of Archy. Chid would have to remember to give Archy a little lecture about getting so chummy with his half-sister. If nothing else, Chid would have to tell the boy not to talk to her during the worship service.

But Chid remembered that Tish was probably in mourning for her parents, and this reminded the minister that he had to give the funeralizations, so when Brother Duckworth finished the expulsion announcements and crouched back down, Chid rose again and said, "Well, brethering and sistering, maybe we've got time before the Lord returneth to take care of this week's funeralizations. The following has done went and westered off lately since our last meetin, and we do hereby commend their souls to the Lord: Malvina Swain Murrison has gone west of old age in her twenty-seventh month; James T. Bourne, beloved son of Millard and Gladys Bourne, in only his third instar, has been eaten by a salamander; the childern of Nolan and Bertha Coe, sixteen in number, in their third instar, has been chewed up and westered by mites;

153

nine of the fourth-instar children of Fred and Florence Chism has been consumed by pismires.

"Let's see, now," Chid went on, searching his memory, "Brother Rodney Stapleton has been eaten by a nightingale. And oh yes, the entire family of Clarence and Beatrice Whitter and their sixteen imago childern, fifteen fourth-instar childern, sixteen second-instar childern, and thirteen newborn nymphs and swains, has all been consumed by a opposum, may Our Lord and Saviour Joshua Crust take them each and every to live forevermore on the Right Hand of Man! Now, let's see, yes, also little Joseph Donald Dingletoon, eaten by a green frog, has predeceased his parents, John or Jack Orville Dingletoon and wife Josephine, logdwellers of Carlott, who was last seen in a beercan in the Lord's cookroom, where they had no business in the first place.

"And last but not least, just a few minutes ago, out yonder in the Roamin Road, before my very own eyes, Brother Luke Whitter was crushed beneath the sole of the Woman of Parthenon! Now, my friends, I wish I could tell ye that She did it of a purpose, that She had seen him and stomped on him to punish him or to rapture him, but I do believe it was pure accidental-like. But who is to say? Maybe Luke didn't care, or maybe he thought he had it coming to him, on account of his wife Nancy. . . ."

Chid detected a murmur running through the crowd, but it was not because of his words. Those in the back of the audience had detected the footsteps of the return of the Lord! Once again, many of the congregation dashed away beneath the rug or pieces of furniture, but once again the majority of them remained rooted and watched in adoration as the Lord walked back to His cheer-of-ease and plunked down into it. Chid was glad to have the Lord back. Why had He taken so long? Maybe he had grabbed Hisself a snack in the cookroom, which meant there might be more crusts and crumbs littering the floor. Yes, a few of the faithful were becoming unfaithful and edging away in the direction of the cookroom.

"Hold on there!" Chid shouted, stopping them in their tracks. "This here service aint over yet! Why, no, my friends, we are hardly started! I've got a real important message fer ye tonight! But first, Brother Chism, supposing ye lead us in a hymn or two?"

Deacon Fent Chism rose and, using both of his sniffwhips to set the tempo, led the gathering in a four-part harmonization of "I'll Meet You in the Morning on That Glorious Shore of the Sweet Bye and Bye Right Along Topside of His Blessed Hand." After four verses and chorus of this, Fent Chism conducted them through "At The Old Shiny Pin Where My Saviour Did Bleed I Shall Lean on Those Everlasting Arms and Get Ready to Leave This World and Go to Gloryland."

Now for the best part, Chid said to himself as the last chorus faded off and he picked up its last word to open his resumed sermon: "*Glory*land! How sweet the sound! Yes, brethering and sistering, we shall all meet in Gloryland! But who will be *waiting* for us there? Why, of course, those I've jist funeralized, what has been eaten by frogs and salamanders and possums and mites and what-all, and them that has westered of plain old age or jist disappeared, but most of all, my friends, I tell ye, the ones that will be waiting to save us a place will be them that have already been dispatched by His Holy Gun!

"You know I didn't mention none of them in my funeralizations for this week. You know *why* I didn't mention 'em, because they don't need no funerals! Nossiree, their souls is already in Gloryland! This past week, the following has not westered a natural west nor been eaten by critters, but has been raptured and *pulverized* into smithereens by the Holy Bullets of the Lord! Brother John Thomas Murrison! Brother Carl Henry Duckworth! Brother Arnold Justin Chism! Sister Jessamine Sue Plowright! Sister Sophronia Marabelle Coe! And Brother Oscar Robert Whitter! These are the saints who have been raptured and sanctified in the fire of His Fire!"

This was the moment that Chid liked best, and he paused for breath, and to let the mood be set for his next words: "Who will jine them tonight? Who amongst ye has already been chosen for the Sacred Fire? Who will stand bravely with head upraised and ask, 'Is it I, Lord?' Search your hearts, I say, and ask yourselfs, 'Am I ready?'" Chid felt no guilt over this contradiction. The best way to hold them, he knew, was to confuse them. Let them be uncertain whether the westering by gunfire was punishment for sin or a rapturing and reward for faith, whether the pulverization into smithereens was to be avoided by clean living or sought as the ultimate salvation. No school of theology had implanted Chidiock Tichborne with this fundamental lesson of evangelism: perplexity is the foundation for faith. Do we live our eastering in order to seek west or avoid it?

Already the more susceptible were whipped into a frenzy of postures and devotions, some of them shouting aloud, "Is it I, Lord?" and "Am I ready?" while still others strained their entire bodies in the direction of Man and declared "It is I, Lord!" and "I am ready!" Surely, Chid thought, the Lord Himself could hear them. He was pleased to notice that Squire Sam Ingledew had stopped grinning his stupid grin and was looking around himself in wonder. And then, as if the young squire could not bear the sight of so much faith and fervor, he slipped away from the crowd and disappeared into the darkness. Good riddance, thought Chid.

It sure would do me a right smart of good, Chid thought, *if the Lord would shoot one of them Ingledews.* It would not only strengthen Chid's power over the unbelievers and the Crustian backsliders, but it would also reduce by one the obstacles to the Crustian takeover of Parthenon.

"Just a little more hubbub," Chid said to himself, "and the Lord Hisself may hear us." He shouted to the crowd, "WHO IS READY?!?" and he commanded them, "PRAISE HIM! PRAISE HIS HOLY NAME!"

A great tumult of sound rose from the congregation, a blending of cries of "I AM READY!" and "CHOOSE *ME*, LORD!" and "BLESSED BE THE NAME OF THE LORD!" And Deacon Fent Chism managed to get a few dozen of them to harmonize on a loud chorus of "Gettin Ready to Leave This World

157

of Sorrow to Head My Gitalongs for the Gloryland Up Yonder."

Even Archibald, Chid was pleased to note, had stopped fooling around with that Dingletoon gal and was getting into the spirit of things. But Chid silently prayed to the Lord to spare Archibald and all the rest of his own family, including especially himself, although he quickly added, "But if it be Thy will, Lord, and You don't need me no more to watch after Yore flock, why then just Rapture me too."

Then, somehow, the tumult of all those prayers and songs, the very loudness of those hundreds of voices raised in worship and supplication, must have reached Him. He closed the book He was reading, and seemed to stare off into space for a moment as if He were thinking about what He had just read, but then He reached up and turned His reading lamp so that it shone full upon the entire congregation. The Lord leaped out of His cheer-of-ease.

"Shit!" spake the Lord, and snatched up His revolver. "BANG!" spake the Holy Gun, and dispatched Deacon Fent Chism to the Gloryland he was singing about. So many of the faithful were so close to the Lord's gitalongs that the Lord began stomping at the same time he was shooting, and westered several at a time beneath his shoes, narrowly missing Chid himself. "KER-POW!" spake the Holy Gun again, and obliterated Ila Frances Tichborne, Chid's wife. "Oh, take me next!" Chid cried, in a curious mixture of grief for his wife and elation at his own imminent Rapture.

But the Lord was not aiming at him. The Lord

was aiming at one in a group of three: Archibald Tichborne, Tish Dingletoon, and Squire Hank Ingledew. "Oh, let it be the Squire!" Chid screamed.

"PLEW!" spake the Holy Gun, and Chid looked to see which of the three was hit, but none of them were. The Lord had missed? Chid looked up, and saw that the Lord's eyelid, the lid of His sighting eye, was covered by a clinging roosterroach! Some blasphemous roosterroach had climbed up the Lord's person and dropped off the top of His head at the instant of His firing, seizing Him by the sighting eye's lid! The Lord had been made to miss!

"AAAAGGHH!" spake the Lord, and dropped His revolver, which crushed the Stapletons, and swatted at His own face, knocking the offending roosterroach away, then raised and clutched His gitalong. The Lord had shot Himself in His own gitalong!

19.

When Tish heard the fourth explosion she thought it was one more discharge of the Lord's Holy Bullets, but how could that be? The Holy Revolver was on the floor, lying atop poor westered Mr. and Mrs. Horace Stapleton, and the Lord Himself was sprawled out on His loafing couch, clutching His gitalong in agony, moaning and cursing. No, the fourth explosion must have been somebody else shooting a gun, but who?

Tish found that one of her gitalongs was en-wrapped by the sniffwhip tip of Archy Tichborne, who was pulling at her and saying, "Come on, gal, let's skedaddle out of here!" He led her through an old bullethole in the wall and into the space behind the walls, a deserted corridor, where they were squeezed together in their hiding. Hiding from what? Tish wondered. Then a fifth explosion sounded, and she jumped, mashing up against Archy, who enfolded her with his sniffwhips and said, "Easy, sweetheart, He caint git us here."

"He's not trying to get us," Tish said. "He's shot. Somebody is shooting Him."

"That aint gunfire any more," Archy declared, knowledgeably. "That's thunder. It's comin on to rain."

"Nobody's shooting Him?" Tish asked.

"He shot Hisself," Archy said. "He was aimin right at *me* but He missed and shot Hisself."

"Is He west?" Tish asked in awe.

"Naw, He jist blasted a big hole in His gitalong and fell on his loafin couch."

"But He's a-westerin," Tish declared with concern.

"I misdoubt it," Archy said. "He jist won't be walkin around much."

"Then why are we hiding?" she asked.

"It's still dangerous out there," Archy said.

A sixth explosion sounded, causing Tish and Archy to jump again and to hold one another more tightly. Even though they knew it was thunder, not gunfire, it was so close, so loud, and so shaking that

160

it seemed as if the walls of Holy House would collapse. There is nothing like danger to promote intimacy, and Tish was surprised to find that she and Archy were such close friends already, almost as if she had known him all her life. Had it been only the night before last that she first saw him at the Carlott play-party, and admired him, and wished he would take notice of her? He was certainly noticing her now. The proximity of their bodies reminded her of that night too, when the two of them had hidden together from the Lord. Was there a cosmic parallel here, that once again they were hiding from the Lord? Or were they only hiding from the thunder? Or from what?

The thunder increased, as if it were seeking them out, and even the confines of the wall in which they hid were no blanket against the flashes of lightning. She could hear now the steady drumbeat of rain high up against the roof and even against the sides of the house and the windowpanes.

After a long time, Tish asked, "Shouldn't we go see?"

"See what?" Archy asked.

"If Man is all right," she said. "If He's not a-westerin."

"We darsen go nowhere," Archy said. Then he gave her a little kiss. "Let's us jist stay here all night." He gave her a bigger kiss.

Tish was thrilled. One thing Squire Sam had never done, even though he had given her a marble, was to give her a kiss. She thought about Squire Sam, and about last night and this morning. But she did not *want* to think about Squire Sam at a time like this.

Her thoughts were already torn between Archy, so close beside her and so increasingly intimate, and Man, who might be in peril and was at least in agony. Archy had such beautiful big eyes. And such an easy-going manner. For a minister's son, he seemed almost indifferent to the Lord's distress and wounding. Or maybe, being the minister's son, he knew things about the Lord that she did not know. He knew, perhaps, that the Lord was immortal and could not wester.

"If He caint walk, how can He get something to eat?" she asked.

"Who?"

"The Lord."

"Oh, *Him.* Is He all you can think about, at a time like this?"

"Like what?"

"Like here and now, like this: I got both my sniffwhips around you, babe." Archy kissed her again, full on the lips.

Tish had believed the old wives' tale that once a girl has been impregnated with a boy's marble, she can't send out pheromones any more. Thus she was surprised to discover that she was giving off a tiny bit of her special perfume, with which, in the closed confines of this corridor-in-the-wall, she could not avoid gently showering Archy.

"Ummm," he said, quivering his sniffwhips in recognition of her scent. "Wow, honeybunch, if you aint keerful I'm liable to start oozin some of my affy-dizzy."

There was one old wives' tale, however, which was sure-enough no mistake: once a girl has taken a

162

boy's marble, she can't take another one. Thus, when Archy's wings rose to reveal a back lathered with affy-dizzy, she was able to resist the temptation, despite her hunger.

"Come on, sweetheart, try a taste," he urged.

"Thank you, I've done already eaten tonight," she lied.

"Huh?" He looked at her strangely. "No gal is able to pass up affy-dizzy, irregardless of how much she's done et," he explained, as if she didn't know.

Inside the wall it was so snug and cozy and romantic. Outside the wall the sound of the thunder went on and on and on, and the steady beat of the rain. In all her life, Tish had never heard, seen, smelled, or felt a thunderstorm like this one, and she began to wonder if it was not merely a great raining but something more. The Lord had shot Himself. The world was changing. Perhaps the world was ending. Perhaps all those dreadful sounds out there were not merely thunderclaps but The Bomb.

Almost absent-mindedly she reached out and dabbed at the affy-dizzy and brought it to her mouth.

20.

Mandamn that preacher all to hell, Doc swore to himself, hobbling among the bodies of the injured and the westered. Then he involuntarily chuckled at the awful irony of his own oath: it had been the Mandamning which had done this. Unfortunately the Mandamning hadn't Mandamned the sonofabitchin preacher but had sure Mandamned the east out of several good folks: there lay the fragmented remains of Fent Chism, beyond all help from Doc. Here were several folks squashed past all recognition, although one of the bodies smelled like old Jonce Ledbetter, and at the edge of a fresh bullet hole Doc picked up a broken sniffwhip and took a good sniff of it and identified it as all that remained of Ila Frances Tichborne, the preacher's own wife. Where was the preacher? Didn't he even care? Maybe, Doc thought, that last shot had got the preacher himself. But no, it was clear that the last shot had gone right smack into Man's own git-along, between the tarsal and the metatarsal bones; the bullet had passed through the shoe, come out through the sole and left one more hole, a bloody one, in the floor. "Sorry, mister, I caint do a thing fer ye," Doc said irreverently to Man, who lay in obvious suffering on His couch. "But iffen I was you, I'd git up and put more than a Band-Aid on thet thang." Doc turned his attention away from bleeding Man to the bleeding roosterroaches, those who still had a spark of east left in them and could use his help. Horace Stapleton had had all his midgut squeezed to soup by the falling revolver-gun and was already west, but his wife Martha was still a bit to the east, her thorax caved in but her abdomen almost intact. Doc soothed her. "You'll be all right, Marthy. Jist lay easy, and don't try to move."

When the fourth explosion sounded, Doc did not twitch, recognizing it for what it was: thunder. Up in the sky. Outside. The greater gods, thought Doc, who believed in greater gods, are firing their pistols. His stargazers were too blind to detect the distant flash of light heralding the fifth explosion, but his main eyes caught it, verifying that it was indeed lightning, and when the boom came, he judged the stormclouds were approaching. *We shore need a good sprinkle*, he thought. Like any roosterroach he loved rain but hated lightning, not because of the noise but because of the light.

Between the booms of thunder, he heard another sound: a moaning, coming not from Man but from a roosterroach. Another survivor of Man's wrath or the preacher's provocation, or both, was somewhere out of sight. Doc tuned his sniffwhips and tried to locate the victim by scent. He was drawn to the proximity of Man's cheer-of-ease; the scents and sounds were coming from somewhere up among the cushions of the cheer, high above. "Who's up yonder?" Doc called, then repeated himself, but got no answer. Either the victim was hurt beyond the ability to reply . . . or else was deaf. More likely the latter, thought Doc. He needed a boost to get up the side of the cheer. He looked around for someone to boost him. Six of Martha Stapleton's sons, Dick, Vic, Rick, Mick, Nick, and Jick, were gathered around her, and a few other ambulatory survivors were wandering around in a daze, but most of the roosterroaches had de-camped back to their frock, smock, or car lot.

Doc would just have to scale the cheer as best he could, unassisted. He reached up with his one good gitalong on the left side, took a grip of the fabric of the cheer, and pulled himself up, then gripped with the two on the right side of his tripodal purchase, and slowly hauled himself gitalong over gitalong up the side of the cheer until he reached the edge of the seat cushion and could stop climbing. Winded, and his heart pounding, he prowled around the edges of the seat cushion until, in the crevice at the very back, he found the belly-up roosterroach he had suspected he would find. The boy was still east, breathing, and still intact, with no gitalong or sniffwhip missing, but he had been knocked into a daze, stunned senseless. There was no serious trauma or visible lesions but a flow of ichor from the mouth and around the pedicel of one sniffwhip. Doc took his pulse, which was weak and erratic. "It's a wonder," he said, "that the blow didn't stun yore tailprongs back into usefulness again." But the poor devil couldn't hear him. He raised his voice. "THAT WAS A BRAVE SMART THING YE DONE!" he shouted at one tailprong. "NOBODY ON EARTH BUT YOU WOULD'VE BEEN ABLE TO DO IT."

The boy focused his eyes and stared at Doc, and tried to smile, then tried to speak, but Doc shushed him. Moving him was out of the question; he would have to remain absolutely still for several hours, which would be critical. "MAYBE YOU'LL STAY EAST," Doc said, even if it was a white lie, "BUT YOU'VE GOT TO JIST LAY EASY, AND TRY NOT TO MOVE." The boy let his eyes fade out of focus, and Doc settled himself down into a crouch alongside, where he could monitor the heart-beat and respiration. He wiped away the ichor dribbling from the lips, and was pleased to see that it did not continue to flow. He forced the sniffwhips into the relaxed horizontal position alongside the body, and patted them gently to keep them from springing up again.

The rainfall could be heard now as well as smelled. The thunder went on and on, and the periodic flashes of lightning illuminated the interior of the loafing room, but the omnipresent sound was of the rain beating down. From his position, as the minutes passed, Doc could see Man but not the floor; he could not tell what was happening among the victims and survivors down below, but he could see that Man had rolled over onto His back, on the couch, and had perhaps passed into unconsciousness, from pain or loss of blood. "YOU'D BEST STAY AWAKE!" Doc shouted at Him, and his patient snapped into watchfulness again, and Doc apologized, "I DIDN'T MEAN YOU. I WAS A-HOLLERIN AT THE LORD. BUT COME TO THINK OF IT, *YOU* STAY AWAKE, TOO."

"Thanks, Doc," the patient mumbled.

"DON'T TALK," Doc yelled. "DON'T EVEN *THINK* ABOUT TRYIN TO TALK. You jist let me do the talkin. Man is all belly-up yonder on His couch, with the awfulest wound in his gitalong. You made Him shoot Hisself in the gitalong, did ye know that? Shut up, don't answer. You didn't do it a purpose, I reckon. When you clumb up onto His haid and made Him miss yore dad and yore sweetheart, you didn't know that if He missed He'd hit Hisself in His own gitalong, did ye? Hush. He orter known better Hisself, a-playin around with that pistol of His'n the way He allus does. He orter known He'd shoot Hisself if He didn't watch out. But maybe you done Him a favor. Yeah, maybe He would've done somethin worse bye and bye iffen ye hadn't taught 'im a lesson. All he's got is maybe a fractured metatarsal bone or two, and no doubt a splintered part of the second and third cuneiform tarsal bones as well, but he won't be walkin again for a right smart spell."

As if to give the lie to Doc's prognosis, Man suddenly heaved Himself into a sitting position, stood up on one gitalong, and hopped, then hobbled, then hopped, right back toward His cheer-of-ease! Doc feared that the Lord would plop His butt right smack down on top of both him and his patient, and he cringed, and debated with himself whether to try to stuff himself and his patient further down into the crevice between the cushions. But the Lord merely came to get His tumbler of bourbon off the table beside the cheer, lifted it to His mouth and drained it off in a couple of swallows, then turned and hopped, and hobbled, not back to the couch but toward the cookroom. He was leaving a trail of blood all over the carpets and linoleum. "YOU EEJIT!" Doc yelled, blasphemy be damned, "GIT OFF THEM GITA-LONGS! TIE A TURNICUT OVER THET THANG!"

As if the Lord had heard him, when He returned, He was bearing in one hand His unopened new bottle of bourbon and in the other hand a linen tablecloth. Flouncing down again onto the couch, He first opened the bottle and drank directly from it. Doc shouted,

"PORE A LEETLE ON THE WOUND, FOR A ANTY-SETTIC!" but he was ignored, or unheard. Man then proceeded to rip the tablecloth into shreds. With one strip of cloth He tied a clumsy, drunken tourniquet around His ankle and tightened it. Then He removed and tossed away His shoe, which bore a gaping bloody bullethole in the instep, another in the sole, and removed His sock, which was soaked with blood. Doc had a fleeting glimpse of the ugly wound before Man began to wrap His gitalong with strips of the tablecloth. Doc winced at the sight of both the wound and the dressing, unsterile rags of linen that would likely establish a colony of staphylococci all around and in the wound, to say nothing of tetanus.

The amateur bandaging finished, the Man took a few more lusty swallows from the bottle, smacked His lips, sighed, then lay back down on the couch and closed His eyes again. Lightning and thunder continued, but the sound of the rain was loudest. A toad-strangling downpour, Doc reflected. He hoped so. He lost no love on toads. He reached out and checked the breathing and pulse of his patient; the breathing was deeper, the pulse was steadier but fainter. The boy was still conscious. *Why do I keep callin him boy?* Doc asked himself. *He's a full-growed feller, stout as a tumble-turd.* "Yeah, maybe you done the Lord a favor," Doc repeated himself, although he was aware that he was not speaking loudly enough for the deafened tailprongs to hear him, "maybe you done us all a favor, if the Lord has learned His lesson not to fool around with that firearm no more." Doc chuckled.

"Maybe you put the preacher out of business with his Rapture thing and all. And maybe," Doc paused and reflected on the magnitude of the notion, "jist maybe there won't never be no Bomb." He was surprised at himself for having such a thought, which went counter to his usual pessimism on the subject, his unshakable faith in the cataclysm that would obliterate the world as we know it.

Unless . . . and this was another, different thought . . . unless this event now, tonight, *was* The Bomb. Perhaps The Bomb was just this one pistol shot into the gitalong of Man, that would start Him westering, if not wester Him off completely for good for once and for all, so that He would no longer be here to provide for His roosterroaches, who would have to seek their salvation elsewhere or starve to west.

"Theology is really complicated," Doc Swain said to his patient, remembering again but not caring that his patient was too deaf to hear him, and as the night hours passed he went on talking. The patient kept his eyes focused on Doc Swain's face almost as if reading his lips, and kept his useless tailprongs erect, and gave the semblance of listening. Doc Swain talked about the Stay More of old, that he had never known but only studied and still diurnally dreamed of, the Stay More populated with almost as many Men, and Women, and Children, as there were now rooster-roaches remaining with the one Man. This Man, our Man, was not even of any kinship to those ancient folk of Stay More; He was a furriner, from distant parts, an outlander, a newcomer, even if He had lived

170

in Holy House longer than all but the oldest rooster-roaches could remember. Doc Swain was one of these: he could remember, as a child, nearly two years before, watching Man move into the old Stay More Hotel, which had once been the home for human Ingledews before becoming a hotel, and had been abandoned for years before Man moved into it and installed the Fabulous Fridge and the pantry and breadbasket and grocery sack and other good things. Although the Man did not dress like the ancient Men of Stay More, or talk like Them, or practice Their customs, He was still Man, and the only Man we had. He might not be as Almighty as the Crustians thought He was, but He was the Lord.

"LORD, DON'T PASS OUT!" Doc Swain called, because it was evident that He intended to anesthetize His pain into oblivion with the bourbon. Doc was tempted to make his way over to Him, climb on Him, tickle Him, try to keep Him awake and conscious, or, failing that, persuade others to join in the effort. To do so, he would have to leave his patient, and as far as he was concerned, even apart from the sense of loyalty to his own kind, if Doc had to choose between Man and Sam, he would pick Sam, any old day.

It was day now. The rain was letting up, but only for a moment, as if pausing to catch its breath before trying harder.

21.

"Hit's pourin down pitchforks, cats and dogs!" Jack observed, flinching from the pelting rain. He didn't mind the wet, which couldn't penetrate his cutin, but the force of the heavy drops kept knocking him off his gitalongs, and the drops were cold.

Josie thought, which kept her from minding the long hike. "Do some folks think that cats and dogs fall with the rain?" she asked, and belched.

"Huh?" said Jack. "Naw, that's jist one a them ole sayins, pourin down cats and dogs. You ever see a dog fall from the sky?"

"I aint never seen a dog," Josie said, and tripped over a pebble of sandstone and fell down.

"You still drunk as a fiddler's bitch?" Jack asked her, helping her to her gitalongs. He wasn't exactly sober himself, but they would never get home if his old lady didn't stop falling down and asking dumb questions and burping like a grasshopper.

"What's a fiddler's bitch?" Josie asked.

"Aw, that's jist a breed of dog," he said. "Now shut up, Maw, and watch where you're going." He raised a limb of grass to clear her sniffwhips, then passed under himself. It was hard going. Ever since the previous night, except for the bright daylight hours which had forced them to seek darkness in an abandoned ants' burrow, they had been making their way slowly homeward from the Lord's Garden and Refuse Pile, where they had been lost for the entire length of time it took them to sober up enough to walk. Jack would never forget the terror of those impossibly long moments he was airborne, inside the beer can hurtling into the unknown, the dregs of beer swirling all around and over them and getting into their mouths and spiracles, and the weightlessness that went on and on, until, with a horrible jolt and crash, the can landed amidst a pile of other cans, not just empty beer cans but cans of emptied pork and beans, cans of emptied pineapple, cans of emptied ravioli, cans of emptied 30 W motor oil. *If I hadn't of been a Ingledew*, Jack told himself, *I would of been westered shore as shootin.* They had spent hours recovering from the crash, sustained by nothing more than whatever beer remained in the can, quite a lot of it, and then they had found their way out through the opening of the lid of the can, which fortunately lay on its side, and had found themselves among all those other cans, the exploration of which, and the escape from which, had consumed all of the rest of their night.

The Lord's Refuse Pile was a fabulous place, and Jack was determined to return with his whole family there on an outing and picnic, some night when the weather was fair. Tonight the weather was awful unfair, and the flashes of lightning had panicked Josie and driven Jack not into complete sobriety but into a partial cure of his hangover. There was so much illumination from the sky's electrical display that Jack feared he would be easy prey for any nocturnal creature, until he realized two things: the nocturnal creatures of prey were just as unsettled by the lightning as he was, and they were all getting wet and seeking shelter. *If I had the sense Man gave to a flea*, Jack told himself, *I'd seek shelter too*, but he knew that if this rain kept going the way it was going, so much of it would fall that the ground would be cut by new rivulets and rills and runlets, and they would never reach home. Already it was a struggle to keep to relatively high ground. Of course Jack was a fair swimmer, and so was Josie, but swimming made slow and tedious progress.

The paths that Man had trod from Carlott to His Refuse Pile, or vice versa, were few and infrequent, and thus the forest of grass and weeds impeded their long journey. The distance could not have been half a furlong, but it seemed like miles, and it was nearly morning when Jack and Josie straggled around a corner of Holy House and espied their native Carlott once again, with a mixture of exultation and weariness.

The last mile of any journey is the hardest, and it seemed they would never reach home before daylight. The cats and dogs stopped falling once they crossed the threshold of their familiar log. All of their children were already self-tucked into their sleeping crannies . . . all except one, the boy Jubal, crouched in the center of the main hall amid a pile of tiny smidgens of foodstuffs, with some of which he was attempting to stuff himself. As the two adult roosterroaches staggered, wet and weary, into the room, Jubal's mouth dropped open and he sprang into full alert. But his sniffwhips recognized the two as his parents.

"*Maw?!*" said Jubal. "*Paw?!*" He rushed to them and passed his sniffwhips all over them and felt them with his touchers. "Air ye still *east?!*"

"Howdy, hon," said Josie. "How's ever little thang?"

"But, but," said Jubal. "But, but, but but but."

"Whar's Tish?" asked Jack.

"But, but," said Jubal, "but *everbody* said you'uns had done went and westered off!" He indicated the pile of foodstuff fragments. "Folkses has done already started bringin the funeral feeds."

"My, my," said Josie, and reached out to sample a crumb of Hostess chocolate cupcake, her very first taste of chocolate, of which so much had been said and rumored and gossiped. Then she tried a pinch of peach fried pie, a snippet of oatmeal cookie, a tittle of zwieback, and a fleck of cough drop. "I never in all my born days dreamt that we'uns was so *popular*!" she observed. She asked Jubal, "Did ye remember who-all brung which-all? Did Sally Dinsmore bring us ary a thang?"

Jubal hung his head. "Yes'm, she brung some whitish lookin stuff, but I done et it."

"Marshmaller!" cried Josie. "How dast ye?" She drew back a sniffwhip as if to slap the youngun.

Jack stopped her. "Whar is yore big sister Tish at?" he asked the boy.

"She did lak ye said, Momma, Tish did. She up and took herself to Partheeny, for to claim kin to the Ingledews."

"Naw!" said Jack and Josie together, and looked at one another and then looked back at Jubal. "Did she *really*, now?" Josie asked. "Why, bless her heart! Here we aint been west two nights and already she's done went and done it!"

"We aint west, Maw," Jack pointed out. To Jubal he said, "When did ye see her last? How do ye know she went to Partheeny? What-all else do ye know?"

Jubal told them everything he knew, or had heard. He had not left the Dingletoon bungalow, because Tish had made him promise to watch out for his brothers and sisters during her absence. When she had passed beyond reach of his sniffwhips, night before last, she was heading toward Hinglerocks, but she did that all the time anyway and she hadn't come home, so Jubal figured that if she hadn't been et by something, she had gone on to Parthenon.

"My, my," Josie said to Jack. "Do you suppose our Letitia is a-dwellin at Partheeny now?"

"If she wasn't et by some critter along the way," Jack said.

"Why, if she has done went and moved into Partheeny, she's probably expectin us to come and visit and stay the night or even forever!" Josie said.

"She thinks you'uns is both west," Jubal declared.

"Let's go susprise her!" Josie urged Jack.

"Not today, Maw," Jack said, stretching and yawning. "We aint goin nowhere in the daylight. I aim to git me some sleep." He took a particle of some creamy looking stuff from the pile of funeral feed, and said, "Jubal, you turn in, now, and leave these here eats alone."

Jack and Josie turned in, too, and slept all day, deeply and soundly, recuperating from their long journey and their ordeal, and woke at the dip of dusk almost completely sober, to greet their assembled offspring, share with them in the consumption of a fraction of the funeral feeds, caution them not to breathe a word to any other visitors bearing funeral feeds that their parents were not solemnly west, and then announce that they intended to sneak off to Parthenon to check up on Letitia and see if she might have prepared the way for *all* of them to move into Parthenon.

The children, between mouthfuls of funeral feeds, cheered and hugged one another and thanked their lucky stars, and wished their parents the very best of luck.

Jubal was still trying to get them to hush up when Jack and Josie disappeared into the still-falling rain on their journey toward Parthenon. Jubal had just lost scent of his parents on his sniffwhips when he picked up a different scent: that of his sister, Tish, returning home from another direction.

22.

She had not allowed him to accompany her *all* of the way home. She didn't want her brothers and sisters to see him, and get wrong ideas about what she had been doing, out all day. She felt wracked with guilt, on several counts, the least of which was she had no business staying away from home so long. But she hadn't done anything wrong . . . not with Archy, anyway. It was funny. They had spent the entire rest of the night together, and even slept together all day, almost side by side, but he hadn't actually given her a marble. Not that he hadn't tried to, and not that she wouldn't have let him at least try, but the process of making connection, as she had already discovered with Squire Sam, was such a complicated procedure of fastening the right latches and hooking the right clamps and putting this thing alongside of that thing, and then the other thing inside of the round thing, that in the process of all the maneuvering and straining Archy had lost his marble. Well, it hadn't been completely lost, it was still there, rolling around on the floor, and eventually they even made a kind of game, playing with it, rolling it around and bouncing it.

Archy had tried to make the whole business seem all right by declaring that he was glad he hadn't been able to take her virginity, that he hoped she would remain a virgin until they got married. He hadn't come right out and proposed to her. He hadn't asked her, "Let's me and you git hitched," or anything like that. He had simply said he wanted her to remain a virgin until they could do it properly with the approval of the church. Of course she hadn't told him that she already had a marble inside her, Squire Sam's marble. She hadn't even mentioned Squire Sam.

As a substitute for the hours they would have spent properly hooked up, joining together, fused, Archy had told her practically the entire story of his life, past, present *and* future: his dreams of adventure, his plans for exploring the world, his desire to travel in search of fabled houses far away, even outside of Stay More. He had talked a blue streak, never showing any concern over the incident of Man's shooting Himself, nor ever once expressing grief over the westering of his mother. Hadn't he noticed? Tish wondered, without asking him, if he had seen, heard, or smelled the erasure of Ila Frances Tichborne by the second bullet of the Lord. Maybe he was happy for her Rapture, or maybe he didn't care; there were countless roosterroaches, particularly males, who felt no attachment to their mothers.

Squire Sam's mother had died when he was in his fourth instar, but Sam had not talked much about her to Tish: one of the very few things Sam and Archy had in common was a reluctance to mention their mothers. Tish had wished they would, so she could talk about hers, so recently westered. She really needed to tell someone how much she had loved her mother, and how much she missed her already. Her father too, of course, but Jack Dingletoon hadn't been much of a family man; he had been a happy-go-lucky drunkard, and Tish had never felt really close to him, not the way she had toward her mother, even if her mother was rather giddy and even silly at times.

There had been moments when Tish had almost blurted to Archy, "Don't you even *care* about your mom?" but she had kept her mouth shut and let him do all the talking. He had spoken a great deal about his father, Brother Chidiock Tichborne, who was his ideal of Manliness and malehood, although Archy had turned a deaf tailprong to his father's attempts to get Archy to follow him in the "preacherin business." Two of Archy's brothers were preparing for the ministry, but Archy had decided against it. Of course, there was always the possibility, if he found himself

179

in some foreign land where the folks needed a preacher but didn't have one, that Archy might change his mind. Tish didn't want to be a preacher's wife, now did she? No, she didn't.

The confines of the corridor in which they laid low throughout the hours of conversation had been snug and cozy for a while but had eventually become stifling and dank. There were strong odors of mouse scat, snail-slime, fly-spittle, termite-trail, and ant-spoor; generations of critters had used this corridor for a passageway, and the offensive smells destroyed Tish's pheromone and were magnified by an increasing humidity because of the rain: yes, the world outside Holy House was being deluged, as the weather station of her sniffwhip told her: a real frog-choker. She loved rain and hated frogs.

She wished Archy would take her out to the porch, such a glamorous architectural wonder, where she had never been, so that the two of them could watch the rain, but she did not suggest it to him. She wondered if he might take her to his home, in the frock, in some distant room of Holy House, and introduce her to his brothers and sisters. Maybe he had sisters who needed comforting because of the loss of their mother. Maybe if Tish comforted them for their loss, they would comfort her for hers. At this thought she had begun to weep, quietly, and finally Archy had stopped talking long enough to ask her why she was crying; had his narration of his childhood and his outlining of his dreams for the bright future made her cry? She could not explain that she was thinking there was no one to comfort her that her mother was west, no one to comfort her that she had foolishly thrown away her virginity, no one to aid her in this time of loss and stress and confusion, no one but Archy, who could only talk on and on about the great world away out yonder that he planned to conquer.

She had fallen asleep. Day was coming anyway, or, if not day, because the stormclouds would never let the sun appear, the time of sleep, almost automatic for roosterroaches, but not quite for Archy, who went on talking for some time before he noticed that she slept, and then he went to sleep himself.

Upon awakening at eventide she had told him that she *must* return to Carlott, to the family log, to see about her brothers and sisters. He had insisted upon going with her, because the rain was still pouring down. They found that three rivers ran around and through Carlott, where none had been before, and no doubt Tish would never have been able to ford these rivers without the help of Archy, who assisted her in swimming across or, in the case of the worse torrent, devised a raft of weedstems and floated the two of them over. The water was nearly up to the level of the Platform, and most of the automotive thingumajigs and doomahitchies littering the ground were submerged. Water was up to the hubcaps of the Lord's nonjunk vehicle, His Ford Torino. Some of the dwellings of Carlott were underwater or washed away, and the refugees, Tish's neighbors, were milling in confusion and fright on patches of higher ground above the village. In the distance she could see her home: the log was not submerged, but waves lapped at its door.

181

"You'd best turn back, and get on home before this rain gets any worse," she told Archy.

"But I'd be proud to meet yore mother," Archy insisted.

"My momma has westered, same as yours," Tish declared.

"Mine?" he said. "What gives ye the idee my momma has westered?"

"You didn't *see*?" Tish asked, and realized, too late, that indeed he had not watched the shooting of Ila Frances Tichborne and, all this time, had no idea his mother was west. Should she tell him? Yes, she had better: "Last night, didn't ye notice, the second bullet of the Lord hit your momma and Raptured her."

"No!" Archy exclaimed. "Don't tell me *that*! When did you hear this?"

"I didn't hear it," she said. "I mean, I didn't *only* hear it. I saw it too."

"Are ye certain it was her?" he asked her. "How do ye know?"

"Everybody knows the preacher's wife," she declared.

Archy continued to appear incredulous, then became credulous, then grew angry. "Why didn't ye *tell* me?" he asked.

"I thought ye knew," she said.

"You mean all this time I been so sweet to ye, all this time I was a-lovin ye and talkin so nice to ye and all, all this time ye *knew* I was motherless?"

Tish could only nod. Then she added, softly, "I'm motherless too."

Archy snorted a hollow laugh. "I was fixin to ast ye to come and meet my momma tomorrow night and have breakfast with us," he declared. "But it don't look like I can, do it?" When she did not respond to this rhetorical question, he said, "Well, I'll see you around, somewhere, sooner or later," and he swung his six gitalongs around to decamp.

"Archy!" she called after him, but he did not turn.

Sadly, she entered her home, finding it waterlogged but all her brothers and sisters not only safe but manic with joy, jumping up and down, hugging one another, and babbling about "Partheeny." The highest up-and-down jumper was Jubal, who exclaimed, "Wal, looky who's here!"

"Hidy, Jubal, how's stuff?" she said.

"I'll tell ye how stuff is!" he exclaimed. "Paw aint west! Neither is Maw! Both of 'em is jist as eastern as me and you!"

"*What!?*" said Tish, and began searching with her sniffwhips. "Where are they?"

"They done went to Partheeny to look for you."

"Me? But I'm *here*."

"But aint ye been to PARTHEENY? Didn't ye claim kin to the Ingledews?"

"Well, sort of," she admitted.

"Aint we'uns all gonna move into Partheeny?" he asked, and the question was picked up and chorused by the assembled brothers and sisters, who kept chanting, "Aint we'uns all?" and "We'uns gonna?" and "Move into?" and "Partheeny?"

"Let me sit down and try to explain," Tish protested, and crouched to the loggy floor and sighed, "I'm wore to a frazzel," and asked, "Could ye scare me up a bite of fungus?"

"Fungus, heck!" Jubal said. "Lookee here at what-all we got to eat!" and shooed aside the mob of siblings to reveal the pile of funeral feeds. Tish recognized them for what they were; it is the dream and dread of every young roosterroach to experience the mixture of grief and delight that comes from a funeral feed.

"This is called 'peanut brickle,' " she knowledgeably explained to Jubal, as she helped herself to a bite.

Not to be out-knowledged, he said, "This is called marshmaller," and showed her a bit he had been hoarding.

The assorted Dingletoon offspring surrounded the funeral feed and dined, while Tish, between bites, attempted to tell them the story of her visit to Parthenon, omitting, of course, her indiscretion with Squire Sam. When she had finished, all the children rattled and blathered, "When air we'uns gonna move into Partheeny?" and "When air?" and "Move into?" and "Partheeny?" and "We'uns gonna?" Tish attempted to explain that Parthenon was the exclusive domain of the Squires Ingledew, and even if the Dingletoons were Ingledews, they couldn't just go rushing all of a heap into that marvelous house.

When she had finished the story of Parthenon, her brothers and sisters urged, "Tell us another'n, Sis!" so she told the story of the latest shootings at the church-meetin at Holy House, one shot of which

184

had wounded the Lord Himself. They could not believe that part. Man is bulletproof, they said; Man is punctureproof, He is holeproof. Not so, Tish insisted; she had seen the Holy Blood. She described it. It was *red*. It was thicker than ichor.

She told of the couch on which the Lord lay, and she detailed the character of the corridors inside the walls and the awful smells of the trails and spoors of critters who crawled and crept in the spaces. She made Holy House sound like both a marvelous place and a terrible place, and the children listened with their glossae agape and their tailprongs twitching.

They would have eaten all the funeral feeds if she had not made them draw a line, a literal line which they were not allowed to cross. She explained that the intended honorees of the funeral, their mother and father, ought to have a share of the feeds unto themselves, and that whatever was left over should be saved and used to present as funeral feeds to the survivors of those who had been westered the night before at Holy House, including Nancy Whitter, Luke's widow and outcast, and the children, including Archy, of Ila Frances Tichborne. She would give Archy the last hunklet of peanut brickle herself.

Near onto dawn Tish talked and entertained her siblings, and then she sent them all to bed. She needed to think. She needed to remember what had been happening to her, and to conjecture what was now going to come of it. The Fate-Thing had plans for her, but she had to make her own as well. The Fate-Thing can make your plans, but you have to carry them out . . . unless you try to carry out plans the

Fate-Thing doesn't have for you: then the Fate-Thing will stop you.

There was that marble of Squire Sam's caught and held within her ovary. How exactly had it come to rest there? Dreamily Tish dwelt upon the mood of the long hours of conjunction, the pleasurable shuttling back and forth between the resistance to the bondage and the giving in to it, with the accompanying necessary tension building to a peak. She reflected upon the shape and form of all the instruments of the bondage, Sam's natural anatomical manacles, cuffs, collars, buckles, trusses, which had gripped and clamped Tish's natural anatomical latches, hasps, hitches, and hooks, holding her fast and tight.

Why that need for bondage? Did the female have to be restrained or did she *want* to be? At no time during the process had Tish felt an actual urge to disjoin and decamp, so why had Man created her body, and Sam's, with all those fasteners? Why was it so pleasurable to be seized, grasped, clutched, held?

Holding is all. All: to hold is to wish to be held. To be held is to hold. To embrace is to enchant. Making love was like making stories, storyteller Tish realized. The story that enchants also embraces. The storyteller wishes to be embraced, as the lover wishes to be loved. The genital clasper grabs hold as the story grabs hold. The story expects resistance, and the resister disbelieves in order to be won over. The holding back, the resisting, the subjection and seduction. . . .

Tish realized that her easteregg was growing within her, starting from nothing as a story starts from nothing, and needing to be fertilized by a touch from the other: Sam's marble released the first of the many copies of himself that it contained, baby Ingledews having a family reunion with their longlost kindred Dingletoon cousins. Even if she could never dwell in Parthenon, now Parthenon dwelt in her.

And began to protrude.

Her thoughts were interrupted by a strange sensation in her body, a rocking motion, an unsettled feeling in her six sensitive knee joints which told her that the substratum was in upheaval. *Is this what pregnancy feels like?* she wondered. Did the protrusion of the easteregg cause the floor to tilt?

"Tish!" cried Jubal, rushing into her room and into her reverie. "Our house is floating away!"

23.

"Godhead above my Man, are you there still?" Chid whispered, and listened, but heard nothing, save the endless droning drumbeat of the rain upon the shingles of the roof. This sound was so loud because he was right next to it, up there alongside the rafters, in the place that he thought of as his private refuge, secret and safe. If he had known of Tish's fondness for Hinglerocks, he would have understood it, for this abandoned dirt dobber's nest served the same function for him: a quiet and magical place to meditate and try to come to terms with the great mysteries of life. For Chid, a central mystery of life was whether or not there might be some force greater than Man, some Absolute Mover and Shaker more Infinite and Omnipotent than Man, some Everlasting Eternal Being who did not drink bourbon or coffee, smoke cigarettes, pass out, fire pistols, write love letters, and urinate. This Supreme Soul Chid envisioned as dwelling somewhere far overhead, somewhere that not even Man could reach. Thus the abandoned dirt dobber's nest up under the roof of Holy House was closer to the Entity whom Chid was inclined to call, for want of a better name, by the name that Chid had heard Man Himself use, when, most lately, He lay on His couch of suffering, pain, and blood, and cried, "Oh, *God*."

Chid had for several long moments refused to accept the possibility that Man could have shot Himself, that He was not only mortal but woundable, bleedable. And once this possibility had established itself in Chid's consciousness, blotting out even the awful event of the atomization of his wife Ila Frances, he had fled, upstairs, upattic, up and up to this haven, this hermitage of rest and contemplation.

The dirt dobber, also called mud-dauber (*Sceliphron coementarium*), is a wasp who makes not the paper nest of the poliste or the hornet but a grouping of cells of clay, or, in places such as Stay More, where there is little natural clay, just dirt and dust from the earth moistened into mud and overlapped into tan tubules. Therein, the female lays her eggs, along with the bodies of spiders caught and paralyzed for the larvae's nourishment. Dirt dobbers had rid Holy House of spiders, and, although they were not above

188

dining upon a roosterroach when they could, they were strictly diurnal and only killed the occasional roosterroach found wandering after dawn. Once a nest has served its function for one generation of wasps, it is never used again, and the rafters of Holy House were encrusted with abandoned nests. Chidiock Tichborne could easily crawl into one and feel snug and safe and meditative.

If the truth be told, his lamentation over his wife Ila Frances was not as great as his grief for poor Josie Dingletoon, who had been, albeit briefly, the true love of his life, at least in terms of compatible sexuality. Ila Frances, after all, had been his own sister, although no one knew this except the two of them.

Sometimes Chid questioned whether Man really cared that Chid had been incestuous. Even Joshua Crust, as far as Chid could recall, had never spoken out against incest. Why, then, did Chid decry it? Because the roosterroach populations of Stay More would decline into no better than termites if they continued breeding incestuously.

No, Man did not care, but there was a godhead greater than Man, some Cosmic Immutable Force Who had planned the whole world more ably than Man could do, and Who had determined that incest was bad for you. This Force was not susceptible to pistol bullets, or even to The Bomb. This Force wanted the roosterroaches of Holy House to move into Parthenon, if need be, after puny Man had westered, or, even if He didn't wester but took up with the Woman, or, even if the Woman moved into Holy House instead of having Him move into Parthenon

. . . whatever, the Force clearly wanted Chid and his followers in Parthenon.

But Brother Tichborne ought to have his contingencies ready; he ought to know his options and be prepared for the time when he would have to counsel his congregation to cease worshipping Man and begin worshipping Woman instead.

As for himself, what was to keep him from worshipping the Force, calling it God, and reserving to It alone the honorific of "Lord"? He didn't have to tell anyone else about God. Indeed, it would be better if he kept God as his own private, personal deity, just as Tish Dingletoon had made a personal deity out of the Fate-Thing. The image of God, in Chid's imagination, was not that of Man at all, but rather an amorphous arthropod with six mighty gitalongs, an infinitely vast head, thorax, and abdomen, and all-knowing sniffwhips.

Would it be hypocrisy for Chid to pay lip service to Man and secretly petition God? All through the night and into the next day, Chid lay in the snug confines of the dirt dobber's nest and ruminated about this matter. The following night, he left his hermitage: he had to comfort the survivors, arrange for further funeralizations, and confer sainthood upon those westered by bullets. He also had to find a bite to eat.

This latter gave him the most difficulty. Visiting the cookroom, he found that it had been stripped, although several fellows were scrambling about trying to scare up some victuals.

"Morsel, boys," Chid greeted them. "Slim pickins tonight?"

"Morsel, yoreself, Reverend," Tolbert Duckworth said. "Aint no pickins of no kind. There aint a gaum of grub to be found nowheres. If rain was syrup, we'd all be gorged, but there aint enough sup to make a housefly floop his snoot."

"Hasn't the Lord supped at all?" Chid asked.

"The Lord aint riz, a bit," Tolbert answered. "He jist lays thar, west to the world."

"I'd better have a look," Chid declared, and hied himself toward the loafing room, where the reading lamp, still burning from the night before, cast its beam vacantly out upon the scene of last night's carnage. The floor was now empty except for the three new bullet holes. Chid peered down into one of them, and stuck one of his sniffwhips down into it, and could detect only the faintest trace of whatever molecules Ila Frances had become. He made the sign of the pin over the hole, and then raised a sniffwhip just in time to detect a roosterroach climbing the side of the cheer-of-ease. The roosterroach had a suspicion of food between his touchers! Chid recognized him as Doc Swain, clawing his way slowly up the fabric on three gitalongs. Chid wanted to call out, "Hey, Doc, where'd you get them eats?" but he held his tongue and decided instead to follow stealthily and see where Doc was taking the provender.

Chid climbed up to one arm of the cheer-of-ease and gazed down upon the cushion, where Doc was urging the food, an ancient sop of bland white bread, upon an injured, recumbent roosterroach whom Chid identified as Squire Sam Ingledew. Squire Sam could scarcely move at all, but managed to raise his head and nibble at the sop and swallow.

Chid realized that injured Squire Sam must have

191

been the culprit who had climbed the Lord's person, causing the Lord to shoot himself in his own gitalong. Of course! Squire Sam must have done it of a purpose, not accidental-like: his father had been in the line of fire, perhaps the Lord's intended target. *Hmm*, said Chid to himself, *I should of knowed; nobody but an Ingledew would've been both fool enough and strong enough to try a stunt like that. Hmm*, hummed Chid, trying to determine from a distance the extent of Squire Sam's injuries. *Looks like he's pretty well banged up. Hmm. Don't look like he could get up and go back to Parthenon and help his father keep anyone who wanted to from barging in and taking over the place. Hmm. I could round up the deacons and elders of the church and we could just walk into Parthenon and run old Squire Hank off. HHHMMM.*

Chid hummed so loudly that he drew the attention of Doc Swain, who turned and caught a glimpse of him before Chid was able to drop out of sight down the side of the cheer. Well, that was no skin off Chid's sniffwhip; Doc couldn't do anything; Doc wasn't in much better shape than his patient.

Chid did not even stop to examine the Lord, or give Him more than a glance, just enough to see that He was unconscious upon His couch, sprawled akimbo and supine and agape, an empty bourbon bottle's neck clasped in the fingers of the hand that had dropped to the floor. For the first time in his life, Chid felt a sort of contempt for the Lord, the drunken fool.

"Wal, Brother Duckworth," Chid said, back in the cookroom, "I do believe you're right. The Lord is west to the world, and no tellin but what He might actually and completely wester off."

192

"Aw, naw!" exclaimed Tolbert Duckworth. "Aint no chance He could do that. The *Lord* completely wester?!? Why, the whole world would wester afore the Lord Hisself would! Naw, Reverend, He's jist sleepin another one off, as usual."

The other fellers in the cookroom, mostly all good Crustians, nodded in agreement but with hesitant conviction, as if waiting to see if the preacher would persuade them otherwise.

"Brethering," Chid said solemnly, "our Lord is all-powerful, He is mighty, He is our rock and our shield, the Lord is our fortress and our strength, yea, Man abideth though the mountains shake and the waters roar—" The preacher's words were underscored by a renewed pouring down of rain outside the house. "Our Man is our refuge and our ark, He is our deliverer and our provider and restorer, praise His Holy Name!"

"Praise HIM!" shouted the brethren, and "Amen!" and "Lord be praised!" and "Blessed be the Name of the Lord!"

"But—" Chid interrupted their hosannas, "though He provideth for us everlastingly, yet might not the case be that with His right gitalong shot nearly plumb off they's *no* way He could git up and feed Hisself, let alone that He could feed the rest of us?" Chid let his question mark hover and flutter and cast uncertainty upon their faces. In one fell swoop Chid was making immortal Man into a mortal, and there was no turning back. "The Man is a worse drunkard than ary a feller amongst us!" Chid pointed out truthfully. "Why, jist in the past twenty-four hours, since

He shot Hisself in the gitalong, He's done already drunk enough hard bourbon whiskey to wester every roosterroach in Stay More! No tellin *when* He'll wake up! No tellin *if* He'll wake up! Could be He won't *never* wake up! Then what'll we do? Huh? Then where will we be? Huh? I ast you, brethering, what'll we be without that *Man*?!?"

The roosterroaches silently stared at him and then at one another, with expressions of anxiety and fear, and perhaps with no little wonder or dismay at Chid's apostasy. One of the younger ones, Jim Bob Murrison, offered timidly, "But we're all gonna go live on His right hand when we wester. . . ."

"What good's His right hand gonna do us if it's westered?" Chid asked. No one answered this rhetorical question, and he continued, "Fellers, I say we had better start thinkin about movin into Parthenon!"

The murmur went through the crowd: *"Partheeny!"*

"There's scads of room and food galore!" one of them shouted.

"Right!" said Chid. "So what are we waitin for?"

"We're waiting for the rain to stop, Reverend," said Tolbert Duckworth. "Aint no way we could make it to Partheeny in this rain."

Chid sighed. "That's a fact, Tol. But I'd 'preciate it iffen ye would git all the other elders and deacons together, to have a special meetin with me right soon, tonight."

The gathering of foodseeking roosterroaches disbanded, to return to their homes in the other rooms of Holy House, in the Frock or the Smock. Their wives and children were greatly disappointed that they returned empty-touchered, without any food. The fellows told their wives of Brother Tichborne's shocking reversal, but the wives, when they heard of his plan to move into Parthenon, realized that it was not so much backsliding as a new understanding of the Gospel made necessary by the prospect this time of great famine. For his part, Chid hoped he could soon deliver a rousing sermon to one and all, setting forth the Lord's shortcomings and inadequacies and worthlessness, and explaining the need for worshipping Woman instead. Yes: Chid looked forward to working up a real sniffwhiplashing peroration on the subject.

24.

"Doc, you know I can't hear, so just answer some yes-or-no questions for me, all right? Just nod or shake your head. First question: am I going to stay east?" A nod, belated and hesitant. "How long do I have to keep lying here? No, that's not a yes-or-no question. Do I have to stay here all of tonight?" A nod. "All of tomorrow night too?" Another nod. "All of the night after that too?" A shrug, a shake of the head, a nod of the head, and another shrug. "Well, have I got any permanent injuries or impairments?" A nod. "What? Where?" A touch of the sniffwhip to each tailprong. "Oh. My prongs. They were already impaired. Nothing else?" A shake. "Doc, did I cause the Man to miss His aim? Did he hit my dad?" A shake. "Did He hit Tish?" A shake. "Why isn't He sitting down in this cheer any more? Why am I staying here, when He might come and sit down on me and squash me? That's not a yes-or-no, is it?" A shake. "Has He left Holy House?" A shake. "Is He out in the cook-room?" A shake. "Is He in His ponder room?" A shake.

"SAM . . ." Doc shouted at his tailprong, then pantomimed what he wanted Sam to do: wiggle his fore gitalongs. Okay. Wiggle his middle gitalongs. Okay. Wiggle his hind gitalongs. Okay. All six of his gitalongs could wiggle. "NOW SCROOCH OVER THISAWAY, REAL EASY AND SLOW," Doc ordered him, and led Sam very slowly and carefully to the edge of the cushion, a distance of several inches, inches of agony and pain. Then Doc pointed. From this vantage, Sam could see out across the room, he could see the Man's couch, with the Man supine upon it, akimbo and agape.

"Is He just west drunk?" Sam asked. Doc shook his head. "He's not *west*, is He?" Sam asked. Doc shook his head, then brought two sniffwhips close together, to signify "a little" or "near" or "almost." Doc pointed to his own gitalong, then pointed at the Man. Sam looked. The Man's gitalong, divested of His shoe, was swaddled in strips of cloth, soaked with blood. Sam understood. "The last bullet . . ." he said. "The last bullet didn't hit Dad or Tish but hit Him in His own gitalong?" Doc nodded, he nodded and nodded. And smiled a bit. Sam couldn't help grinning a bit himself. "I see," said Sam.

In a flash the scene of the night before returned to him, the impulsiveness of his own deed, the precariousness, the harrowing moment: the quick dashing climb straight up the Man's back, across His collar, up through His hair to the summit of His head, then clutching onto His forelock until just the right moment, when he dropped down, at just the right angle, to seize the eyelash and then the eyelid, hoping that the right eye was the *right* eye, the sighting eye, not the left, as is sometimes the case with binocular shootists, and then the awful stunning pain of the back of the Man's hand slamming against Sam, knocking him off, and through the air, and into the cheer, where he had lain ever since. The Man had been his adversary, and still was, and Sam shouldn't feel any pity for him, but still there it was: this wave of fellow-feeling.

"Isn't it dangerous for Him to be in a coma from booze when he's so badly hurt?" Sam asked Doc, and Doc nodded vigorously. "Can you do *any*thing for Him?" Doc shook his head, sadly. "Couldn't you go and tell others what the situation is, and maybe get some help to try and wake Him?" Doc slowly nodded his head. "Where's my dad?" Sam asked. "Find my dad, and get him to help, too." Doc nodded, and then lay his sniffwhips down heavily upon Sam's, indicating he should rest and be still. Then Doc left.

Only after Doc had gone did Sam begin to think of an endless string of additional questions that he wanted to ask. Did anyone else know that Sam was convalescing up here? Where was Tish? What had become of her after the incident? She had been with Archy Tichborne; had she fled with him? What had

become of Tichborne's father, Chid, who had instigated the disaster? Perhaps "instigated" was the
wrong word; yet Sam, being able only to watch but
not hear the minister's ranting exhortation of the mob,
had had the impression that Chid had *willed* the
shooting.

Sam began to feel sorry for himself, not so much
because he was weak and unable to get out and discover what was going on in the world, but because
he was deaf and had no business trying to discover,
let alone control things. He should remain an ob-
server, not be a participant. But if he had not acted
when he did, either his father or Tish might be west
at this very moment. How had he known that the
third bullet was directed at one of them? How had he
known the instant when he needed to spoil the Man's
aim? Maybe, he told himself, there *was* a Fate-Thing,
and he had been acting as the Fate-Thing's agent.

If so, it was not his father but Tish whom the
Fate-Thing was protecting. The Fate-Thing had great
plans for her. If nothing else, she was destined to
become the mother of the next generation of Ingledews, perhaps a generation of Ingledews who would
lead Stay More through the post-Bomb period and
pave the way for a new Golden Age. Perhaps his job,
his whole reason for existence, had been simply to
plant that marble in her. Perhaps all the countless
meals he had found and eaten had been simply sustenance to keep him alive for that responsibility of
propagation.

His purpose in life, he realized, was now to protect Tish from the bullets of Man or from whatever

other dangers awaited her. He was the Fate-Thing's lieutenant and aide-de-camp. But where was Tish? Why had she taken leave of him and of his Clock without any further word (or sign) to him? Perhaps their sexual linking, wonderful though it had been, had been too soon, too sudden. Their hours of "talk" in sign-language had made them as familiar with each other as they would ever be with anyone, but still, wasn't it wrong to fuck on the first date?

During the interminable hours that Sam was required to lay immobile, convalescing, helpless, his mind dwelt upon all these things, over and over again. It replayed for him those hours of that one act of lovemaking, when their bodies were joined end-to-end together, and the alternatively slow and fast rubbings of all the points of contact, each in a different tempo, counterpoint and syncopation, building slowly to an almost unbearable pitch. . . . Thinking thus, Sam began to realize something important about Larry and Sharon. Larry had known Sharon in some distant place, had experienced one or more sexual couplings with Her, and, when She returned to Stay More, to the world of Her youth, He had followed Her, because He loved Her and wanted to experience again the act of Their lovemaking, or even, if denied the chance to do that, to watch out for Her, to protect Her. Larry, Sam realized, was the lieutenant and aide-de-camp of Sharon's Fate-Thing.

But now, because He was injured, She should help Him. *Who am I talking about?* Sam asked himself. He was talking about all four of Them: Larry and Sam and Sharon and Tish together. He knew that Sharon

199

had to help Larry. And he knew he could certainly use some help from Tish, if nothing else, to help him understand what was happening in the world, to be his surrogate tailprongs, to "translate" into sign language for him what others were saying. But where was Tish? And where was Sharon, who had been so strangely absent from Her room when he had last been there?

Sam kept his sniffwhips tuned to the room he was in. The comings and goings of roosterroaches down below registered dully on his olfaction. He lost track of time. He slept, even during the night, which he had never done before. He slept, of course, all the daylight hours. He had a dream, which he did not know was a daydream or a nightdream, of Tish as captain of a ship. Waking, he tried to interpret it: he had seen her clearly, on the quarterdeck of a brigantine or something, giving orders to the boatswain. The vessel was being tossed on the waves, and was in peril of being dashed against rocks. Maybe the vessel was called Fate-Thing, though Sam could not read that name clearly across the bow in the dream. The ship was swarming with deckhands trying to heed the boatswain's orders, relayed from Captain Tish. Was that boatswain Archy Tichborne? No, he was younger. Sam went back to sleep and tried to follow the rest of the dream, but it drifted downstream away from him.

He woke to a scene that seemed even more a dream, another swarm of deckhands, but they were not scurrying over the rigging of a ship but over the rigging of a body, Man's. The captain was not Tish but Squire Hank, and the boatswain was Doc Swain. The deckhands, Sam recognized, were non-Crustians, every one of them, and thus not hindered by the impious act they were performing: trying to wake Man. They were crawling on His face, floundering through the thickets of His beard, tickling His eyelids, stomping in and out of His gaping mouth, creeping in and out of His nostrils, in and out of His ears. Surely He was not insensate to such unbearable tickling. Squire Hank was shouting orders, urging them on, although his voice did not move Sam's westered tailprongs. But there was no effect whatever upon Man, except the slightest involuntary twitch of His facial muscles. Man was not totally west, yet. Goading them on to renewed effort, Squire Hank himself leapt into the rally, climbing Larry's lip and disappearing into His mouth.

Sam discovered that he was standing up now, though his gitalongs were weak. He was standing and cheering, rooting for his father.

Abruptly Man's jaws clamped shut.

INSTAR THE FOURTH:
The Consequence

25.

Doc was at a loss. The Patient's skin was moist, clammy, cool, and it had, in what light fell upon it from the reading lamp, a distinctly morbid grayish hue. The Patient's pulse was weak, almost imperceptible, but quite rapid, so rapid that the pauses between beats could barely be detected: more a hum than a pulse. The Patient's respiration was hardly discernible. All of the symptoms of shock were present, but, Doc was the first to admit to himself, he had no experience with shock in human beings, and shock in roosterroaches manifests itself in somewhat different sequelae. Quite possibly the signs here were of shock exacerbated by intoxication, or vice versa. Whatever the exact condition and its prognosis, the Patient, in addition to His other traumas and pathology, now had a *Periplaneta* lodged in the oral cavity somewhere between the palatine papilla, or the palatine raphe, and the sulcus terminalis linguae. The immediate concern, as Doc saw it, was that the patient might swallow, involuntarily, with unfavorable consequences to both the Patient and the *Periplaneta*, who could become lodged in the esophagus or, worse, the trachea . . . or, worse still, as far as the *Periplaneta* was concerned, end up in the stomach. Even if the *Periplaneta* remained in the anterior oral cavity, the prognosis was especially complicated by the possibility that *Bacillus tetani* had entered the gunshot wound of the patient and might within forty-eight hours release tetanospasmin toxins, resulting in rigidity of musculature around the jaw, or lockjaw. Doc checked for any sign of *risus sardonicus*, the sardonic smile sometimes seen in the early stages of the disease, but the particular twist of the patient's mouth could be the result of a natural sardonic smile, not the onset of lockjaw.

Examining up close the configuration of the smile, Doc thought to holler, "HEY, HANK, ARE YE IN THAR?" but the Patient's teeth and lips were so firmly clamped as to preclude any sound escaping from behind them. Nor could Doc's sniffwhips detect any scent of the Squire, overwhelmed as it was by scents of bourbon whiskey, unbrushed teeth, nicotine, and a general effluvium of westwardliness.

Should efforts continue to wake the Patient? Thus far everything had failed, including the attempt of the squire himself to excite the interior of the Patient's mouth. "Boys, we might as well take a rest," Doc called to his helpers, who were still clambering upon Man's face. If the Patient woke too suddenly, He might gasp, indrawing air that would swallow Squire Hank. Better to just keep an eye on things and *think*, Doc told himself.

Hours passed. Doc wondered what his friend the

squire was doing. If it was me, Doc told himself, I would be a-kickin and a-jumpin and carryin on and doin somersaults and backflips even. But knowing Squire Hank, he was probably just laying low, keeping as still as could be, not wanting to make any move that would cause Man to swallow. That, or he was already in Man's stomach, being slowly disintegrated by the juices there. Even if he weren't swallowed, Squire Hank's body would be diluted by salivary secretions and possibly even decomposed by the enzyme ptyalin.

One possibility eventually occurred to Doc: perhaps Man had one or more missing teeth. If so, and it were possible to determine where the missing tooth was located, the lips covering that spot might be forced apart, with the combined efforts of all his helpers, sufficiently to permit Squire Hank to squeeze through. Roosterroaches are, after all, designed to flatten their bodies for passage through the most narrow openings; the squire could easily pass through the space of a missing tooth. But was a tooth missing?

Doc sent his helpers to spread the news throughout Holy House and Carlott, and to ask if anyone could recall having seen the Lord's face close enough to determine whether or not a tooth was missing. Several individuals reported back that, yes, they had seen the Lord's face only recently when he was lying in the grass of Carlott, but he had not had his teeth bared. A fellow was located who claimed to have been still awake one morning, in the Lord's washing room, when the Lord was brushing His teeth, but he had not been able to see the teeth because they were all covered with the white frothy and foaming tooth-paste.

Somebody reported that there was an image of the Lord on the wall in the ponder room, and the teeth were exposed in a smile. Doc himself went to investigate, instructing his helpers to keep a close watch on Man's Adam's apple, in case Man showed any signs of swallowing. Doc had never been to the ponder room before, and he was impressed. The walls were lined with books, the several filing cabinets climbing halfway up the wall, Man's great oak desk topped with the black creature of fifty eyes staring upward, a "typewriter" it was called. On one wall, sure enough, there were several glass-covered images, icons, representations of Man alone and Man with other Men and Women, Man with rows of other Men, Man holding an infant, Man delivering a lecture in some kind of arena. Only in this picture did Man have His mouth open, but His teeth were not visible. But there was one portrait, the only picture of Man alone, in which Man was smiling, and His teeth were visible, His front teeth at least. It was not exactly the sardonic smile that Man naturally wore; it was more of a forced, artificial, obligatory smile; edges of the first molars were visible, all of the bicuspids, canines, and incisors, none of them missing. Doc sighed.

While he was in the ponder room, Doc could not resist, as long as he had climbed up the wall to take a close look at the picture, climbing further along the wall to the bookshelves, and examining Man's library, which, from what little Doc knew of literature, was almost exclusively concerned with poetry: complete sets of complete works of complete poets, incomplete sets of incomplete works of incomplete poets; poets of all centuries, major poets and minor poets, biographies of poets, and critical studies and interpretations of poets. Even the few prose writers were those who wrote poetically. In what seemed a place of honor near Man's desk were double copies or triple copies of four titles: *Where Knock Is Open Wide: The Life and Work of Christopher Smart*, by Lawrence Brace; *Yet What I Am Who Cares: The Life and Work of John Clare*, by Lawrence Brace; *The Heart without Story: A Sort of Life and Work of Richard Jefferies*, by Lawrence Brace; and *Life Is Whose Song?: The Wrong Life and Right Work of John Gould Fletcher*, by Lawrence Brace. There were six copies of the latter, and Doc concluded that that was all that had been printed.

The desktop itself was a mess, surrounding the typewriter, the black creature with fifty eyes, which, Doc discovered on closer examination, were not eyes but, rather, nodules imprinted with letters of the alphabet, numerals, and doodads. A strange steady purr came from the machine. Doc observed that one of the elongated nodules bore at either end two contradictory messages: "On" at the depressed upper end, and, at the raised lower end, "Off." Beside the typewriter were piles of white note cards, small slips of paper, some of them blank, others scribbled with an indecipherable handwriting, and a stack of books: *The American Heritage Dictionary of the English Language, Roget's International Thesaurus*, and Clement Wood's *Complete Rhyming Dictionary*.

Wrapped around the roller of the typewriter was

a sheet of paper, which had typed at one corner of the top, "Stay More, Arkansas," and beneath that, "Lawrence Brace," and in the center of the page, "Myth, Meaning and Narrative in the Poems of Daniel Lyam Montross," and then the beginning of a sentence, "What are we to make of" The rest of the sentence was incomplete . . . or at least Doc, losing his footing on the paper and sliding off the roller down into the innards of the typewriter, could not later recall having read more than that. He climbed up out of the machine and returned to the loafing room, where Lawrence Brace had not changed position upon the couch, had not moved, had not stirred, and was wearing the distinct beginnings of a sardonic smile, with parts of two upper bicuspids visible. Neither tooth, alas, was missing. But there was a minute crack between them, and Doc was able to press up to this crack and yell, "AHOY, SQUIRE HANK, AIR YE ANYWHERES ROUND ABOUT IN THAR?" Quickly Doc stuck a tailprong anent the crack, and heard his words echoing eerily in the chamber of the oral cavity.

Then came a voice, muffled, liquescent, irritated, but calm, "Is it daylight yet out yonder? Can I go to sleep yet?"

"Naw, Squire, it's still night, but gittin onwards to dawn," Doc called in answer, conversationally. "Are you all right?"

"Wal, it's purty damp and all," Squire Hank allowed. "Too wet to plow, I'd say."

Doc laughed. "Have you seen the White Mouse?" he called.

"There's somethin real furry in here," Squire Hank said, "but I think it's His tongue."

Doc laughed again but asked solicitously, "How's yore outsides? Any itches or irritations? Anything that feels like it might be a-sloughin off?"

"Hard to tell, Doc," Squire Hank answered. "Hit's so blamed dank and cloudy, I caint tell what's mine and what's His'n."

"You jist take it easy," Doc called, "and we'll figger out some way to git ye out of thar." Then he asked, "Could ye sort of feel around and see if any teeth are missing?"

There was a long silence, and then Squire Hank replied, "Wal, my uppers is kind of wobbly, but there're all here."

"Not *your* teeth, Squire," Doc said. "*His* teeth. See if one of 'em's missing big enough for you to crawl through."

Another long silence, then Squire Hank answered, "Yeah, they's one of 'em gone, but it's way down in the back."

"Third lower molar," Doc said to himself, "the wisdom tooth." He called out to his helpers, "Okay, boys, here's what we got to try to do." He explained to them the plan, and then he explained it to Squire Hank. A dozen of the strongest fellers would simultaneously press against the lower lip at its corner, forcing it downward enough to uncover enough of the missing molar for the squire to squeeze through. It would have to be well-timed, because they could only exert so much force for just a fraction of a second. Doc selected, from his knowledge of their medical histories, the twelve strongest fellows, and arranged them in position, and said, "Now, when I give the signal, shove as hard as ye can!"

Doc gave the signal and everybody shoved, with much grunting and groaning, and managed to move the corner of the lower lip a tiny fraction of a millimeter, not even enough to reveal the edge of any gap of any missing molar.

"Hey!" came the voice of Squire Hank from within. "Which side of the mouth are you fellers on?"

"The left," Doc Swain hollered back.

"Which left?" Squire Hank answered. "Your left or *His* left?"

It took Doc more than a moment to figure it out, wiggling his left toucher and then his right toucher, and he realized he meant, scientifically of course, the Patient's left, that is, Larry Brace's left, which would be Doc's right side as Doc faced Him. That would also be Squire Hank's left, assuming Squire Hank was facing this way.

"Wal, the tooth that's missing is over on the right side," Squire Hank informed them. "*His* right side."

Doc directed the Stay Morons to shift position from the left side to the right, and once again he gave the signal and called "SHOVE!" and once again they strained and grunted and squealed and managed to move the right lower corner of the mouth back and downward a larger fraction of a millimeter, just enough to uncover a distant view of a missing molar, behind which Squire Hank's face was expectantly waiting.

But it was not enough. The gang collapsed, panting and sighing, and the corner of the mouth snapped back into its original sardonic smile. Doc realized he needed some stronger roosterroaches. Who was the strongest roosterroach in Stay More? Why, Squire Hank, of course, but he was on the wrong side. Who was the second strongest roosterroach in Stay More? Unquestionably that would be Squire Hank's only son, Squire Sam, but he . . .

Doc realized with a pang of conscience that he had been so busy attending *this* Patient, Larry Brace, and then trying to rescue Squire Hank, that he had woefully neglected his original patient, Squire Sam. Excusing himself from the company once again, and reminding them to keep a close watch on the Adam's apple for any sign of swallowing, Doc made his way down from Larry Brace and over to the cheer-of-ease, and up it to the seat cushion, where Squire Sam lay as before, near the edge, taking in the view of the bustling activity on the couch across the way.

"How you doing?" Doc asked, but received no answer because Sam couldn't hear him. He checked Sam over. Respiration normal. Pulse normal. He tested Sam's reflexes. Reflexes normal. Eyes okay. Prongs deaf. Sniffwhips straight and keen. He poked at Sam's thorax and abdomen, to test for any internal injuries, but Sam did not flinch, nor wince. He spoke closely to one prong: "HOW YOU FEEL?"

"Hungry," Sam admitted.

That was good, but Doc Swain had nothing more at hand to feed him, and everybody in Holy House was grumbling with hunger. Maybe Doc could persuade some of the folks to give up their funeral feeds for the worthy cause of nourishing convalescent Sam. Doc wondered how to explain to the deaf boy the task that was expected of him. "THINK YOU CAN WALK?" Doc asked loudly of one prong.

Sam nodded, and said, "I've been watching. You want me to get over there and help, is that it? I've just been waiting for the doctor's permission."

"YOU GOT IT," Doc said. "CAN YOU STAND UP?"

Squire Sam stood up. His six gitalongs were rickety and wavered a bit. Slowly Sam walked around in circles on the seat cushion, then widened the circle with stiffer gitalongs. He really oughtn't to be exerting himself, Doc realized, but it was a matter of life and death for his father. He motioned for Sam to follow as he led the way down the side of the cheer.

It was slow going, getting Squire Sam down off the cheer-of-ease to the floor. They could've flown, but the landing would've been jarring for both. Sam clung frantically to the fabric of the side of the cheer and lowered himself tail first, an unusual and clumsy manner of descent. They crossed the floor to the couch, and prepared to ascend a leg of Larry Brace, but were met by a mob of Crustians blocking the way, with Preacher Chid in the forefront.

"Morsel, Chid," Doc said, and eyed him warily.

Chid did not return the greeting, but intoned solemnly, "The Lord is west."

"Not yet he aint," Doc replied, but wondered if in his absence Lawrence Brace's vital functions might have ceased. He moved to get a closer look, but Chid blocked the way.

211

"Yea, verily I say unto ye," Chid raised his voice, addressing not just Doc but the entire crowd of Crustians and non-Crustians alike, "our Lord has westered off and abandoned us. I don't aim to preach His funeral. But the elders and deacons of my church has decided, and I agree, that we will have to move on out of Holy House and seek our salvation elsewhere." A chorus of affirmations went up from the crowd, folks yelling, "You bet!" and "Shore thang!" and "Yessirreebob!" and "Yo're darn tootin" and "Tell it, preacher!" and "Amen" and "Let's eat!" Chid waved his sniffwhips for silence, and went on, looking straight at Doc Swain, "And there is only one place for our salvation, and that is *Parthenon*."

"So?" said Doc Swain. "How does this concern me? I got a few patients here to take keer of, including one who's got his body all covered with a Man's mouth."

"Wal, that 'un's west too, as far as we're concerned," Chid said. "Aint no way you can git him out." He pointed at Squire Sam. "And aint no way that this one can stop us by hisself from taking over Parthenon."

"Chid, you're lucky he cain't hear ye," Doc said. "He'd make ye eat them words iffen he could hear ye. Now step out of my way, so's we can git up yonder and see about them other two patients."

"Deef, is he?" Chid looked curiously at Sam, and then spoke to him, "Did you get yore prongs hurt as punishment for what ye did to the Lord?"

Squire Sam, of course, could not hear this question, but Doc answered for him, "That wasn't what

212

did it. And he may be deef, but he's still powerful enough to keep ye out of Partheeny."

"Keep *us* out of Partheeny?" Chid said, and scornfully laughed. "Heck, Doc, you don't understand. You got it backwards. It's gonna be *us* keepin *him* out of Partheeny, once he ever gits thar. Time he gits thar, we'll already have the whole place to ourselfs. Right, folks?" The crowd of hungry followers of Chid chorused, "Yeah Brother!" and "I mean!" and "Betcha boots!" and "Pon my word!" and "Let's eat!" Chid took six or twelve dramatic steps in the direction of an exit hole out of Holy House and shouted, "What are we waitin fer? Let's go!"

Tolbert Duckworth exclaimed, "Wait, Preacher! Half the country between here and Partheeny is under water!"

"And more comin down," someone said.

"Pitchforks, cats and dogs," added a third.

"WE CAN SWIM, CAIN'T WE?" Chidiock Tichborne screamed.

As if in answer to this question, as if the Lord Himself, west to all the world, had spoken a final word, a word of protest against His people abandoning Him, there was a sudden near flash of lightning, followed instantly by the most enormous crack of thunder anyone had ever heard. It literally knocked the multitudes off their feet. The light of the reading lamp, the only illumination in the great loafing room, went out. The electricity throughout the house went out. Clocks stopped. The Fabulous Fridge westered. The typewriter went off.

In addition to the three patients he already had,

Doc had to minister to several ladies and one or two males who had fainted. The rest of them, those who could get back on their gitalongs again, dispersed, either to their favorite hiding places or to places where they could pray to their Lord, who, Doc was both gladdened and disturbed to notice, showed signs of rousing from His coma, as if the thunderclap had awakened Him. There was not a minute to lose: Doc grabbed Sam by a gitalong and the two of them scurried up the body of Lawrence Brace to His face, which was twitching in imminent threat of preparation for one big swallow. They fought their way through the thicket of hairs in His beard.

Chid, when he recovered from the thundershock, declared bravely, "Well, I can swim to Parthenon by myself, if need be. Anybody going with me?"

Only a half-dozen Crustian deacons volunteered to accompany their minister on his brave outing, and they exited through a hole in the front of Holy House.

Doc pantomimed the force he wanted Sam to exert against the corner of Larry's mouth, and Sam went at it, with all his strength, which was still considerable despite the weakness of his convalescence. With fractions of a millisecond to spare, Sam threw his body against the right corner of the lips of Larry and pushed the flesh back just enough to uncover the missing tooth, making a gap through which Squire Hank instantly squeezed with an exclamation of deliverance.

Man swallowed.

Squire Hank did something he had never done before and might never do again: he embraced his son.

26.

"If you cain't shet yore mouth, Maw," Jack warned, "you're liable to git a midge caught in it." For the longest time, from the moment they had first entered Parthenon, Josie, even in her sleep, had been hanging her mouth open like a nymph gaping at a swallowtail butterfly. There weren't any butterflies in Parthenon, but the things Josie kept gawking at were no less stunning, if stationary: furniture of brass! tables of teak! machinery of mahogany! and shelves, ledges, benches, brackets, blocks, bends, knobs, pulls, handles, cribs, cubbies, curtains, and clothes! The walls were covered with images! Patterns, pictures, pretties everywhere! Neither Jack nor Josie had ever, even in their dreams of the houses of Man, conceived of anything like it. Jack himself, who had sense enough not to hang his mouth wide open as his wife was doing, still wondered if perhaps they might have westered after all and were now in heaven. But if this were heaven, they were not going to sit on the right hand of Man . . . or Woman, who clearly had the run of the place and didn't look as if She had any intention of bending over and placing Jack or Josie or anybody on Her right hand.

Their best instincts told Jack and Josie to stay out of Her sight, and they did. They waited until She was asleep before exploring the house, and then they seemed to have it all to themselves. There was no sign or scent of their daughter, Tish. What was more peculiar, there was no sign or scent of the Squires Ingledew, who, everybody knew, were the lords of the manor. For the longest time, Jack, without expressing his doubts to Josie, had feared that they might have entered the wrong house, that *this* was not Parthenon, that there was a *third* inhabited house in Stay More . . . but there were certain clues that this was the right place. In the cookroom, for example (a fabulous wonderland that put the cookroom of Holy House to shame, nay, to utter disgrace), they discovered a hidden apartment that obviously was the personal lodgings of Squire Hank, but without Squire Hank in it.

Maybe, Jack decided, after waiting hours in the cookroom for the squires or Tish to return, the squires had taken Tish off to tour the rest of the fabulous castle. He decided to search elsewhere in Parthenon for them, but first he and Josie had to rest up from their long hike—and their swim—from Carlott, a more perilous journey than their recent attempt to get home from the Lord's Refuse Pile. Jack realized he wasn't in the very best of condition—hadn't Doc said something about his pigeon tubes being squoze up by fatty bodies?—and he had traveled more in the past three nights than in all the rest of his life put together.

Their first night at Parthenon, Jack and Josie dined lavishly in the cookroom on an assortment of particles they found beneath one of the stoves (there were two: an old woodstove and a modern electric range) and spent the rest of the night confining their explorations to the cookroom alone. Since Squire Hank appeared to have it to himself, except for occasional forages from the son squire, and the two squires could not hope to consume even a fraction of the scraps that the fastidious Woman overlooked, there was still an untouched bounty of edibles here and there, in cracks, crevices, and beneath things. Not alone on the floor beneath the stoves but on the countertops too, their sniffwhips kept drawing them to fresh discoveries of snippets of food.

"Close yore mouth and eat," Jack commanded his wife, but she was too awe-struck even to speak, let alone eat, and Jack could not remember when Josie had ever been at a loss for words.

It was away along in the second night before a situation arose which finally moved Josie to close her mouth and speak. This night, after the Woman had climbed into her great fabulous brass bed and her slumber-scent wafted across the room, Jack and Josie began to explore this room and a small room adjoining. Josie's mouth opened even wider at the sight of such things as a large oval rug braided of strips of colored wool, and Josie spent an hour just running around the grooves of the braids like a racehorse on an oval track.

The adjoining room, the Woman's washing room, contained a marvelous dresser, which Jack and Josie climbed, to explore such things as the Woman's hairbrush, comb, and bottles from which emanated exotic fragrances. From a corner of the dresser they had a view of a pool of water, enclosed in a white porcelain bowl framed in a wooden oval, which gave them much wonder and conversation. It looked like a private swimming pool, but one much too small for the Woman. Did she have a pet fish? Or perhaps it was a birdbath—but there were no birds inside of Parthenon. Josie closed her mouth in fear of the water.

They resumed their tour of the house, but when the Clock, in foppish tones, uttered "TUTTI-FRUTTI," Josie's mouth fell open again. Ever since entering Parthenon, they had been hearing the chiming of the Clock, although not close enough to distinguish "NOUGAT" from "ECLAIR." But now, Josie exclaimed to Jack, "Did ye hear what that thing called me?"

"Aw, now, he wasn't speakin to you personal, Maw," Jack assured her. "He probably calls everybody that."

Nothing would do but that they climb up the mantel and explore the Clock themselves, finding it every bit as enchanting as their daughter had, several nights previously, and finding even a trace of the scent of their daughter. Jack was smart enough to figure out that the interior of the Clock, with its library of edibles and the little wardrobe of Sam's moults, was Sam's apartment, and had been inhabited, at least overday, by his daughter. But where was she? Where was Sam?

They left Sam's apartment and explored the rest of Parthenon. Next to the Woman's room was the great vacant room which had once been the general store and post office of the humans of Stay More, but was now unused, dusty, moldy, cobwebby, and contained only a few pieces of furniture attesting to its former use: the antique wood-and-glass post-office boxes and the postal counter, empty shelves, a couple of glass showcases, spool cabinets, and, on the walls, a variety of old advertisements for Garrett's Snuff, Brown Mule Chewing Tobacco, Carter's Little Liver

Pills, Putnam Dyes, and Lydia Pinkham Remedies. This room, lost in time, was as foreign to Sharon Herself as it was to Jack and Josie Dingletoon. There was scarcely a thing to eat here that had been overlooked by previous generations of Ingledew roosterroaches or by other scavenging creatures. Indeed, there was no evidence of other living creatures in this room; even the Cobb spiders had long since given it up.

Their third night in Parthenon, Jack and Josie convinced themselves that they had the place all to themselves, except for the Woman, who had a regular schedule: She was finished with Her supper and the washing of its dishes each night when Jack and Josie awoke, and then, while they had breakfast, She sat on the porch in Her rocking cheer until dark, watching lightning bugs, then spent the balance of the evening, before bedtime, sitting in Her cheer-of-ease with a book, and listening to music not at all like the Purple Symphony, music of many instruments and voices that came from two separate large boxes placed on the floor of Her listening corner. The third night, Jack left Josie in the cookroom and sallied forth into the Woman's room while the Woman was still awake and listening to the music. He kept out of sight along the edge of the wall, then crawled beneath Her cheer-of-ease, where he was able to perceive the reason there were *two* boxes from which music came. He discovered, by placing his body so that each of his tailprongs received the same amount of sound from each of the separate boxes, that the music surrounded him, it seemed to come not simply from the boxes but from the four walls and ceiling of the room, and it captivated his tailprongs. For a long time he listened to the music, which, whenever it came to a long silence, the Woman would start up again by turning over great circular black plates.

But once the Woman stopped the music before it came to its silence; She interrupted it, made it stop, because the giant black ant perched on the giant black beetle, who had given Tish such cause for wonder, was now making a discordant music louder than the music from the boxes. But Jack, or Squire John as he truly ought to be called when sober (and he had endured nearly four nights now without a drop), understood that these were not insectile creatures but mechanical, metallic thingumajimmies.

For three nights he had heard the Woman muttering aloud, talking to Herself, indistinguishably, in entire paragraphs, but now She was speaking aloud, clearly, into one end of the thingumajimmy.

"Hi, Gran. Just fine. No, not yet. Yes, I know. Um-huh. Wouldn't you think? Yeah. Well, I couldn't. That's right. *If* I did. Sometimes. You've got me. Of course. Soon, I hope. You're kidding. Well, possibly. Oh, come on. No, Gran. Never. Don't say that. Huh? Ah, me. So what did you say? That bad, huh? You *didn't*. And what did she say? Oh, no. Well, I'll be. Um-huh. Unt-hum. Hunt-uh. Maybe. Who knows. Tomorrow morning. But not last night. If we get one more drop, I'll go nuts. Did it? Well, you never know. If I don't, he would. Yeah. What I'm telling you. Could be. Any time. Right. Bye-bye. Sleep tight."

Squire John sat for a long moment puzzling over the significance of what he had heard. At a loss, he returned to the cookroom, where he had left Josie feasting upon a bit of strawberry shortcake fallen from the Woman's supper dessert, and repeated to Josie, word for word, what the Woman had said. Then he asked, "What do ye make of that?"

"Wait a jerk, and let me git this straight," Josie said. "What did She say right after 'But not last night'?"

"She said, 'If we git one more drap, I'll go nuts.'"

"That's what I thought ye said She said," Josie said, and resumed munching her strawberry short-cake.

Squire John waited. At length he said, "Wal? What do you think?"

"I think this strawberry shortcake is the best thang ever I et," Josie declared.

"I *mean*," said Squire John, "what d'ye make of Her words? You're a female, like Her. What-all kind of womenfolk talk is that-all?"

"Wal," said Josie at length, finishing her food and cleaning her chops, "hit's plain as the sniffwhip on yore face that She was a-talkin to Her grand-mother. What did the Other Lady look like?"

Squire John tried to explain that there were no pictures, only words, on the thingumajimmy. Josie was dubious, but she explained to Squire John, "The Granny-Woman asked Her how She was doing, and She said She was doing just fine. Then Grandmaw says, 'You haven't gone to bed, have you?' and the

221

Woman says, 'No, not yet.' Grandmaw says, 'The ten o'clock news said that Sheriff Tate was defeated in the run-off,' and the Woman says, 'Yes, I know.' And Grandmaw says, 'Did you vote for him?' and the Woman says, 'Um-huh.' Then Grandmaw asks . . .''

Squire John's mouth was hanging open; he listened in amazement as his wife, with a female intuition beyond his grasp, told him word for word the conversation between the Woman named Sharon and the Grandmother named Latha. The subjects covered, in addition to the aforementioned county election, were: the use of rotenone as a duster for vegetable crops, the progress of Sharon's strawberry crop, the approaching visit of Sharon's Sister coming from a place called California, the Sister's divorce from her Husband, an earlier conversation on the telephone between the Grandmother and the Wife of Sharon's Brother Vernon, the current duration, amount and possible future of the rainfall, and, finally, the current status of the ongoing relationship, or lack thereof, between Sharon and Man Our Lord of Holy House.

His wife, Squire John decided, had some intelligence that he had not given her credit for.

Josie had a troubled look. "It don't appear that neither one of them Women has any idee that Man shot Hisself in His gitalong."

But here Squire John's sniffwhips detected the scent of roosterroaches, and he spun around, expecting to see the Squires Ingledew and Tish.

Instead he saw, coming into the cookroom as if they owned it, three Holy House deacons, led by the preacher, Brother Chidiock Tichborne.

"Morsel, Reverend," Squire John said, and added, "Morsel, boys," and spat, marking his space.

"Good morsel to ye, Squire John," said the parson, and spat too. Each of his confederates also spat.

27.

Would this redundant rain ever stop? All her life, or at least since the first cold rain she could remember, from her childhood back in November, Tish had loved the rain, its power to magnify all the scents of the world, its ability to quench thirst simply through the vapors it left in the air, to be squeezed from one's sniffwhips. Without this moisture she would not have grown, no less than the zillion plants whose roots were constantly nourished by the water. But enough was enough, the rain had been falling constantly for five days, and continuously since the ark of Tish's log home had come to rest atop a sandbar called Ararat many furlongs down Swain's Creek from Stay More.

Would she ever find her way home again? Did she even *want* to—to reveal to all the world this easter-egg that kept edging its way out of the end of her abdomen? Maybe the Fate-Thing had intended the rain to wash her and her house away until the easter-egg dropped off the end of her abdomen and was hidden somewhere, or abandoned, or at least left her body unmarked and disemburdened.

Jubal had been the first to notice it, and during the downstream voyage, when it was clear he had

223

nothing better to do than take his attention away from the roiling current to observe the condition of the passengers on the vessel, had remarked to her, matter-of-factly, "Looks like somebody has done went and knocked ye up." She had flinched and been unable to say anything or divert her attention from the direction of the current that was carrying the log down the now-raging creek. Others of her brothers and sisters had remarked, "Tish is in a family way," or "Tish is p.g.," or "Tish has got a cake in her oven," or "Tish has swallered a turnipseed," or they had said that she was any one of the following: teeming, heavy, ketched, gravid, great with child, anticipating, sprung, pizened, or coming fresh. But mostly they said that she was "prego," and Tish thought she would go crazy hearing them ask, "Are you prego, Tish?" and "How did you get so prego, Tish?" and "How prego are you, Tish?" and simply, "Preg, oh, Tish?"

But if it had not been for their interest in her easteregg, they might have been more frightened than they were by their plight, the undirected wandering plunge of the ark down the stream. In the course of the voyage nearly all of them had become seasick, and, despite all their mother had taught them about the need for puking in solitude, they had vomited in one another's presence, openly and unashamedly, and now nobody could stand to go near the remainder of the pile of funeral feeds. Nobody had any appetite.

Despite her best efforts to captain the ship and keep everybody safe, Tish had lost several passengers. It wasn't her fault. She had urged them all to stay off the top of the log, to keep inside of it, and they had, but the log kept crashing into rocks, or the shore, or tree limbs or roots, and each time this happened Tish would count heads afterwards and discover one or more passengers had been dislodged from the vessel and fallen into the tide, never to be seen again. The population of her brothers and sisters was now down from forty-two to thirty-one, and Tish wondered if Brother Tichborne could even keep track of all their names in his next funeralization.

Tish realized that the next funeralization was going to have to run all night and maybe have a matinee. Not alone for roosterroaches but for all critterkind: the stream was full of the corpses of every conceivable insect. Not just insects of every possible configuration of soggy sniffwhips and drenched wings, but furred and feathered creatures too: when the brothers and sisters were not busy making remarks about Tish's pregnancy they were observing and commenting upon the westered wildlife floating past. They saw drowned birds, they saw drowned rodents, they saw a drowned pig, a drowned possum, even a drowned fish. There were drowned frogs and drowned snakes and drowned turtles, and then, when the ark landed and lodged on the sandbar, there came a drowned mouse.

It was not just *a* mouse which washed up beside their log. It was the Great White Mouse himself . . . or maybe herself, nobody had the nerve to approach near enough to check, even if it was clearly drowned. The shore of the sandbar was littered with other corpses, drowned bugs and beetles and spiders, drowned slugs and leeches and snails, drowned ants and moths and flies, but the only drowned mammal on this stretch of shore was the Great White Mouse. Although she had never seen it before, Tish knew it at once, because she had heard many stories about it, and had in turn told many stories about it to her brothers and sisters, so that simply her hushed utterance of "The Great White Mouse!" at the sight of it sent thirty of them scurrying into the innermost recesses of their ark.

"Looks west to me," declared Jubal, who alone beside Tish had not hidden himself.

"You don't want to step over there and find out, do you?" she said.

"Me? I aint that dumb. Let's jist wait and see if it moves."

Tish and Jubal watched the Great White Mouse for a long time. He (they began to assume it was male) lay on his side, one gitalong bent at an odd angle, his eyes closed tight, his albino fur thoroughly soaked and grimed and matted.

"Do you smell any westwardness?" Tish asked Jubal.

He waved his sniffwhips slowly, turning them and tuning them closely. "Jist only all them other west critters. Pew."

She could not detect any mammalian westwardness on her sniffwhips, but perhaps it was too soon; perhaps the Great White Mouse's heart had stopped beating only within the past hour and the corpse had not yet begun decomposing. Tish stepped down from the entrance of the ark onto the sands, and took a few steps closer to the Mouse.

226

"Watcha *doing*?!" Jubal cried. "Don't ye git no nearer to that thang!"

"He looks bad hurt," Tish observed.

"Don't ye jist hope he's hurt *west*?" Jubal said. "*I* shore hope he's hurt as west as ye can go! Now git yoreself back in here!"

But until a renewed pouring down of the rain drove her back into the log, Tish stood and stared at the Great White Mouse, and even from the shelter of the log she continued to watch the Mouse, having tired of watching the rain long ago. Eventually her vigilance was rewarded.

Beside her, Jubal jumped an inch and exclaimed, "Did ye see *that*!? His tongue crope out a bit!"

Sure enough, the Mouse's tongue, as pink as the interior of his ears and the edges of the closed eyes, had poked out one corner of his mouth. Then, more unmistakable, the tip of the long scaly tail twitched ever so slightly.

"He's still east!" Tish said, and realized she was whispering, as if the Mouse might hear her.

Then they began to hear a sound coming from the Mouse: a high-pitched nasal whining, a sort of squeaky hum coming from the throat and larynx and nasal passages all combined. The one intonation of this hum rose into a higher note and then piped into a droning, unmelodious melody, slightly liquid and gurgling because of all the water the animal had soaked up.

The Great White Mouse slightly opened one eye, which seemed to attempt to focus upon Tish and Jubal. The eye was pink all over, and turned up at the edge evilly like a snake's. The Mouse hummed a feeble

227

word, which sounded like "Mawris?" Tish and Jubal exchanged glances, and mumbled the word to each other, questioningly. Then the Mouse hummed, "Mawris, juicy da lim?"

"What?" Tish said aloud, although Jubal frantically tried to hush her. "What did ye *say?*"

The eye attempted to look at her. The great head attempted to lift from the sand. The voice, humming, droned, "Juicy da lim what bunked me?" Then the voice faltered another hum of "Mawris?" and the head lifted, then fell, and the voice moaned, "Ya aint Mawris. Who ah ya?"

Tish understood this question, and she answered, "Letitia Dingletoon."

"Anudda friggin cockroach," hummed the Mouse. "Way's Mawris?"

"Mawris *who?*"

"My brudda," hummed the Mouse. Then the rain stopped. The Mouse hummed, "Comere alidda closa, toots. I can't see ya."

Although Jubal grabbed at her to stop her, Tish shook him off and moved closer to the Mouse, not close enough for him to reach her, unless he was just pretending to be injured. "Are you hurt?" she asked him.

"A tree lim bunked me on da head," he said. "Juicy it?"

"No," she said. "Can I do anything for you?"

"Howsbout sum teet?" the Mouse hummed.

Tish could not understand him. It was a very peculiar foreign language that he was speaking. She had to ask him to repeat himself, and then she repeated it to Jubal, "Howsbout sum teet?" and Jubal thought at first the Mouse was referring to a tit, or teat, which mammals have. But that was not it.

At length, Tish asked, "Are you askin for somethin to eat?"

"What I said awready," hummed the Mouse. "Whatcha got? Come alidda bit closa, kiddo."

Jubal whispered behind her, "He wants to eat *you*, Tish! Don't go no nearer than that!"

Tish returned to the log, but only long enough to search the pile of funeral feeds for a scrap of something, which she carried in her touchers bravely within chomping distance of the Mouse, who could have swallowed her up whole, but did not. Instead he took the offering in his teeth. "Cheese I know," he said. "Velveeta?" He gulped it down. "Say, dat's simply delish, snooks. If ya'll ponny spression."

She fetched him another morsel, a cupcake fragment. And then another. She even took him a tad she had been saving for herself: the last bit of peanut brickle.

"Dis I don't know," he said, humming appreciatively. "But it takes da cake. If ya'll ponny spression."

She carried to the Mouse every last crust and crumb remaining in the pile of funeral feeds, and then she announced, "That's all. There's not any more."

"Donkey shay, angel. Way ja get all dat stuff?"

Tish attempted to explain to the Mouse the custom of the funeral feeds, and further to explain that although the funeral feeds had been intended in observation of the westering of her mother and father,

229

they weren't actually west but had only been presumed to be, and that she and her forty-two—no,
now it was only thirty-one—brothers and sisters had
been adrift on their log home for nights, until now,
and were all too seasick to eat any more of it, so the
Mouse was welcome to it, and it was hoped that he
had had enough to eat that he wouldn't feel like eating
any of *them*.

"Hey, *right*, lambchop," the Mouse commented.
"So why should I wanna eat my *benefactors*, fa crissake,
if ya'll ponny spression awready?" He successfully
raised himself into a sitting position.

Tish did not know "benefactor," but assumed it
was another of this foreigner's strange words. "You
sure talk right funny," she observed.

"Jeez, chick, ya sound fahrin yasself, ya know,"
he said.

"Fahrin," she repeated after him, and then she
understood it, and pronounced it her way, as if cor-
recting him: "furrin." She said it again: "Furrin."

"Awright, furrin," he said. "Whatcha say ya
name was again?"

"Letitia. Everyone calls me Tish. What's yours?"

"Hoimin. Please ta meetcha." He extended one
clawed paw as if for a shake, but of course she could
not take it.

"How do you spell 'Hoimin'?" she asked.

"Lady, I don't spell, period."

The rain was starting up, once more. Tish wanted
to invite the Great Mouse into the shelter of the log,
but she was hesitant. "Don't you generally eat
roosterroaches?" she asked.

230

"Do which? Na, I genly eat jiggers, bedbugs, cooties, whatevah. Cockroaches I don't like. Dey gimme gas, if ya'll ponny spression."

Still she was hesitant, but she invited him in, out of the now drenching downpour. It was a tight squeeze; he took up almost all their loafing room, leaving no space for her brothers and sisters, who wouldn't come out of hiding, anyway, except Jubal, who kept jumping around nervously from one gita-long to the other, as if he had to go potty.

Hoimin really liked to talk. As he lay there, snug in the dry confines of the log's main chamber, he told to Tish, and to hopping Jubal too, his story. He talked most of the night. Jubal crept off to find his brothers and sisters and urge them out of their hiding places. "His name is Hoimin because he's always hummin," Jubal explained to them excitedly, "and now he's hummin the beatinest story ever ye heared!" One by one the brothers and sisters crept within earshot—or rather prongshot—of the Great White Mouse and listened to his story.

He had been born and raised in a great city, far away to the east—and "east" meant not "alive" to him but merely a direction he called "Dataway." East Dataway was a city of zillions of human beings who lived in houses stacked one atop another until they reached to heaven. Hoimin had been born in a cage high up in one of these fabulous towers of East Dat-away, and along with his brothers and sisters he had lived the life of someone named Riley, well-fed and cared for, but once Hoimin had reached adulthood, full size, he was daily subjected to certain indignities, and he chronicled each of them for his listeners, followed by the question, "Hodda ya like dat?" He was stuck with needles; Human Beings picked him up and stuck needles into his "butt" and injected some kind of fluid into him. "Hodda ya like dat?" He was put into boxes with labyrinthine passageways that he was required to find his way out of. "Hodda ya like dat?"

Tish was not certain how to answer his repeated question. She *did* like that, in the sense that she liked the telling of the story, but she did *not* like that, in the sense of all the strange things that were done to Hoimin. So each time he asked "Hodda ya like dat?" Tish would usually reply, "I don't like that."

Eventually Hoimin plotted his escape from the Human Beings who were doing crazy things to him. There was a Man who each day brought into Hoimin's room a flattish box called a "briefkez." This Man, whose name apparently was A. Sun Poddy, as Hoimin referred to him, sometimes left the briefkez open, and one day Hoimin saw his chance when A. Sun Poddy's back was turned, found his way completely out of the labyrinth in which he was caught, and snuggled into a pile of papers in A. Sun Poddy's briefkez. Later that day A. Sun Poddy shut up the briefkez and it remained closed for several days, during which Hoimin experienced sensations of being carried, and then of flight, and being carried again, and then more flight, weightlessness almost, in the deafening roar of great engines, and then being carried again, until, at last, the briefkez was opened on a table top and Hoimin emerged to see many Human Beings standing around him, including A. Sun Poddy, who exclaimed, "What the shit?!"

The Humans tried to grab Hoimin but he leapt off the table and gained the floor and made it out through a door and into a long corridor and down some steps and to the curb of a street where many four-wheeled vehicles were dashing past. One of them stopped at the curb and its rear door opened and a Human stepped out and Hoimin jumped in. He hid beneath a seat in the vehicle and rode for two nights and a day until the vehicle came to a stop, and he jumped out and found himself on the dirt road that led to Stay More, the strangest country he had ever imagined.

For over a year now Hoimin had attempted to adapt himself to life in the woods and fields of Stay More, encountering all sorts of creatures and having countless close brushes with west, experiencing enough adventures to keep his listeners entertained for a month of Sundays. But now the sky was lightening up in the east, dataway, and the sun would soon rise, and Hoimin intended to get caught up on his sleep.

Tish yawned and realized it was bedtime for herself and all her brothers and sisters too; and she realized something else—the rain had stopped, for good, or at least for a long long time. But before she could think of sleeping in the same log with a rodent creature who ate insects, she had to ask him a question. She remembered all the stories of Doc Swain's encounters with the Great White Mouse, and assumed it was Hoimin.

"Didn't you ever try to eat a roosterroach?" she asked Hoimin.

"Yeah, once, maybe," he admitted. "A sun poddy what tried to bite off the tip of my tail."

"That wasn't A. Sun Poddy!" Tish said. "That was Doc Swain."

"Huh? Lisn, buttercup, he was a sun poddy what took a bite on my tail! Hodda ya like dat? But I dint try teet da bug, I was ony goin skeer da bejeesus outa him. If ya'll ponny spression."

Tish yawned again, and said, "Well." She shooed all her brothers and sisters off to bed. "Tonight we've got a long way to go. We can't float this log back upstream, so we're going to have to walk." She spoke these words to her siblings but loud enough for Hoimin to hear, and then she said to Hoimin, "If we're not here when you wake up, you can have our house. We won't be needing it any more."

"What izzis, toodlum? Ya don't like my looks maybe? Lemme go witcha, awready, hey? Just lemme grab a few Z's first, okay? Den we'll talk. Gimme a break. So I'm a type person what's hod to know maybe but just gimme a chance, hey, lidda dew-drop . . . ?"

Still babbling, the Mouse drifted off to slumberland.

28.

Parthenon surpassed the wildest stretches of his fancy, Chid thought, and he had seen only the cookroom so far. When would Josie offer him some of that strawberry shortcake? (If she didn't invite him to taste it soon, he might have to come right out and *ask* her.) Parthenon was a heaven on earth; no, it was not even earthly, it was kingdom come, the promised land, the world above. It surpassed his most vivid preachments. It was a mansion in the sky, the hereafter come hither.

Chid realized he was drooling. He glanced at his deacons, and they were drooling too. That hike-and-swim all the way from Holy House to Parthenon would have given anybody an appetite sufficient to eat a loaf of bread. And Parthenon was clean and tidy compared with Holy House; there was no dirt, no clutter, no grime or filth to require one to wash oneself unnecessarily. Chid realized he could probably get by with only two baths a day when he lived here.

The three drooling deacons, Brothers Sizemore, Ledbetter, and Stapleton, represented only half of the party who had started out from Holy House on the expedition to Parthenon; the other three deacons had been drowned on the perilous voyage. There had been moments when Chid himself had doubted his ability to stay afloat, moments when he had prayed, not to useless Man, nor even to anticipated Woman, but to God, Chid's private solace and salvation. The fact that Chid had survived, and was now standing east and whole in the Paradise of Parthenon, seemed to indicate to him that there *was* a God who was concerned with his well-being.

"Josie," he said, in the same seductive voice with which he had persuaded her nearly a year ago to sample his affy–dizzy, "do ye reckon ye could see yore way to let us fellers have a taste or two of thet thar strawberry shortcake?"

"Why, jist look at me!" Josie exclaimed, lashing herself on her face with her sniffwhip. "Aint I awful? Here I've done went and fergot my manners! Jist hep yoreself, Reverend, and take all ye want."

Chid attacked the strawberry shortcake, and, with the help of the three deacons, reduced it instantly to nothing. His stomach stopped raising a howl and putting up a squawk. He was so grateful to Josie that he decided to spare her when he executed her husband.

He turned to the latter and observed, "Wal, Squire John, it 'pears like ye aint done went and westered off, atter all, don't it? How did that come about? I've done already preached yore funeralization."

"Wal, thanks a heap, Reverend, I 'preciate it," Squire John replied, "but what happened was, that thar beer can didn't never drown me nohow, nor did it wester me when it crashed, as was thought."

"Good to hear it," Chid lied, and then wanted to know, "Does anybody else know you're still east?"

"Only Josie," Squire John said.

Chid told Jack and Josie the story of recent events at Holy House up to the swallowing of Squire Hank by Man.

"Wal, strike me three shades of pink, if that aint the beatinest thang ever I heared!" Jack declared, when Chid finished the story. "I'll be switched!"

"So it appears that the Ingledews are no longer masters of Parthenon, but rather you, Squire John, are the lord of the manor now."

"Is that a fack?" Squire John said with wonder, and glanced vaingloriously at his wife, who was all worshipful toward her husband.

"And our blessed Savior and Redeemer is no longer Man, whose gitalongs were of clay, who has been weighed in the balance and been found wanting, and who was drunker'n a tinker besides, but instead Woman, most fair, most mighty, most graceful, most merciful and most perfect!" Chid enjoyed these new intonations coming from his mouth. He turned to Squire John and asked, "Where is She?"

"Reckon She's sound asleep in Her bedroom yonder," Squire John said.

"Show me, that I might pray unto Her," Chid requested. Squire John led him toward the bedroom. The others started to follow, but Chid turned and said, "Josie, why don't ye give our brethring a tour of the cookroom?" He wanted to be alone with Squire John.

Chid had not yet determined the best way to perform murder upon the person of Squire John. He could, conceivably, simply bite Squire John's thorax, and chew into the vitals, but that might be messy. And it might not look like an accident. No, better to wait, bide his time, proceed with caution.

The Woman was not, they discovered, asleep. A kerosene lamp burned on Her night table, and She was propped up against Her pillows, holding in Her hands sheets of paper, which Chid recognized as the sheets upon which Man had composed letters to Her.

237

Squire John suggested to Chid that they climb the mantel to the mantelshelf, where they had a good view of the Woman, and they watched Her: She would read a few sheets of paper, then refold them, put them into an envelope, return them to a box, and take out from the box another envelope and unfold its sheets of paper. Often She smiled. Occasionally She laughed aloud, causing Chid to jump. He realized She had not received a new letter from Man but was merely re-reading His old ones. Chid had never heard Human laughter before. Man had never laughed, and rarely even smiled.

If the Woman's little bursts of laughter caught him by surprise, he was in for a bigger one. Right behind him, a huge voice clanged, "ECLAIR!" causing Chid to leap several inches in the air and then fall off the mantelshelf to the floor. All the way down he screeched a loud wail of "HHHELPPP!" But the loudness of his scream was not enough to reach the Woman, who would not even have noticed him had She not been staring in that direction to confirm the clockhands' verification of the aural announcement of the hour.

Her eye, glancing at the Clock, saw the black roosterroach fall, and Her laughter at Her reading was interrupted by noises of fright and disgust. She sprang out of bed, put Her gitalongs into coverings, and then began attempting with those coverings to stomp upon Brother Chidiock Tichborne. The fall from the mantelshelf had not hurt him in any way, only stunned him momentarily, but now he was compelled to seek an avenue of escape from Her stomping gitalongs. He was reminded of the last Rapturing by Man, whose shoe-clad gitalongs were more fearsome than Woman's slipper-clad gitalongs. Perhaps it would be more of a Rapture to be trampled by Woman's slipper than by Man's shoe. He was almost tempted to give in, to yield to the experience of the Rapture, to see what it was like. But Chid could not give in to a Rapture so soon after moving into Parthenon, not without experiencing the other joys the great house had to offer.

Seeing his chance, he stopped darting to and fro and made a beeline for the underside of the Woman's bed. There, She could not stomp him. She got down on Her knees and tried to see him, where he crouched panting and wheezing, but it was too dark for Her to see him, although he could see every configuration of wrath and disgust upon Her lovely face, which hurt his feelings. He was grievously insulted by Her attitude. He had intended to pray to Her, to worship Her, to pay Her lip service unendingly, but now he scowled at Her and said, "Woman, you aint a damn bit better than me. Yore shit stinks the same as mine. God is gonna wester *you* one of these days."

As if She had heard him, She rose up and disappeared. She passed entirely out of range of his sniff-whips. She was no longer in the room. Chid remained hiding under the bed for a while, then crawled out from beneath, grabbed hold of the coverlet, climbed the bed, marched upon the sheets, the bedsheets as well as the lettersheets; he was close enough to read the lettersheets, the florid sentiments that drunken Man had poured out to Her, His eloquent expressions of yearning, His hopes for their life together, His

239

extravagant similes comparing her to the pastoral springtime unfolding around Them. Chid spat upon the sheets. He spat upon the lettersheets as well as upon the bedsheets.

He climbed upon the Woman's pillow and squatted and squeezed his haunches and deposited a black pellet of feces upon Her pillow. He was about to squeeze out a second one when She returned, coming back into the room, holding in Her hand a can. Chid darted beneath the pillow and watched Her. It appeared to be a can like the cans of beer that Man drank, but it had some sort of button-like gadget on top that She began to push with Her thumb, creating a most noxious spray. She got down on Her hands and knees again and sprayed the underside of the bed. The poisonous fumes rose and assaulted Chid's sniffwhips, and he crept deeper under the pillow, and remained there, sheltered from the worst brunt of the gas, but still he smelled it, and knew it to be fatal.

At length the Woman stopped Her spraying and sat down upon the side of the bed, speaking aloud, "There, you vermin, I hope that dissolves you into goo."

Chid was not dissolved into goo, but the vapors from the spray were so strong that some of their molecules penetrated into his hiding place and knocked him out. When he woke up, much later, he did not know where he was. He felt a tremendous pressure bearing down on him, almost but not quite squashing him, almost but not quite like he imagined the rupture of Rapture to be. He squirmed out from beneath it, and freed himself from the confines of the pillow. The pressure, he discovered, came from the

Woman's head, which was lying upon the pillow. Still dizzy and disoriented from the poisonous fumes, and suffering a terrible hangover from them, he could not at first determine what his attitude toward Her should be: should he hate Her for trying to gas him? Or had he been westered by the gas and was now in the promised heaven of his afterlife? He climbed upon Her right hand. The muscles in the hand twitched but She did not wake. Chid sat there for a long time, waiting for his wits to return to him, waiting for his hangover to go away, waiting to see if there was anything really pleasurable about sitting on the right hand of Woman, but he ultimately decided that it was not pleasurable; in fact, it was terribly boring. He could not conceive of spending eternity on the right hand of Woman.

The sun rose. Chid watched the dreaded rays streaming into the room. He gazed at the mantelshelf, where the machine which had startled him into falling off the mantelshelf was now rumbling, and now clearing its throat, and now crying, "SCONE!"

"Scone, yoreself," Chid said back to it. His gaze scanned the mantelshelf for any sign of Squire John, but there was none. Most likely Squire John had succumbed to the deadly fumes of the Woman's spray, but where was his corpse?

Later, the mantel machine crooned, "SUGAR-PLUM!" but Chid was not charmed. He ignored it. The Woman, however, stirred, and began to rise. Chid jumped off Her right hand and scurried beneath the sheets. The Woman did not leave the bed, She just sat there, Her knees drawn up to Her chin and Her eyes gazing at nothing off in some corner. Then

Her reverie—and Chid's watching—were invaded by the screaming blare of the giant black beetle with the giant black ant on top of it. Chid watched in awe as She lifted the ant and held it against Her face.

"Good morning, Gran," he heard Her say to the ant.

But this grandmother ant was mute, or else she communicated extrasensorily, while She kept speaking as if in reply to her. "No, that's all right," the Woman said. Then She said, as if answering a question, "Just this morning." Chid listened with growing fascination as She went on: "I've decided that my letter probably angered him, he doesn't want to be nagged, he doesn't need me commenting upon his drinking habits. He probably thinks it sounded like a bribe: I'll talk to him *if* he stops drinking. I guess it *is* a bribe, come to think of it. And of course he has no intention of stopping. So instead of answering my letter, he's just giving me the silent treatment. Well, let him. I've been here longer than he has, and I intend to stay here after he's gone, if he ever goes. Sometimes I wish he would. But maybe he intends to do the Montross book first. Yes, I think maybe one reason he hasn't answered my letter is that he's going back to work on that paper about Montross he was planning to write for *The Southern Review*. It could be he has sobered up enough to write it. At least I haven't heard him shooting off his pistol for several days now. That *must* mean he's not drinking too much. What? Um-huh. Unt-huh. Well, yes. Maybe you're right, but I hadn't thought of it that way. Could be. Well, I'll tell you what, Gran. I think I'll wait until the end of this week, just to see if he *might* answer my letter, okay?

I don't want to seem pushy, or anxious. I'll wait until the end of this week, and if he still hasn't answered my letter, I'll write him another one. How does that sound? I'll write to him again, and sort of apologize, if I offended him. Yes. Um-huh. That's right. Well, thank you, Gran, I really appreciate it, I surely do.

"And listen, one other thing. I think I *do* have a roach problem. I saw another one. It was climbing on my mantel, and fell off, or jumped off. I tried to mash it underfoot, but those things can really scoot, you know? It ran up under my bed. I tried to find some bug spray, but I don't have any. All I could find was hair spray. I don't know if it worked or not, but I didn't see it again.

"Don't laugh. Anyway, after I sprayed the hair spray, I poured myself a drink, to calm my nerves. A *hard* drink. It's the first one I've had since the last time he was over here. I wanted also, and you'd better not laugh at this, to see if I couldn't find out, by drinking, why he likes to drink so much. No, I didn't discover any answers. But I might try it again. Do you want to come over this afternoon and have a gin-and-tonic with me? Oh? Well, tomorrow then? . . ."

29.

If only you were with me, Tish, to be my interpreter. If only I had you here to tell me what these guys are saying. They are all talking at once, and have been at it for nights. One great difficulty that we deaf souls have, Tish, is that we lose selective hearing: we cannot single out a particular voice or sound to concentrate upon, but instead hear only the general hubbub of all sounds merging into one confusing noise. Your sweet cute tailprongs have the power to focus upon the voice of your choosing and banish all others into background noise, but my poor prongs cannot discriminate among the voices of: Doc Swain, my father, Archy and other youths, meddlesome Crustians and busybody butt-ins. Everybody talking at once. Where are you, Tish, my love?

Everyone is discussing what can be done to help the helpless Man. For indeed He is helpless, if not beyond all help, not just from us but from His fellow men in this world, if there are any, and I'm sure there must be, other than Sharon. He is still east. Sometimes He even opens His eyes. His mouth, that dungeon from which my father escaped, with my help, is dry and parched and cracked. But He is immobile, confined to His couch, drifting in and out of consciousness, mostly out, terribly thirsty, and Doc Swain keeps shaking his head, to himself, just at the sight of Him.

The atmosphere is distinctly unpleasant, the air of the loafing room muggy with the must of west, the fetors of rot and gangrene and disease, and the foul odor of Man's incontinence, which has soaked His couch. If He once had worshippers, they no longer find anything worth worshipping in Him. No one prays to Him or venerates Him or propitiates Him. The Reverend, His Holiness Tichborne, had abandoned Him already, and has not returned from, I suppose, Parthenon, where he is up to who knows what mischief—I almost said "Lord knows what mischief," but the "Lord" knows nothing. The Lord has been invaded lately by bedbugs, bloodthirsty little creatures, dumb and determined. We search and destroy among them, but not fast

244

enough to keep them from gorging themselves on the helpless Man's blood.

Because I cannot hear, I can only talk. One more voice, and a loud one, in the general clamor. But everyone listens to me. They listen as if I alone know the answer to this predicament, and maybe I do, but if I do, I haven't quite discovered it yet myself. I have made a number of suggestions. They have been considered, and examined, and debated, and argued, but none of them have been tried. . . .

. . . except my suggestion that, before beginning to eat one another, we attempt to break into the cartons of the cookroom's cabinets. We had been reduced to eating soap from the cookroom sink's soapdish and from the bathroom shower's soapdish. Have you ever eaten soap, Tish? Depending on the brand, it is edible and even palatable, and of course it contains essential nutrients and minerals: fats, alkali, potassium, glycerides, whatever, and there are Stay More legends of roosterroaches who survived the ancient depopulation of the village by discovering old bars of lye soap, terribly caustic but tastier than the perfumed modern stuff.

Doc Swain and I are both proud of our collections of foodstuffs, but I'm sure that neither he nor I want to share our larders with all of our fellow villagers, except as the very last resort. Doc himself was with us the other night when we were gathered around the cookroom's soapdish, having a supper of sorts, our mouths ludicrously foaming with suds and all of the fellows making jokes (which I could not hear) about the taste of the meal and our appearance or whatever they joked about.

I told the others of my plan: to climb up into the cabinets above the cookroom's counters and see if we couldn't chew

245

our way into some of the containers of cardboard, paper-board, pasteboard, whatever, and find something edible and more tasty than soap.

We did, and there are, we discovered, enough boxes of cookies, crackers, wafers, chips, pretzels, Melba toasts, saltines, etc., etc., to sustain the populations of Holy House, and of Carlott too, until, and possibly beyond, doomsday. There will never be any need for these folks to invade Parthenon in search of salvation for their stomachs or their souls. Doc Swain yelled at my tailprongs the information that the roosterroaches of Stay More have been so overjoyed at the discovery revealed by my suggestion that they have referred to this immense treasure of sustenance as "samfood." My own gratification over my resourcefulness, and my pride, are dampened only at the thought that you are not here with us, Tish, to share in this endless banquet. Where are you, my darling? Your Carlott neighbors, who have moved, one and all, into Holy House, report that nothing further of you, or any of your family, has been seen. Your new "boy-friend," Archibald Tichborne, is almost as pining for you as I am; every night he goes out and searches Stay More for you. He comes home, shaking his head slowly, drooping his sniffwhips, languishing, anguishing. I am almost tempted to commiserate with him, but we are rivals, after all.

The general jubilation over the discovery of samfood threatens to make us complaisant, sated, and indifferent to the plight of Lawrence Brace, who westers slowly. But Doc Swain and my father and I, at least, and a few others, even Archy, when he's not out sniffing around for you, continue to discuss and plot ways to get help for Man.

I suggested that we attempt to get word to Woman, to

Sharon. I proposed that we attempt to write to Her. All my life I wanted to write a love letter to Sharon, but there was no way to make the words. Not even with the help of all the strongest roosterroaches, including my mighty father, could we even lift the cumbrous log of a pencil, let alone manipulate it.

"Ink, maybe," Doc suggested. "The old-timey kind that comes in a bottle and Humanfolk used to dip a goose-feather in."

Hunting through and upon Lawrence Brace's writing desk for nonexistent ink, we discovered—or rather I should give Archy proper credit for it, for it was he who first climbed the machine and summoned the rest of us to observe it—the IBM Selectric, with its "on" button still engaged and its vitals humming. Doc told the others some things I could not hear, concerning his previous exploration of the machine and his own theories of its use and function. The several of us climbed all over it, hopping from letter-button to letter-button, reading the letters and numerals there. It was Archy who realized that if enough pressure was exerted against the buttons, it would cause the machine to impress a letter upon the sheet of paper which contained only the words already impressed: "Stay More, Arkansas," and "Lawrence Brace," and "Myth, Meaning and Narrative in the Poems of Daniel Lyam Montross," and then the fragment of a sentence, "What are we to make of."

Archy began jumping up and down on the "I" key, yelling "THIS ORTER DO THE TRICK!" But for all his efforts, nothing whatever happened. The machine went on humming, but remained inactive. Your young fellow Archy is strong, stout, and agile, Tish, but for all his acrobatics—jumps, backflips, somersaults—his weight was not enough to budge that "I" key. I tried, myself, and in all modesty I am the strongest of us all. I too jumped high and came down hard, and, while I could not do backflips and somersaults like Archy, I could exert more downward push upon the key. But to no avail. My father, the second-strongest roosterroach in all Stay More, tried to climb up and join me, but the key would scarcely accommodate both our bodies, and one or the other kept slipping off. We could, however, push downward on its edges, and, with Archy jumping up and down on the top, and Doc pulling down on one side too, we managed, with much grunting determination and super-physical exertion, to depress the key!

The type-ball jerked, clattered, and slammed against the page. We fell down, panting, sighing, but victorious. There it was, our handiwork upon the page.

What are we to make of I

"Now, a comma, quick!" I exclaimed, exulting.
"WHAT'S A COMMA?" Archy asked.
"Down there!" I pointed, and he leapt upon the comma key, followed by us three others, and we got it down, down, down:

What are we to make of I,

"Where's the 'W'?" I asked, scampering about, and we all hunted.
"UP OVER THAR!" my father called, and we joined him two rows up, and used all our strength to complete a three-letter word, "WHO." Getting that "O" down

248

nearly exhausted me, and we fell to the bottom key, which wasn't a key at all, but the space bar, an easy bar to depress, but, for readability, an essential bar.

None of them had the energy to heed my command, "Now let's find the 'A' key!" They crouched and rested on the space bar, and then my father suggested we all needed a bite to eat to recoup our strength. After a visit to the cookroom for a heavy snack, the lot of us returned to the writing machine and continued our labors for another hour, until the whole bunch of us were exhausted. I began to wonder if this was really the afterlife, the prophesied Hell, in which we non-Crustians, true to predictions, had to work. We were all working for the first and only time in our lives, and it was not pleasant.

A major difficulty occurred when the typing of the words reached the extreme right of the page, and we were at a loss for the means of moving the type-ball back. We could not budge it. Again it was clever Archy who figured out that the very large key inscribed RETURN might have something to do with moving the type-ball. But even with six of us crowded upon it and jumping up and down in unison, we could not depress it. Archy squeezed between the keys and discovered that the underside of the RETURN key was attached to a bar which, if a dozen strong rooster-roaches pulled down on it at the same time a dozen others piled on top of the key, would cause it to lower sufficiently to activate the violent return shuttle of the type-ball.

After hours of this hell, we observed our creation, and it was good:

What are we to make of I, WHO AM HURT BADLY SHOT MYSELF IN GITALONG CAN'T MOVE PLEASE HELP SEND HELP AT ONCE

I studied it, and wondered if, grammatically speaking, we shouldn't have put in some more punctuation, but decided it wasn't necessary. The several of us, after another big meal and a rest, and the recruitment of additional help from other Holy House and Carlott males (we had to threaten to withhold their samfood unless they helped), began the laborious task of chewing through the remainder of the sheet of paper and removing the written portion from out of the writing machine.

Then came the tricky part. We had to take the message, now freed from the machine, carry it like an enormous sheet, forty or fifty of us holding it around the edges, down from the machine, down from the desk to the floor, across the floor, out of the ponder room, through the loafing room to the front door, which was shut tight; but, like all doors, with a narrow space between the bottom of the door and the top of the sill. By careful manipulation—a couple dozen or so went out through a bullethole and tugged from the opposite side—we were able to slide the sheet under and onto the porch.

I collapsed. A combination of relief and weariness enfeebled me. I still had not fully recovered from the ordeal of several nights previous, when I had been hit by Man, the same Man whom I was now so determined to save. Doc Swain hobbled over to my side and told me to stay put for a while. I had overexerted myself, writing the message and supervising its removal from Holy House. Now, Doc said, he and my father would supervise the carrying of the message to Parthenon and leave it there where the Woman would see it, providing, of course, that they didn't encounter much opposition from Chid and the deacons who, it was presumed, had laid claim to Parthenon. Doc said I should stay and rest. There was only an hour or so until dawn, and the "messengers," fifty strong, had to get the message to Parthenon before daylight. The rain had stopped, the Roamin Road was now reasonably dry, and fifty valiant roosterroaches carried the sheet of paper down into it, and headed for Parthenon.

I could only watch. I wanted to help, or at least to go with them, but truly I was tired unto west. So I remained on the porch and watched the message procession. The white sheet shone in the moonlight as it moved slowly along the Roamin Road.

Then a morning wind uprose, and I could feel its force along the length of my sniffwhips, which also told me that it was a dry wind, not a rain wind. Good weather was coming . . . but for our purposes, bad weather, because the wind itself, a gentle but firm breeze, swept up under the sheet of the message and snatched it loose from its carriers— or from most of them; some, a dozen or so, clung desperately to it, and were carried aloft. Most of these dropped away and fell safely to earth, but a few, including my father, continued clinging to the sheet as the wind lifted it high like a kite into the night sky, westward out across the so-called "Lord's Garden and Refuse Pile," out across a fallow field, out toward a line of trees bordering Swain's Creek, then downward over the creek, off into the night, out of sight. Whether the precious sheet of paper had landed in the creek or sailed beyond it, I could not tell. As author of the message, I could only feel the frustration of having no ultimate reader of it.

Eventually, the dejected messengers returned to Holy House. Doc Swain hobbled over to where I was crouched, and sank wearily down beside me, shaking his head and sighing almost audibly. I could not speak to him, because of my disappointment, and he could not speak to me, for a long time.

Dawn came. Doc went to watch over his "patient," who, we were convinced, was now in the last day of His life. I slept. I dreamed, around noon and thereafter, of you, Tish, and of my father, and of skyscrapers, and fabulous food, and of all the things I have ever dreamed of, but mainly of you: you and my father were meeting by a creek bank, and you were saving him, or he was saving you. I dreamed of an angellike snow-white rodent. I dreamed, finally, of the Woman, Sharon, and of a person who was both myself and Lawrence Brace.

The vividness of the dream woke me. It was still daylight, but I discovered that Doc and Archy too were already awake, unable to sleep or troubled by their dreams. Despite the full daylight, we began to wake the others, and to assemble in a hubbub of complaining and of discussion. Archy came up with the bright idea of setting the house on fire, in hopes the fire would attract Her attention. When Doc scoffed and said the fire might burn the Man and most of us before it was noticed, Archy suggested that we might set fire instead to the old three-hole privy out back beyond Carlott. Okay, but how? There were kitchen matches, and these could be carried laboriously, two rooster-roaches at each end, up to the privy, where we could attempt to create enough friction on one of them to ignite it, possibly at the expense of igniting whoever made the effort. But what if we simply could not get the privy to burn?

I grew tired of trying to listen to all of this. "All right, fellows, that's enough," I said firmly. "Now listen to me. I want every able-bodied roosterroach of Stay More—ex-

252

cluding, of course, those who are already at Parthenon—to
assemble here in the loafing room immediately. Is that clear?
Wake up all of those who are still asleep."

My order was promptly carried out. Within minutes
I had an audience of a thousand.

"Neighbors, friends, and good folks of Stay More, all
of you," I began. "Crustians and non-Crustians, Smock-
roaches and Frockroaches, and Carlotters, the future of Stay
More is in your hands, or rather in your gitalongs, which
are needed today as they have never been needed before, not
to run and hide but to march, purposefully and resolutely,
in order to save the life of the Man Who established this
home and Who nourished most all of you from infancy. You
Crustians once adored Him and praised Him and asked
favors of Him, and you non-Crustians who were indifferent
to Him still fed from the crumbs fallen from His table. None
of you would be east were it not for Him!"

I paused, both for dramatic emphasis and to gauge their
reactions. Many of them were nodding their heads in agree-
ment, but all of them were eagerly awaiting the heart of my
message. I went on. "We have different beliefs, different
religions, different customs, and different opinions, but one
thing we all have in common: we share Man's table! His
habits are always such that He has leftovers, and we clean
up the leftovers. Even you Carlotters, ye wretched of this
earth, who have not until recently been able to dine on
Man's foodstuffs but instead scavenged in His back yard,
you have chosen your proximity to Him! Why not live in
the remote forest, far from Man? Because everything in you
desires that nearness to Him, that occasional sight of Him,
despite the abuse that He has occasionally heaped upon
you.

"Let's face it, we love Him! In spite of ourselves,

almost, and certainly in spite of Him, we love Him. And yet He now lies westering, and we do nothing. Oh, the bravest of us have tried to help and failed, but there is something remaining that all of us can do.

"And this is what it is. The Woman of Parthenon, who alone can summon help for Him, and provide help for Him that we cannot, does not know that He is westering. We must inform Her. How? Here's what I propose: all of us should go immediately down the Roamin Road to Parthenon, where She always sits on Her porch in the hour of gloaming, before it gets too dark for Her to see us. We will form ourselves, all our numbers, into an arrow, which will point in the direction of Holy House and begin moving slowly but steadily back in this direction, drawing her attention this way."

My words were interrupted by a great murmur of protests. I could not hear any of it, but I could see that they were all talking at once, to each other, and in my direction. Some of them shouted questions at me, a few of which I could hear. How did we dare journey to Parthenon while it was still daylight? The diurnal creatures—birds and reptiles and mammals—would devour us all! We would all be eaten!

I waved my sniffwhips for silence. "Not if there are so many of us!" I cried. "In our numbers is our strength! In our numbers is our safety!" My eyes searched the crowd for a sign of bravery, and fell upon a cluster of young damsels. In other circumstances I would have been petrified by shyness in their presence, but this was an exceptional situation. "Girls," I said, "don't you remember your 'train' on the night of the play-party, just the other night? The Cerealia? Don't you remember how the sight of so many

254

of you scared all other creatures out of your path? And gave a heart attack to a toadfrog?"

The girls of Stay More, at this reminder, raised their heads proudly, then raised their sniffwhips to volunteer, one and all. Above their upraised sniffwhips, the windows of the loafing room presented me with a view of the setting sun.

"We don't have any time to lose!" I cried. My lieutenants, at a signal from me, began distributing crumbs of chocolate chip cookies, high in energy. Everybody had an early breakfast as I concluded, "Fellows in the vanguard, ladies in the train, children last! Our cry shall be, 'SAVE HIM!' Okay, let's go!"

"SAVE HIM!" shouted the multitude and finished the breakfast, then headed for the exit holes of Holy House.

On the Roamin Road to Parthenon, we did not yet form ourselves into any figure, file or shape, but rushed in a body, myself leading, toward the house two furlongs away. Birds circled over us, and some of them dived for a closer look, but none dared attack. Snakes slithered out of our path. A possum couldn't believe his luck, but then was afraid to, and scampered off. A tarantula leaped frantically to get out of our way. A praying mantis prayed, but not for prey. We reached Parthenon without the loss of a single roosterroach.

As I expected, Sharon sat on Her porch, in Her rocker, one hand holding a drink, which She raised to Her lips. She was listening to music coming from within Her house, and Her gaze drifted toward Holy House.

Quickly I directed my lieutenants, Archy chief among them, to arrange everybody into a shape:

I myself took the position at the extreme front point of the
arrow, with Archy at the lower point flanking my right
and Doc Swain hobbling along at the upper point on the
left. I counted cadence: "Hup, two, six, twelve! Hup, two,
six, twelve!" The crowd yelled "SAVE HIM!" continuously. We moved steadily but not slowly in the direction
of Holy House until I was sure we were out of sight, then
we broke ranks and rushed back to the yard of Parthenon,
reformed, and repeated the whole process. The third time
the arrow was formed, I relinquished my position to Archy

and rushed to the porch of Parthenon to observe the arrow from Sharon's vantage, and, more importantly, to observe Sharon, to see what She was doing.

She was doing nothing. If She even saw the arrow, I could not tell. Her gaze was not directed downward toward the yard, toward the road, toward the huge throng of marchers, but rather outward toward Holy House. I thought of rushing up into Her lap to attract Her attention, to shift Her gaze out of its fixation on Holy House and downward, but I decided it wouldn't work; it would only perhaps scare Her and make Her rush into Her house.

Dusk was rapidly approaching. Soon it would be too dark for Her to see the arrow even if She looked in that direction. I was at a loss, and becoming hopelessly dejected.

Suddenly the entire mob making up the arrow began rushing back toward Parthenon. I thought at first they were coming back to reform one more time. But they were running in fear from a creature who was not intimidated by their numbers or their arrow-shape. A great white mouse. The Great White Mouse. And following the mouse was a female roosterroach who, my eyes and then my sniffwhips told me, was you.

30.

Doc didn't follow. He abandoned his position as leader of the left flank, broke rank, and stood aside on his three weary legs to watch the frantic retreat. He felt rage and helplessness, futility. These folks had not been frightened of the snake, the tarantula, the mantis, the birds, and the possum that had been in the path to Parthenon, and yet they were now running from the Great White Mouse. He didn't blame them, but Doc had told himself that he would never run from it again. In all his idle hours he had plotted and planned what he would do when he met up with it again, and now he was ready. "Forehead to forehead I meet thee, this third time, White Mouse!" he yelled at it, and stood his ground, albeit standing on only three gitalongs, having lost the other three to the aforesaid Mouse on the aforesaid occasion.

"Don't skeer all those folks, Hoimin!" a female voice called, and Doc saw that there was a girl standing right *behind* the White Mouse. The girl was Tish Dingletoon, reported drowned days ago; daughter of Jack and Josie (reported westered in a crash days ago); reported sweetheart of Squire Sam, who was now running toward her from the north, also unafraid of the White Mouse; the same Tish who was, Doc recalled, also the reported sweetheart of Archy Tichborne, who was now running toward her from the south, also unafraid of the White Mouse.

"TISH!" shouted Squire Sam and Archy simultaneously, and ran to embrace her.

The poor girl could not look in both directions simultaneously, but she had one sniffwhip fixed on Sam and the other on Archy. Doc had both of his fixed on the White Mouse, who, however, was not paying him any attention whatever.

Then Tish did a very strange thing. She introduced the Mouse to Doc. "Hoimin," she said to it,

258

"I want you to meet Doc Swain. You owe him three apologies."

The Mouse spoke to Doc! "Haughty," it said. "If ya'll ponny spression. Please da meetcha. Da lidda pigeon says ta me I should big ya poddon I ate ya legs off. It was mistook identity, belive me. I taught ya was a *edible* bug, ya know?"

Tish and Squire Sam were doing some kind of dance with their sniffwhips. The Mouse kept on talking to Doc. Doc thought he was dreaming. Suddenly from down the Roamin Road came strolling Squire Hank Ingledew. Doc *knew* he was dreaming.

"Like to skeered yore other three gitalongs off, I bet!" Squire Hank said to Doc. "Aint this some critter? Name is Hoimin, which is jist the way he misspeaks Herman. Got a story as long as my right sniffwhip, but he caint talk good English. Lissen to him!"

The injunction was hardly necessary, because Doc couldn't avoid listening to him; the Mouse wouldn't stop talking. Every other utterance seemed to be "ya know?" or "if ya'll ponny spression" and the Mouse kept asking Doc, "Hodda ya like dat?"

"Where did ye find *this*?" Doc asked Squire Hank, and reached out to touch the white fur.

"Tish found him, down the creek a ways," Squire Hank said. "Doc, I got a long story to tell, myself. But what's a-gorn on here? What's all these folks doing? Trying to deliver another message?"

When Squire Hank had been brought up to date on events, he commented, "Now that is the pure-dee dumbest notion ever I heared!" and he turned to his

259

son and said, "Sam, boy, why in blazes didn't ye jist try writin another message on the typin machine?"

Squire Sam looked blankly at his father, not hearing him. Then the younger squire turned to his girlfriend and asked, "What did he say, Tish?" and Tish waved and wiggled her sniffwhips into all sorts of odd positions, and Sam said, "Oh," then he said to his father, "There wasn't time, Dad. And there wasn't any guarantee the wind wouldn't have blown the second message away too. We've got to get Her attention before dark!"

"Wal, why don't ye jist run up thar and hop in Her lap?" Squire Hank asked.

Tish seemed to be taking the older squire's words and translating them into some kind of sign language for the younger squire.

"What good would that do?" Sam said to his father. "You've told me never to reveal myself to Her, and if I did, it would just frighten Her."

Tish spoke, timidly but with conviction. "I have an idea, sirs. What if we had Hoimin march at the front of the arrow? The Woman would see Hoimin because he's *white*." As she spoke, she expressed this in her sign language for Sam's benefit.

The two squires looked at each other, then looked at Doc, and Doc looked at them and then at Tish and at Archy and at Hoimin, who was looking at each of the others in turn and saying, "Hey, ya know sumthin? Da lidda sweety is positively kerspang on da button, ya know? Attawaygo, beby!"

If he were dreaming, Doc did not want to wake up. The reason he knew he was dreaming was that there was no possible way a fellow who had endured all that he had been through for the past several days could even hope to stay awake. He had to be asleep. He hadn't had a good day's sleep since the day before the night Lawrence Brace had shot himself in the git-along. Doc was somewhat ashamed of himself for falling asleep right in the middle of the most dramatic and essential portion of the rescue operations, but it couldn't be helped. He was asleep, and here was this preposterous daymare of this great nemesis of his, the White Mouse, who was suddenly speaking like a laboratory rat with a Brooklyn accent and who was about to become the hero of the whole affair.

The nice thing about dreams is that you don't really have to exert yourself and be active. You can sit back and just watch all these things happening to you and to others, and you don't even have to respond, if you don't feel like it. Doc wasn't even required to resume his position at the left flank of the arrow. Squire Hank took that place, and Doc just stood over to one side—or, if he was dreaming, just crouched asleep over to one side—and watched.

The arrow of hundreds of roosterroaches of Stay More, under the direction of Squire Hank and Squire Sam, and Tish, the latter practically riding on Hoimin's long pink scaly tail, reformed itself in the yard of Parthenon, right beneath the porch upon which the Woman sat, gazing at Holy House. The arrow began moving out across the yard, with Hoimin at the head, or point. "Hey, lookit me!" Hoimin hummed. The arrow followed Hoimin. "C'mon, *Lady*, lookit me!" Hoimin squealed, over his shoulder. "Fevinsakes awready, Lady, willya *lookit* me?!?!"

And the Lady looked at him. When Her gaze

shifted downward, caught by a ball of fur hopping, skipping, bouncing, and dancing, someone—it appeared to be Squire Sam—dropped back and arranged the last few hundred roosterroaches into a new formation:

A great philosophical question which had often preoccupied Doc Swain in his casual musings was the possibility that in dreams not only is the dreamer dreaming but also every participant in the dream is dreaming. If I dream that you are there, you in turn are dreaming that I am here. *Therefore*, Doc reflected as he watched this procession, *every last one of those roosterroaches out there is only dreaming that he (or she) is doing this, and also, of course, the Great White Mouse is dreaming.*

. . . and also, of course, the Woman was dreaming. Surely She Herself had to think that She was dreaming, seeing this strange sight. (I think I dream, therefore I dream I think I am. Et cetera. Philosophy was complicated, Doc realized.)

So the Woman went on thinking She dreamed, as the procession slowly wound its way down the Roamin Road toward Holy House. But then the Woman stood up, unsteadily, and put down the glass of whatever had been responsible for the dreaming. Then, instead of going out into Her yard to follow the arrow to Holy House, She turned, and went into Parthenon. She was gone for a moment, and then returned, muttering loudly to Herself, "Goddamn Newton County Telephone Company!" She raised one hand to become a visor on Her forehead, and peered out across the Roamin Road into the gathering dusk, where the arrow was fading into the direction of Holy House. She took a step down Her front steps. "Gran, I've only had four gin-and-tonics," She said to the air. "Well, maybe it was five. But I'm not drunk. I swear. I know what I'm seeing. Unless I'm dreaming."

She took the rest of the steps down into Her yard and began walking in the direction of the arrow. "Well, it wouldn't hurt to just go *see*, would it?" She asked.

"No, it wouldn't, Ma'am," Doc said. "You'd be mighty surprised what You would discover. Hurry!"

The Woman began walking rapidly, as fast as She could. Doc followed. Hobbling for all he was worth, he could not keep up with Her. The procession of the arrow had almost reached Holy House. As the Woman caught up with it, it was already at the steps to Holy House, where, as the Woman reached it, the roosterroaches disbanded and decamped. The Woman climbed the porch of Holy House, knocked at one of the three front doors, knocked again, and disappeared inside. Doc had scarcely reached his own clinic, half-way between Parthenon and Holy House, when he watched the Woman enter the latter.

He kept going, but was still a hundred yards short of Holy House when the Woman came out of it again. She looked up and down the Roamin Road as if looking for someone else, but saw no one. Then She began running. Not toward Parthenon but in the opposite direction, toward the Man's mailbox. But She did not stop at the mailbox. She kept running out into the county road and across the WPA low-water bridge.

She disappeared in the direction of the old canning factory. Doc could not understand what reason She might have to go to the abandoned canning factory. But maybe She was going beyond it. What was beyond it? Far beyond it, up the mountain, lived other humans, or so the old legends told. But they were a long way off. No, nearer beyond the canning factory was the old schoolhouse. But why was She going to the old schoolhouse?

Before he could figure it out, Doc heard the

sound. He had never heard it before, but had heard from oldtimers who had in turn heard from their ancestors what the sound was like. "BOMMBBB!" it said. The sound reverberated all over everything and seemed to drip from the trees. There was an instant's interval to let the sound rumble and roll all over Stay More valley, and then a slightly different sound pealed. "DOOMMM!" it said. Doc noticed that not he alone but all the roosterroaches in sight were standing frozen, their tailprongs erect and tingling from the sounds.

"BOMMBBB!!" the great sound came again. "DOOMMM!!" Doc understood what was producing the sound, and who was causing it, and even how.

"BOMB!" "DOOM!" Doc decided he wasn't dreaming, after all, because in dreams you don't hear such sounds. In dreams you don't hear sounds you've never heard before.

"BOMB!"

"DOOM!"

There was, Doc reflected, a kind of irony involved in the meaning of the words the bell spoke. "Bomb" suggested that indeed the advent of The Bomb was at hand, or that, as Doc had suspected, The Bomb consisted only of Man shooting Himself in the gitalong. "Doom" suggested that now we were sure in for it. But the Bombing and the Dooming were sounds that meant help and hope, and a solution to the problem of Man. Doc understood why the Woman was ringing the bell.

"BOMB!"

"DOOM!"

Wasn't the Woman's arm getting tired, pulling the bellrope? It went on and on. Then Doc's tailprongs began to pick up a different sound: the engines of cars and pick-ups, converging on Stay More from every direction.

INSTAR THE FIFTH:
The Woman Pays

31.

Squire John Dingletoon/Ingledew, *pro tempore* lord of
the manor of Parthenon, began to suspect that his
house guest, the Reverend Chidiock Tichborne, was
cooking up murder. The minister's behavior was such
that Squire John believed he was plotting to commit
insecticide, possibly upon Squire John's own person.
Squire John this morning had even voiced his suspi-
cions to the lady of the manor, Josie, but Josie had
replied, "Huh? Now what-for would Brother Chid
want to do a thing like thet for?"

"For to git rid of me," Squire John patiently
explained. "So's he could be the boss squire of Partheeny, and have all these goodies to hisself."

"Why, we've got more'n a plenty, hon," Josie
pointed out. "He don't have to wester nobody to git
all he can eat. He don't even have to ask. I'm always
tellin 'em, 'Jist hep yoresefs.' " Josie yawned. "Now
it's way past our bedtime, Squire John."

Squire John did not believe he could sleep. Long after the sun rose, and Josie had drifted into the arms of slumber, he crouched awake, his sniffwhips raised and waving steadily to and fro. He wondered, but doubted, if Chid and the deacons were asleep. Chid, when last seen and smelled, just before midnight, the hour of Tutti-Frutti, had been evacuating upon the Woman's pillow. Squire John had been offended and angered by Chid's rudeness, and had started down from the mantelshelf toward the bed, fully intent upon first removing the pellet of feces from the Woman's pillow and then removing Chid from the bed, and, if need be, from Parthenon itself. But then the Woman had returned to the room and done something to the air. The beer can she held had fizzed, but the fizz hadn't been like any beerfizz Squire John had ever smelled before. It was globulous and sticky and Squire John knew that it would asphyxiate him. He had fled as fast as his gitalongs could skedaddle, but not fast enough. He had decamped the room entirely, but the fumes of the fizz had already, if not asphyxiated, intoxicated him. He had become drunker than an Englishman, whatever one of them was. The rest of the night he had spent in the abandoned store part of Parthenon, the old post office, wandering around in a kind of hallucination, in which he envisioned that Chid was stalking him with a variety of murder weapons: a candlestick, a knife, a lead pipe, a wrench, a revolver, a rope, and poison. When the effect of the fumes had eventually worn off and the hallucinations ceased, Squire John had returned to Josie in the apartment they had made for themselves in a cabinet beneath the cookroom sink. The Woman had come and fixed Her breakfast, left a few traces of it behind, and left the cookroom.

Like most Carlotters, Squire John could not read, and thus was not able to decipher the labels on the containers with which he and Josie shared the cookroom cabinet beneath the sink: Drano, Lysol, Oxydol, Ajax, Electrasol, Dawn, Drench, Pledge, Behold, Future, Glory, Windex, Fantastik, Spic and Span, 409, Mop & Glo, and Mr. Clean. None of these, Squire John could tell by sniffwhipping alone, was potable or edible. Sheer instinct led him now in the throes of insomnia to conceal himself behind a can of Lysol and spy upon the boudoir where Josie crouched in slumber.

Soon Chid Tichborne stealthily entered the cabinet through a crevice and advanced upon the master bedplace. He carried a wrench. No, Squire John corrected himself, a lead pipe, in any case some instrument with which he intended to murder sleeping Squire John. But Squire John was not asleep, and he stepped around from behind the Lysol and said, "Morsel, Reverend, have ye lost yore way home?"

Whatever the murder weapon was, it disappeared. Chid wheeled around to confront Squire John, coughed, gulped, and stammered, "Why, hidy, Squire John, I figgered ye would be asleep."

"I aint," Squire John observed.

"Wal, I was jist checkin up on ye," Chid declared. "Jist wanted to make shore that both of you'uns was comfy and cozy and all, you know. It's a hot day, aint it?"

"Real hot," Squire John allowed.

"Couldn't sleep a wink, myself. Got to wonderin if you and Josie was comfy and cozy and all, what with all this heat, you know. Seems like it's too hot fer roosterroaches or beasts."

"Aint it, though?" Squire John agreed.

"Reckon ye seen as how I nearly got trompled by the Woman in yonder," Chid said. "And I aint been able to sleep good, since."

"Was that how come ye to crap on her bed piller?" Squire John demanded. He realized the noise of his voice threatened to waken Josie, who began to mumble in her sleep. "Let's step outside," Squire John suggested.

They resumed their conversation on the cook-room floor. They were beyond prongshot of Josie but still Chid kept his voice low, conspiratorial. "Squire John, I have some terrible news for us all. The Woman aint holy and divine, after all. She aint the Lord, or even the Lady. Maybe She's a Witch. Anyway, She's in cahoots with a giant ant that is probably Her grand-mother, and She talks to it."

"Is that a fack?" Squire John said. "Are ye shore it's a ant?"

"I'd show ye," Chid offered, "but I aint a-gorn back in yonder again. I tell ye, it's nearly enough to sour a feller on religion forever. First, our Man turns out to be undependable and worthless, and now the Woman turns out to be a Witch."

"Looks like you might be out of business, Rev-erend, if you aint got nobody to worship or preach about," Squire John reflected aloud. Then he asked,

"Did ye notice, was that there 'ant' connected to anything?"

"Connected? Yeah, now you mention it, the ant had some kind of real long tail that run all the way down to the beetle, and the beetle's tail run down to the floor and out through a hole."

"Them wasn't tails, Reverend. Them is called 'wires.' Like all the 'lectric wires in Holy House, only they aint quite so electrified."

Squire John was about to explain the mechanics of thingumajimmies to the minister, but the conversation was interrupted by the quivering of the substratum that warned of the approach of Woman Herself. The two roosterroaches had just enough time to scurry beneath the cabinet's toeboard before the Woman came into the cookroom. They watched as She removed two bottles from Her Fridge, along with a small green fruit of some kind, and then a tray of ice cubes from the freezer. On the countertop She began mixing the first of the drinks She would have that day. She took Her glass, to which a wedge of the green fruit had been added, back to Her room and thence out to the porch of Parthenon.

Both roosterroaches waved their sniffwhips and picked up the distant aroma of the liquids she had mixed. Brother Tichborne suggested, "How about a sample, Squire?" and the two of them scooted up the cabinet to the counter. A lone housefly was already there. Neither roosterroach had had much experience with the diurnal housefly or could understand its strange dialect. Among the many other things that roosterroaches have in common with human beings

271

is their mutual disdain for houseflies, who lack other insects' sense of personal hygiene and are careless disseminators of baneful microbes—not to mention their sheer ugliness: the hoglike snoot, the huge goggled eyes, the pudgy, bristly body. "Shoo, fly," Squire John said to it, and jumped at it. The fly, likely alarmed at the encounter with an unfamiliar and nocturnal creature, flew.

Squire John and Chid sampled the juice of the green fruit cut open on a cutting board, and found its sharp, tangy citrus flavor interesting but not exciting. They sampled a droplet of one of the two clear liquids, which the minister, from his experience at Holy House's cookroom, identified as quinine, reputed to be a good cure for mosquito bite, not that he himself had ever been bitten by a mosquito. They approached, finally, a spilled droplet of the other clear liquid.

"This here is called 'gin,' " Chid explained. "Not being the drinking sort myself, Squire, or not usually, anyhow, I'll have to pass on it, and let ye have it all to yoreself."

Squire John tasted it, and jumped an inch. It was powerful stuff. It had a kick like nothing Squire John had ever tried. Chism's Dew was like Kool-Aid by comparison, not that he had ever tried Kool-Aid. The merest taste of the gin sent shivers through his brain. "Great jumpin Jehoshaphat!" he exclaimed. "A whole drap of that stuff would wester a feller!"

"Oh, I don't know," Chid said. "Try it and see."

Squire John began to suspect that Chid was trying to poison him, but he couldn't resist the beverage and its scalding bite. Before he knew it, he had magically

272

shrunk the preacher to the size of a third instar rooster-roach. "*Ex*-preacher," he corrected himself, for it was apparent that Chid Tichborne no longer had a reputable deity to venerate. If Chid gave up preaching and became just an ordinary feller, he might not be such a bad sort, after all. He wouldn't be any better than Squire John. Already he wasn't half as big as Squire John. Squire John and him could be good pals, if they gave it a try.

"Come on here there," Squire John urged the shrinking ex-preacher, slurring his words, "and try a leetle snort of this here gin yoreself."

"It's all your'n," Chid declined. "Take the whole drap."

"Don't mind if I do," Squire John remarked, and proceeded to lap up the entire droplet of gin. The preacher shrank to nothing.

Nighttime came at broad day. How awful, that a feller in bad need of sleep, and thinking it the west middle of the daytime, should suddenly find it night-time, after all. But Squire John didn't care. He just drifted off to dreamland. Blackness surrounded him. Even with his good night vision Squire John could see no trace of the ex-preacher. Jack Orville Dingle-toon was Boss Squire of Parthenon and had it all to himself and could dream his whole life there, a cock-roach in the Land of Cockaigne, the floors paved with pastry, the walls of barley sugar and cakes and pies.

When he woke, and discovered that his old head felt as if his sniffwhips had been pulled wrongside out, it was indeed nighttime, or at least completely dark all around him. His supersensitive night vision could see nothing, not even his sniffwhips in front of his face. He could only attempt to feel his way around, and it was hard going, terrible going. He had a vague memory of having been on a countertop in the Parthenon cookroom, but that was not where he was now. He was surrounded by substances. Sticky stuff, gooey stuff, coarse stuff, slime and gaum and gunk and goop and glop: garbage, yes, it was some kind of hodge-podge of sheer garbage that surrounded Squire John. A feller ought to be able to find paradise in garbage, but Squire John thought he had gone to hell. None of this was really edible: coffee grounds, black and damp and murky, foul-smelling. Chicken egg shells. The squeezed pulp and rind of a fruit that he identified as the green stuff the Woman had put in Her drink. Several strands of the Woman's hair. Floor sweepings of dust, grime, dirt, and only a particle or two of edibles. With his touchers and sniffwhips Squire John explored further and found unrecognizable messy substances and liquids, and he found the body of the housefly he had encountered earlier. It had been crushed by a swatter, and stank to high heaven. Elsewhere in this prison were empty cartons, containers, and crumpled pieces of paper. The walls of this prison were of some resilient shiny smooth material, black as pitch, which Squire John could not bite through. He heaved himself against it, and it gave with his weight, but only slightly, and sprang back, mocking him. He explored in every direction, but the shiny smooth black material had no exit. The one place where it puckered and narrowed to an apparent exit was bound tightly from without.

"Josie?!" Squire John called, pathetically, futilely. "Chid?!" he wailed. "Anybody?!" he tried. He was alone, and had the worst hangover he could ever have imagined, and although he was not west, he might as well have been, because there was no way out, no escape, no going back to the world of folks and love.

"What did I do to deserve this?" he cried aloud. There was no answer. Not yet. And then came one. As he crouched in abject despair, convinced that he had gone to Hell, he had his conviction confirmed by the sound. "BOMB," it said to him. "DOOM," it added.

It kept saying the same thing, over and over.

32.

She knew that Archy wanted to take her far away. His belief that the world contained fabled houses far better than Holy House or Parthenon was confirmed by the sudden presence, in and around Holy House, of so many human beings. A dozen or more, she couldn't count them all. Big and little, male and female, thin and fat, young and old. Tish had grown up being taught that there was one Man, and only one, who was supreme over all creatures. She had loved that Man as her Lord, and prayed to Him, and expected that when she went west she would live on His right hand forevermore. Then she had come to know that Man was just a man, large and drunk and prone in the grass of Carlott, lonely and vulnerable and somehow lovable in a different way. But now Man was west and being carried out of Holy House by other Men, Who looked more handsome and lordly than our Man, and Who lifted Him up and removed His body from Holy House and carried Him out to a vehicle, which took Him entirely away from Stay More, just as His own vehicle had done every now and again, but with Him driving. Now He was not driving, but lay spread out in the back seat of another Man's vehicle, and the door was closed upon Him, and He was driven away. The Woman got into one of the other vehicles, which another Man was driving, and it too gained the county road and disappeared. One by one, the other Human Beings, hanging back at Holy House to explore it and then to lock it up, returned to Their vehicles and drove away. The roosterroaches of Stay More, and the one rodent of Stay More, watched all this to its conclusion.

The sniffwhip-spelling sign for "west" is the same as that for "belly-up": a turning over of the two sniffwhips to signify the turning over of the body into the belly-up position. Tish went up to Squire Sam, who was talking to Doc Swain and his father, and in sign language she asked Sam, "Is He west?"

With his sniffwhip gestures Sam answered her, "We don't know. Doc didn't have a chance to check His pulse before They took Him away. Doc was too busy helping us try to get help for Him."

"What are you two talking about, thataway?" Doc asked her.

"I was asking him if Man is west," Tish said to

Doc, "and he told me that you didn't have a chance to find out before They took Him away."

"But didje notice," Doc said to others around him as well as to her, "one of them Men who drug Him out of the house had one of these here things around His neck, I do believe it's called a stereoscope or something like that, that listens to the heartbeat. There's one of 'em a-hangin on the wall in my clinic, covered with dust. Anyhow, He had the business end of that stereoscope up against Man's chest, and He was noddin His head yes, as if to say yes, He could hear that Man still had some heartbeat."

This information was spread from mouth to prong throughout the crowd, until everyone in Stay More understood it.

"What d'ye reckon They're fixin to do with Him?" Squire Hank asked Doc.

"Where are They taking Him?" Tish asked. She was still busy "translating" Doc's words into signs Sam could understand, and she was slowly spelling out s-t-e-r-e-o-s-c-o-p-e.

"Wal," Doc said, "I'll tell ye. I used to hear it told that far off and away, beyond the mountains, there is a big old kind of house, not a house where Humanfolks live, but a big house where the Humanfolks take keer of Their sick and the lame and the westerin, and this house is called a House Pittle. I reckon They've took Man to the House Pittle, to keep 'Im until He gets better."

Tish was aware that Archy stood to one side, watching her intently, curiously, and somewhat jealously.

Sam too was aware of Archy, and he signed to her, "I'm sure you've got things to discuss with him too"—he imperceptibly pointed a sniffwhip in the direction of Archy—"so why don't we get together alone later? We've got so much to talk about."

"Yes," Tish agreed. "I've got to tell you how Hoimin helped me hide my easteregg."

"*Hide your easteregg???*" Sam duplicated the signs with emphasis but added three question marks with a rhythmic flourish of his sniffwhip tips.

In sign language, "See you later" is a combination of the conventional "see" with "you" and a flip of one toucher over the other in a forward direction indicating "later." She gave this to him.

Then she went to Archy and asked, "Do you want to talk?" The last of day was gone now; night, the element of roosterroaches, had come fully again, and they were in it.

"I caint wiggle my sniffwhips like he can," Archy said.

"You don't have to," she said. "Because you've got good hearing, I reckon."

"But I aint nobody around here lately, in all this excitement," he observed. "Yore squire has been runnin the whole show."

"With your help, Archy," she corrected, trying to be encouraging. "He couldn't have done it without your help."

"And yours, and the big mouse's," Archy pointed out. He smiled. "Did ye know, you're the famousest gal in the whole town, now? You're quite a shucks. All the other gals is green-eyed with envy."

Tish blushed, and protested, "Aw, Archy, they're all green-eyed anyway." Which was true, because all roosterroach eyes are that color. But she had to admit to herself that she enjoyed being the center of attention; she relished having these two males competing with each other for her favor. The other girls of Stay More were whispering among themselves all over the place, and casting covetous looks at Tish. Wouldn't her parents be proud of her! But where were her parents? "Have you seen my folks?" she asked Archy.

"No, nor mine neither," he said, with an insinuation of reproach, because he remembered painfully how she had been the one who had informed him of his mother's west, and she remembered that the last time she saw him she told him that she was motherless too.

"I heard they went to Parthenon, lookin for me," she said.

"Well, that's a coincidence," Archy declared. "My dad has gone to Parthenon, too. Why don't we jist mosey up yonder and see what's what?"

So Tish and Archy began a little journey to Parthenon, and it was along the way that he told Tish he wanted to take her not just to Parthenon, but far, far away.

"I don't reckon as how that Man will ever come back," Archy said. "Even if He aint west, They'll keep Him in that House Pittle for the rest of His east. Even if They let Him go, He won't come back here. Holy House is a-gorn to be deserted like the other houses of Stay More, and then where would we be?

279

No, I think it's gonna be every feller for hisself, and Mockroach take the hindmost, and I don't aim to hang around and wait to see if Man ever comes back."

"Just which way do you plan to go?" Tish asked him.

"I've thought about it." He gestured with one of his sniffwhips toward the mountain, to the west, that some folks had called Mount Staymore. "I'd like to head thataway. I hear tell there's People up yonder live in fine houses."

"I've heard tell," she said, "that the nearest house, up that way, is a dozen furlongs off, and several creeks to cross."

"What of it?" he said. "Nobody never got nothing in this world without a little effort. It might take us a week or more to get there, but it'd be a good trip for us."

"Us?" she said.

"Me 'n you," he said mildly. He stopped. He entwined her sniffwhips almost playfully with his own. "Tish, honey, I wouldn't even start in to think about going by myself, without you. I'd lief as stay here in Stay More if you wouldn't go with me." He studied both her eyes up close, and added, "You *will* go with me, won't you?"

"Why, Archibald Tichborne, you haven't even proposed to me, yet," she said.

"What do you think I'm doing, right now?" he asked.

"I don't hear you saying it," she said.

"Don't make me put it in words," he protested. "I caint jist come right out and *speak* of marriage."

"Why not?"

"Wal . . . it's not . . . it's not manly."

"*Manly?*" She wondered if he meant manly in the manner of Lawrence Brace.

"Aw, heck, shoot," he complained, and kicked at pebbles with one fore gitalong. "You know what I mean," he protested. "It aint proper I should git down on my knees and perpose to ye, like folks used to do in the old-timey days."

"How do folks do it nowadays?" she wondered aloud.

"They jist git hitched," he said.

"And how do they do *that*?" she asked innocently.

"Wal, they find 'em a preacher, and he preforms the ceremony."

"The only preacher's your dad," she pointed out.

"That's right," he said. "And yonder he is!"

Their stroll had taken them to the yard of Parthenon, right back to the point where the procession of the arrow had originated, but now, instead of the Woman sitting in Her rocker on the porch, the porch was dominated by Brother Tichborne, who crouched on its edge as if he owned it, and crouching beside him was Tish's own mother! Keeping to the shadows behind them were three deacons of the church, Brothers Sizemore, Ledbetter, and Stapleton.

"Momma!" Tish squealed, and ran up the steps to greet her.

"Poppa!" Archy called, and ran right behind Tish, overtook her, and was the first to embrace his

281

parent. "I didn't know if you had drownded, or what!" Archy said to his father.

"I didn't know if you had drowned, or what," Tish said to her mother.

"I shore didn't know where-at you might've drownded yoreself," Josie said to her daughter. Then she asked, "Where's all yore brothers and sisters?"

Tish hung her head. "Jubal and them are down at Holy House," she reported. "*Some* of them. There aint but thirty-one left now, Momma. Our house got washed away in the flood, and we lost Julie, Japhet, Jenny, Jick, June, Jay, Jill, Jock, Jarvis, Jewel, Jayne, Junior . . ."

"Never mind," Josie interrupted her, and announced solemnly, "There is worse news. We have all lost your father."

"No!" Tish cried, and searched her mother's face for the truth of this, but her mother lowered her eyes. Tish looked to the preacher, who was solemnly nodding.

"The Woman destroyed him," Brother Tichborne announced. "She westered him, and threw him out with the garbage. I saw Her do it with my own eyes. Let us pray," he automatically added and lowered his head in prayer but instantly raised it again. "Wait a minute. There aint nobody to pray to. Man is west, aint He?" He glanced at his son.

"They don't know," Archy said, and related to his father the recent events at Holy House. "Didn't you'uns see the arrow? Didn't you'uns see the Great White Mouse?" he asked his father, the deacons, and Josie.

"Arrow?" they said. "Mouse?" they said. Archy

explained. Archy's father appeared to be distressed at the news that Squire Hank was still east.

Archy concluded, "Dad, didn't ye hear the bell ring? When the bell rung, it brought Human-people from all over the mountains down into Holy House, to get the Man and take Him to a House Pittle. It's jist like I been tellin ye, Dad, there aint one Man but many of 'em. The world's full of 'em!"

"I know, I know," Brother Tichborne said solemnly. "And Women too. And Woman is the worst. Before He drunk Hisself silly and shot Hisself in His own gitalong, Man was great, Man was good, Man was our King. But Woman . . ." The preacher's eyes shone with malice and there was a murderous rumble in his throat. "Woman is vile, and evil, and unmanly; She is not a Queen, but a Witch. I won't never worship Her."

"Then you aint a preacher no more?" Archy inquired of his father.

"I'm afraid not," Chid said. "I'm fixin to stay right here in Parthenon, but I won't never bend one knee in worship to Woman! I won't never go back to Holy House! I am now the Boss Squire of Parthenon, and I don't aim to let the Ingledews git it back! I will—"

The preacher ranted onward, but Tish could not listen. All she could think about was her westered father. She discovered that she was weeping.

When the ex-preacher paused to catch his breath, Archy interrupted, "Dad, if you aint a preacher no more, I don't guess you can marry me and Tish. If you aint a preacher, who is? How are we gonna git married?"

33.

Chid was stumped. Not by the question of his no longer being of the cloth, as it were, nor by the question of who else might still be a minister—Chid assumed that elsewhere in the world there were other ministers, albeit of different religions, Hindoo and such, none of them Crustian. In Stay More, Chid had been the only minister, the only direct spiritual descendant of Joshua Crust Himself. If he denied Man, wasn't he denying Crust also? This was a tricky question, but it wasn't the question that stumped Chid. The question that had Chid stumped was how his son could get married to Tish Dingletoon, who was, all unbeknownst to him, his sister, or at least his half-sister, offspring of that long-ago congress between Chid and Josie.

But what was wrong with that? Somehow, incest didn't bother Chid the way it had when he was still a parson and servant of Man. Now that he didn't have any evangelical responsibilities, it seemed to Chid that incest was just fine. Sisters and brothers, fathers and daughters, sex was sex, and a heap of fun. Thinking of it, he became impatient to enjoy his rights and privileges as Boss Squire of Parthenon, including his right to move into Josie's boudoir and act out that sexual paradise he kept conjuring up in his itching fantasies. He sure would like to give Josie a marble. For that matter, since he was going to enjoy *le droit du seigneur*, or *Jus primae noctis*, among his other rights as lord of the manor, he wouldn't mind giving a mar-

284

ble to Tish too, who was a whole lot younger and fresher and prettier than Josie. Chid licked his chops, appraising her.

And then he said to his son, "Well, Archy, I don't reckon I've forgot how to do a weddin. After all, I've married everbody in Stay More that ever got married, for the past year or so. If you and her aim to jine in wedlock, I can give ye the bonds of matrimony right here and now. Only it won't be *holy* matrimony. Might even be unholy matrimony, ye might say."

"Whatever's legal," Archy said.

"Son, anything *I* do, from here on out, is legal," Chid declared solemnly. "Okay. Dearly Beloved, we are gathered here tonight, not in the sight of Man, who is west or leastways gone off some'ers, nor in the sight of Woman, who—"

"Wait!" Tish said. "I haven't even said I will."

"That comes later," Chid pointed out patiently. "First, I have to ask *him*. Do you, Archibald, take this gal, Tish, to be yore lawful wedded wife, to have and to hold, in sickness and health, till west do ye part?"

"I do," Archy said.

"Okay. *Now* then, Tish, do you, Letitia, take this fine feller, Archy, to be yore lawful wedded husband, to love, honor, cherish and obey, in sickness and in health, till west do ye part?"

"No, I do not," Tish said.

Chid wondered if his tailprongs needed cleaning. In all the weddings he had officiated—four hundred or more, he had lost count—not once had the bride ever said anything other than a modest "Ah do" at this point in the ceremony. He regarded Tish with curiosity. Possibly, he realized, she was feeling be-reaved for her father, and was in mourning, and not really herself. "You don't?" he said.

She nodded her head. But then she shook her head. She was confused, obviously, and he tried coaching her, "When I ask that question, you're sup-posed to lower yore head and smile real sweet and say, 'I do.' Okay? Let's try it again. Do you, Letitia, take this feller, Archibald, to—"

"No," Tish said. "No. Stop. This aint a weddin!"

Chid looked to Josie for help, as if Josie might be able to put some sense into the poor girl's head.

"Hon," Josie said to her daughter, "watch yore manners. You're embarrassin me."

"Mother, I don't want to get married tonight," Tish protested. "How could we even have a weddin when we ought to be having Daddy's funeral?"

"Yore father done had his funeralization a week ago," Josie pointed out.

"But he wasn't west then," Tish said.

The girl had a point, Chid admitted, but it was academic, and besides, he wasn't in the mood for preaching any more funerals. For that matter, he wasn't in the mood for preaching the rest of this wed-ding. He didn't have to have the girl say "I do." As Boss Squire and Lord of the Manor, Chid had the right, among all his other droits, simply to decree the marriage, without the consent of either party. "Well, Dearly Beloved," he announced, "since we aint gittin full cooperation in this matter, looks like I'll jist have to git it all over with. I now pronounce you'uns husband and wife." He added, to Archy, "You may kiss the bride."

Archy tried to do his duty, but Tish pushed him away. "You can't do this!" she protested. "I aint married! I don't want to be 'Tish Tichborne.' It sounds like somebody clucking!"

The girl was probably in need of a good marbling, Chid decided, but it could wait until *noctis*. Meanwhile, the girl could probably use a good meal. Traditionally in the Ozarks the groom's family is supposed to sponsor the enfare, or wedding feed, which occurs the night *after* the wedding night, but the bride's family is responsible for the refreshments immediately following the wedding. Chid did some mental calculating, and determined that *he* was both the groom's family and the bride's family, since he was the bride's actual father, so he ought to be the host for all the eats. "Let's have the wedding feed, folks," Chid announced, and led the way into the Parthenon, towards the cookroom.

But the problem was, the Woman, confound Her witchy bones, had skipped supper. Maybe because with all of those gin-and-tonics She was sipping all afternoon, She hadn't had any appetite. Anyway, She hadn't had a blessit thing to eat for supper, and the floor of the cookroom contained not the faintest trace of crust or crumb, and the countertops had nothing except the lethal drops of gin and the unfilling tonic water and lime. When would the Woman return? It didn't appear that She was coming back tonight.

Chid's sniffwhips told him that *some*where in Parthenon was a cache of crusts and crumbs, but whenever he tried to fine-tune the direction of the signal, it only seemed to come from the vicinity of that same mantelshelf he had fallen off of, when the machine had said "ECLAIR!" so rudely to him. Perhaps the machine ate crusts and crumbs, and had a supply of them, but Chid wasn't about to climb up there again and mess around with it.

"Brother Sizemore," he said to one of his deacons, "suppose ye scoot up yonder to the mantelshelf in the Woman's sleepin room and see if ye caint find out where the smell of all them goodies is a-comin from?" Chid realized he would have to think of a better name for ole Leroy Sizemore than "Brother," because, without religion, they weren't brethering and sistering any more.

Leroy Sizemore climbed the mantel, with his sniffwhips flicking in every direction, and homed in on the source of the scent of the yum-yums. As he approached the Clock, it greeted him loudly with "NOUGAT!" and he duplicated exactly the plunge that Chid had taken the night before, off the shelf and down to the floor. After picking himself up, he sheepishly claimed, "Lost my balance," and then he said, "Shore nuff, they's a power of victuals up yonder inside thet machine."

They waited until the machine had chimed its nine bongs, then Chid dispatched Brothers Ledbetter and Stapleton up to investigate, and they returned with their mouths and touchers full of exotic foodstuffs.

"Stop!" Tish yelled angrily. "That's Sam's blancmange!" And she tried to pull Brother Stapleton's mouthful away from him. "This is Sam's prize mammon chiffon!" she cried. Any roosterroach who encounters another insect attempting to interfere with his feeding will quickly swallow whatever he's got in his mouth, and Brother Ledbetter nearly choked getting down his mouthful. "Oh no!" Tish cried. "You've eaten Sam's brazo demercedes!"

Chid wondered what was bothering the girl, but before he could put his concern into words, his son beat him to it. "Tish!" exclaimed Archy. "How do you know so much about Sam's stuff?!" The question seemed to stun the girl into realizing she had given away some secret; she hung her head and could not answer. "Have you been up to the Clock before?" Archy demanded of her. She continued silent, but feebly nodded her head. "*When?!*" he asked, but she would not speak. "Maybe," he said, "you and me had better have us a little talk." He took her by one of her gitalongs and said, "Excuse us, folks," and led her away, into another room.

"So that," Chid observed, staring upward, "is Squire Sam's famous Clock?"

"Yeah, and it's jist chock full o' goodies!" Brother Stapleton declared.

"Well, we might as well start the weddin feed without the principals," Chid declared. "Gene and Stan"—for so he had decided to begin calling Stapleton and Ledbetter—"you fellers scoot back up there and jist git all the food out and kick it off the mantelshelf, and we'll stack it up right here."

Soon the floor beneath the mantel had a sizeable little pile of assorted tidbits stacked up, and Chid was attempting to sample all of them, remembering, of course, his manners, and offering Josie a sample of each also.

"My, my," Josie commented, eating. "Did ye ever? If this aint the. I swan. Fancy! Lord a mercy. Mmm-mmm. Hot diggety dog! O sweet papa."

Chid was mildly concerned that the transfer of the arsenal of food from the Clock to the floor of the Woman's sleeping room might increase the danger that the Woman, returning, would sweep it all away. But he dismissed this thought for several reasons, one, the Woman didn't look as if She intended to return, not tonight, anyway; two, the wedding party would probably consume the whole pile before morning, anyhow; and three, he wasn't a damn bit afraid of the Woman, Who didn't scare him in the slightest. But just as a precaution, he said to Brother Sizemore, "Leroy, eat yore fill, and then git out thar on the porch and keep a eye out in case the Woman comes back." Leroy gobbled his fill and did as he was told.

The others settled in for some serious eating, making determined inroads on the pile of wedding feeds. Archy and Tish had better get theirselfs back before too long, Chid chuckled, or else they wouldn't get nary a bite! Chid was determined, for once in his life, to gluttonize. God, who had created him, had intended for him to be an eater. God had given the roosterroach a svelte, streamlined, trim body only to enable him to squeeze into tight places for purposes of escape. Chid had no further intention of running away from anything or anyone; he didn't need to be skinny; he could afford, at last, to reach his full girth.

And Josie, his new consort, always somewhat pleasantly plump, could now afford to take on the dimensions of a Queen of the Colony. Just as the Queen of Termites, their remote cousins, was an obese giantess compared with her subjects, it was proper that Chid's queen outweigh all the other females of Stay More. She didn't have to look like a roly-poly, let alone the grotesquely bloated Termite Queen, but it would give Josie a certain stature in the eyes of other Stay Morons if her volume came to match that of the—yes, Chid permitted himself to use the word, the King. "King," he said aloud, testing the sound of it.

"What did you say, hon?" Josie inquired.

Chid liked the little endearment she attached to the end of her question. They were going to get along together famously. "Mmmmph, um," he replied, and passed her another piece of the mercedes, or whatever Tish had called it.

Still and all, Chid reflected, as his imagination allowed him to step deeper and deeper into the waters of monarchy, he was going to miss certain aspects of the ministry. As King, how would he ever find time to continue his hobby of local history and genealogy? No, he would have to give up interviewing little old ladies and learning the pedigrees of all the Stay More folks. He wouldn't mind giving up the tedious preaching of funeralizations and weddings and baptisms and Wednesday-night prayer meetings, and he certainly wouldn't miss attending the teas of the Ladies' Aid Society and giving pep talks and sermonettes to the Crustian Young People's Fellowship.

But he was going to miss—yes, he had to admit it—he was going to miss his special relationship with the Lord. Never mind that the Lord had turned out to be a nondeity: a drunken wastrel unworthy of simple love, let alone veneration. All his life Chid had devoted his time and his energy and his thoughts to the service of that Man; he had come to identify with that Man; he had believed that that Man had created him, Chid, if not in His own image, at least in the image of what He, Man, deemed the most intelligent and best-designed of all insects. For all His foibles and frailties and flaws, it was still sad to lose Him.

"DIVINITY!" cried the Clock, and Chid knew that this time, without question, the Clock or whatever Cosmic Force controlled it was speaking directly to him. He spat out his mouthful of blancmange.

"What's the matter, hon?" Josie asked. "You find a fishbone in your food, tee hee?"

"Divinity," said Chid, with much feeling.

"Naw, that aint none of that," Josie observed. "Tish said it was 'block mash,' or somethin. That there is the divinity." She reached out and grabbed some white stuff off the pile and offered it to him.

Chid rejected it. "Divinity," he said again. "The Clock said 'divinity' to me. I have lost divinity."

"Aw, he wasn't speakin to you, personal," Josie said. "He calls everbody that."

But Chid prostrated himself and prayed. His prayer was interrupted by the return of his son. Archy did not have Tish with him, and he looked terrible. He was grumbling and mumbling a string of profanities and obscenities. Josie offered the white stuff to him, but he declined with a curse.

Chid was disturbed by his son's indelicate language. "What's eatin ye, boy?" he asked.

Archy raised his drooping head and regarded his father with large eyes that were stricken. "Tish aint a virgin," he declared.

"How could ye tell?" Josie inquired.

"She told me. She confessed. Her and Squire Sam have done went and done it. Right up yonder in that Clock. Reckon you'll have to unmarry us, Dad."

"Divorce aint so simple as that, boy," Chid said. "You have to take it to court, and get a Justice of the Peace to approve."

"Who's the Justice of the Peace?" Archy asked.

"That would be ole Doc Swain," Chid announced.

Archy hung his head again, and muttered, "Wal, I might as well git on down to see him, then."

"Where's Tish?" Josie asked.

"I don't keer," Archy said. "I don't honestly keer. She could be in Hell for all I keer."

"Son, don't take it so bad," Chid attempted to comfort his boy. "Maybe it would make ye feel better to know that Tish was your half-sister, so it would've been incest anyhow."

"*What?!*" Archy demanded.

"Aint that right, Josie?" Chid said.

"*What?!*" Josie demanded.

"Why, Josie, don't ye remember?" Chid asked gently and fondly. "Don't ye remember that night when me and you was out in the grass after my brush arbor meetin, last fall?"

"Huh?" Josie said, and seemed to try to recall. "Was that *you*? Whoever it was, I couldn't see him because we was jined end to end, the way it's supposed to be, you know. Was that *you*, Reverend?"

It was the first time anyone had called him "Reverend" ever since the late lamented Jack Dingletoon had employed the title, and Chid realized he missed it. "Why, of course it was, Josie, and I gave ye the marble that Tish come out of."

"You couldn't a done that, Reverend," Josie replied, "because I had done met up with handsome Jack Dingletoon, and he had done sweet-talked me into having his marble, and, as anybody knows, once a lady has took a marble, she can't take another'n."

"*What?!*" Chid demanded.

This interesting discussion was interrupted by the abrupt appearance of Leroy Sizemore, the lookout, who was scampering into the room, calling out, "Chid! Chid! He's coming!"

"*He?*" said Chid. "It was *She* I tole ye to look out for."

Leroy was all out of breath and he had to insufflate noisily through all his spiracles before he could continue, "Naw, I don't mean Him. I mean *him*."

"*Whom?*" Chid demanded.

"Squire Hank! He's comin this way, up the Roamin Road. He's comin *home!*"

"Who's with him?" Chid asked. "Is Sam with him?"

"Nossir, he's alone."

"Then what are we worryin about?" Chid demanded.

294

34.

Sam went out for a stroll. It was after midnight, the air was clear and clean, the sky was black and spangled with a zillion zillion stars. *I might be one of only two squires in Stay More*, Sam reflected, *but there are a zillion zillion other squires in Arkansas alone, and that's just a little part of this world, which is only one of a zillion zillion worlds circling through the universe. Is it not enough to learn one's own garden?* Sam noticed that the heavy rains had nurtured the burgeoning of plants, and particularly weeds, the roosterroaches of the plant kingdom, eating up the spare, leftover patches of soil not taken by the cultivated plants. Dandelion, plantain, dock, horsenettle, toadflax, sowthistle: their names, to Sam, suggested unwanted, creeping, striving, but thriving things, like roosterroaches, despised by man but useful, each with its purpose in the grand scheme. When he was a child, Sam used to climb the tall ragweed, a beautiful, large-bladed, spreading, rank, and succulent plant, as high as a dozen feet or more above the ground; he had felt an affinity for it even before he learned that it was a pest, like himself.

A drought was coming, Sam knew. The one thing certain about too much rainfall was that it would be followed by too little, or none. Meanwhile, the weeds took hold, and thrived, and perfumed the night air with their vegetable voices. Sam hoped he would live long enough to understand the peculiar communication of one plant speaking to another in the night, by fragrance alone. He needed no tailprongs to study the voices of plants. But thinking of tailprongs made him think of what he was deliberately avoiding the thought of, with all this meditation on stars and weeds: Tish, and her power to talk gently to him in signs. There were now only two persons he could "hear": Hoimin with his thrumming boom, and Tish with her soft gestures. How could he hope to exercise his duties as squire of Stay More if he could not hear his townsfolk? Even with Hoimin's help, with Tish's too, he could not listen to his people . . . or minister to them, and he realized that now that Chid Tichborne was abandoning the faith, he would have to replace him, not as an espouser of the Crustian religion but as a pastor of sorts in a confused pastoral populace. If not a pastor, a kind of schoolmaster, perhaps. . . .

His eye fell upon the distant little tower of the schoolhouse. Sam found himself stopped in the middle of Roamin Road, with two directions to turn, a choice to make: north toward Parthenon, to reclaim his Clock and his girlfriend, or south toward the schoolhouse, to reclaim his hearing. If he chose the latter, he would not return before dawn. And he had no guarantee that the expedition would succeed, little faith in the efficacy of the cure.

He could not decide. While he stood immobile in Roamin Road, turning first toward the north and gazing with longing at Parthenon's roof, and then turning south and trying to make out the belfry of the ancient schoolhouse, another roosterroach approached him, and his sniffwhips told him it was his father. "Morsel, Dad," he said.

His father said something he could not hear; he

assumed it was simply a return of the greeting. But then his father began talking, and Sam could tell from the expressions on his father's face and the gestures of his sniffwhips that he was not simply making idle conversation; he was talking seriously to his son. Futilely Sam strained his tailprongs to hear.

His father's tone indicated that now his father was asking him a question, and Sam had to remind him, "Dad, you know I can't hear very well."

His father looked irritated, and then committed a mistake that many of normal hearing make toward the hearing-impaired: he began to pronounce each word slowly, tonelessly, in an artificial rhythm that made it impossible for Sam to re-create a coherent sentence from the sounds. "How," he thought he heard his father say, "come" seemed to be the following word, "her" was pronounced imperfectly, "to" seemed to open up one end of an infinitive that went on infinitely, followed by a rising inflection of a question mark following "that."

"I'm sorry, Dad, I just can't tell what you're saying," Sam declared.

His father's expression changed to disgust, and then he attempted a crude sign language of his own: Squire Hank pointed at himself, he pointed at the road, he pointed in the direction of Parthenon, he made the motions of walking, and he said one word Sam could hear clearly: "home."

Sam was able to determine that his father was declaring his intention of returning to Parthenon. The decision that Sam was having so much trouble making was being made for him: he would have to go with his father, to help his father overcome any resistance from Chid and the deacons. But Sam was forced also to confront his reluctance, not to tussle with Chid, but to find that Archy might have proposed to Tish. He realized that he did not want to see Tish until after she had successfully escaped from Archy, if she wanted to, and returned to him.

His father made one more unintelligible statement, then turned to go. "Dad, I'll go with you," Sam offered, and walked alongside. But his father stopped, shook his head, said something else, and gestured for Sam to return to Holy House. "No, Dad, you might have trouble with Chid, and you'll need me," Sam protested. His father again shook his head, stamped his gitalong, and pointed at Holy House, then left his son standing there as he moved at a rapid clip toward Parthenon.

Sam felt ashamed, both of his own indecisiveness and his inability to hear his father. He muttered, to his father's disappearing back, "The next time you see me, I'll hear you."

Then he turned and marched resolutely in the direction of the schoolhouse.

The journey to the schoolhouse took the rest of the night. No roosterroach in recent memory had made the journey, and there was no scent of anyone's spit anywhere along the trail . . . or along the way, for there was no trail. The footsteps of the Woman had mashed down the grass and weeds in places, but not enough to clear a path for Sam, who walked under and through the thick forests of grass. He encountered hostile crickets, and was required to box a few of them out of his way. He encountered a fearsome Santa Fe, and had to fly above it. He was caught in the net of a funnel-web spider, and had to fight and kill the spider before he could laboriously break loose from the sticky ropes. Then, within prongshot of the schoolhouse, if there had been anyone there to hear his cry, he was pounced upon by a tarantula, who surely would have crushed him in its jaws, had he not danced a wild tarantella, whirling beyond the creature's grasp.

He was exhausted, and the first slice of dawn was served upon the distant ridge when he gained the steps of the schoolhouse and collapsed upon them to rest. He did not rest for long. Soon, he entered the building and found his way to the bell-rope, so recently burnished by Sharon's hands and therefore still smelling strongly of Her. He climbed beyond Her scent.

The bell-rope was coarse and easy to cling to, but it seemed to rise forever. He had climbed only half-way, too far to fall but still too far to go, when he felt but could not hear, bouncing off his prongs and his very cutin, the shrill echo that is broadcast by the vicious *vespertilionidus*, the big brown bat, in search of its prey by echo-location. Sam saw the bat at the same instant the bat located Sam—not only with bouncing echoes but with vision—and prepared to strike. Sam's reflexes were much too slow to avoid the flying mammal. The bat's needle-sharp teeth were opening to strike, and the evil eyes and ears were both focused on him. Sam did not even have time for his whole life to flash through his memory.

At the instant Sam braced himself for his fatal

impalement on the bat's teeth, a great insect interceded! A broad-winged roosterroach, screaming a curse that drowned out the bat's echo-signal, flew into the space between the bat's teeth intended for Sam, and bit the bat on the lips! Then bit the bat again! And again! The bat's wings were in disarray as it tried to stop its flight and reverse course, and the great-winged roosterroach kept attacking it. The turbulence of the thrashing wings almost blew Sam off the rope, to which he clung desperately. Now the vicious bat was totally frightened and cowed into a frantic retreat, but as it tried to fly away, the roosterroach kept striking and biting until the bat decamped. Then the roosterroach flew back to Sam, and hovered before him like a hummingbird.

The roosterroach was a stranger, to put it mildly; at least Sam had never seen him around Stay More before, or at least not in conscious "reality"; perhaps Sam had seen him in dreams or in stories. He was the most powerful-looking, not to say the handsomest roosterroach that Sam had ever seen, dreamt, or imagined, but the look he gave Sam was enough to freeze the ichor in his veins. He spoke. "You may proceed." He motioned for Sam to continue his climb up the bell-rope. Sam was stunned to realize that he could hear these words clearly, although the stranger had not raised his voice. It took a moment before Sam could raise one gitalong above the other and continue his climb up the bell-rope, and the roosterroach flew along beside him, in complete defiance of the known fact that the flight of a roosterroach may never last more than a few seconds.

Sam was not convinced that he *was* a rooster-roach, but Sam continued climbing until he reached the bell, and stood precariously on the iron arm where the rope terminated. The stranger alighted and confronted him. With his wings at rest, the stranger did not seem quite so large; still, he was much bigger than Sam.

"Who are you?" Sam asked.

The stranger laughed. It was the first laughter that Sam had been able to pick up on his weakened tailprongs in a long time; it was almost a tonic, to hear laughter again. Then the stranger introduced himself by saying, "Most of your kinsmen call me the Mockroach, but that is not my name."

"You . . . you're Satan?" Sam asked.

Again the laughter. "Old Scratch. Old Split-foot. Old Harry. I go by many names."

"You don't look like the Devil," Sam observed.

Again, the hearty guffaws, which made Sam understand why the creature was called the Mockroach. Was the laughter mocking? "How does the Devil look?" the Mockroach asked.

"Well . . . diabolical," Sam ventured. "Sinister. Fiendish. You could almost pass for a nice guy."

The stranger scarcely stopped laughing. "I'd like to think that my intentions are benevolent, not evil."

"You saved me," Sam said.

"For a while there you were doing just fine, handling whatever came your way. But that bat was a different proposition."

"Then you've been looking out for me?" Sam

turned the observation into a question at the last moment. "You know everything that's going on?"

The Mockroach bowed, and smiled, but said nothing.

"I can't believe you're real," Sam declared. "But here you are, aren't you? When I was little, I heard the wildest stories about you. I suppose they're all true. I didn't believe them, but nobody would believe me if I told them how you scared that bat away." The Mockroach continued his almost mocking smile. "Can you tell me," Sam requested, "if Man still lives?"

"Mankind still lives," the Mockroach said.

"But Lawrence Brace . . . does *He* live?"

The Mockroach would not answer. Instead he said, "Behold the bell," and gestured at it, the huge, bronze, black shape beside them, its shape comparable only to that of certain flowers Sam had seen in bloom, canterburies and lilies, but hard, impervious, and infinitely larger than any flower. "Read it," the Mockroach commanded him.

Around one edge of the rim of the bell were letters cast into the metal, and Sam read these aloud: "Samuels Foundry Works, St. Louis."

"Not those," the Mockroach said. "Higher up."

Higher on the rim was an inscription in Latin, which Sam could not even pronounce, let alone understand:

Nunquam aedepol temere tinnit tintinnabulum
Nisi quis illud tractat aut movet, mutum est

"Now what does that mean?" Sam asked.

"You'll find out before this story is done."

"Story? Is this only a story?"

"Everything that I become involved in," said the Mockroach "is only a story. To hear them tell it." He laughed once more, at his own joke this time, and then reminded Sam, "Don't forget what you came up here for," and at the instant Sam remembered, the Mockroach flew away as quickly as he had come.

For a long time, before he could continue on the errand that had brought him here, Sam pondered whether the Mockroach had been "real." But certainly that bat had been real, and Sam would not be "real" himself any longer if the bat had eaten him.

The basic structure of the bell and its housing was much less complicated than that of his Clock: cast into the top of the bell was a large bolt which rested and balanced upon cradles in the mountings at the sides of the bell, from one of which sprang a metal lever attached to the end of the bell-rope, the pulling of which caused the bell to rock back and forth. Its motion was lubricated by grease in the cradles: this grease was very old, and dried, and caked, but the friction of its recent employment had thinned and solved the grease enough that Sam could daub a bit upon his touchers and taste it; it must have been rendered from hog lard; it was rancid and bitter. But he chewed off enough of it to smear along the lengths of his tailprongs. He anointed his prongs thoroughly. Nothing happened. He felt foolish. One of Doc's old wives' tales of a home remedy, that was more likely to dissolve his tailprongs than to treat them. Sam wondered how long he was supposed to wait, or whether the treatment required repeated applications at intervals; he became impatient and nervous. Daylight was in full upheaval now; somewhere roosters, toward whom he felt not even the affiliation of part of his generic name, were crowing an announcement he could not hear: WORK THE HERD OF LURKING DIRTY BIRDS!

The long ordeal of his journey to the schoolhouse and up the belfry, his encounter with the Mockroach, and now the uncertainty, took their toll, and he realized how many hours had passed since he had fed, but had nothing to eat now except vintage hog lard. He was hungry and tired and impatient and nervous and felt foolish.

At last he fell asleep, resting upon the framework of the bell housing, and a pigeon flew down and studied him and said to him, "You! You! You!" but Sam did not hear, nor wake. The pigeon decided he was not edible, and did not eat him . . . or perhaps the Mockroach was still protecting him.

He slept all day, and when he woke at evening, it was because he had been awakened by the music of katydids, and the melodies of cicadas, and, yes, the sweet strains of crickets, and, yes yes, the lovely tunes of frogs, and yes yes yes, even the far-distant aria of his very own Clock calling, "EGG"—the last song it ever sang.

35.

Eight o'clock, Doc thinks idly, or even unconsciously, or conscious only of the fact that it is the
time the Loafer's Court usually begins to assemble on
his porch, but now he has the porch all to himself.
Has? "Ortent thet to be 'had'?" he wonders aloud,
trying to get the tense correct. No, he has the porch
to himself, and it is the present. The eighth hour, and
the night after the leaving of Man, and of Woman.
Neither has returned, and the Woman has not been
home to tend to Parthenon, to wind the Clock, which
is an eight-day affair that was last wound nine days
ago, and now, with the strike of "EGG," has breathed
its last.

There is no more time, in the counting sense, for
Clocks or roosterroaches, and Doc Swain sits, or
crouches, on the porch of his clinic, removed from
time, aware that the Loafer's Court is not convening
at its usual hour—or, wait a minute, the days have
gotten longer and the nights shorter, and it's still daylight at eight o'clock, this night in early June, and the
Loafer's Court might or might not come along later.
Fent Chism will not be there, because he's west, and
Squire Hank possibly won't, because Squire Hank,
the fool, has gone home to Parthenon and likely got
hisself westered by the preacher and his gang.

Nobody but me and the spiders, Doc observes, and
even though it is still daylight at eight o'clock, the
spiders have gone to sleep for the night. This is the
way things ought to be, he reflects. This is how Stay

More should be all the time: no excitement, nothing happening, a full belly, and the cool of the evening (but it's a mite too dry and don't look like it aims to rain again for quite a while), and the old familiar sounds out there in the yard and the road and the grass a-stirrin themselves up into the Purple Symphony. Doc Swain could just sit here forever, and hardly even breathe. Maybe spit now and again, not to mark his space, nor because he's chewing tobacco or anything, but just to spit for the pure cussed sake of spitting.

Now that the Clock has stopped, Time is resting. It isn't the Woman's fault, for Her failure to wind the Clock well before leaving, nor for Her failure to return and wind it again. In the stillness, Doc reflects that the Woman ought to have returned today, if not late last night, after seeing that the Man was safely in the House Pittle. Is She required to stay in the House Spittle too? Is She giving blood transfusions? Is the Man's heart hooked up to Hers? Or, perish the thought, if Man has westered, or was already west to begin with before They took Him from Stay More, is the Woman simply busy handling the funeral arrangements, or the arrangements for the shipment of the body to whatever place Man had come from before? Doc cannot understand why the Woman is not returning. He can detect no sign of life over at Parthenon . . . . although he knows that there is *some* roosterroach life there, Chid and his gang cavorting around and stirring up mischief.

One other possibility occurs to Doc, to explain Woman's non-return: She is so fond of Man that She is staying by His side. *Yeah, that's probably it,* Doc says to himself, and wishes there were others around, any of the old loafers, to say it to.

As if in response to his wish, one of the old loafers appears, but he is clearly more a patient than a loafer. Leroy Sizemore is missing two gitalongs, and dragging two others behind the two that will still work; one of his sniffwhips is cracked in two, with half dangling uselessly across his face. The remains of his wings are in tatters. He cannot even climb up to the porch where Doc is crouching, but halts out in the yard, barely able to raise his head and groan, "Doc, I've got some complaints."

"It shore looks like it, Brother Sizemore," Doc observes.

"I aint 'Brother' Sizemore no more," Leroy declares. "I aint no brother nothin." He takes three more steps in Doc's direction, and collapses into the dust, lacking only the belly-up position to appear completely west.

Doc hobbles down off the porch and feels for Leroy's pulse, which is still faintly beating. "What happened to ye, son?" Doc asks.

Without raising his head from the dust, Leroy narrates, "We was mobbed by Squire Hank. He come into Partheeny and druv us all out."

"All seven of you?" Doc asks.

"They wasn't but four of us," Leroy protests, as if the reduced numbers made the story more likely. "Not countin Chid's boy Archy, I mean. Just us three used-to-be deacons, and Chid. The other three used-to-be deacons is used-to-be, period. I reckon they westered in the flood. But just me and Stan and Gene,

307

who aint deacons of nothin no more on account of Chid has done went and did away with religion, and we was about to resign from whatever fellowship Chid had in mind for us, when Squire Hank come back home to Partheeny and threw us all out."

"*Threw* you out?" Doc asks.

"Yeah, sort of. He flang ole Gene right out the door, and picked up ole Stan and chunked him off the porch, then he lit into me, and I was stupid enough to try to fight back, and look what he done to me!"

"What did he do to Chid?" Doc asks.

"Lord knows," Leroy says. "Naw, the Lord don't know, does He? Wherever He is. Archy says some human beans come and took His body away. He aint in Holy House no more, is He?" Doc shakes his head, and Leroy asks, "Do you think I'll easter long enough to see Holy House again, and my wife and kids?"

"You ort to be in the House Pittle," Doc declares.

"Say what?"

"Let's see if we caint git you inside, so's ye can lay easy and rest a good bit," Doc says, and helps Leroy struggle up the porch and into the infirmary. A canopy of cobwebs rises above Leroy's bed, but the spiders have gone to sleep for the night, and they won't bother Leroy anyhow. In fact, those ordinary house spiders will help, because the sticky strands of their webs are good for binding and dressing Leroy's wounds.

Before the night is over, Doc has two other patients in his house pittle, ex-deacons Gene Stapleton and Stan Ledbetter. The former lapses into unconsciousness and possible coma, but the latter is able to talk enough to corroborate Leroy's story of the eviction of the three of them from Parthenon by Squire Hank, and, although he had not witnessed it, the presumed banishment of Chid too.

"What about Archy and Tish?" Doc asks.

"Him and her is hitched," Stan declares, "so the Squire tole 'em they might as well stay in Partheeny for their honeymoon."

Doc does all he can for his patients, although it appears that Gene Stapleton is a goner. Doc wishes he had a nurse or two to help out. What's a house pittle without a nurse? Doc doesn't even have a receptionist. In his mind's eye he sees the House Pittle where Lawrence Brace lies, attended and waited on by a receptionist, a secretary, a registered nurse, a practical nurse, a nurse's aide, a respiratory therapist, a dietitian, and the health insurance officer, not to mention twelve different kinds of doctors, and an orderly. The human race is quite a bit advanced over the roosterroach race, Doc reflects, and allows himself a fleeting moment of self-pity.

But there isn't all that much to be done in his house pittle, and he knows it. Once the missing git-alongs are swabbed and cleaned and wrapped in cob-web to regenerate (or, like Doc's own unregenerate legs, have healthy stubs), and the patient is made comfortable and given an occasional temperature check and pulse check, there really isn't much to do. Often Doc can return to his porch and watch the world go by, or what little of it happens to be going by on this dull, still, typical lazy night. A youth, Freddy Coe, is ambling along the way, and he pauses just long enough to wave his whips and say, "Morsel, Doc."

"Morsel, Freddy," Doc returns.

The boy stops, and twitches his whips. "You got some sick folks in thar, smells like?"

"Yeah, got me a regular house pittle," Doc says, with no little pride. A thought occurs to him. "How'd you like a job, as orderly?"

"Job?" says Freddy. "Orderly?"

"It don't take much," Doc assures him. "I got three fellers banged up kind of bad, and I need somebody to help me look after 'em."

"Maw says I'm right *dis*orderly," Freddy confesses.

"Wouldn't ye like to be a doctor when you grow up?" Doc suggests. "I could train ye how."

"Grow up?" Freddy says, offended. "Doc, I done reached my imago last week, didn't ye notice?"

Sure enough, the boy is full grown, in imago, but it's hard for Doc to realize that children like Freddy, who had been coming to Doc for treatment ever since Freddy was in his first instar, have a habit of getting mature and old. "All the more reason I can use ye," Doc says.

"Wal, I reckon there are worse things to do," Freddy allows, and climbs the steps.

And Freddy is right. There are worse things to do. Thus childless Doc Swain, without sons of his own to follow in his footsteps, acquires a protégé, pupil, and intern. His first night on the job, Freddy is green and slow to learn. He wonders if he should remove the cobwebs from the house pittle, and has to be instructed in their uses. He is told the names of the sleeping spiders but is not eager to be introduced to them when they wake. He is shown the store of edibles and given a feeding schedule for the three patients, or rather the two who can eat, but he is not able to resist consuming a share of the food himself. But the patients like him, and they ask him to run an errand for them: go to Holy House and summon their wives and children to come to the house pittle during visiting hours.

Freddy asks Doc, "What did ye say the name of this business is?"

"House pittle," Doc tells him again for the third or fourth time.

"Okay. When is visiting hours?"

Doc hasn't decided, and he tries to decide, but remembers that Time is resting, the present tense is with us, and we are stuck in the here and now, without any hours. "Oh, just whenever," he tells Freddy, and Freddy receives permission to run his errand.

Almeda Sizemore comes from Holy House with her twenty-three children to visit Leroy, Claudine Ledbetter brings her seventeen children to visit Stan, but poor Gene Stapleton the goner is also a bachelor and has no visitors except his old mother, Hester. Even villains have mothers, not to mention wives and children. Did you ever think of that?

"What?" says Freddy.

"In any story," Doc tells his pupil, "the bad guy, regardless of how bad, still has mothers and sweethearts and wifes just like all the rest of us, jist as much as the good guy, if not more so."

311

Freddy mulls over this philosophy. With the house pittle full of visitors, he would just as soon sit out here on the porch with Doc, watching the world go by and mulling over philosophical thoughts. "You may be right," he allows, to his teacher.

The world goes by. A stately, strong-looking roosterroach comes up the road, his head held high. "Morsel, Doc," he says, and climbs the porch.

"MORSEL, SAM," Doc says, raising his voice so much that Freddy jumps. To his student he explains, "Squire Sam is deef as a post."

"What's a post?" Freddy wants to know.

"A figure of speech," Doc says. He asks of Squire Sam, "HOW'S EVERTHANG OVER AT HOLY HOUSE?"

"I haven't been over there since last night," Sam says. "I thought maybe you could tell me, but I see you've moved back to your clinic."

"IT'S A HOUSE PITTLE NOW," Doc declares, and attempts to pantomime the care and treatment and feeding of patients. Freddy joins in with the pantomime, especially the feeding part, but is overdoing the pantomime to the point of clowning. "He's just deef, Freddy," Doc cautions. "He aint stupid." To Sam he invites, "COME LOOK WHO WE GOT." He leads Sam into the house pittle and shows him the three villains.

"What happened to them?" Sam whispers,

Doc does not whisper. "YORE DAD WHOPPED THE SOUP OUTEN 'EM."

"Oh," Sam says, and manages to figure it all out, without any further yelling from Doc or pantomiming. The ladies are looking accusingly at Sam, as

312

if he were the assailant who had mutilated their loved ones. Sam returns to the porch, and crouches. He stares in the direction of Parthenon.

"His sweetheart is up yonder at Partheeny," Doc explains to Freddy. "Squire Sam don't know it, but his sweetheart has done went and married another feller, Archy Tichborne, the preacher's boy, and they're up yonder honeymooning at that house." Doc raises his voice and asks Sam, "YOU FIXIN TO GO HOME?" Sam doesn't answer for a while. Doc says to Freddy, "I don't know if I should warn him, or not." Freddy shakes his head.

"Maybe not," Sam says at length. "Maybe I ought to just go live in Holy House, and watch out for things in this corner of Stay More."

"GOOD IDEE," Doc says. "YORE CLOCK HAS DONE STOPPED ANYHOW."

"Yes," Sam says. "I know." Doc wonders how he knows. Has someone told him? He can't hear the Clock striking, or rather he can't hear the Clock *not* striking, which is even harder to hear than the Clock striking. Sam adds, "We're stuck in the present tense."

"That's what I figured," Doc agrees. "But maybe not forever. Maybe the Man and the Woman will come back." He realizes he isn't raising his voice, that he has wasted his words. He starts to repeat himself, "THAT'S WHAT I—" but Sam interrupts.

"The present tense can't be cured by starting the Clock again, or by restoring what has been lost. The present tense always creates a mood of expectancy. But maybe expectancy sometimes lasts forever."

"Freddy, are you payin attention?" Doc asks of

313

his protégé. "That's pure-dee genuine philosophy, and Squire Sam is going to be our philosopher. We've had enough of preachers and religion. Now we're going to have some philosophy!" Doc wishes he could volunteer to be a deacon in whatever kind of church Sam is going to establish.

"Is Man gonna come back?" Freddy inquires of the new philosopher.

"You'll have to ask it louder," Doc tells Freddy. "Speak up, so's he can hear you."

"Yes, Man will always come back," Sam says without waiting for Freddy to repeat himself. "But that's future tense." Then, seeing that Doc looks astounded that he can hear, he adds, "Doc, you know, that grease from the mountings of a bell recently rung really works."

INSTAR THE SIXTH:
The Convert

36.

Though they do not exactly sleep together, Tish and Archy retire for the daylight hours in each other's company to the inside of the vanity in Sharon's bathroom, where they hide before the wrath of Squire Hank, who has banished the three deacons from Parthenon, has chased Chidiock Tichborne from one end of the house to the other without catching him, and has told Archy that he and his "bride" are welcome to spend the day but must vacate the premises at sunset. Tish has tried to protest to the Squire that she and Archy are not actually married; she has wanted to return to Holy House in search of Sam and her good friend Hoimin, but Squire Hank, in a foul mood, hasn't listened to a word she has said. Now she and Archy, not before having a newlyweds' quarrel that has virtually estranged them and left her in copious tears, are attempting to sleep inside this vanity, and Archy at least has been able to fall into fitful slumber.

Archy has declared his intention to get them unmarried as soon as he can present the case to the Justice of the Peace, who is Doc Swain. As soon as he gets them unmarried, Archy intends to strike out alone for Mount Staymore or the world beyond. It has been his fondest wish to take Tish with him, but he does not want a nonvirgin even as a traveling companion. Now he feels no love for her. "I wouldn't give ye a marble if you begged for it!" he has declared.

Did she err in telling him of her brief affair with Squire Sam? He had demanded the whole truth; she had had no choice, but stopped short of telling him she had borne an easteregg. She had had to explain how she knew the names of all the collectibles in Sam's food treasury. Archy had already guessed that there was something going on between Sam and Tish, what with the way Sam had saved her life by spoiling Man's aim of a bullet at her, the consequences of which had created all this turmoil in Stay More. Archy had even become friends with Sam during the nights they attempted to do something for Man, and, while Sam had told Archy nothing about his feelings for Tish, Archy guessed that they were "sweethearts." Tish simply had to confess to what Archy already suspected, and Tish had never told a lie in her life.

She can understand Archy's bitterness and it hurts her, for she really likes Archy. If Sam had not come into her life, she would have been thrilled at the prospect of being married to Archy. Any girl in Stay More would give her right sniffwhip to be Archy's wife. Compared with Sam, Archy is so matter-of-fact, down to earth, commonsensical, not to mention much more handsome. Sam's not bad-looking at all, but he just doesn't have Archy's big eyes and firm mandibles and sleek wings. And somehow Tish feels much more comfortable with Archy. Sam, even apart from his deafness, seems somehow remote, unnatural, not of this world. He is not "just folks," the way Archy is. He is too different, even though it is unlikely that he will ever want to live again in that peculiar apartment inside the Clock, now that the Clock has stopped.

Will Sharon ever come home and wind the Clock? What would life be like for Tish if she stayed here in Parthenon when Sharon returns? Even if Sharon returns, and Tish doubts it as much as Archy does, Tish is not certain she would want to live with Sam in Parthenon (assuming, of course, he ever asked her to). She would get lonesome for the folks of Carlott and Holy House, for her brothers and sisters, her mother and f—. Tish thinks again of her westered father, and sheds another tear.

Unable to sleep, she climbs to the top of the vanity and explores it, half-blinded by daylight and stumbling among the paraphernalia that Woman uses to prettify Herself, although Tish cannot at first determine the function of each of the items: the brush and the comb are obviously for the hair, but what are all the plastic rollers for? And the board with thousands of grains of sand stuck to it? Is that for cleaning the teeth? The various bottles and jars, tubes and cylinders, vials and compacts intrigue her, and, although she can read, she can only guess at their contents and uses.

She is not alone. She turns and sees Archy approaching her, stiffly, his gitalongs moving strangely along the countertop, and, more strangely, her sniff-whips detect the unmistakable odor of his slumber-scent. He is asleep, yet walking! His eyes are vacant. As he moves toward her, he murmurs in sad, despairing tones, "West! west! west!"

She is so startled she cannot speak, but she is not afraid of him. She waits. He comes up to her, and lifts her up in his strong touchers with the aid of his fore-gitalongs. He carries her.

"My wife—west, west!" he says.

He carries her toward the edge of the countertop. Does he intend to throw her off? Or, in his dream, does he imagine he can fly away with her? Is the "west" he keeps repeating the west of his intended directional destination, or is it the west of nonexistence? What is he doing with her? At the edge of the countertop he stops, holds her even higher for a moment above his head, and she has a panoramic view down below of an oval pond of water enclosed in a glistening white porcelain bowl elevated above the floor, a pool of crystal water framed in its wooden shore.

She tries to speak, but he silences her with a kiss, a profound, passionate, and yet anguished kiss. Then he heaves her out into the air! And she drifts down inexorably toward the waiting waters. She beats her nonexistent wings futilely and kicks with her gitalongs and manages to cry, "Oh, Archy, how *could* you?" but the last syllable and the question mark are strangled in the water.

Tish does not panic and drown. She treads water with her gitalongs and keeps her sniffwhips dry. The shore is too high, but the wall of the porcelain bowl, aglint in the afternoon sunlight, is not far, and she swims slowly toward it, reaches it, and seeks purchase with the tips of her gitalongs, but the wall is smooth and impervious; she cannot grip anywhere. She scrambles, she claws, she lunges and crawls, but cannot clutch hold of the wall. It is the same all the way around, an unbroken bank of mockingly white and pure enamel. "Archy!" she calls upward, hoping to wake him and summon his aid, although she cannot imagine what aid he might give her. But he has disappeared, he has gone back to wherever he had begun his dream, to finish it, or he has wandered sleepwalking into some other part of Parthenon.

She floats. She does not tire, yet, and she keeps as calm as she can, telling herself that the merest thought of despair might weaken her or unsettle her, and let her drown. Time passes, or, since time has ceased to exist, and it is only the present tense, the tense presence remains definite, suspended and endless. Daylight passes. Tish feels hunger and knows that it's breakfasttime. If the Clock still worked, it would say "EGG," but the Clock is west. Tish thinks of Egg, she thinks of Easteregg, she wonders how her sixteen babies are coming along, growing steadily in their capsule in the place where she and Hoimin hid it. Another long month or so will pass before the capsule hatches, cracks, and lets the sixteen out into this cruel world. Will any of them find their way back to Stay More and will anyone in Stay More tell them

319

of their mother, drowned and westered in a—, in a—? Tish has been in this water so long, she has gradually fathomed its purpose: it is not a reservoir of drinking water, or washing water, but a water which has been forced from some subterranean source like a spring and will return to a subterranean location to carry away the wastes of Woman. It is therefore a water potty. Will anyone tell those sixteen poor babes that their poor mother westered in a water potty?

When will Sharon return to find a black bug, perhaps still alive, floating in Her water potty, and cause the water to flush the bug away? For that seems to be Tish's only fate. Thinking of fate, she remembers her fairy godmother, the Fate-Thing, and wonders why that kind protectress wants to wester her in this fashion. Perhaps, Tish reflects as night comes on, the Fate-Thing knows that everyone must wester eventually, and the Fate-Thing has chosen for Tish this dramatic, exceptional, extraordinary west.

From time to time, or, since there is no Time but only a sense of the necessity of repetition, Tish calls out, "HELP!" She cannot know that her father, presumed west himself, is also occasionally, between bites of lime peel and egg shell, summoning the strength to holler, "HELP!" In this same household, their cries go unheard, the father's because his is encased and muffled by thick plastic bagging, the daughter's because hers is confined within the solid walls of the porcelain bowl, which indeed serves as a megaphone directing the cries of "HELP" upward, if only there were someone to hear her. . . .

There *is* someone to hear her. He appears,

320

perched like a guardian angel on the edge of the round wooden seat, peering down at her. It is not Archy. Tish tries to sign "Help me," with gestures, but she cannot work her gestures in the water. She tries to sniffwhipspell "H-E-L-P," but her sniffwhips are too wet to spell. She can only moan, in exasperation and relief, "Oh, Sam!"

"Tish," he says. "Mrs. Tish Tichborne. You know, it sounds like someone clucking."

"I KNOW! I KNOW!" she yells, hoping he can hear her. "BUT I'M NOT! HONEST I'M NOT!" She sobs, and having used up the strength of her voice, can only sigh, "If you could get me out of here, I could explain it to you." She talks to herself.

"Explain it to me now," he says, as if he has heard her.

"You can't hear me," she declares, "and I'm too tired to holler or try to spell with my sniffwhips."

"I can hear you," he declares.

"You can?"

"Yes, Doc prescribed something for my prongs which apparently works. I can hear whatever you have to say."

"Oh, that's wonderful!" she exclaims. "So listen careful." And she begins to talk, as fast as she can. She relates to Sam the whole story of her recent dealings with Archy, and of sleepwalking Archy's unconscious attempt to wester her by throwing her into the water potty. She is careful to explain that the wedding took place without her consent or active participation, that the marriage was practically *decreed* by the groom's father. She is also careful to express her opinion that Archy did not deliberately intend to wester her, but was only acting unconsciously out of some deep-seated frustration or disappointment. She concludes the entire story by remarking, "I don't really think we're married. Do you?"

"Not if the officiant was a defrocked Frockroach, as it were," Sam says. "Chid had no authority to perform the marriage." Sam relates to Tish how his father, Squire Hank, is at this moment looking all over Stay More for Chid. Chid dare not return to Holy House, for the roosterroaches there feel that Chid has abandoned them, and they are in a mood to wester him if he ever shows up there again. "But as for Archy . . ."

"I think Archy has gone west," Tish declares. "I mean *westward* west, I mean thataway." She attempts to gesture. "In any case, I don't care if I never see him again."

And now, having said this, Tish is surprised to discover that Squire Gregor Samsa Ingledew is proposing to her. "Tish, will you marry me?" he has asked. Has she heard him correctly?

How can he propose to her in such an unromantic place as a toilet? "You'd have to get me out of here," she replies. "And you can't."

"I'll get you out of there," he says, and for a moment he disappears from the wooden rim of the seat, but reappears beneath the seat, on the edge of the porcelain bowl, which he is scratching at with his gitalongs.

"Don't try to climb down!" she cautions him. "You'll get stuck yourself, and we'll both drown."

"Then I'll drown with you, because I don't want to live without you," he says. "Listen. I'm going to try something. I don't know if it will work, but we can try. I'm going to *fly* down there, see, and then you catch hold of my rear gitalongs, and I'll fly you out of there!"

"But you can't fly that long!" she protests. "No roosterroach has ever flown for more than three full seconds."

"Time has stopped," he says. "There are no seconds. But assuming there are: one second down, one second for you to grab hold, one second to get you out. Okay? Let's try it. Here goes!"

And before she can further protest, dear Sam springs off the edge of the bowl, his wings fluttering frantically in the clumsy way that roosterroaches have of using their useless wings on rare occasions, and he comes steadily through the air down to her, until he yells, "Grab hold!" and she bites into one of his rear gitalongs, firmly enough to hang on but not so tight as to bite off his gitalong, and then she can actually hear the beat of his wings! He thrashes his wings, and she can feel herself being lifted, slowly, out of the water! But so slowly! Surely three seconds have passed already. He rises upward, beating his wings until it would seem his heart would give out, and she herself senses that the three seconds have expired. Time is up, Time is out, Time is over, and if she continues clinging to him she will wester him. And just in the instant before his heart can fail, she releases her bite on his gitalong, and drops, falls, back down into the water, and he has strength only to give his wings one last solid beat that lands him back on the edge of the wooden seat.

He collapses there. She collapses into the water, shaken and with only enough of her wits remaining to remember to keep herself afloat. She can hear Sam panting and wheezing, and it seems to take forever for him to regain his voice and ask her, "Why did you let go?"

"If I hadn't, you wouldn't have made it," she says. "You know that."

He seems to know that. "Well, let's try it again," he suggests.

"No," she says firmly. "You've already used up your strength. You couldn't possibly succeed on the second try."

"Well," he says, "I suppose I can just sit here and try to keep Sharon from flushing you away whenever She comes back."

It takes Tish a while to realize that Sam is attempting to make a kind of half-serious joke. She does not laugh. "When do you think She'll be coming back?" she asks.

"The question is not when but *if*," Sam says. "There is some doubt that She will be coming back at all. But I for one *know* that She will, eventually."

"And when She does, She'll flush me."

"Not if I can help it."

"Sam, Sam, listen, in case She flushes me, I want to tell you where my easteregg is hidden—*our* easteregg, because it's yours too—I want you to find it, and make sure our babies get back home to Stay More, and then someday you can tell them about me." The

324

pathos of this declaration makes Tish begin to cry.

"Hoimin's already told me how to find it," Sam says. "We'll find it. You and I will find it, and when our babies hatch we'll give a party."

The prospect of that almost comforts Tish; she snivels and tries to summon up the Fate-Thing to keep her company during the coming hours.

37.

Sam will always remember the toilet seat as the place where he got religion. It is of golden oak, with chrome hinges attaching it to the back of the bowl, and he has spent hours and hours on it, either perched at the edge, talking with Tish, or impatiently, anxiously, nervously walking around it, around and around and around it, as on a racetrack. He must keep talking to Tish, so she won't fall asleep, because if she falls asleep she will drown.

"Funny," she has remarked to him, once, trying to sound light, "all that time my house was floating down the creek, and so many of my brothers and sisters were drowning, it never occurred to me that I might ever wester by water. And now . . ."

He is desperate with worry, and it is precisely such states which drive some folks into religion, although this is not to say that there aren't many deeply and truly religious persons who have never been worried, or frantic, or feeling so utterly helpless. Not once does it ever dawn on Sam to pray—not to Man, certainly, or to Woman, or even to God, although he is well aware of the presumed fact of God's existence, a fact which all generations of Ingledews have steadfastly denied. And Sam is not about to become religious in the sense of accepting that fact, let alone praying to God. No, Sam is about to become religious in the sense of believing that there is not one Man, or one Woman, but many of Them, and They have not perished from this earth, and never will, and if we continue to worship Them, and honor Them, and love Them, They have the power to keep all of us staying more, forever and ever, amen. Call this religion polytheism or myriotheism; call it secular humanism, even; Sam is about to become a passionate convert to it, and eventually a preacher of it, and he will always remember (and relate to his audiences) that his conversion took place on the seat of a toilet wherein his true love floated in peril of drowning or being flushed away.

To pass the time while they wait for an outcome unknown, a fate unimagined, Sam even tells Tish of his conversion, his new belief, and his plan to preach it. Tish laughs, perhaps at the thought of him preaching. It is good, at least, to hear her laughing.

But now his tailprongs pick up a sound he has not heard since he first began to lose his hearing: the engine of an automobile. He runs to the front porch and sees a car driving into the yard. From the passenger seat, Sharon emerges, and, before closing Her door, speaks at length with the Driver, Her voice too distant for Sam to hear. Nor can he see the Driver.

Sharon closes the door. The automobile leaves. Sharon turns and approaches Her house. She begins to climb the steps. Squire Sam rushes back into Her bedroom, telling himself to keep calm, at all costs. *Do not panic*, he says to himself, more than once. *But think*, he says to himself. *Think. Think!* There must be some way to keep the Woman out of Her bathroom, or keep Her from flushing the toilet.

The Woman enters Her bedroom. She flings Herself across Her bed, and simply lies there, face down. Sam from this low perspective cannot see Her face. Are Her eyes closed? He waves his sniffwhips for a long time, trying to detect Her slumberscent. There is none. Is the Woman silently crying? Has Man westered, after all? Is Sharon alone in this world? For the longest time, or, since Time has stopped and the Clock sits west and silent on its mantelshelf, there is no movement or sound from the Woman.

Sam begins climbing the coverlet. He will not let Her see him, but he wants to get as close as possible to Her. He wants to see Her beautiful face, to tell if he can if She is grieving, if She is mourning the west of Man. Yes, Her eyes are open, but She looks not at him or at anything but off toward the general direction of the mantel, not looking at it but just toward it. If there is grief or even sadness in Her face, Sam cannot tell. She looks simply tired, very tired. "Sleep," he says to Her. "Why don't you sleep?"

If only She would fall asleep, he could have a grace period in which to make one last effort to save Tish. Sam has decided that if he cannot prevent Tish from being flushed away, he will go with her. Even if it is to westwardness and oblivion in a subterranean septic tank, he will join her on that last journey. If there is any chance in this world that the pipe leads not to an enclosed septic tank but to a drain field or even to the creek, there is always the chance that Tish could survive, if he is with her, to help her and guide her. But his many walks and hikes in the vicinity of Parthenon have never shown him any hole which could be the outlet of the drain, so probably its outlet is within the tank. Probably he and Tish both would drown before they reached the tank. But whatever her destiny, it shall be his too.

The Woman lies prone, staring vacantly into space for a very long time. If She remains much longer, inevitably She will have to get up and go use Her bathroom. As he is thinking this thought, Sharon moves. She turns over, raises Her upper body, and sits up. But She does not stand. Sitting on the edge of the bed, She reaches for the telephone, holds it to Her ear and listens for a long moment, then pokes Her finger into the dial and turns the dial, then again, several times.

"Gran," Sharon says, "I'm home. Yes. Vernon drove to the airport and got me. Are you all right? How long have I been gone? I would have called you from Little Rock, but Vernon said he talked to you. That's right. Yes. Um-hmm. Yes. Unt-uh. No, he didn't. That was before. Probably Friday afternoon, they said. I hope. What day is this? It *is*? Gosh, Gran, are you sure? It seems like time has stopped. Just completely stopped. I'll look. Yes, it says eight o'clock, isn't that ridiculous? I'll wind it. I thought something was funny, because it hasn't bonged once since I got home. I don't know. Are you sure you don't want me to . . . Well, thanks, yes, I guess. Of course I paid all his expenses, the doctors' bills too, and all. The least I could do. Well, I'll let you know. Thanks again. Goodnight, Gran. Sleep tight."

Sharon puts the phone back where it was. Now She stands. Sam jumps off the bed and heads for the bathroom, intending to place his own person between Her and the bathroom door. But She does not move to the bathroom. She moves to the mantel. She opens the Clock face, lifts the key, inserts it into the Clock, and begins to wind. Sam can hear the old familiar scritches and grindings of the Clock's internal vitals. Sharon continues to wind. Soon the Clock will be east again. Soon the Clock will run. Soon Time will . . .

38.

. . . shift entirely into the future tense, because Sharon winds the Clock too tightly, too far, too easterly, too much: the mainspring will go haywire, the secondary gear will slip off the tertiary gear, something will snap, and the Clock will begin to keep exceptional Time, Time too fast and all future: it will be Time which will not have happened yet but will always stand in possibility of happening.

Sharon will exclaim, most unladylike, "Oh,

shit." Then she will sigh and say, "Oh well, I'll just get a new one, an electric one that doesn't have to be wound. Maybe I'll just get a clock-radio for the bedside."

Then, at last, she will head for the bathroom. She will see a cockroach standing in her path to the bathroom. She will gasp, and then she will stamp her foot, but the cockroach will just stand there, as if he is not afraid of her, as if he's trying to block her way to the bathroom.

"Out of my way, Alfonse," she will say, "or whatever your name is."

Will it be just her weariness that will make her think the cockroach will be speaking in reply to her? Will she just fancy the bug will be trying to talk to her?

Since he will not budge, she will step over him, resisting an impulse to step *onto* him, and in her bathroom she will discover *another* cockroach floating in the toilet bowl, alive and kicking. "You little buggers really think you can take over my house while I'm gone?" she will say. "What are you trying to do?" She will stare down at the bug in the water, who will be staring back at her. She will impulsively reach for the handle which flushes the toilet. The first cockroach, the one she will have called Alfonse, will fly into the air, and hover above her hand without quite touching it, and she will draw back her hand, exclaiming, "Jesus! I didn't know cockroaches could *fly*!" She will watch Alfonse fly down and land in the water of the bowl where the other roach will be. Now there will be *two* roaches in her toilet bowl.

"Are y'all trying to commit suicide, or something?" she will ask them. "Or is this just your idea of a skinny-dip, huh, Gaston?" She will have decided to address the other one as Gaston, the lesser of the two; it has no wings like Alfonse. But then she will say, "Oh, I get it. You are a female, huh, Gaston? Then I'll call you . . . I'll call you Letitia, which means happiness." Sharon will smile to herself, and look at herself in the vanity mirror, the dark circles under her eyes from lack of sleep, the unkempt hair. She will speak to her image, "I am being *so* silly."

For the briefest instant, she will reach once again for the handle that makes the water swirl and lower and disappear in the bottom of the bowl of the toilet. But she will not. Instead, she will wad up a handful of toilet paper, and she will hold the wad down close to the water, close enough to touch the bugs or be touched by them, and she will suggest to them, "All right, Alfonse and Letitia, climb aboard." The two cockroaches will not; they will seem to be conferring with each other about the meaning of her gesture; they will seem to be trying to back away from the offered wad of tissue.

But finally the one she will be calling Alfonse will actually nudge Letitia, pushing her toward the wad, and the one Sharon will be calling Letitia will climb onto the wad of tissue, and Sharon will lift the wad out and hold it close to the floor and give it a shake, and Letitia will be on the floor. Then Sharon will return the wad to the bowl and hold it close to the other one and she will say, "And now, Alfonse, you climb on too." And he will. And then she will set him down on the floor beside Letitia.

The two bugs will seem reluctant to decamp.

331

They will almost seem to be having a discussion on whether or not to decamp.

But then they will walk together, side by side, out through the door, and Sharon will be alone.

Before going to bed, she will set out a saucer with some milk in it, and a cookie on the edge of it. She will study the saucer for a while, as if she will be waiting to see if her cockroaches will come to it. They will not.

In the morning, she will look to see if any of the milk will be gone. It will not be. Nor will the cookie appear to have been sampled. She will throw the milk into the sink, and untie the garbage bag to put the cookie into the garbage. When she will untie the garbage bag, a cockroach will leap out of it, startling her. "Alfonse?!" she will cry. But there will have been no way the cockroach she will have called Alfonse will have been able to get inside that tied garbage bag.

The cockroach liberated from the garbage bag will make a beeline for the front door, and the porch, and she will follow, watching the cockroach scamper down from the porch and off in the direction of Larry's house. The same direction that the whole horde of cockroaches had seemed to point, that evening, oh so many evenings ago.

She will be tempted to follow, for she will intend to be going that way, anyway, soon. But first she will have her breakfast, and an extra cup of coffee, to dispel the remnant of the possibility that she will be imagining things.

Still, she will be edgy and nervous when she will at length walk to Larry's house, and the sight of his car parked behind the house will cause her to stumble and grab a tree for support, until she will remember that the car will never have been moved. Or will it have?

It will be a beautiful morning in Stay More, a gorgeous morning, one of those sunny springtime (or early summer) days, more rare than June is rare, and she will be almost reluctant to go indoors. She will want to stay out here in the sunshine, breathing the nice air. It will be unpleasant inside the house.

It will be unpleasant inside the house: it will be unpleasant on the porch, as she will climb it. As she will climb the steps, she will see a strange little thing: right in the way, at the top of the steps, stuck into the wooden porch floor, there will be a cockroach impaled upon a straight pin. It will be a fat cockroach, much fatter than her Alfonse. The way the pin is stuck through the roach's body and into the floor will remind her of the bug collection her brother Vernon kept inside a cigar box. But Vernon will not have done this. Larry *could not* have done it . . . unless . . .

The cockroach, fat and stupid-looking, will somehow arouse a fleeting pity in Sharon, pity that she will not have felt if it will not have been for the pity she will have taken on Alfonse and Letitia, sparing them. This dead, impaled cockroach, over which she will step as she will have stepped over Alfonse the day before, will cause her to recite aloud some old snatch of an elegy she has read in school: "And now I live, and now my life is done."

Sharon will not know why she will be saying that aloud, but, thinking of poetry, she will be not

333

totally unprepared for what she will find inside the house, in Larry's study, in his typewriter: a poem. She will have known, of course, that he sometimes attempted poetry when he wasn't analyzing it, and she will assume, even before reading it, that this will be his own creation. His black IBM Selectric will still be running, still be ON. She will reach down to feel how warm it will be, and in doing so she will cause to fly up an enormous cockroach. This will not be, cannot be, Alfonse, nor the one she liberated from the garbage bag, nor any other cockroach she will ever have seen; it will be too large, and although she will have discovered, just yesterday, that cockroaches *can* fly, this one will be flying all over the place, like a bird, like a bat, and she will be much more afraid of it than of any insect she has ever seen. But it will at length fly through the door and away, and she will never see it again.

She will have one more fright before she can read the poem. She will see a mouse. If it will have been a black mouse, or a gray mouse, it will have made her cry out and jump, but it will be a white mouse, and it will not be totally a stranger, because it will be the same mouse who led the horde of cockroaches in their directive arrow and message.

The white mouse will be on the floor near Larry's desk, and it will be looking at her, twitching its whiskers and bobbing its nose. And then it too, like the oversize roach, will decamp.

Sharon will return her glance to the poem, and read its title and begin reading it.

We will see her standing there, at Larry's desk,

reading. It will be almost like a painting by Vermeer. The lovely lady, the wonderful morning sunlight which seems to caress her face and her hands and the white, white sheet. She will read. She will smile.

And when the reading will be done, she will raise her eyes from the poem in the typewriter, and she will address the house: "Larry?"

IMAGO:
The Mockroach's Song

If roach were man and man were roach,
the subjects both would brood and broach
are love, dependency, survival.
We trust you in your rearrival
to read this fable in reverse
and keep the world from getting worse.
We are the scurry of your ugly
despisèd motives—humble, bugly,
but not so bad we should be *kaput*.
You shot yourself in your own foot,
went nearly west. We kept you easter.
Before you blast off your own keister,
wise up, stay more, re-ken your kin.
We know you out, we know you in.
We drink your nectar, eat your shit.
We haven't had enough of it.
You think you pine with love and grief?
Yet think how pitiful and brief

we are, your small, unloved familiars:
our hearts will bridge the Void. Will yours?
Some say your world will end in fire
and ours survive. Not so. No choir
can hymn or hum inhumanly.
Thou needest us. We needest Thee.
Grow up, earn Love, like us conceive
a God to pray to and believe.
Ring out bomb-doom and ring us true.
You live, we are, you die, we do.
Ding-dong the dang dumb don'ts to soundless hell.
In purple sympathy we twain shall dwell.

LaPorte County Public Library
LaPorte, Indiana

Harington   L F 89 07153

The cockroaches of Stay More

1995*

DISCARDED BY THE
LA PORTE, INDIANA
PUBLIC & COUNTY LIBRARY

SIGNATURE

FICTION CATALOG

LA PORTE COUNTY PUBLIC LIBRARY
904 INDIANA AVE.
LA PORTE, IN   46350

INPUT